Roger Radford is the author of two previous novels, *The Winds of Kedem* and *Schreiber's Secret*. The former was a bestseller in Israel, while film rights were sold for the latter. *Informed Consent* is a polemical thriller revolving around the trauma caused by invasive spinal procedures. Radford, a former foreign correspondent for the Associated Press and journalist with Reuters, has suffered from adhesive arachnoiditis, an incurable and debilitating spinal condition, since 1998.

'Roger Radford is unputdownable. He has the gift of leaving you wanting more.'
MANNY ROBINSON, *London Evening Standard*

Also by Roger Radford

THE WINDS OF KEDEM
SCHREIBER'S SECRET

ROGER RADFORD

Informed Consent

Booklocker.com, Inc.
2002

*I dedicate this book to the many silent victims of
invasive spinal procedures.
Their voices deserve to be heard.*

The author wishes to express his gratitude to fellow members of
the Circle of Friends with Arachnoiditis
whose courage and fortitude were the inspiration for this novel.

'Medicine used to be simple, ineffective and relatively safe. It is now complex, effective and potentially dangerous.'

The dean of one of Britain's leading medical schools.

CHAPTER ONE

The wife whose husband had murdered seven men screamed in agony.

'Just a bit more, there's a good girl, I can see the head,' Martin Townsend cajoled. The consultant obstetrician was worried. He could see Teresa Kelly was in pain and he knew she shouldn't be. He swept the sweat from his brow with his sleeve, and cursed under breath that still bore the imprint of a night on the tiles. The bloody epidural had gone desperately wrong. He'd had to jiggle the damn needle around before it finally went in. The good doctor silently chided himself for not having left it to a junior, somebody to whom he could pass the buck.

'Why am I hurting so much, doctor,' Teresa gasped. Beads of sweat began to meander down from the damp red hairline and across the myriad freckles adorning her soft Celtic features. Most women did not look their best in the throes of childbirth but, despite her pain, she retained the prettiness that would soon be enhanced by the first flush of motherhood. She gripped her husband's hand more tightly and smiled thinly at his worried face. 'Don't fret, Kieran,' she mouthed silently. After all, childbirth was no big deal for an Irish Catholic. They were born to raise big families. She was only twenty-seven and had already spawned three kids. All had been relatively difficult births. Sian, the first, had been a forceps delivery. She could never forget that labour. Excruciating, it had seemed to take forever, and she'd vowed never to go through it again. Three daughters later, she was going through it again. Only this time, and against her better judgement, she'd consented to have an epidural. She had never liked confronting the laws of nature, but they'd assured her the procedure was safe. This time, it just had to be a boy. Kieran wanted a boy. Kieran was desperate for a boy, someone for whom he could have dreams and aspirations; a boy with whom he could play football over the local park; a boy who would one day captain his club and country, a united Ireland. As long he was there to carry the Kelly line. It was a Celtic thing.

Kieran Kelly looked on, a familiar anger burning within him. He knew enough about modern medicine to understand that an epidural was supposed to anaesthetise the pain of childbirth.

'Why is she in pain, doc,' he said threateningly. 'You said she wouldn't feel a thing.'

Townsend grunted noncommittally. He hated it when the husbands insisted on being present.

'Can't you do something, doctor?' The Irishman hated the desperation in his voice. He abhorred being beholden to any man.

'Oh, Kieran,' Teresa gasped again, curtailing his musings with troubled, confused eyes. She gripped his hand more tightly as the contractions increased. They'd said she wouldn't feel any pain with the epidural. Then why was she hurting so?

The Irishman could sense that scant attention was being paid to his wife's pain by the medical menagerie surrounding her. He began feeling the familiar pounding in his head that in the past had presaged physical violence. He was a man of black and white. Once committed, whether to kin or to cause, he remained dedicated to their welfare. Ever since the end of the Troubles, Kieran Kelly had worked all the hours God gave in order to provide for his family. Despite an IQ of 180, he was a man of thwarted ambition, desperately seeking to escape the drudgery of his job as a security guard and the working class suburb in which he lived. Peace in Northern Ireland, religion and a fourth child were conspiring to prevent him from realising that aim, although he would be the last to admit it. God's grand design could not be questioned. *He* had once commanded him to become a hit man for the Provisional IRA's Internal Affairs. Now it was *His* wish that he lead a life of relative anonymity, to forsake his native Belfast for the comparative safety of the sprawling metropolis that was London. Memories were still long back home, and there were plenty of enemies who might seek to exact the sort of revenge he himself had meted out in the heyday of the Troubles.

Teresa saw her own pain reflected in her husband's eyes. She must not let him see how much she was suffering. She must be brave. It wasn't the contractions; she could hardly feel those. It was her back. Her back felt as if it was splitting in two, and rivers of fire were running down her legs.

2

He stroked her moist red hair. 'Nearly there, now, *a gradh mo croidhe,*' he said soothingly. She was indeed the light of his heart.

Teresa suddenly became aware of the antiseptic aromas in the delivery room. The white tiles, pristine and frigid, glared at her as if affronted by her whinnying. Those tiles had witnessed so much pain and joy that maybe they had a right to be disdainful. The insistent bleeps of the monitoring equipment seemed to be shrieking like a demented mobile phone. For the first time in all her pregnancies, she felt a sense of total vulnerability, albeit mixed with the thrill of expectation that this was to be Kieran 's moment. Indeed, her very raison d'être was geared to this moment. There, with her legs splayed unappealingly on stirrups and the very quick of her displayed for all the world to see, Teresa Kelly was about to give birth to the most beautiful boy in the universe.

'The baby's coming now, my dear,' came the lilting voice of the West Indian nurse, plump and motherly. 'Start pushing.'

Teresa winced as she put all her effort into the task. She wanted to scream but knew she wouldn't. It was not her way. She looked beseechingly at the obstetrician. Everyone had told her to have faith in the doctors and nurses. 'You've been through it all before, Teresa,' they'd said. 'This time you won't feel any pain. Trust the doctor.'

Martin Townsend could see the baby's head begin to part the labia. Its dark hair was besmirched with blood, and also by faeces released by pressure on the rectum. The bleeping cardiotocogram gave no hint of complications. The obstetrician placed his right hand on the perineum, the area between the anus and vagina, and then applied gentle pressure to prevent tearing. Two contractions later and he was cupping the head of the baby, its face turned from him. Technically, it was still an 'it.' Aided by moderate pressure down into the bed, the anterior shoulder began slipping under the symphisis, where the two bones of the pelvis join. Almost at the same instant there was a 'plop' and baby Kelly entered the world. Weighing in at seven and a half pounds with full cheeks and brackish dark hair was the one gift from God Kieran Kelly desired above all others. His lineage was safeguarded, but at a terrible price of which he was unaware, for although Teresa Kelly was not dead at the point of her son's birth, she might just as well have been.

Meanwhile, consultant obstetrician Martin George Townsend just wanted out of there.

It was three months later when Townsend, still affected by the Kelly birth, entered the portals of the Royal Society of Medicine at number one, Wimpole Street. It was the last Friday in the month, the occasion for a gathering of consultant obstetricians and gynaecologists. There were usually fifty or so who could make it on a regular basis. Most others, including Townsend himself, were infrequent visitors to this venerable institution. This time, however, he felt an urge to discuss the matter with some of his more illustrious colleagues. There were always a few leading surgeons present, those who operated in the major teaching hospitals and had lucrative private practices in nearby Harley Street.

A familiar voice called out as he entered the bar. It was Len Jameson, an old college pal who was currently working at Guy's under the tutelage of the great Sir John Peabody himself.

'Long time no see, old boy,' said Jameson, pumping Townsend's hand. 'How are you?'

'Fine, Len,' said Townsend unconvincingly.

'It's a good thing you've come tonight,' his colleague enthused. 'Peabody is here. He's giving a talk.'

Townsend could not share in the enthusiasm and his companion sensed this immediately.

'What's up, Martin? Your face is as long as a kite.'

'It's been a rough few months.'

'Nothing that a couple of shots wouldn't fix, eh?' said Jameson. 'Your usual?'

Townsend nodded and leaned against the bar while his colleague ordered a Scotch and dry for both of them.

'Now,' said Jameson, handing Townsend his drink, 'tell all to Uncle Len.'

Townsend sighed deeply. He had kept his own counsel about the Kelly birth. His marriage had ended in acrimony two years earlier. Not that being still married to Jane would have made much difference. For the last five years they had barely talked. First it had been separate beds, then separate rooms and, finally, separate homes. As usual, most of the angst was about who got what. He was thankful there had been no progeny to further complicate matters. After fifteen years of living a sham, he had found himself alone. Most of his friends had been hers and, naturally, had taken her side. He compensated by ploughing into his work. He knew he was a workaholic, but there *was* nothing else. Medicine was his life. He saw himself as a perfectionist, which made the Kelly fiasco even harder to bear. He thanked God he could find some semblance of peace at the bottom of a bottle.

'Well,' said Jameson, 'it can't be the end of the world, can it?'

Townsend circled the rim of his whisky glass with his forefinger. 'I delivered a baby a few months back,' he said flatly.

'Lost it did you?'

'No, nothing like that. The poor woman had an epidural, and I think it went wrong.'

'These things happen, Martin,' Jameson said soothingly. 'It's down to the anaesthetist or whoever. It's not your fault - does she know?'

'I don't think so. The last I heard, she'd been to some doctor who told her there was nothing wrong with her, that it was all in her head.'

'Well, then, that's okay.' But the look on his colleague's face told Jameson that all was not okay.

'I gave her the epidural myself,' Townsend said, his voice barely audible. 'I think I've fucked up her central nervous system.'

Jameson clasped his colleague's shoulder consolingly and whispered in his ear. 'See no evil, hear no evil, speak no evil. Forget it mate. You win some and you lose some. Just remember what the insurance companies tell you: admit nothing.'

A world away from the illustrious portals of the RSM, Kieran Kelly wiped away the residue of another sleepless night. He stared blearily at himself in the mirror. The piercing blue eyes that had once struck fear into his adversaries now bore a patina of pain and incomprehension. It was all about control. During the Troubles, *he* had been in control. *He* had called the shots. *He* had decided which traitor was to be executed and the manner in which that execution would be carried out. Some might have called him a professional killer, but he disdained that title. A professional was usually paid for his work, but he, for one, never killed for money. He killed to protect a cause. Meticulous in the planning, each killing - seven in all - had not been accompanied by torture. It was not his way. There were plenty of psychopaths out there who had killed for fun. He was not like Kenny McClinton, the latter day fundamentalist preacher who had become a celebrity but once advocated beheading Catholics and impaling their heads on railings in the Shankill. McClinton and his ilk had tortured young and old alike. Poor sods like Thomas Madden, an inoffensive middle-aged Catholic who was uninterested in politics but was ritually carved into a gargoyle. None of the hundred and fifty stab wounds to his body was sufficient to kill him and he had died slowly of strangulation, suspended from a beam by a slowly tightening noose. This was the sort of thing that made him hate them still. In his war there had been rules of engagement. He despised those who had carried out sectarian killings. Each of the men he had killed had been guilty of crimes against his own people. They had deserved to die, but they had not suffered. Not like the love of his life who was now too ill to get out of bed, too sick to lift their new baby. She was suffering, oh, how she was suffering. Her spinal cord was shot to pieces and nobody cared. For the first time in his life he felt totally helpless.

'Kieran, Kieran,' whimpered Teresa, her plaintive voice puncturing his morbidity. He splashed some more cold water on his face, dried himself off quickly and entered their bedroom. Teresa smiled at him wanly.

'Did you get the children off to school okay?' she rasped.

'Yes, my darling, don't worry.' He leaned over the bed and kissed her dank brow. He knew that she'd had another rotten night, despite the plethora of painkillers she took to try to alleviate the pain. Nothing seemed to assuage this illness with no name.

'I'm so sorry, Kieran.'

'What do you mean, darling?'

'I'm so sorry for being such a burden to you.'

'Don't be silly. You'll never be a burden to me, Terry. We'll beat this thing together, I promise you.'

Kelly could feel the doubt creeping into his voice. They had tried alternative therapies. Osteopathy and chiropractic had made her worse, while acupuncture had made no difference. Two faith healers had lightened their patient's pocket rather than her agony. Meanwhile the great National Health Service meant they would have to wait six months before Teresa could see a specialist neurologist. Their own GP had given them the referral reluctantly. The ignorant pig thought all Teresa's symptoms were psychosomatic. Post-natal depression, the man called it. His wife was depressed all right; anyone in her position would be.

'I can't stand to see the kids watching me suffer, Kieran. I can see the pain in their eyes. They want their ma back.' Tears began to meander down into the corners of her mouth, their saltiness almost a comfort.

The Irishman kissed her mouth gently. 'I've had a word with them. Believe me, they understand. They're brave, just like their ma.' He was thankful that his job allowed him to work nights, thus allowing him to be home in the mornings in time to prepare breakfast for their three daughters and drive them to school. He then usually cooked something for Teresa before climbing into one of the children's beds to get some sleep. The girls were aged seven, five and four. Sian, the eldest, had taken her mother's illness the hardest. She couldn't understand why having a baby should leave her mum bed-bound and whimpering in pain. She was old enough to feel guilt and perceive rejection, while Sinead and Kerry were still too young to fully comprehend what was happening. Teresa had now been ill for three months and he felt drained. She could barely walk. He had had to attend to her every need, keeping the children and the house clean, cooking for them all and, at the same time, holding down an overnight job that played havoc with his metabolism. Hard as he tried, he could not understand what Teresa was going through. When she spoke of her body feeling as if it was being cremated, he could not really imagine what that was like. At one point he had thought of running a blowtorch up and down his legs. Such was his love for her that he was prepared to do the unthinkable: maim himself in order to feel what she was feeling. Yet he knew that while burns would heal, whatever had been pumped into his wife's spinal cord had caused the sort of damage that could never be repaired.

She motioned for him to help her. He knew how much of an effort it was for her to even reach the toilet when he was not there. She clung to him and groaned as he lifted her gently from the dampened sheets that stood testament to a night of torture. 'Try to walk, my darling,' he said, gently lowering her legs onto the floor. 'It'll be good for your muscles.'

She stood up gingerly and leaned against his sturdy six-foot frame. How she adored him. She'd fallen for Kieran within a week of their meeting at a pub in the Falls Road. Once most men had the demon drink inside them, they either became violent or silly. But Kieran was different. He was always the quiet one in his circle of friends; quiet, yet incredibly strong. He was the proverbial icon: tall, dark and handsome. His hair was jet black, his jaw square and set beneath high cheekbones that lay astride a nose that was ever so slightly hooked. But it was his eyes that captivated her. They were pools of azure in whose depths lurked a mystery that she had found utterly irresistible. Their courtship had lasted six months before he had spoken the words she had longed to hear. The ten-year difference in their ages had mattered little. Although she had barely turned seventeen, she was mature enough to know what she wanted. During those first six months they had barely been apart. Only on a couple of occasions had he left her for a few days, each time travelling to Dublin to visit some relatives. She'd been wise enough not to tie him down against his will, always believing that the looser the shackles, the tighter the chains. She sighed at the irony of the phrase. The chains were tight now all right. Her illness was strangling him with them. Everyone tried to behave as if their lives were normal; as if 'her upstairs' was the same woman who had laughed and danced her way through life, the same woman about whom others would say, perhaps with a trace of envy, 'she's got a marriage made in heaven and kids to match.' One lousy injection had ruined her and their lives and, of course, everyone kept saying that no one was to blame. But Teresa Kelly knew who was to blame. She was. She was overwhelmed by guilt for what she had done to her loved ones. It weighed on her like a lowering Belfast sky. But this was London, not Belfast, and any Irish sky was better than the one above the English capital.

Kieran had been unemployed in Belfast when, almost without warning, he had decided that London would offer them more opportunities. She'd not wanted to leave, but she knew she would follow him to the ends of the earth if necessary. Three years ago they had made the break. If she were honest with herself, she had never really settled in east London. The sagging terraced house in Leyton was damp and dismal. Belfast, especially a Belfast no longer at war, was infinitely better. She missed her family, especially her mother, who was devastated when they left. Her father had died absurdly of a heart attack at forty. Perhaps that was why she had married someone ten years her senior.

She clung to him more tightly and brushed her lips against his cheek. 'Kieran,' she said weakly, 'I want us to return home. I want to be near my family. It would mean so much to me.'

Kelly quivered. He had dreaded these words ever since the birth of Patrick. How could he deny her when he loved her so much? And yet he knew that a return would probably mean his death. There was a contract out on him, peace or no peace. Teresa knew nothing of his extra-curricular activities, or anything of the double life he had lived for the ten years prior to The Agreement. He would happily have killed any man who told her, but he knew there would be no whistle-blowers amongst his comrades; each had sworn to take his secret to the grave. Even if an enemy would somehow divulge the truth to Teresa, he would deny it and that would be an end to the matter. He knew that she had more faith in him than she had in God. In fact, he doubted whether her faith, once so vibrant, was still intact. Whilst he was still a believer, after a fashion, she had decided that God had forsaken her and no longer deserved her faith. All suggestions of having a priest visit were swept aside by an expletive; so unlike her, yet so understandable. Pain was like that, whether it was the physical torture of her illness or the sort of mental torture associated with being a despised minority in one's own land. The Irish always won by sacrifice. It was in the genes. Yes, he knew pain, and he would gladly have sacrificed his life for her and the children. Not like a Protestant. The Protestants had a horror of death. Death was the end of everything for them whereas for Catholics it was only the beginning. While the Catholic fought for the future, the Protestant was immersed in the past. The Catholic had the confession, the opportunity of forgiveness, of the sacrament that they didn't have. The Protestant hadn't got the resources to get rid of his guilt and know that his repentance had been accepted. It must have been a lonely thing to be a murderer if you were Protestant. Yet, he himself now felt more alone than at any time in his life. For the first time he felt truly afraid for the future.

'Kieran,' she groaned, shaking him from his morbid mood, 'I want to go home.'

'Of course,' he lied. 'Of course we will.' She was bent double with pain as he led her carefully to the toilet. He gently lowered her knickers and sat her down. 'Call me when you're ready, my love,' he said before closing the toilet door. She deserved the dignity of being left alone there; at least that.

Teresa gasped. The medications she was taking caused her severe constipation. But at least this was one place where she found she could think more clearly. It was womb-like, safe and free from the prying eyes of those whose unswerving love only emphasised her own feelings of guilt and worthlessness. Kieran's and the children's very goodness made her feel even more inadequate. She'd noted the inflection in his voice that told her he did not mean for them to return home. But she had said nothing. She knew it was wrong to inflict more upheaval on their lives. The children had made new friends, especially Sian. Her daughter was so vulnerable, and she could see the pain in her eyes, the hurt and guilt that came with having a mother who was a cripple. The children, apart from the baby, who was too young to care, were living a daily nightmare. How desperate they must feel when they hear their mother screaming the house down. She didn't know what was worse: the spasms which locked her into a foetal position, the nerve pain which felt like being devoured by millions of ants or, when she showered, the beads of water that flayed her legs like air rifle pellets. Then there was the numbness in her pelvis, the chronic pain in her rectum and finally, and not least, the affect all this was having on her concentration. Some days she could barely think straight, fighting to find words that came out only as gobbledegook. Although Kieran said that this was the effect of the painkillers, she knew differently. He was right when he said that the whole of her central nervous system was shot to pieces and that no one, apart from her loved ones, really cared. No one deserved this merciless cruelty.

Several miles southwest of the epicentre of Teresa Kelly's torture, the man ultimately responsible for public health in the United Kingdom was in a hurry. Stephen Sellars slammed the door of his chauffeur-driven

Jaguar and strode purposefully through the portals of Richmond House. Under the right arm of his ample frame was an early edition of *The Times* he had picked up on his way to the office. It was his newspaper of choice, and he always liked to read it on his way into town from his Buckinghamshire home. The rest of the papers could wait. He could rely on the mandarins of Whitehall to have outlined any stories that might have remotely interested their Secretary of State for Health.

'Have you read this, Richard?' Sellars boomed, thwacking his desk with the rolled up newspaper. 'Bloody *Times* again.'

Richard Whiting, Principal Private Secretary and a man not noted to fluster under pressure, surveyed his Minister with tired grey eyes. He was an able young civil servant. While still relatively junior, he knew he was marked out for rapid promotion. The Department of Health was all about putting out fires and this one would be no different than the rest. While the NHS was in constant disarray, the beef fiasco had come and gone and the possible detrimental effects of genetic engineering were simmering on the back burner.

'It'll blow over soon enough, Minister,' he said soothingly. 'It's not as if it's of major interest to most people. It's not like Thalidomide.'

True, thought Sellars. Babies being born with no arms or legs was about as emotive as one could get, while this thing was an intangible. Everyone suffered pain at some time in his life, but pain was something you felt rather than saw. It was different with missing limbs. Nevertheless, it paid to be prudent about matters of pubic health. He would hate to be put in the same position as Stephen Dorrell, a former health secretary who had been forced to admit he misled the public about the dangers of beef and BSE. He also knew he must keep a tight rein on the wannabe mandarins, some of whom had admitted shredding incriminating files. 'Maybe it will blow over, Richard,' said the Minister pointing to the broadsheet, 'but this rag has a habit of getting its teeth into things. The opposition might table a question in the House. I want a meeting fixed for eleven o'clock. Round up the usual suspects.'

Whiting winced. He hated getting the circus involved. As far as he was concerned, the plethora of other private secretaries, special advisers and even the Minister of State just got in the way. Although he was very much the servant of both political and official heads, his access to the boss gave him opportunities to acquire information and influence. It was his job to take a pre-view of all drafts and memoranda and offer suggestions to make them more acceptable or convincing to Ministers. He prided himself on being his boss's eyes and ears, an efficient link between the Secretary of State and the government machine. He knew that Stephen Sellars was a man in a hurry and already being touted as a future Prime Minister Thus a certain Richard Whiting was not going to do anything that might loosen his own grip on the big man's coat tails.

It was almost midnight when Kieran Kelly arrived at the BBM building in London Wall for the overnight shift. He was an hour late. Fortunately, his colleagues understood. They knew what had happened to Teresa. He nodded to his colleague, Bill Parsons, and sat down beside him at the bank of screens that gave coverage of all twenty floors.

'All action tonight,' Parsons said jokingly.

'You mean same as usual - half a dozen offices ransacked, the vault broken into and the chairman's love letters to his mistress stolen.'

'Got it in one, Kieran.'

Kelly slumped in his chair. How he hated his job. The routine was always the same: arrive - read a couple of newspapers - check the outside of the building - check the inside of the building - read a couple more newspapers - check the outside of the building - check the inside of the building - read some more newspapers.

It was about five o'clock in the morning when he began flicking through the previous day's copy of *The Times*. The new day's papers did not usually arrive until after he'd clocked off. It was the only way he kept himself abreast of events. He hardly watched television, his off-duty hours being devoted completely to Teresa and the children. Suddenly a headline caught his attention. Unusually for *The Times*, it bore just one word in large bold letters: OUTRAGE.

Kelly folded the broadsheet in two and began reading:

Thousands of people in the UK continue to be maimed through the use of invasive spinal procedures, *writes Robert Robinson*. These carry a high potential risk for a public that continues to remain uninformed.

This is indeed an outrage that must be addressed in a proper manner by a government that should know better.

I am a former foreign correspondent who has covered wars in central Europe and Asia. Now, as a newly diagnosed sufferer of the spinal disease arachnoiditis, I am currently engaged in my own battle to force the Government to compensate the disease's victims and set up an inquiry into what I believe is the greatest medical tragedy of the late twentieth century. Along with twenty-five million other people in the past fifty years, I have had an injection of an iophendylate oil-based dye to discover if I had a slipped disc. Now, eighteen years later, that x-ray procedure has come back to haunt me.

An innocuous slip on the stairs apparently caused the dye to leak onto the arachnoid membrane around my spine. Suddenly, normal life has been replaced by incessant pain.

It can be any time of the day that the soldier ants begin their attack. Voracious of appetite, they brook neither opposition nor offer even a modicum of mercy; their little jaws working ceaselessly to tear my flesh apart. No amount of flailing on my part has any chance of halting their advance. At first, they begin circling my waist. Then, with the diligence of an army well versed in the art of blitzkrieg, they strike out along my limbs. Within seconds they reach the soles of my feet. Worse is to come. Not satisfied with torturing my lower extremities, they then head for the very core of my manhood. My genitals are being eaten alive.

No, these soldier ants are not real, but then they aren't exactly imaginary either. They are just some of the symptoms of a disease named after a creature not so far removed from the insect world: the spider. Adhesive arachnoiditis is a cruel spinal disease that produces the pain of cancer without the release of death. My life will not necessarily be cut short by the disease of, but knowing that I must suffer it the rest of my days is the hardest thing to accept. On 'flare-up' days I may burst into tears, not only because of the pain, but also because of the quality of life I have lost, because at the age of 52, life's dreams are mainly redundant. Because of its constancy, pain from arachnoiditis is uniquely more depressing and debilitating than more intense pain that is short-lived. Outwardly, I look 'normal,' a picture of health, inwardly, I die a little every day. Only fellow sufferers and the few doctors worldwide committed to our plight really understand the effects that this awful disease can have upon the human body and psyche.

I am the victim of an iatrogenic (doctor-caused) tragedy. No, I am not one of those high profile victims of a misplaced scalpel, oxygen starvation or transfusion of the wrong blood type; cases in which compensation for disability and suffering can sometimes run into the millions. I am one of the many uncompensated victims of perhaps the greatest international disaster in the history of medicine. I suffer from an iatrogenic disease which has been perpetrated on the unsuspecting and of which, I guarantee most of you have never heard (even my own GP professed ignorance). I also guarantee that many who read this will one-day experience some form of this disease. In most cases it will be put down to a bad back, rheumatism, bad circulation, or maybe even just plain old age. The number of these sufferers probably runs into many millions, and the numbers who will be completely disabled over the coming years may well run into hundreds of thousands. Arachnoiditis has been an ongoing epidemic, a social catastrophe by which other similar tragedies of life pale in comparison.

And yet, to all intents and purposes, this entity barely exists! There are few papers written about it and none printed in lofty publications such as The Lancet or the British Medical Journal. No money is being allocated for research into it. In fact, many so-called physicians will throw you out of their surgeries claiming it's all in your head. The reason why few of them will admit it exists is that to do so would mean admitting that they have been culpable in creating the tragedy. The Government declines to act, maintaining that it does not have the necessary statistics to do so. Because so many doctors either cannot or do not wish to recognise the symptoms, arachnoiditis is probably the most under-reported of illnesses.

The tobacco fiasco has ably demonstrated that where there is culpability, there is cover-up, and that where there is cover-up, there is denial.

Hundreds of thousands of sufferers now demand that their anguished cries be heard so that the carnage can be truly recorded and that future generations will not be subjected to the catastrophic application of dangerous spinal procedures.'

The article captivated Kelly. There was so much that now fitted into place. He learned that arachnoiditis was the inflammation of the fine and fragile arachnoid membrane surrounding the spinal cord and brain; that it was this membrane which produced the spinal fluid to keep the central nervous system nourished and healthy. He learned that diagnostic dyes had crippled more than a million people. But his eyes were transfixed by two paragraphs:

'Still more people, pregnant mothers, are offered an epidural to ease birth. When my wife was about to give birth to our daughter (now aged 24), she was offered an epidural. She was about to agree when, at the last moment, a Sister told her that it carried a small risk. My wife had second thoughts and declined.

Most anaesthetics and pain-killing steroids contain preservatives that have the potential to be highly toxic. An injection in the wrong place (and we are talking millimetres here) and the patient may never be able to experience another peaceful moment for the rest of his or her life. The victim will suffer the unrelenting agonies of arachnoiditis. He or she will also have a hell of a time getting an accurate diagnosis. This is the biggest insult. I, myself, was turned away by one 'specialist' who said my symptoms were psychosomatic. Another arrogant physician scratched his head when he saw my plight. What should I do? I pleaded. 'Ambulatory and Perambulatory,' was his cynical reply.'

Kelly learned that while oil-based dyes were no longer used in the West, their legacy lived on in the guise of steroid preparations, the most dangerous of which appeared to be a drug named Triamerol made by a company called Parados Pharmaceuticals. His ire increased as he read on.

'It took Parados Pharmaceuticals at least twenty years to finally warn doctors in the US that the steroid should not be injected into the spine. Meanwhile, hundreds of thousands are likely to suffer a fate worse than death, because its effects can sometimes take years to appear.

The profit motive means that Parados has so far resisted calls for this explicit warning to be duplicated in the UK, Australia and elsewhere.

15

The drug is banned for use on dogs and horses, but doctors can use it if they believe it will be of benefit to their patients. At a few hundred quid a shot, it can also benefit their pockets.

The evidence on Triamerol is not hard to find. Much of it has been uncovered by Dr David Wellington who is a world-renowned neurologist and one of America's leading experts on the uses of the drug. He says: 'No doctor should ever use Triamerol epidurally.' He has been warning about the drug for nearly twenty years.

'We are in deep, deep trouble,' he recently told an American TV reporter. "'I'm talking about hundreds of thousands of patients who will be paralysed. This stuff can take between eighteen months and four years before it exerts its paralytic and painful effects in our patients. We are sitting on a time bomb. What's going to happen is the biggest medical story of our time.'

He said the constituents of Triamerol were, in effect, a mixture of alcohol and detergent. He said it was 'like old-fashioned anti-freeze.'

'Now, would you let someone open up one of your nerves and pour that stuff on it? It's going to paralyse you - you can't put that anywhere near a nerve.'

Dr Wellington's studies show that, even if the needle is correctly placed in the epidural space, the drug can seep through the dura into the spinal fluid.

'If any of it leaks, one hundred percent of these patients will get arachnoiditis.' He said the results could be catastrophic.

'If you're numb from the rib margins down and lose your bladder function, and you lose control of your legs, and leak faeces the rest of your life, that is serious.'

In many cases, the pain and emotional damage is more obvious than the outward signs of injury. This makes it easy for doctors to pass off the problem as psychological and to suggest that the patient is malingering. Once the damage has been done, many doctors drop the patients like a hot potato.

After more than twenty years of campaigning, Dr Wellington and his colleagues forced Parados into issuing instructions to doctors not to use Triamerol in epidurals. But in the UK, Australia and New Zealand, no such instructions have been issued.

The warning on the drug packets outside the United States, says Dr Wellington, 'is much more passive. In effect, it says, "don't put it where you're not supposed to."'

He added: 'That's just like a lorry's about to hit you and I whisper get out of the way. It's laughable.'

Why do American patients get the benefit of a strong warning, while UK patients have to take their chances? It seems Parados's decidedly soft position here has clearly left doctors with the impression that the company is prepared to turn a blind eye to what they are doing and let them get on with it.

'I think that Parados has approached the problem of Triamerol with a great deal of self-interest,' says Dr Wellington. 'They should have banned it (for epidural use) years ago.'

Oil-based dyes and Triamerol. Different drugs. Same story.

The greatest medical tragedy of the late twentieth century is continuing unchecked into the new millennium.

This outrage must cease. Now.'

The article also dealt at length with what it termed the 'culpability, cover-up and denial' by successive British governments. At the end was a box outlining the newspaper's aim to campaign for an inquiry into invasive spinal procedures.

Kelly slowly lowered the newspaper onto the desk. He stared at the console in front him. 'Bastards,' he muttered. The familiar anger welled inside him, anger that in the past had had only one outlet.

'What's up, Kieran?' It was Parsons. 'You look like you've seen a ghost.' The bespectacled security man leaned over and just managed to catch a glimpse of the headline and opening paragraph before Kelly rolled up the newspaper and thrust it under his arm.

'Mind the shop, will you Bill, I'm going home half-an-hour early. Tell them I didn't feel well.' With this, Kelly hurried away towards the exit. The first light of dawn was infusing life into the City of London but scant relief into the person of Kieran Patrick Kelly.

As he drove home, the Irishman reflected on the article in *The Times*. While on the one hand it meant that the guilt for Teresa's condition had several addresses, there was comfort, scant though it was, in the fact that her disease now had a name and that she might be able to share her pain with other sufferers, those who knew exactly how she felt.

Within fifteen minutes and a couple of jumped red lights, Kelly had drawn up outside his home. He could barely contain his eagerness as he unlocked the front door. It was five-thirty in the morning. All was still. Should Teresa be asleep, he would not disturb her. He'd allow himself to give her a peck on her forehead, that's all.

Even the creaking stairs seemed to be heralding the important news he held in his hand. He glimpsed into the children's bedroom. Sian was snoring gently. How sweet was that sound, he thought, before creeping into his own bedroom. Thankfully, baby Patrick was also sleeping soundly in his crib.

The Irishman stepped gently towards his own bed. Teresa had left the curtains open and the dawn light played on the carapace of her gentle face. She was indeed asleep, but she must have had a hard night, for despite its serenity, the face was pallid. Her striking red hair was damp with sweat. For a few moments he stared at the delicate contours. Then a seed of concern began to sprout in the pit of his stomach. He felt his heartbeat begin to race, the tingling flush of fear tightening every muscle. Half-fearing the worst, it was another few seconds before he knelt beside the bed and kissed her forehead.

In an instant, Kieran Kelly found his body flinging itself backwards against the bedroom wall in a paroxysm that vented itself only in a dry scream.

CHAPTER TWO

The Everglades

Professor Jonathan Tring first sank to his knees and then launched his not insubstantial frame to lie prone on the prow of the airboat. With the huge fan switched off, there was a deathly silence, save for the rustling of the saw grass and reeds as he thrust aside a couple of large clumps. The lamp from his hard-hat pierced the darkness and played on an area about a yard ahead.

'Can you see one, Jonathan?' whispered the familiar Southern drawl of his companion. 'Take care now, ol' boy. They'll have your pecker if you ain't careful.'

Considering why they were there, the joke might have seemed to some to be in poor taste. Dr Eugene Smith, however, possessed a winning way and Tring was more than grateful for a little light entertainment. Events of the last six months had driven him almost to distraction. The Proctors, especially, had contrived to lead him a merry dance. He was beginning to wish he'd never met them.

'Don't worry, Eugene,' said Tring soothingly, 'I can see it now. It's a three-footer.'

Tring was a pukka thirtysomething Briton with an accent that was pure Received English. His grey-green eyes and thick, blond wavy hair combined with ruggedly handsome looks to leave the native girls drooling. This helped make his not infrequent trips to the States so invigorating. If only the world knew what scientists did when they let their hair down.

The Englishman had arrived in Florida a week earlier, his research sponsored by Parados Pharmaceuticals, his employer and a medium-sized player in the drug market worldwide. Tring was the company's new medical director and there were already some who saw the brilliant professor as a future chairman of the company. He was more

19

circumspect, preferring the excitement of the leading edge of research to the internecine warfare of the boardroom.

Tring dipped his hands into the black murky waters either side of the prow. This was his third trip to the Everglades and he never ceased to be amazed by the place. From the air, it seemed a vast, mysterious world of land and water at the edge of which civilization seemed to stop. From the highway, it appeared as an endless prairie above which birds flew in winter, while in summer towering storms deluged the land, giving sustenance to the swarms of mosquitoes and their prey. Here life teemed, water flowed and creatures struggled for survival in miraculous cycles that had been repeated over and over since prehistoric times.

Only today there was a difference. Now the cycles were dependent on humankind, on those who had tamed the waters and channelled the streams and, as a result, held the survival of this beautiful, fragile region in their hands.

Tring knew that man, as usual, was screwing things up. All the water feeding into the region was being controlled by artificial means. The complex food chain of the Everglades that had always been dependent on natural cycles of rain and drought was now at the mercy of those who manned the pipes and dykes to meet the demands of Florida's ever-growing human population. Two major highways, remarkable feats of wetland engineering, now cut across the once-pristine, free-flowing river of grass. Fertilizers and insecticides, so important to farmers yet deadly to many creatures of the wild, were threatening to upset the fragile balance of nature.

This was why Tring was here. Parados was sponsoring research into what these pollutants could do, and he was part of a scientific team called in to investigate the declining number of alligators.

'I've got it!' the Englishman hissed. With his right hand clasped tightly around the baby alligator's neck and the left holding the tail, he hauled the reptile aboard the boat. The scientist whipped it over onto its back. The animal, seemingly impervious to the indignity to which it was being subjected, made little effort to break free. The lamp from Eugene Smith's hard-hat played on the creature's dank white underbelly. The American inserted his little finger into a hole and hooked out the alligator's stunted phallus.

'Jesus!' Smith gasped in exasperation at the seventh deformity of the night. 'This one also ain't never gonna be no daddy.'

Tring shared his colleague's desperation. What was happening in the Everglades was mirrored in his own country, albeit not to the same extent. Nevertheless, there was no doubting that the human population in the UK was being affected by water pollution. Sperm counts were down and getting lower by the year. The chemical companies and all those pouring effluent into the rivers had much to answer for.

The indignant ringing of his mobile phone interrupted the Englishman's thoughts. It was the hotel switchboard.

'Sorry to trouble you, sir,' came an apologetic female voice. 'We have an urgent fax from your head office in the UK. Shall I read it?'

'Yes, go ahead,' Tring replied, wondering what on earth could be so important that it could not wait until later.

'It reads: "Return UK immediately. I will be incommunicado until you arrive. JP."'

'Is that all?'

'Yes, sir.'

Tring thanked the girl and tugged on Eugene Smith's sleeve. The American was still bent over the belly-up alligator. 'Eugene, old boy, throw this one back and let's vamoose. They want me back in the UK pronto.'

'They damn well might have chosen better timing,' Smith grunted, still holding the alligator's miniature phallus between thumb and forefinger. 'Did they say why?' There was a tinge of disappointment in the American's voice. He would miss the gangling Limey.

'No,' Tring replied, scratching his head. 'And it seems they don't want me to know...yet.'

A day later and the scientist was back across the Pond. His boss had apparently been singing his praises, although it was said that when Jack Proctor lauded you, your letter of resignation was already written.

'Smart people with smart ideas make for smart business, and that's why I brought Professor Jonathan Tring into this organisation.'

The compliment was made by a man who commanded attention, not least because of his vocal and physical attributes. John Albert Proctor was a Yorkshire terrier who looked and growled like a bulldog. He was stocky and muscle-bound, with gimlets for eyes, a couple of unsightly warts either side of his pug nose, and jowls that hung like heavily laden coat hangers. Snatch away his pinstripe and he could have been a market trader dealing in bone china seconds. That he ruled Parados Pharmaceuticals with an iron fist would have surprised nobody acquainted with the history of other leaders of men who were, in the parlance of the politically correct, vertically challenged. Being a middle-aged multi-millionaire, it was also little wonder that he had availed himself of a wife half his age, and that she was stunningly beautiful.

Tring smiled diffidently at Proctor's compliment. The scientist was more at ease with molecules than with mankind, his taut six-foot-two-inch frame and craggy good looks suggesting a man with a physical rather than a cerebral occupation.

'We have been called the fastest-growing pharmaceutical company in this country,' Proctor continued, the pug face beaming with bonhomie. 'And in order to keep it up, we have to be at the leading edge of research and development. We're now in the twenty-first century and the pace of technology demands constant application. You have a hard act to follow, Jonathan.'

The faces around the boardroom table nodded in acquiescence. They had all benefited from the expertise of the late medical director, Dr Martin Locke, who had developed several drugs that became market leaders. His suicide had shocked the industry and curtailed a talent that was about to enjoy its finest triumph. Worse still, it had caused Parados shares to drop a few points. The one thing Jack Proctor abhorred was a drop in the index. Although he was the majority and controlling shareholder, he liked to keep the others happy, and, in general, they had been kept very happy indeed.

'Nevertheless,' Proctor went on, 'I have the fullest confidence that Professor Tring will add a new dimension to our efforts. We must not remain complacent. While we've bucked the trend by coming up with new products to replace the high-profit drugs going off patent, it does mean that others see us a target for acquisition. Companies big and small are tangoing with each other, but let me say categorically that they'll dance to my tune and that the only acquiring around here is going to be done by me.'

The chairman's determined missive did not go unappreciated by his audience. They knew that any takeover of Parados would probably cost them their jobs. Many companies had reacted to new and tougher times by slashing their workforce. One out of six jobs had been lost since those who paid the drug bills had been in open revolt over the high cost of medicine. Although the directors of finance, distribution and sales and marketing may not have liked Proctor, they knew where their bread was buttered. Merger mania had gripped the industry. Giants like Glaxo and Wellcome, Pharmacia and Upjohn had amalgamated. In the past few years alone, drug companies had put together more than a hundred billion dollars worth of major mergers or acquisitions. Some companies, such as America's Merck and Britain's SmithKline Beecham, had decided that if you couldn't beat them, you could buy them. They bought up prescription-management companies that sold drugs at lower prices. Then, to cap it all, Glaxo Wellcome had merged with SmithKline to become the world's market leader. The once gentlemanly industry, in which hostile deals were almost unknown, had turned vicious. And should there ever be a Pill Inc., then the men around the boardroom table would prefer Jack Proctor to be at its head. The old hands present could sense their boss was getting up a head of steam.

'While we've made good profits from producing generic brands, we must continue to make sure we keep being innovative.' Proctor shook his stubby fist to emphasise the point. 'The weakness of big companies is that size is no guarantee of success in developing new products. Huge firms lose flexibility and creativity. We are middle of the road and that's just about the best place to be right now.' The chairman took a beat to allow affirmation from his audience, then, 'but our great company is only as good as the people in it. And that means you, each and every one of you. Leaders must steer those under them to perform at their best by making them feel comfortable and rewarded, not just by salary but also by recognition and positive reinforcement. You should each increase your levels of competence in information technology so that it is a productivity tool and not simply an intellectual toy. To keep abreast of what's happening in world markets; you need a perspective that extends beyond the borders of the company. Change is also vital. No company can afford to stand still. Some of you probably know the story about the flea circus.'

Tring noted the faces around the table remained blank although he had a distinct feeling they had heard all this before.

'You put a bunch of fleas into a box,' the chairman went on, 'and they start to hop up and down. When you remove the lid, they all continue to hop up to the same level. They don't want to hit their heads on the ceiling that still exists in their own minds. And that's exactly how it is in an organisation. If the ceiling is gone, managers must make this clear to their colleagues. People in organisations are programmed just like the fleas. They know how high they can hop without getting hurt. But this says nowt about their abilities. They, and you, can hop higher!'

Jack Proctor pounded the table as he finished his rally and then stared disconcertingly at Tring. The breast-beating was over. Everyone knew the real reason for the meeting, except, it seemed, the professor. The Yorkshireman took out a copy of *The Times* from his briefcase and looked sternly at his new ward. 'And now, lad, let me tell you why I had you recalled.'

Tring listened attentively while Proctor read out the newspaper story in full. It was soon clear to him that his boss wanted a damage limitation exercise.

'Jonathan,' he said conspiratorially, 'I want you to be our front man on this. You will liaise with the media and the government. Basically, you will be the voice of Parados.'

'But you know I'm busy with the new product,' the professor protested. The last thing he wanted was to get involved in a slanging match over something he had neither introduced nor worked on. He was a scientist. Triamerol was an old product and, anyway, it had been a previous incumbent's baby. The machinations revealed by the newspaper article were something for which he felt no responsibility.

'You're the best man for the job, Jonathan,' Proctor said bullishly. He was the boss and would not be put off by his ward's protestations. 'I want you to work on a strategy to handle this. The last thing we need is a scandal that will hit our share price and leave us open to predators. I have my own ideas, but I want to hear yours first.'

With this, the chairman arose, zipped up his briefcase with an exaggerated flourish and waddled out of the boardroom.

Tring looked forlornly at the rest of the board members. He sensed that no help would be forthcoming there. 'Rather you than me,' he thought he heard one mutter.

Still pondering the task set for him, the scientist took time out for a coffee in the boardroom lounge. Glad none of the others had joined him, he reflected on his short time with the company. During his first few weeks, he'd spent much of his time exploring the impressive headquarters of Parados Pharmaceuticals. Twenty years earlier a huge tract had been carved out of the Essex countryside near Harlow in order to provide a Greenfield site conducive to the well being of staff. The glass edifice allowed an extraordinary amount of light to enter its innards. The chairman believed that neon lighting made people drowsy, thus reducing their capacity for work.

The location of the company gave easy access to the country's main motorway routes. It was situated a few minutes from the M25, which made it possible to circumnavigate London and spin off at all points of the compass. The site also lay adjacent to the M11 and an easy forty-five-mile run to Cambridge, repository for many of the finest young scientific minds in the country. All had conspired to give sustenance to a workforce of three thousand, although two-thirds of these were employed in the company's foreign subsidiaries.

The Proctors, leaders of this motley crew, had left for a month-long series of worldwide conferences the day after his arrival. 'Get to know your staff and get to know the company,' Jack Proctor had counselled. 'The real work will start when I get back. Nobody gets owt for nowt in this company.'

Thus Tring had immersed himself in getting to know the firm's products and his immediate subordinates. Each seemed eager to please their new director, although he felt an immediate rapport with one of them. Harold Spencer was a bluff Mancunian who was in charge of clinical research. Rotund and middle-aged, he had a ready wit and a general irreverence for the serious business at hand. His preference for wearing brightly coloured bow ties was his sole eccentricity. Yet he felt instinctively that this antithesis of the beetle-browed scientist was in fact a past master at his job. Clinical research was part of the complex procedure to demonstrate the effectiveness and safety of drugs and other products of the pharmaceutical industry. It required the collaboration of many personnel with a variety of skills and their leader had to be someone they could trust. Drug researchers did not like to think of themselves as the scientific equivalent of the National Lottery; hurling a huge range of compounds at a disease in the hope that one of them will cure it. They preferred to believe that rational thought rather than blind chance lay behind their successes. All members of the team, including secretaries and administrators, had to be made aware of the procedures of clinical research and, in particular, the rules placed upon their actions by Good Clinical Practice and Standard Operating Procedures. The professor had noted that the research team at Parados appeared to be both knowledgeable and contented, which was not entirely unexpected. The company was expanding exponentially and most of them held shares that were ever increasing in value.

'A penny for your thoughts.'

Tring was startled from his musings, but then relaxed on seeing that it was Harold Spencer. 'Unprintable, Harold,' he joked.

'He's quite ruthless, you know,' Spencer said. 'Oh, don't worry, Jonathan,' the florid Mancunian added, carefully pouring his superior a steaming beverage. 'I'm generally right about who I share my confidences with.'

'I'm sorry, but who are you talking about, Harry?' Tring asked somewhat disingenuously.

Spencer raised his thick eyebrows in mock surprise. 'The man with the Midas touch, the Pit bull terrier of our industry, el supremo. Need I go on?'

'I would think that a man in his position would need to be like that.'

Spencer shrugged quickly. 'Sure. I mean the shareholders are happy, most of the staff are happy. Uncle Tom Cobbleigh and all are happy.'

'So what's the problem?' Tring queried, accepting the steaming mug from his colleague and gingerly savouring the first sip of piping hot coffee.

'He killed him you know.' The reply was almost matter-of-fact.
'Killed who?' Tring's voice was tinged with apprehension.
'Old Lockey.'
'Sorry.'
'You know, the guy you've replaced.'
'I'm sorry, I still don't understand. Everyone knows it was suicide.'
Spencer leaned back and half sat on one of the canteen tables. 'Maybe. Proctor would be nothing without Locke. Martin was here at the beginning. He was a good man. He developed the drugs that helped make this company a world leader. Sure, Proctor gave him some shares to try to keep him happy. But it was like feeding a dog a bone. Fine to get your teeth into but ultimately not very fulfilling.'
'I still don't understand,' Tring said weakly.
'Let me put it like this,' Spencer went on, 'it was like putting a Pit bull in with a Chihuahua. Lockey was run ragged. Once Proctor gets his jaws into you, he doesn't let go. The man is so consumed by power that if he senses a weakness, you're finished.'
'But Locke was here for twenty years. He could have left at any time.'
'Sure. I used to think the same. But Martin Locke was a complex character. He was a quiet man, always willing to please. Proctor took advantage of this and pushed him to the limit. Proctor always wanted more and better drugs and sometimes I wondered whether Lockey had a home to go to.'
Tring scratched his temple. Locke had topped himself at fifty-five. In the enthusiasm of his new job, Tring was already putting in fourteen-hour days, but he was damned sure if he would sell his soul to his new employer. There had to be a perspective on everything.
'Anyway,' Spencer went on in an accent as wide as the ship canal, 'I think Proctor had something else on Locke.'
'What do you mean?'
'I don't know. Nobody knew much about Locke's private life, what little he had of it. There were rumours. You know, a middle-aged bachelor and all that.'
'I'm still a bachelor,' said Tring, eager to allay any doubts about his own preferences.

'No, I mean Lockey *was* a bit effeminate. I know that doesn't necessarily mean anything nowadays, but the rumours persisted. It's just a hunch. Anyway, he killed himself because of anxiety about something, sex or overwork, or both.'

'What about Mrs Proctor?' Tring was eager to change the subject. 'I only saw her once, on my first day. She certainly is a looker.'

'Ah, Mrs Proctor, our very own Southern belle,' Spencer gestured expansively. 'I have a collection of aphorisms to describe our Sharon. It was Emerson who said that a man's wife had more power over him than the state. And remember, it's the woman who chooses the man who chooses her.' The Lancastrian chuckled and tweaked his purple bow tie. 'Can't recall who said that.'

Tring smiled, adding an aphorism of his own. 'So she's the power behind the throne.'

'I guess so. Nobody really knows for sure, but I think you should know that Jack Proctor is an insanely jealous man. As far as his wife is concerned, it's a case of you can look, but you can't touch. Every ugly old man with pots of money would be on his guard with a woman like that. Besides which, she's American.'

'So.'

'I don't like Yanks much. They're all gold-diggers.'

'I hope you restrict these comments to people you can trust,' said the new medical director. He was worried that Spencer was being a little too patent.

'Humph,' growled the older man, 'if he sacked me tomorrow, he'd be doing me a favour. I've had enough anyway. I've spit blood for this company, and I might take early retirement. My wife's been pushing me to pack it in for a couple of years.'

'Meanwhile, it's back to the grindstone, old chap,' Tring said, deciding to change the subject. 'The molecules are waiting.'

As Tring watched his colleague leave the lounge, he couldn't help wondering again why his predecessor had taken his own life. There were many things he didn't know about Proctor and his company, among which was the listening device hidden in a switch to the right of the coffee maker.

In Whitehall, Stephen Sellars faced the motley collection of his minions with the air of a man who was used to getting results. Power might be the capacity to make others do what you wanted, but he also knew that as a politician, it was much better to foster relationships through persuasion rather than command 'Well, gentlemen,' he said, peering above rimless Armani spectacles, 'you've all read the article, you've all been briefed and you've had plenty of time to come up with some suggestions. I'm sure they'll be good ones.'

With others hesitating, Richard Whiting decided to take the initiative. He needed to earn some kudos and he'd done enough research on the matter to know about as much as anyone present. It was also important, of course, to remain the moderator of this particular set of in-house prima donnas, each of whom coveted sole possession of the Health Secretary's heart and mind. He cleared his throat to signal his intentions, only to hesitate upon seeing the vein on his boss's temple rise like a blue worm. It always held a fascination for him. The delay proved costly.

'Secretary,' Brian Bingham, the parliamentary private secretary, rasped, 'I have investigated this matter fully and it is my belief that we should stick to the tack taken in the past by our predecessors.'

Damn it, thought Whiting, didn't this ginger-haired idiot with his adenoidal croaking know there was a pecking order. It galled him even more that the man had come to the same conclusion as himself.

'Elaborate, Brian, please,' Sellars requested. His soft Highland accent was edged with steel. He'd already done his own homework, although there would always be some things he could not know; that's why he had this lot around him.

'Well, I've looked up previous Hansard's and even the Tories managed to get themselves out of a sticky situation over this matter in the past.'

'Presumably, that's when we were in opposition,' Sellars proffered.

'Er, yes.'

'What did we have to say about the matter, then?'

Much to Bingham's chagrin, he accidentally dislodged the stack of papers in front of him. It was enough to put his presentation out of kilter.

Whiting took his chance. 'If I may, sir,' he chimed smugly, 'I think my colleague is referring to nineteen ninety-three, when David Blunkett was Shadow Health Minister.'

'What did he say?' Sellars queried. The blind politician was an old friend and colleague, but was no longer in government having lost a relatively safe seat in the last election. The Party was still scrabbling around to find him an even safer seat somewhere else.

All eyes around the long table were fixed on Whiting. The Minister's Principal Private Secretary cleared his throat. What he now had to say was about as embarrassing as it could get. 'Er, well, sir, he called for emergency action on arachnoiditis. He referred to the damage caused to innocent people's health as a needless tragedy and said there was the need for a clear statement of precisely what action has been taken.'

'And what action did the Tories take?'

'Well, nothing, naturally, sir. You see, there was a court case in motion. About four hundred patients were suing Glaxo, the maker of a diagnostic dye called Myodil, which was injected epidurally or intrathecally. They settled out of court in nineteen ninety-five, with Glaxo denying liability.'

'Did Blunkett say anything else in parliament?'

Whiting took a deep breath. This was the double-whammy. 'Yes, sir, he called for specific steps, including the establishment of a full inquiry, no-fault compensation for the victims and all invasive procedures carried out in the course of spinal treatment to be immediately replaced with safer procedures.'

Sellars smiled knowingly, 'And you're going to say that, now we're in power, we can't afford to take that stand.'

'Er, yes, precisely, sir.' Whiting could feel his collar begin to tighten.

'Why not?'

'Because it would be too costly. There are millions of people with back trouble who would come out of the woodwork and make a claim. We'd be snowed under.'

Sellars pondered his adviser's words. Admitting anything would indeed open a Pandora's box, but he still needed more information. 'How many people are suffering from this disease in the United Kingdom?'

'We have no real idea, sir.'

'Why not?'

Bingham watched with undisguised satisfaction as Whiting's triumphant intervention began to wilt. The man didn't have the answer.

'If I may, sir,' Bingham said taking his cue, 'arachnoiditis is under-reported. Because it's iatrogenic, doctors have, understandably, been somewhat reticent about reporting it.'

Sellars was beginning to feel irritated. The blue vein on his temple was becoming positively rampant. 'Damn it, man, is it in the thousands or millions?'

It was Whiting's turn to revel in his colleague's discomfort. 'If I may say so, Minister,' he interjected, 'the condition is unlikely to be affecting more than a few thousand individuals. It is quite rare.'

'How do we know that, if it is under-reported by doctors?' the Scotsman fired back. The set of blank faces before him spoke volumes. Secrecy was the not the exclusive domain of the medical profession. Ted Heath may have been a Tory, but the former Prime Minister was right when he pointed out that Britain was the most secretive of all the Western democracies and that the habit of telling its citizens as little as possible was ingrained in the ruling classes, whatever their political persuasion. There was no greater citadel of secrecy than the Department of Health. His predecessor was given a remit to follow a path of more openness and accountability, but it counted for nothing. The system was the system and he was not about to buck it. He already knew what he must do. As much as he sympathised with the sufferers, they were in a no-win situation. He was determined that this would not become another scandal like BSE or Thalidomide.

By the end of the day, a press release was winging its way to the media.

This Government does recognise that arachnoiditis is a very painful condition. There is no dispute about the suffering it may cause. As there is at present no known cure for the disease process, it is for doctors to decide, in individual cases, which treatment will best alleviate the symptoms of this condition and help to control the pain.

There is also no dispute that arachnoiditis can be a side effect of invasive back procedures like myelograms and epidurals. However, no treatment is completely risk-free. It is for the clinicians to use their knowledge, skill and experience to weigh carefully the likely benefits of any procedure against the anticipated risks for the individual patient and, following discussion with the patient, to exercise their clinical judgement accordingly.

There has never been a cover-up on arachnoiditis. It has been a known possible side effect of certain medicinal products like Myodil *and* Triamerol. *Therefore this Government does not intend to hold any form of inquiry into arachnoiditis nor to award compensation to those suffering from the disease.*

CHAPTER THREE

Belfast, 1993

Father Seamus O'Hare was popular with sinners, and understanding of sin. But the role he found most harrowing was performing the Last Rites. Ministering to the sick, injured and dying was part of the covenant he had made with the Holy Father, and was something he could accept as part of his calling. What he could never bring himself to accept was what he was now being asked to do. It sickened him, and yet he knew he was being left little choice. Priests were not immune from bullets.

'Don't try to be heroic or we'll kill both of you. Just get on with it.'

O'Hare looked into the speaker's eyes, the only features visible from within a woollen balaclava. They were a piercing blue and icy cold, two anonymous sentinels in a field of black. It was the voice, however, that struck a chord. The priest knew that voice. Somewhere in the deep recesses of his mind was stored the name of its owner, for when one sat behind the confessional screen for so many years, one developed an innate recognition of voices.

'Well, what are you waiting for?' The utterance was as threatening as the pistol pointed at him.

'Let us alone, please,' said the priest quietly. It was an appeal to a mind that he knew was tortured, severed from the soul. These paramilitaries had usurped God. They had declared that they alone had the power of life and death. And yet they relied on the confession to absolve them of responsibility.

'Two minutes, and that's all,' replied the voice. 'He's already made his confession to us and this will be his last.'

Father O'Hare watched the gunman and his two masked accomplices leave the dingy room. He despised these active-service Provos who went to daily Mass and communion, did their novenas, went home, put on balaclavas and then went out with the gun. He was sure they had a

33

prayer to St Joseph in their pockets for a happy death and a small wooden cross to protect them from evil. It was the theology of the just war. These people did not regard killing as a sin.

The good priest sighed before turning his attention to the unfortunate victim. The man's face was slightly bruised and his lips swollen, but he did not look as if he had been tortured, as was usually the case. He was young, probably no more than twenty. Tied to a chair, he seemed to have long given up the struggle for freedom.

'Please help me, Father.' The words were almost inaudible.

The priest's eyes filled with tears. There were two victims in the room, but only one was about to die. 'God is with you, my son,' he whispered unconvincingly. 'Do you want to confess?'

'Yes,' said the young man, suddenly finding an inner strength. 'I betrayed my friends, Father. Our family is poor. We needed the money, and the British - oh, what difference does it make now? I'm going to die. Isn't that right, Father?'

The priest put his arm around the informer. There were those so-called holy men who would have applauded the action that was about to take place; that a rat, however young, deserved to die. But he was there to offer God's absolution and comfort, not to preach to those who would not listen.

'My son,' he said, placing his hand on the dank thatch of blond hair, 'I absolve you of your sins in the name of the Father, and of the Son, and of the Holy Spirit.' His voice was breaking, his soul ruptured almost beyond repair. It was a hideous event. Yet for a priest the confessional extended into all aspects of life. He could not be judge, jury or law enforcer. Those roles would make people feel that a priestly confidence was worthless. He could comfort the dying, offer God's absolution, and confront violence with Christianity, but the moment he stepped outside of that framework his role as a priest was compromised. It might be seen by some as a cop-out, but what was the alternative?

The young man began to sob quietly. Just as O'Hare straightened, there came a knock at the door. In one last act of comfort, the priest clasped the victim's shoulder and turned towards the door. The man with blue eyes opened it and beckoned for him to leave the room.

'This is against the law of God,' O'Hare protested weakly, as he was led from the derelict building.

The reply was as contrary as it was final: 'You look after the law of God, Father, and we'll take care of business.'

With this, the priest was bundled into the back seat of a car in which sat other masked members of the Provisional Irish Republican Army. Within fifteen minutes he was back in his church, kneeling in front of the Madonna and Child. He may not have heard the shooting which despatched the young informer, but he was now able to put a name to the voice of the terrorist leader.

'May God have mercy on your soul, Kieran Patrick Kelly,' he prayed.

Kelly stirred. Memories of death in times past had flooded his dreams, leaving him bathed in a cold sweat. Still curled in a foetal position next to the chilled and lifeless body of his one true love, he began to luxuriate in the ether between waking and slumber. It was a time when wishful thinking still dominated reality; a time when the white knight always rode to the rescue, plucking the fair maid from the gnarled grasp of the Angel of Death; a time for the family Kelly to celebrate love, unity and wholeness. They were indestructible. And yet the sound of a baby's distress began to invade his idyll.

It was several seconds before the Irishman opened his eyes. The pressing demands of baby Patrick went unheeded as he stared at the ceiling, willing it to come crashing down and put an end to his misery. Death was no stranger to him, for in the past he had been its harbinger. He had been the nemesis, the instrument that God had used in order to punish those who were godless in their perfidy. Stool pigeons, informers, traitors, they had all deserved to die, but not Teresa Kelly; not this woman of such selfless devotion to her family, such innate goodness, such piety.

He leaned over her inert form and picked up the empty bottle of painkillers from the side table. He stared at the innocuous brown container. How much torment must she have endured to have taken an action so anathema to her religion? He cursed himself for not recognising the signs, and yet, if he were honest, there were none. She had borne her illness with such fortitude, always putting the concerns of her husband and children before her own.

Kelly rose slowly from the bed and crossed wearily to the crib. He gently cradled his new son, whose sobbing pierced his heart like the devil's trident. Only then did he allow his own tears to flow, for anger was rapidly becoming the dominant emotion. One thought now consumed Kieran Patrick Kelly: revenge.

Later that day, Professor Jonathan Tring was sitting uncomfortably before his chairman. 'The best thing to do when dealing with the press is to take the wind out of their sails, JP,' said the scientist somewhat tentatively. He felt not a little discomfort as Proctor fixed him with a cold, inquisitive gaze that was matched by that of his wife in the huge portrait painting hanging on the wall. The enigmatic Sharon Proctor's steel-blue eyes seemed to be reminding visitors who the real boss was at Parados.

'Stunning, isn't she?' the Yorkshireman said in a tone which implied forbidden fruit.

'Er, quite,' Tring stuttered. He felt himself blushing like a naughty schoolboy caught peeping into the girls' changing room. The scientist sought to quickly return to the matter in hand. 'We must issue a statement without further delay.' It had not taken the professor long to ascertain that the company had been less than forthright about ensuring the safe use of one of its products. No law had been broken - yet.

'You mean like the government has done,' Proctor growled.

'No, I think we have to go a little bit further. We have to bring the instructions on the use of Triamerol into line with those issued outside the U.K.'

'Wouldn't that mean admitting culpability, lad?'

'No, I don't believe so. Legally we were under no obligation to advise doctors not to put it anywhere. It is, after all, a drug that has produced some benefit in epidural use. Apart from the US, we have always left it to the medical profession to use its discretion.' Tring felt uneasy. The company had taken almost two decades to issue the new edict across the pond. The press had not been slow to point this out, but statistics, or more pertinently, the lack of them, could always be used to extricate the company from a sticky situation. He knew that none of this was lost on his chairman.

'So what do you suggest, lad?' Proctor queried.

Tring produced the press release he had spent hours formulating and placed it face up on the chairman's table.

Proctor slowly withdrew reading glasses from an inside pocket of his tweed jacket. He placed them at the end of his pug nose, where they threatened to keep slipping off.

Tring watched his boss dissect every word. They both knew that any mistake would be picked up by the media and used to slaughter the company and, more importantly, the share price. Basically, he had written that while there was no statistical evidence to prove that Triamerol was more dangerous in epidural use than other drugs of its type, the company would now advise doctors worldwide that this use was not indicated. However, the company could not be held liable if individual doctors believed the epidural or intrathecal use of Triamerol would be of benefit to their patients. Tring knew that this was a cop-out. As long as Parados never said the drug *should* be used for epidural or intrathecal use, then the blame for its use could always be landed at the door of the medical profession, which would, in turn, claim that there was not enough statistical evidence to support its contra-indication. When in doubt, obfuscation was always the best policy. Tring had agonised over the task set him. Perhaps he should have resigned from a company that had shown such a cavalier attitude towards the public, and yet he knew that by staying on the inside he could now do more good. He could attempt to rein in the Machiavellian machinations of the man before him by making sure the company trod a more ethical path in future. Meanwhile, he had little choice but to play his master's game.

After what seemed an eternity, Jack Proctor slowly lowered the sheet of paper onto the table and then pushed it towards his chief scientist. 'Publish and be damned,' he said with finality.

It was slightly less than a month later when Kelly drove into the car park of a halfway house hotel just off the M1 motorway near Leicester. It was the sort of nondescript watering hole used by many organisations that needed a venue suitable for members who might live as far apart as Land's End and John O'Groats.

The Irishman switched off the engine of his ten-year-old VW Golf and sat for a few moments to luxuriate in the spring sun as it beat on the windscreen. The cocoon-like feeling brought him a rare moment of solace from the torment of the past few weeks. Closing his eyes, he imagined that Teresa was still alive, that his children were playing in the garden, that it was a Friday evening and she was calling them in for tea. Poached cod and mashed potatoes topped with mushy peas. He could taste it even now; so much better than the cardboard upon which he now subsisted. Junk food in a junk life. As melancholy once more swept over him, he could taste the salt tears of his daughters as he relived the funeral of their mother; tears that were repeated when he had flown them to Belfast to hand them over to their Aunt Mary. He knew that he could not raise three children on his own. Terry's sister and her husband were childless and the children could not have been in better hands. He spoke to them by phone every evening and intended to fly to Belfast every second weekend to see them, as long as this did not conflict with his plan. Nothing, not even his own children, must stand in the way of his destiny. He slapped the steering wheel as if to reinforce his belief that what he was planning to do was right and just.

A voice filtered through his half-open window. 'Have you come for the meeting?'

Kelly looked up from his dashboard to see a dapper middle-aged man who was standing next to a woman in a wheelchair. The Irishman nodded.

The dapper man opened the driver's door of the Golf. 'Follow us,' he said.

Kelly climbed out of his car and the three of them were soon in the hotel lobby.

'Are you a sufferer yourself?' the wheelchair woman asked.

'No, it's my wife.'

The wheelchair woman sighed. 'Nurse was she? So many nurses are sufferers. They do their backs in helping others and then get crippled by their own profession.'

They entered the lobby and approached a table at which sat two female committee members. Kelly knew this because of the badges they wore. One of them was extraordinarily beautiful with blonde hair swept back into a bun and mesmerising turquoise eyes. He thought she must have been in her late twenties. He was surprised when she spoke, for her voice bore a German accent.

'You must be Mr O'Donaghue,' she said. Her voice was kind and her smile generous.

'How did you guess?'

She laughed and handed him a badge with his name on it. 'You told us you were coming, and you're the only new person here. You're originally from Belfast, aren't you?'

'Yes, and your good self?'

'Austro-Hungarian,' she said proffering her hand. 'Countess Magda von Esterhazy.'

Kelly took her delicate hand in his and brushed it with his lips. 'Charmed, I'm sure. My first real live Countess.'

'A real gentleman, Magda,' enthused a rather portly lady sitting next to the Countess.

'Mr O'Donaghue is married, Linda. It's your wife who's a sufferer, isn't it, Mr O'Donaghue.'

'Call me Kieran,' Kelly replied. 'Yes. Unfortunately she was too ill to come today.'

The Countess sighed. 'There are so many who are too ill to travel, Kieran. We have about five thousand members of our Circle of Friends with Arachnoiditis, but we get only a fraction along to our annual meetings. There are probably only about sixty here today. Anyway, it's always good to welcome new members. There are so many out there who have not got a clue what they are suffering from or how they can get advice and support.'

Kelly noticed a flicker of pain cross his hostess's eyes. It was only then that he realised she was sitting in a wheelchair. He knew she must be in torment but was too proud to show it. 'That's why I'm here,' he said. 'I've come to find out as much as possible.'

'Yes,' the Countess said through pursed lips, her high cheekbones suddenly flushing with anger. 'Something must be done about it.'

'Something *will* be done about it,' said Kelly, his voice suddenly cold and distant.

Both sets of eyes, differing in shade but equally as piercing, met in mutual defiance, not of each other, but of the insanity that had ruined both their lives. The voice of the woman named Linda broke in, 'I think we're all here, now. We can start the meeting.' She stood up and began to wheel the Countess towards the dais. Kelly followed and sat in the front row facing a table at which were seated five committee members.

Linda nodded deferentially to the Countess. 'If I may, Madam Chairman, I should like to welcome everyone here to our eighth annual general meeting. Most of you know one another. We have one new member to introduce to you. He is a carer whose wife is a sufferer and unfortunately cannot be with us. Welcome, Mr Kieran O'Donaghue from London.'

Kelly nodded as all eyes turned towards him. He could not help feeling that if he had known about this support group earlier, Teresa would not have felt so desperately alone. Two weeks after the funeral, he had bought himself a computer. It had taken him a further week to master it enough to surf the World Wide Web and garner all the information on the disease that had wrecked his life. He had discovered COFWA and had applied to join immediately, albeit under a fictitious name.

'And now I should like to ask our chairperson to inform us of the latest developments in our fight for justice,' said the beaming Linda, and moved the microphone in front of the Countess.

'Welcome friends,' the Countess began, 'I really do wish that I could have more positive things to report, but as you know the Government continues to be, how you say, obdurate. The press, too, seems to be avoiding the issue. We had a brief flurry of support from *The Times*, but they, too, now appear to be putting our plight on the, er, what is that English phrase ...'

'Back burner,' came a voice from the back of the room.

'Yes, back burner.'

Kelly found himself mesmerised by the Countess. She possessed a classical beauty that reminded him of Catherine Deneuve. It seemed criminal that she should be reduced to a life of pain in a wheelchair.

'Anyway,' the Countess continued, 'you can rest assured that the committee will not give up the fight. We are continuing our postcard blitz on the Prime Minister's office and the Department of Health, and of course we urge members to carry on lobbying their MPs.'

'But they don't give a toss,' came the voice again. 'They're all in the pay of the pharmaceutical companies whether they be politicians, papers or doctors.' The accent was East Anglian and belonged to a rotund middle-aged man whose ruddy face was swelling with indignation. With obvious difficulty he struggled to his feet and leant on his stick. 'Madam Chairman,' he continued, 'we've been pussyfooting around for nigh on seven years. We have to become more aggressive. Everyone here knows nothing will ever be accomplished by being nice to these people. They're all corrupt.

'What do you suggest, Ronald?' the Countess asked kindly.

'I for one would be willing to go on a hunger strike. I can't take the pain anymore, Magda. I can't.' Tears began to well in his eyes. 'Something must be done,' he muttered and slumped back in his chair.

'Does anyone here feel the same as Ronald?' queried the Countess.

The response was mute. It was clear to Kelly that most of the sufferers would love to imagine themselves carrying out such an action. But hunger strikes were for healthy people. They were for political ideologists like Bobby Sands and the other IRA heroes who had sacrificed their lives for the cause. These people were too sick to have the strength to starve themselves.

'I'm sorry, Ronald,' the Countess continued, her turquoise eyes shining with compassion, 'I know how frustrated you must feel. The fight for justice is a long and lonely road, but we have a saying in German: *Das kleinste Haar wirft seinen Schatten*, the smallest hair casts a shadow. I assure you that we will prevail in the end.' She hesitated a little, knowing they desperately needed reassurance, some semblance that progress was being made somewhere, somehow.

'My dear group,' she went on, 'I have read every post, every single word that has been written to me by sufferers since I became chairperson. I've laughed, cried and prayed more than anyone will ever know. I have been challenged by those words, alternately depressed and uplifted. But despite the suffering we endure, we have a common thread that has brought us all to this time and place. Along with all the, er, baggage as you say, we bring experience, strength, hope and a multitude of skills and gifts to offer each other. There are many sufferers out there who are too shy to make contact with us. They may be unaccustomed to talking about themselves for fear of sounding like complainers or far too ill to write or telephone.' .

Kelly was spellbound by her eloquence, finding it all the more remarkable since English wasn't her native tongue.

'I propose,' she went on, 'that we set up a buddy system such as the Americans have, so that there will always be someone somewhere to whom a newly diagnosed sufferer can reach out. This is an extraordinary network of mentally and emotionally strong and giving people, many of who may not be able to hold down a job because of their illness, but yet have definite skills and something to offer. Where it should have treated us with respect and compassion, the outside world has conspired to beat us down. But we must never give up the battle. As I said before, we *shall* win in the end.'

There was a moment's silence before the audience broke into enthusiastic applause. The Countess blushed. She knew that fine words were the only thing she could offer them. There was no research being carried out to find a cure for their condition. Alternative therapies sometimes offered palliative remedies, but there was only anecdotal evidence for this. She went on to mention a few of them before passing the chair back to her colleague.

While Magda von Esterhazy's delivery was as beguiling as that of the most consummate politician, the voice of the woman named Linda grated on Kelly like a squeaky pub sign on a windy day. After what seemed an eternity of the sort of mundane minutiae that infected most meetings, the Irishman was visibly relieved when the obligatory raffle was announced. It was one of those where everyone was a winner. Kelly won two small prizes and promptly put one back into the pot. He kept the lavender bath salts for himself.

Following the raffle, squeaky Linda brought the meeting to an end and group members, some hobbling and others in wheelchairs, began to make their way to the exits. Kelly, too, was about to leave the hotel, but thought it polite to wish the Countess well. He approached her through a melee.

'Ah, Kieran,' she said, 'just the man I wanted to see. You said you live in London.'

'Yes.'

'Where.'

'Er, Tottenham,' he lied.

'Oh, good, a north Londoner like myself. I live in Hendon. I wonder whether you can give me a lift home. The person who drove me here has to continue on to a business meeting in Leeds. There are several members who are from London, but they live south of the Thames.'

Kelly found he couldn't help staring into her eyes. They were truly extraordinary, blue-green lagoons surrounded by milky skin that was pulled tight over proud cheekbones. For a moment the two sets of orbs were locked together, frozen in time and space. The Irishman, suddenly realising this, coughed self-consciously. He glanced down at the wheelchair.

'Don't worry,' she said, 'it's one of those that folds up quite small. Anyway, I can walk a good few yards if I have to with the help of this.' She smiled and waved a walking stick at him.

Kelly smiled. 'I'd be glad to,' he said genuinely. If truth were known, he was desperate for some feminine company, albeit more in the intellectual than in the physical sense.

Within fifteen minutes they were heading south on the M1. Rain began to lash down and the metronomic moan of the windscreen wipers seemed to curb any desire they might have had to converse. Kelly wanted to know more about his charismatic passenger, but hesitated to make the first move.

'Do you know how much was spent last year on researching arachnoiditis, Kieran,' she said suddenly.

'Can't say that I do,' he replied, relieved that the silence had been broken.

'Seven thousand pounds.'

'That's ridiculous.'

'We estimate that there are at least two million sufferers in the United States, Britain and Australia. That works out to a third of a penny per victim.'

'The whole thing stinks, Magda,' Kelly said, leaning forward to peer through the windscreen as the downpour intensified. 'It's a gigantic cover-up.' She was silent for a few seconds, so he began to pluck up the courage to ask her about herself.

She beat him to it. 'I have a castle in northern Hungary, you know. The family was forced to flee when the Communists took power. The village has invited us back, but it's not the same. I couldn't afford to run it, anyway. Once my parents moved to Linz in Austria, we were virtually barefoot aristocrats.' She laughed. 'They used to call me the Barefoot Countess, but that's another story.'

Kelly was intrigued. He wanted to know all about her. 'Please, go on,' he implored, 'I'd love to hear your story.'

'I don't want to bore you, Kieran,' she said, a sudden shooting pain making her wince. 'You must have enough to cope with.'

'No, please go on,' he insisted. 'Is your family still in Linz?'

'It's a sad story, I'm afraid,' she sighed. 'My parents and younger brother were killed in a car crash seven years ago. I was twenty-two and had just finished university where I got a first in English.'

'I'm so sorry,' Kelly said. 'You must have felt terribly alone.'

'Yes, we were a very close family - like you Irish. My only living relative was my mother's older sister, an elderly spinster who lived in Chicago. Can you believe it, within two years I was already married.'

Kelly scratched the back of his head. It was a defensive gesture, as if the thought that she had a husband somehow represented a threat.

'The worst mistake I ever made,' she said quickly. 'No, perhaps the second worst. The worst was when I slipped on the ice outside our home and fractured my spine in seven places.'

Kelly winced and gripped the steering wheel as if his life depended on it. He could not imagine the pain she must have been in.

'Anyway, they had an experimental surgical procedure whereby they injected Chymopapain into my spine. It's an enzyme from the papaya. It destroys the discs. You know, some idiots are still using this procedure today.'

'Nothing surprises me any more, Magda.'

'I was in constant pain,' she went on, 'but once my plaster corset had been removed after about six months, I was able to function again. That was all my husband cared about, you know. He was a Texan oil executive who was twelve years older than me. Everything was fine as long as his exotic aristocratic wife could play the dutiful hostess to his business acquaintances. Otherwise, it would have to be *Aus den Augen, aus dem Sinn.* Out of sight, out of mind.'

Kelly grimaced. The man sounded like a complete shit.

The Countess found herself staring at her companion's profile. The slightly hooked nose counterbalanced his other, finer features. He was extraordinarily handsome, exuding the kind of masculine power she so yearned for. Yet she realised this man named Kieran O'Donaghue was spoken for, a husband who obviously cared deeply for his disabled wife. For the past five years Magda had been alone, preferring to shun the possibility of romance in the fear that the world was full of men who desired only a trophy wife like William J. Buckridge. She felt herself blush as Kelly caught her staring at him. 'Don't worry, Kieran, it gets worse.' She laughed self-consciously. 'One year later, I was bending over to remove some muffins from the oven and could not straighten up again. I went to see an orthopaedic surgeon who told me he would perform a spinal fusion by removing a piece of bone from my hip and grafting it onto my spine. He said I should be home within ten days and dancing within a month. My whole being screamed danger, but I chose to listen to my husband who wanted me patched up and ready to entertain again as soon as possible.'

'They gave you a myelogram, right,' guessed Kelly, eager to use his newfound knowledge.

'Yes. They tilted the X-ray table so that the contrast dye could flow to the head. At that point I passed out. They then gave me a triple spinal fusion, and during the operation I apparently died three times. Four months later I had another myelogram and further surgery. Six months after that, scar tissue was strangulating my spinal cord. In all, I have had eighteen major surgeries on my spine. My husband dumped me like a hot potato, as the Americans say, and left me almost penniless. He transferred to Houston, which is the only state that does not have a maintenance law. I went through thirty-three court hearings, but William and his rich lawyers were too clever for me. Thank goodness we were childless. I would have hated any child to suffer the trauma of a bitter divorce and a disabled mother. The newspapers called me the Barefoot Countess. I couldn't wear shoes because of the pain in the soles of my feet. It was like walking on broken glass. My back pain was so severe that I would have terrible spasms. You know, I once broke my neck during my sleep.'

Kelly's brain pounded in indignation. 'Please, Magda, I don't think I can hear any more,' he stuttered.

'I'm so sorry, Kieran. I didn't mean to depress you. It's so insensitive of me - your poor wife and all. Just tell her she is not alone.'

During the rest of the journey, Kelly heard a potted history of the von Esterhazys: how she had decided to begin a new life in London three years before and how, despite her continuing pain, she was now more content than she had ever been. He listened with rapt attention as she described how she had found the support group and had been quickly ensconced as its chairperson. It seemed it was useful to have a Countess as spokesperson even if the dynasty was somewhat esoteric, not to say truncated. He believed it unlikely she could bear children, so a line that had stretched back some six hundred years looked like ending with this remarkable woman.

Thankfully the rain had eased off as Kelly pulled up outside her home, a nondescript three-bedroom bungalow in Hendon. He helped Magda out of the car and tried to assist her towards the front door.

She shrugged him off gently. 'Don't worry, Kieran, I can sometimes manage short distances with my stick.'

Kelly unloaded the wheelchair while the Countess opened the front door. As he wheeled it towards her, he knew that however much he would like to get to know her further, it would only complicate matters. He was used to playing charades, but not with a person as genuine as Magda von Esterhazy.

'Would you like a cup of tea, Kieran,' she said as they both stood in the hall.

'I'm sorry, Magda,' he answered reluctantly, 'I must be getting back to my wife.'

46

'Of course,' she said warmly. 'Thank you so much for the lift.'

'Will you be all right?'

'Yes, my carer should be here shortly. She's a lovely West Indian girl. I couldn't manage without her.' She suddenly began to rummage through her handbag. 'Ah, here's one.' She held out her hand. 'This is my card. Please feel free to contact me at any time. All of us need to have someone, how can I put it, neutral to whom we can pour out our hearts. Someone who understands exactly what you both are going through.'

Kelly took her hand gently in his and then stooped to brush it delicately against his lips. 'It's been a pleasure meeting you,' he said warmly.

'You too,' she said with feeling. 'By the way, are you on the Internet?'

'Yes.'

'You'll see that my card also carries my email address. Please let me know how your wife progresses. I have also written on the back the Internet address of a sister support group based in the States. They are always a mine of information on the latest drugs and treatments etcetera.'

'Thank you, I'll look them up.' He then gave her a short wave. '*Ciao.*'

'*Auf Wiedersehen*, Kieran,' she smiled. 'May the angels be with you.' It was her catchphrase. She believed everyone had angels who guided him or her through life.

'I'm sure they will be, Magda,' he called out as he opened his car door. Angels were certainly with him.

Angels of death.

CHAPTER FOUR

Dr Martin Townsend felt the familiar pangs just as his last patient left his surgery. He swivelled in his chair to stare balefully at the lights of Harley Street from his fourth floor window at the junction of the bustling Marylebone Road. It was already nine in the evening and the normal phalanx of traffic along the east-west artery had dwindled to a relative trickle. Not that he had far to go. Unlike most of the consultants who plied their skills on probably the most famous street of medical professionals in the world, he lived above the shop. While others might have had a house in the country or a town house not far from their private practice, Townsend had used the money left him by his stockbroker father to buy the top floor for himself.

'I'll be going home now, Martin,' a voice called from an adjoining office. It was Margaret Brown, his secretary for the past fifteen years. A plain woman, Mrs Brown knew everything about him. Well, almost everything. She knew he was a workaholic, a lonely middle-aged man who was so dedicated to his profession that any kind of social life was out of the question. However, she had no idea of the secret that was wrecking his life.

'Okay, Margaret,' he called back, 'I'll see you on Tuesday.'

Townsend waited for the click of the front door and then a few seconds more. Only when he heard the lift on its way down to the ground floor did he permit himself to swivel one hundred and eighty degrees and unlock a deep drawer in his desk with a key that he guarded jealously. A full bottle of Chivas Regal stood silently, invitingly, in front of another that was either half-full or half-empty depending on your point of view. It was a ritual within a habit. He would buy a new bottle and drink about half in one go. He would then place it behind the second bottle, the contents of which he would then drain. In this way he figured he would never be in the disastrous position of staring at a drawer containing only empty bottles. Thus the tortured logic he employed to perpetuate his addiction remained unassailable.

The good doctor always delighted in opening a new bottle. The tactile swivel of the top, the pent-up aroma of the nectar as it burst forth from captivity, the heady delight of expectation about to be fulfilled. Mentally, Martin George Townsend was shot to pieces and he knew it. He was one of the fifty-eight per cent of men who regretted entering medicine. He had done it for his father, learning at a tender age to be an obsessive, compulsive over-achiever who readily accepted that ignorance and expressions of emotion were signs of weakness. He had quickly developed a misplaced, arrogant certainty about medicine, unrealistic expectations of his future and tunnel vision towards an impossible goal. He had developed a carapace of relaxed brilliance to help him appear competent when he knew that he really did not have a clue. He was now combining private practice with stints at St. Thomas' Hospital and, on alternate Mondays and Fridays, at Whipps Cross in east London. Thus he assuaged his guilt about doing a job he loathed by working even harder, encouraged by the fact that workaholism was seen by his peers as an attribute rather than an illness. He had lost the capacity to think, reflect, feel and articulate with any depth. Like most addicted doctors, he hid behind his status to conceal his habit. He knew that his colleagues, even if they suspected a problem, often did not raise the alarm. Action might only be taken if a clinical disaster happened, or if he was caught driving while under the influence.

Townsend lifted the neck of the bottle to his lips and proceeded to take large gulps of the golden fire. Tomorrow was Saturday and he was off duty. Nevertheless, he would never drink more than a bottle of whisky in any one day. This gave him the feeling that he was in control of his problem rather than the other way round. Soon he would lapse into melancholy, the usual precursor to oblivion. He was haunted by images of colleagues and students alike whispering to each other about him in the corridors. His career had seen a catalogue of errors, although one in particular haunted him. He knew he was responsible for the death of Teresa Kelly. She may have taken her own life, but he was the catalyst. He'd found out about her demise only because one of the nurses at Whipps Cross was an acquaintance of hers. He had expressed his sorrow but no more, for the medical profession and the whole NHS system colluded in concealing errors in order to protect staff. See no evil, hear no evil, and speak no evil as a colleague had once told him.

The doctor took a few swigs until the bottle was about half-empty. He then placed it back into the drawer and withdrew the second bottle. Rising unsteadily, he clasped the Chivas to his chest and made towards the stairs that led to his three-room apartment. A half-bottle later and he would be comatose, yet safe in the knowledge that a new day would find him a different man, for he had learned the trick of appearing sober even with a distillery coursing through his veins.

Thus did Martin George Townsend, although a fool to himself, continue to fool others. All, that is, except one man. And that man had tracked the good doctor for the past week, logging and photographing his every move. He, too, was a professional, albeit in taking lives rather than saving them. But then it could be argued that an incompetent doctor was more dangerous to society than a killer who murdered only those within his circle of violence.

It was the heavy hand of loneliness that weighed upon the Irishman as he sat in the lounge of his home, a home that had once throbbed to the happy shenanigans of his children. Facing the cold and impersonal screen of his computer, he would search for solace by surfing the net. All life was to be found there, but in reality it was as inanimate as granite. He desperately missed the human touch of his family, but realised that longing must be subsumed by his strategy for revenge, the tactics of which he had already put in motion. He reckoned it would take about six months of careful planning before everything would be in place. Research and logistics had always given him infinitely more pleasure than execution. Hits were a clinical anti-climax that gave him no satisfaction. But this time it was different. It was personal. Really personal.

Kelly stared at the card in his hand. Countess Magda von Esterhazy was truly as exotic as her name. Try as he might, he could not blot out the vision of this beautiful yet horribly maimed woman. It frightened him that her visage had replaced that of Teresa. So soon. Too soon. The two women were so disparate physically: Teresa, red-haired and freckled, a typical Irish colleen, and Magda, a blonde of almost brittle elegance. Perhaps it was the fact that the two women had shared the same illness that created the empathy within him. But he knew it was more than that. Only now, in the confines of his own home, could he really admit to himself that she had caused a stirring deep within him. The feelings scared him, and he was a man not easily frightened. He knew he must suppress them, for the fewer complications over the next half-year, the better. The Irishman sighed the deep sigh of a man faced by forbidden fruit. He flicked her card over and read the newsgroup address she had written. The handwriting was neat and sculptured. Within a few seconds he was receiving emails from the group that appeared to be based in the United States. He clicked on the first. It was from a woman named Michele who lived in Connecticut.

It takes so much courage to move along not knowing what the future holds. We are often the last to know what the f*** has happened to us! I was told I was experiencing a post myelogram reaction that would go away. Ya, right. Let me tell you eighteen years later this ROTTEN, STINKING REACTION HAS NOT GONE ANYWHERE.
Love, light and peace.
Michele from CT

Kelly switched on his printer and ran off copies of each email he opened. Soon he had a selection that he felt served his purpose.

My name is Andrew and I am twelve years old. I was diagnosed with a tethered spine at eight. I had two spinal surgeries and ended up with arachnoiditis.
  As soon as I wake up I have to use a catheter, as my bladder doesn't function. I take sixteen pills a day. If it's a good day, I can usually have a friend over for an hour. I like to build Lego models. I used to draw a lot but have trouble with tremors now, so I only do it on good days.
  I just want people to understand me...that I'm just a kid who has really bad pain. I may act like I feel OK, and look OK, but I'm not OK. You need x-ray vision to see what is really going on inside of me. I deal with all my pain by thinking of my body as a video game, and the hero of the

game is getting the stuffing kicked out of him. I have been told that I am a gifted child, but what good is being clever when you are in constant pain?
Andrew

Hi, my name is Edward. My Mom is Dinah and I am writing on how it feels to have a family member (Mom) with arachnoiditis.

It hurts me a great deal to see my Mom live in such pain and discomfort. She has such a great soul and could do such great things for this world. I even check to see if she is still alive when she is sleeping or resting because my greatest fear is that she will take her own life to escape the pain. I know she wants to live, but a person can only take so much.

I love my Mom so much it scares me to know everything that this illness causes to the body. It scares me to this day that I am going to lose my Mom some day and I fear of how I will continue in this world without her. I even pray that I may take the illness from my Mom and transfer it to me so she can live.

I also want to say thanks to you all in this group that my Mom has such a network of fine people that she can talk to and learn from. She still has so much to offer.

God bless you all.
Edward

Hi y'all,
Guess what? When I had my awful reaction to the epidural, the doc told me it was normal. A whole bunch of docs told me that. They told me that I just had to suffer those things in order to get better, just suffer through all that and in the end I would be better. Well, like a BIG DUMMY I did. I was in agony, thrashing around in the bed. The docs said HANG IN THERE, it'll get better. Yeah, with my left leg dragging behind me! And it did, it went away and I felt pretty good for a few days, and then CRASH right back to the same old thing.

I did this over and over. Oh yeah, talk about DUMB! I had at least nine or ten of those damn epidurals. They kept saying that it was normal and that one of these times it would do the trick and I would be home free.

Yeah, right!! I thought I was being brave. I thought that I was better off going through all that pain in order to get better. I thought it was worth it to get better. It would have been, IF it were true!! Catch my drift? They kept on saying NO Pain, NO Gain.........boy was I manipulated? What a sucker!

And then they say they don't know why I have this pain. It's just a mystery to them. Epidurals don't cause things to get worse, they said. No, the surgery was done properly. We just don't know why you have this pain. POOP! I'm embarrassed that I was so stupid!

Just last week the doc was disgusted with me because all I wanted was pain medication and no epidural. Can it be that he makes a lot more money each time he injects or am I being too cynical? He acted like I wanted the drugs because I like them. My hubby was so mad he nearly decked the guy and my hubby is not a violent man.

I was about to give up when I found this group. Everyone here has gone through similar things. I know I have been easily led. NO MORE. I AM IN CHARGE HERE and I WILL educate myself and not be manipulated again. CASE CLOSED!

Thanks for listening; I didn't intend to be so long winded. I had intended to help. Heh, I tried!

Pat in Oregon

Hello All,

I have just been diagnosed with a kidney disease that is directly linked to the drug Triamerol *'s main ingredient, ethylene glycol. IT'S POISONOUS AND CAN KILL!*

I am told I may probably have to have dialysis. I have a desperate need to talk with anyone who has developed kidney stones, metabolic acidosis or a disease known as hydronephrosis. The goddamn doctor injected the steroid directly into my subarachnoid space and it caused this damn A. I developed excruciating headaches and had two unsuccessful blood patches. I currently take these meds: oxycontin, diamox, neurontin (almost pure acid to those who don't know), prilosec, restoril, flexerill, lactulose, cytotec, cipro, phenergen and maybe another I'm forgetting. Does anyone else have pain in their throats, chest, stomach, severe constipation, loss of appetite, head pressure and pains in the neck, inside

of the elbows and, of course, in the back, hips, legs, feet and groin? Is there any goddamn place left free of this curse?
My wife, God bless her, is staying with me so far, but my illness has taken a toll of her too. Our relationship seems to be slowly falling apart. SOMEONE OUT THERE HELP ME!
Wilbur

Hi Group
I've had A. since two back surgeries in 1985. Soon my daughter will be having our first grandchild, and I want to be able to hold the baby and play with it. Also this condition has practically eliminated the intimacy between my husband and me. I am afraid I might have another breakdown if I don't get some relief soon. Even my faith in God has started to wane. I am worn down and feel defeated.
Sue

Dear friends
It's a little after 5 a.m. I'm up, wide awake, hurting so bad I can hardly stand it. I really don't think my mind and body can take much more. My feet and legs are crucifying me. This damn disease is so awful. I look like a fish. My skin is scaly, parched and dry all over. The pain in the mornings is worse. My back and hips feel like they are broken. God, please help me! I can't take much more. Can anyone really go on like this, when there is no quality of life? My head is so full of emotions that I don't know whether to scream or cry. I am usually such a very strong person, trying to encourage others that we can overcome this, fight for our rights, for acknowledgement, for justice. We have got to stand up and shout out loud and clear that this cruel, unnecessary pain must be stopped. Where do we go? Who will listen to us?
Take care and God bless you all.
Donna

Hi dear friends,
I have finally crawled out of the hole where I have been hiding, because of this last flare. I sometimes wonder if these doctors ever understand what we are going through. Their famous blank looks are the ones that

really get me. You know, it's that deer in the headlights look. I think I would feel one hundred per cent better if I could just grab one of them and shake him real good. I don't think anyone outside this group could understand the crap that we endure as A. patients. The other thing they're famous for is to tell you that you're anxious and depressed. How could someone who hurts all day not be depressed? I get so tired of the roller coaster rides of highs and lows. I thank the Lord every day for this little group.
Lots of Love, Debbie

Hi, folks,
Well, I am having a rough time at present mentally as well as physically. The pain in my legs and back are causing me so much agony. I have had enough. I just feel like enough is enough. I don't want to live the rest of my life like this. I feel like I am sentenced to a living death. I get so upset knowing that there is no cure. Why can't someone help us? Why can't the pharmaceutical companies who have caused us this misery recognise our plight? Why can't our government help us? Government of the People, by the People for - some of the People. Why didn't my surgeon warn me about the dangers of myelograms and multiple spinal surgery?
   Thank you for listening to me. I didn't know where to turn.
Carol (Brisbane)

Dear friends
I think I am having a nervous breakdown. I am so sick of this disease. I cannot stop crying. I feel so angry and hurt for what they have done to me. There is a storm inside of me and it's called arachnoiditis. It is dark, so dark. And I am all alone.
Jody Marie.

Dear group,
Last June, I gave birth to a beautiful baby girl by caesarean section under epidural. Shortly after the operation, I started to suffer from severe headaches. Upon examination, I was told that it wasn't uncommon and to carry on with the prescribed painkillers. By September, I was at my wit's end with the burning sensations and pain going down my legs,

muscle spasms, cramps, numbness in my arms; also feeling like I'm walking on broken glass, sleepless nights, pain on lying n any position, bowel and bladder dysfunction, difficulty swallowing, dry throat and so on and so forth. I'm sure you've all heard it before. But how does one get on with life? A private neurologist seems to find nothing wrong with me, yet each day I find it's getting worse. Now it's getting difficult to even pick up a kettle or drive my car, yet my family needs me.

  Someone please help me.

Lorraine

Dear All

I don't know what's happening to me. I've never felt like this before. Everything from my waist down hurts. My legs feel like lead, my hips are frozen. I can barely lift my legs onto a footstool. My head feels like it's lead and my eyes are throbbing. I live alone. I'm so afraid, so scared. Please tell me what to do.

Lori-Beth

Dear Group

I have had arachnoiditis for seven years now. I went into hospital to give birth to my son. I was a young healthy 26-year-old. I received an epidural as I was having a very difficult birth. Unfortunately the midwives had all been drinking the night before as my son was born on New Year's Day. They were quite happy to tell me that if they had done their jobs properly in the first place, I wouldn't have needed an epidural.

  It has taken me five years to suspect that I had arachnoiditis and seven years to be sure. So many things started to go wrong within hours of receiving that injection that I just knew it had to be the cause. Doctors told me that this just doesn't happen and that I probably had a slipped disc. Because I was so green I placed them on a pedestal. Not any more. When I had my first body seizure I was told that a lot of people have one attack with no specific cause and that it doesn't happen again and the neurologist discharged me.

  Two years after I received my epidural I started looking for my own diagnosis and doctors laughed at me when I told them what I thought was wrong with me. I had tests done and was told that I didn't have a slipped disc and that I didn't have epilepsy. When the attacks got worse and I was admitted to hospital for excruciating back pain and muscle spasms and passed out. The doctors then had to sit up and take notice.

My seizures now last up to an hour, although every attack I have is longer than the previous one. I get little or no warning and I have fallen and broken my nose at the start of one attack.

There are times when I am very confused and disorientated and tiredness or depression just comes over me like a wave. Ignore all those doctors who accuse you of being mad or unable to take pain. Let them suffer just one moment of this hell and they will see the light.
My thoughts and prayers are with you all.
Elizabeth

Dear All
I've had it. I can't take it any more. I won't get any more pump refills, any more meds, or anything. Time's up! Game's over! I now understand why people go ballistic. Now it's my turn. I'm taking matters into my own hands. What with doctors who don't care about their patients, and being in the amount of pain I'm in all the time, it's time to become judge, jury and executioner. Thanks, group, for all you have done, and don't be jealous, because where I'm going there isn't any pain. Thanks, for the last time.
Paul in Denver

Dear, dear Paul
I think I know where you are. It is the most terrifying place anyone can endure. We feel alone and helpless. No one understands. The pain won't stop and it's impossible to think about going on. Why even try? No one could live like this. The doctors don't really care. They have nothing to offer. No one knows this pain that fills your body, mind and spirit. No one feels the anger we feel at everyone and everything. No one knows what it's like to lose control of your pain-wracked body. No one except those of us with this damned disease. But dear, dear Paul, don't turn the anger on yourself. Yes, scream it out. Scream and scream, because it is the fear and emotional pain that makes you feel so angry. We've almost

all been where you've been. Some probably did give in to it. I didn't. I'm still here although I admit I wanted to die real bad. I stood there with a razor blade at my wrist and a lot of pills in the cabinet. But then I figured that with my rotten luck, it wouldn't work and I would just end up in worse shape. I can't change your mind, Paul. That is something for you to consider. But you are not alone in your agony. You have friends here, people who know the agony you're in.
Please don't give up.
Lou

There were a few more emails listed, but Kelly stopped, arrested by the power of memory. He was almost overcome by the flood of emotion coursing through his body. They were all hurting, just like his Teresa. If only his dear wife had shared with him her terrible thoughts, he might have been able to prevent the tragedy. He'd always looked upon Teresa as a strong woman, a woman who could shine through any adversity. Yet it seemed that weaker people, those who were not afraid to cry or voice their anguish, were those who survived. To take one's own life was the ultimate in foolish courage, the ultimate in waste. Yet who was he to judge? He had never been in their position. He had been the harbinger of death for others and in mortal danger himself on many occasions, but suicide· was as far removed from his lexicon as the stars from Mother Earth.

With his blood turning to ice, the Irishman switched off the computer and removed a file from his desk. He withdrew three items: a six by eight photograph of Dr Martin Townsend and two newspaper cuttings that he had circled in red. The first showed a picture of the Secretary of State for Health and the second displayed a thumbnail portrait of Professor Jonathan Tring alongside a story outlining his company's position on Triamerol. He then collated the printed emails, stacked everything together and returned them to the file. All was now in place for the next stage.

Kelly looked at his watch. It would soon be time to go to work. He was still grinding out intensely boring shifts as a security guard. Besides providing a source of income, it gave him the organisational flexibility that he needed. Nothing, however, could be achieved without the help of his friends. All would depend on their reaction to his plea. That was why he was flying to Belfast that Sunday morning. The meet was all arranged. The two of them would be there; men who, in the time of the Troubles, would have been prepared to lay down their lives for him. But peace was a funny thing. It turned men soft. Once the cycle of violence was broken, priorities changed. Men returned to mundane jobs like his own or completely turned their lives around to become pillars of society. Others lapsed into dissolute and undisciplined ways. He knew of cases where men, robbed of the armed struggle that had become their raison d'être, had slipped into the unforgiving world of alcoholism and vagrancy.

The Irishman had been out of touch with his erstwhile compatriots for almost a year. He knew they had understood his need for anonymity, but he also knew that the burden he was about to place on them would stretch their friendship with him to the limit. While one of them was bachelor and a loner who had no strong family ties, the other was happily married and a father of four. How would they feel now about jeopardising their futures, and possibly their lives, in order to help him exact revenge? If necessary, he'd be prepared to go it alone, although he knew the logistics of his plan would make failure almost inevitable. He knew that to make this thing work, he needed them as never before.

Kelly walked pensively over to the mantelpiece above the gas-fire grate in the lounge. He picked up a newly taken photograph of his children and kissed it. It pained him that he'd be able to spare them only a few hours during his visit, but he would make sure this would be quality time. Once his mission was completed, they would be a family again. That or he would be dead.

CHAPTER FIVE

Jonathan Tring was feeling more than a little apprehensive. The last couple of weeks had been refreshingly free of the contrivances of his chairman. But now the Proctors were returning from their sojourn in one of the world's more exotic locales. The professor, peering out of his office window at the November mist enshrouding the executive parking bays, caught a glimpse of their Rolls as it swung past the imposing granite obelisk which bore the half-metre high chromium letters announcing *Parados Pharmaceuticals*. As if in defiance of yet another grey English morning, the lettering seemed to project an eerie luminescence.

The chauffeur, tall and lean, moved swiftly to open the offside rear door. A leg, slender and shapely, announced the first to alight. The driver, no doubt used to the etiquette demanded of him by his master, offered the company's First Lady his hand and then stood stiffly to one side as Jack Proctor joined his wife. It was the first time Tring had seen her in the flesh. The portrait of her in Proctor's office did her scant justice. She was achingly beautiful. He blinked at the incongruous sight before him: a statuesque blonde, all of six-feet in her heels, linking arms with a man who was a foot shorter and a foot wider. Tring, suddenly reminded of Spencer's cautionary words, moved out of their line of sight. To be caught staring at the Odd Couple might be tempting fate. The scientist chided himself for being unduly paranoid.

An hour later, Tring was flicking through the pages of the latest edition of The *Pharmaceutical Journal* when his intercom buzzed. It was Jack Proctor.

'Jonathan,' the chairman growled, 'come into my office, will you.'

'Right away, JP,' the scientist responded. Proctor had told him that he preferred to be called by his initials. 'It lets people know who's boss,' the old man had said, 'but it's also a term of endearment. My people love me.' Tring had not sought to disabuse him.

The scientist took the lift to his chairman's office. He'd been there only once when the Triamerol affair had been top of the agenda. There had been no personal assistant to negotiate, for Proctor believed he should remain instantly accessible to all his minions, most of whom were too scared to come anywhere near him. Tring knocked quietly on the solid oak door.

'Enter,' came the gruff response.

'Good morning, JP,' Tring said as warmly as he could. The chairman's head remained buried in some papers. 'Did you enjoy your trip?'

'I didn't go half way round the world to enjoy myself, son,' Proctor replied testily. 'Take a seat.'

Tring, making sure to keep his eyes averted from the portrait of Mrs Proctor, felt instinctively that he was about to learn more about Jack Proctor's attitude towards business.

'How have you been settling in, lad?' the slit-eyes inquired.

'Fine.' Tring's reply was firm, although a quick scratch of the nape of his neck betrayed his apprehension.

'You did a fine job on the Triamerol thing. Paper tigers, the press.'

'Thank you, JP.'

Proctor burst into a guffaw. 'Paper tigers, get it?'

'Of course, JP,' Tring replied blandly.

The laugh that creased Proctor's ill-favoured features disappeared in a flash. There were more serious matters at hand. 'You've now had plenty of time to see the set-up here. Impressive, isn't it?'

'Yes, sir.'

'Did you go over the work Locke was doing before he died?'

'If you mean the work on a male contraceptive, yes, I did. It was pretty thorough.'

Proctor grunted. 'Locke was good man. But in the end he couldn't stand the heat, so he got out of the kitchen the easy way. I can't abide weakness.'

Tring was just about to comment when he thought better of it.

The pug-face grimaced. 'Anyway, he let us all down. He was on the verge of a breakthrough that would have brought us millions, maybe billions. And then he bottled it.' The gashes that were his eyes narrowed even further. 'You won't bottle it, will you Jonathan?'

'Er, no JP,' Tring replied apprehensively. 'Although it would be nice to know the parameters you're setting me.'

'I'll set you some parameters, son,' said Proctor, the bleached teeth bursting forth from his holiday tan like white mischief. 'The female Pill is soon going to be as dead as a doornail and I want a new male contraceptive to replace it within a year.'

Tring was fully aware that, since the warning by the Committee on Safety of Medicines that third-generation Pills actually doubled the risk of blood clots, more and more women were opting out of taking any oral contraception whatsoever. However, besides developmental constraints, there was another major factor that prevented the evolution of a male oral contraceptive. 'But men don't like taking pills, JP,' the scientist said boldly.

'Who said anything about pills?' Proctor countered. 'So far our competitors and we have been concentrating on pills, injections or implants. I want you to develop a hormone that can be delivered by patches.'

Tring's eyebrows arched. The idea of patch delivery was not new. It was just that most scientists regarded it as being in cloud cuckoo land. Hundreds of men in ten countries had already volunteered to test the male pill and the results so far had been positive. But there were drawbacks. The Pill worked by giving men an extra dose of testosterone, which sent a message to the pituitary gland suggesting that too much was being produced. This confusion culminated in the blocking of hormones needed to stimulate the testes into sperm production. Weekly injections of testosterone would then be needed to stop the loss of other male characteristics, such as facial hair. Everyone was trying to find a male pill that did not involve weekly injections. Patches were way down the line.

Proctor disregarded the scepticism in the professor's eyes.

'Look, Jonathan, there's nothing a man hates more than fiddling around with a condom. A lot of men refuse to wear them. Now women are refusing to expose themselves to the side effects of the Pill. It's up to us, the pharmaceutical industry, to come up with a solution. And you know that in our business, the early bird catches the worm.'

'But, JP, I'm not sure we're six months away from cracking the formula, let alone getting it approved for the market. And anyway, we're not geared up for patch technology.'

'I don't need excuses, Jonathan,' said Proctor, his face screwing itself into a rictus of wrath. 'The bottom line is that we're number one in hormone technology and our main products look like flying out of the window. I shouldn't have to tell you that unless we come up with something new, this glorious edifice you see around you will begin to crumble. You should never forget that there are thousands of people out there who rely on the likes of you and me to keep them secure and happy. We can't let them down, and I'll tell you something more. I would do anything to keep this company successful, d'yer hear. Anything.'

Tring had little doubt that Jack Proctor meant every word he said.

Abe Klein withdrew a nine-iron and carefully positioned himself for a shot that would take him to within easy putting distance of the sixth on the gently undulating course at Abridge. It was a crisp Sunday morning and they were alone, apart from a couple of figures he could make out at the eighteenth tee. Abridge was predominantly a Jewish club, and Jews did not like cold weather. That was why back home they left the borscht belt in New York to spend their twilight years in Miami.

The American smiled confidently at his playing partner. They had been the closest of friends since he'd been a Yank at Oxford. They had shared the same dreams, the same adventures and, sometimes, the same women. Life had been a ball then, as now. They were scholars and gentlemen, the sort that university and industry prided themselves on.

Klein had had a premonition that one day he would be in the forefront of pharmaceutical technology and now that dream had come true. KleinKinloss was a small player in a big market, but one product, and one product alone, was sending the company's shares through the roof. Folitac, his brainchild and the object of seven years of intensive, energy-sapping research had answered a need for millions of women worldwide. Indeed, it had become a fad. Women everywhere were donning their Folitac patches for a regular daily dose of folic acid and other supplements. It was both a safe and a sure way to prevent the devastating neural tube defects which affected about two thousand pregnancies a year in the UK and God knew how many throughout the rest of the world. People seemed to prefer patches to pills. The boy wonder from Brooklyn had arrived.

The concept of a 'bandage' to deliver drugs through the skin for systemic rather than local activity had been around for years, but the expected rush of hundreds of drugs being delivered in this manner had never materialised. The initial euphoria had given way to the realisation that the theoretical ideal of a controlled delivery method was not necessarily appropriate for all drugs. KleinKinloss had been quick to see the potential in a new delivery system, but the trick had been to develop a method by which folic acid could be released through the skin. The trick, once accomplished, was now making a fortune for Abe Klein and his cohort, Kevin Kinloss, an opportunist Scottish businessman who had guessed correctly that the talented American was his passport to riches.

Klein, dapper and bespectacled, scratched a shining pate that had shed its locks suddenly in his early twenties. Fellow students at Oxford, in honour of Ernest Bilko, called him 'the Sarge'. Gripping his club tightly, he shuffled twice before unleashing a swing that struck the ball with perfect aplomb.

'Not bad, Abe,' said his playing partner, peering towards the green to ascertain the lie. Jonathan Tring was nothing if not truly appreciative of his closest friend's copious talents.

'So how goes it, buddy?' Klein asked as they walked towards the hole. 'I hear that your new boss is a bit of a monster.'

Tring grimaced and rubbed his chin. 'Yes, he does take a bit of getting used to, although it's strange...most of his people would walk through fire for him.'

'Maybe that's just vested interest, Jonathan.'

Tring shrugged. 'Could be. Anyway, he is a bit of a slave driver.'

'And if he drives you *meshuggah,* you can always rely on the Sarge.'

Tring knew what his friend was getting at. Klein had always insisted that he would love to have the professor on his team. Hitherto, Tring had resisted, believing that a professional relationship might spoil a personal one. 'I'll bear it in mind, Abe.' It was his stock answer to any unsolicited approach.

'We're really going places, Jonathan,' Klein enthused. 'Folitac is a winner, and there are rumours one of your biggest products may be withdrawn.' The American knew just how far he could go. There was no question of discussing the chemistry of rival products or marketing plans. They only ever talked about what was common knowledge.

Tring knew his friend was referring to Triamerol. He shortened his stride and then turned to face his fellow scientist. 'Look, Abe, I've been set a challenge and I aim to give it a try. Anyway, you've got a good man in Derek Sutton. He's been with you since the early days.'

Klein continued walking towards the green. It was true. Although he was nearing sixty, Sutton was an excellent scientist and had been mainly responsible for the development of Folitac, but there was an old-new reality. The man was an alcoholic. 'You know about his problem, Jonathan,' the American said quietly.

'I thought he was on the wagon.'

Klein sighed. 'He was paralytic every day last week and I don't think I can carry him any more.'

Tring could see that the situation was hurting his friend, whom he knew always believed in holding the moral high ground. 'What about Michael Bannister?' the professor inquired, referring to Sutton's deputy.

'He's been pushing me for Derek's job, but I don't think he's up to it. I'm not sure of his true commitment.'

'What does Kinloss think about the situation?' Tring asked, aware that Klein's partner was more concerned with profit than personalities.

'He says Sutton is a liability and has to go, although he agrees with me about Bannister. Basically, we both want you.'

Tring remained silent until they neared the hole. He took out his putter and crouched to check the run of the green. It was a puttable eight-foot shot. 'I'm giving Parados a try,' he said without looking up. 'If things don't match up to my expectations, I promise I'll take up your offer.'

'I can't ask for more than that,' Abe Klein said resignedly. The American's attention was suddenly attracted by three disparate figures making their way to an adjacent green. One he recognised instantly as an old playing partner who was both a member of his local synagogue and a captain of British industry. The other two looked familiar. 'Heh, Jonathan, isn't that your boss over there?'

Tring narrowed his eyes against the sun. There was no doubt the squat figure was that of Jack Proctor.

'So it is,' he said quietly as the three men moved away without looking his way. The professor also recognised one of Proctor's playing partners. It was none other than Stephen Sellars, the Secretary of State for Health.

The Falls Road area of Belfast was technically in the same nation as the green swathe of middle class affluence that was Abridge, but there the similarity just about ended. While professor Jonathan Tring was hitting a nine-iron towards the eighteenth green, the man who intended to become his nemesis sat stern-faced in a small grimy back-to-back belonging to one of his former cohorts. Kelly now faced his moment of truth.

'That's a lot your asking of us, Kieran,' said the owner of the house, a thin-faced wiry man approaching middle age. Sean Callaghan looked into the younger man's deep blue eyes. He knew nothing would sway Kelly from his course. Nothing ever did.

'Sean, you know that if you turn me down, I'll not resent you for it. I'd never expect either of you to do anything against your will.'

Callaghan looked away and towards the third man in the room. Gerry O'Connor had put on a little weight since he'd seen him last. Family life seemed to be agreeing with him. 'What do you think, Jim?' he asked quietly.

'I think I might have a lot of explaining to do to my wife and kids,' replied O'Connor, a stocky man in his mid-thirties, who would look at home propping up a front row. In fact, rugby was just about as violent as it had got for him over the last few years.

'You'd just be away for a couple of days,' Kelly rejoined. 'You know me. Everything will be planned to the last detail. You'll be in and out and back home before the shit hits the fan. Nobody will ever be able to connect you with me.'

It was true, thought O'Connor. When Kelly had invited them to join his maverick cell during the Troubles, he'd sworn that he would never divulge their identities, even under torture, whether from his own side or

66

from British Army Intelligence. The man was extraordinary, a chameleon who practised his own rules, some of which were in direct contradiction to the terrorist handbook. They had never been caught. In five years, they had succeeded in evading their pursuers, friend and foe alike. In fact, the authorities didn't even have a clue who they were. Kelly had had the knack of always staying one step ahead.

''Tis true that what they did to Teresa was criminal, Kieran,' O'Connor said compassionately, aware that he too would be consumed by revenge had his wife been maimed in such a way. 'But kidnap a British Minister..' he whistled through his teeth.. 'That's big league.'

'All I'm asking is that you help me capture these guys,' Kelly said. 'As I said, your job'll then be done. Whatever happens to them after that will be my responsibility and mine alone.'

'When do you expect you'll be needing our help, Kieran?' Callaghan asked, playing nervously with one of his long sideburns.

'I reckon it'll take me between three and six months to organise everything, the safe house and all. I still have to work, so I'll be doing everything in my spare time. Sean, you'd be the driver.'

Callaghan laughed. 'Yeah, I'm getting too old to be a heavy.'

'I suppose that's where the prop forward comes in,' said O'Connor.

'If things go to plan, they'll be little need for the rough stuff,' Kelly said.

'Pity,' said O'Connor, smiling through teeth that were worse the wear for years of contact sport, 'these guys sound as if they need a bit of re-shaping.'

There was a pregnant silence while Callaghan poured himself and the others a further pint of Guinness. The wiry fellow then raised his glass. 'You can count on me, Kieran,' he said. 'Life was becoming too boring, anyway.'

'Thanks, Sean, I appreciate it.' Both men then looked towards the third in the room.

Gerry O'Connor first scratched his cauliflower right ear and then his balding pate. After what seemed an agonised few seconds of contemplation he, too, raised his glass. 'To the loving memory of Teresa Kelly,' he said quietly. 'May she rest in peace, and may her tormentors go to hell.'

Kieran Kelly was both relieved and apprehensive as he strode the few blocks between Callaghan's place, small and soulless, and the passion of a home that hummed with the happy voices of children; his children. His two comrades had done him proud. Their friendship had still meant something even though the cause for which they had fought no longer counted for much. And yet he was only too aware that he bore a heavy responsibility. If he thought for one moment that their lives were in jeopardy or that their identities would be revealed, he would scrap his mission without a moment's hesitation.

'Da'! Da'!'

The excited squealing of his youngest daughter pierced his musings, returning him to the warmth of the present rather than the cold uncertainty of the future. He scooped her into his arms and revelled in the clammy wetness of her kisses, as a particularly cold gust of wind almost blew them over.

'Are you sure you're dressed warm enough, my pretty one?' He fussed and pulled her bobble cap further over her ears. A single lock of red hair poked from beneath the rim. A few more strides and he was already over the mantle and into his sister-in-law's home.

'Hi, Mary,' he called out. 'It's me, Kieran.'

Mary Quaid stepped into the hall from the kitchen. By her side and holding her hand was Sian Kelly, reticent and unsure.

The Irishman put down his youngest daughter gently and stood silently for a few seconds. Mary was so like his beloved Teresa it almost took his breath away. He moved the few steps between them and kissed his sister-in-law warmly. He then knelt beside Sian. Taking her hand in his, he brought it to his cheek and then to his lips. He knew she was still hurting and that his prolonged absences had done nothing to help her overcome the trauma of losing her mother.

'Take me to Patrick, my darling,' he said kindly.

Silently, she led him to the baby's crib.

Kelly picked up his son and clasped him to his breast. He glanced at his watch and damned the fact that he could spend only a few hours with them all.

The following morning, Jonathan Tring arose earlier than usual. His sleep had been fitful, punctured as it was by the implications of Klein's offer and the spectre of an admonishing Proctor. The prevailing image, however, had been that of Mrs Proctor. The perfectly sculptured face and body had seemed to both summon and dismiss him.

Women had always been a dominant feature of the professor's life, yet in an ethereal way. It might be said that he held a certain ambiguity towards them, loving them for their bodies and yet finding their minds unfathomable. His mother had been the resolute wife of a City stockbroker, steadfastly ignoring his father's philandering in favour of charity work for the local townswomen's guild in their village just outside Canterbury. Tea and crumpets might have seemed a poor substitute for love, but Margaret Tring was never one to show how much it hurt. In fact she rarely showed much emotion at all, even to her own children. Jonathan and his twin brother, Robert, had been packed off to a boarding school in Broadstairs at the tender age of eleven, thus distancing them even further from a woman who remained somewhat of an enigma. The professor's feelings towards his mother could best be described as vague, and it concerned him that he had felt strangely unmoved by her death. It was said that stress was a major cause of cancer, and he believed a whole life spent hiding emotion was responsible for her premature end at sixty. His dissolute father had expired a year later, leaving the Tring twins an inheritance decimated by gambling debts. That was five years ago. Now Jonathan was a respected scientist and Robert, who was also still single, was a major in the army based in the Falklands. He had recently written of his frustration at having mainly sheep for company.

Tring chuckled as he recalled his brother's plaint about the lack of serviceable females on the islands. 'It's so bad, my boys use sheep in an emergency. I caught some of them racing towards the pen the other day. Well, nobody wanted to get the ugly one, did they?'

The professor suddenly felt much better. Within a few minutes he had showered, shaved and dressed and was already heading towards Harlow from his bachelor pad in Loughton. The journey took about twenty minutes, during which time he attempted, somewhat unsuccessfully, to wipe all thoughts of Sharon Proctor from his mind.

'Where's Tring?' Jack Proctor growled, his corpulent figure blocking the doorway of the lab. He was doing his morning rounds to make sure noses were hard against the grindstone.

'I think he's with Mrs Proctor, JP,' Harold Spencer replied while gingerly transferring a yellowish liquid from one test tube to another. 'She buzzed him a few minutes ago.'

In a single movement, almost graceful but not quite, the chairman turned on his heels and moved with unusual alacrity towards the nearby lift that would take him up two floors. Within less than a minute he had reached his office, the hub of his dominion and the repository of various items of state-of-the-art surveillance. With key already in hand, Proctor sank into his leather chair and stooped to unlock the centre drawer of his desk. Inside was a tape recorder that had already been voice-activated. He fixed an earphone securely into his right ear, folded his arms and then sat back staring at the wall-clock directly opposite. His early-morning rounds could wait, for when one commanded an empire, one commanded time.

'...So how are you settling in, Jonathan?' the silky drawl of Sharon Proctor inquired of the man she had summoned. Her smile, displaying two rows of perfectly formed teeth, exuded complaisance. The lips, full and sensuous, bore a hint of cinnamon that complemented the classic lines of her cream Armani suit. Tall and lean, she carried herself with a confidence found only in women well able to defend themselves.

Tring shrugged. 'Fine,' he said and sat a little less stiffly. He was still blushing from the sudden realisation that he was staring at her. Everything about Sharon Proctor's face was perfectly proportioned. The hair, which ended in a graceful arc either side of a delicately pointed chin, was cut to accentuate the porcelain it circumscribed. The cheekbones, which peeked tantalisingly from within her satin tresses, were high and proud. But it was the grand steel-blue ellipses that held him in thrall. They lay astride a finely contoured nose and shimmered like a peacock's tail.

'I believe you know the U.S. well,' she ventured. The soft drawl was pleasant to the ear, like a Schubert serenade.

'Yes, I've been several times, but never to Savannah. I believe that's where you hail from.'

'Yeah, good ol' Savannah, Georgia. Time warp town. Sittin' on the porch, sippin' mint julep and listenin' to the Mockingbird.'

'Do you miss it?'

The quintessential Sharon Proctor smile revealed a mixture of disdain and cynicism. 'Have you ever picked cotton, Jonathan?'

'Can't say that I have.'

'People have such a romanticised view. You know, the negra pickin' and singin' in the fields. But let me tell you that plenty of poor white folk also worked their butts off. And when it's cotton pickin' time in the fields around Savannah, it's hotter than a sinner in hell. And if the sticky heat don't get you, the damn gnats will. And when you pull that cotton boll from its pod, your fingers become so damn sore they bleed. I don't know what was redder, the blood or the earth. The fields are all red clay in Georgia. It gets everywhere, and that's why we're called Red Necks, whatever they say about it being the sun on our necks and all.'

Tring could see that she was hurting. He watched her eyes mist over as she delved deeper into reminiscences of what he realised must have been a traumatic childhood.

'In the old days,' she went on, 'the women and us children from Waynesboro used to carry large sacks made out of burlap. We'd sling it round our necks and fill it with cotton. Soon it would drag along the ground like a dead weight. My Mom always wanted me near her and was forever warning me not to get lost among those high sticky plants. She feared someone would grab me. I did it anyway, and I remember my heart a-poundin' each time. One time I ran upon some bloody clothing in an abandoned hut. I reckoned a man had killed someone in that hut and I was drawn to it like a magnet. Shortly after, I was playing near the hut and I ran right over a man who was sleepin' in the field. Didn't see him because of the tall plants. I started screaming and ran off like a headless chicken. I don't know who was more frightened, that poor man or me. I was only ten years old.'

Tring sat transfixed by the lilt of her voice and the images it conjured. She was an extraordinary woman.

For a moment Sharon Proctor seemed lost in the mists of time, then, 'We had nine miles of cotton between my back yard and the road, so I never gave it a second thought to work out in the yard when the sun came up. Around my fourteenth birthday, I was out in my see-through nightgown in the early dawn light when a crop duster spotted me and gave quite an air show. I dared not stand up or *I* would have been the one giving the show. Just when I thought it was safe to make a dash for the veranda, he fell outta the sky. He was so close to the ground, I could see him smile as he tipped his cowboy hat to me as he flew by. He did the same thing for the next three years until I left home. You see, I might have been a crop duster's girl.'

'But you were destined for much better.'

'Yes,' she said wistfully. 'You know, I used to catch lightning bugs at night – I think you call them fireflies here. I'd put them in a bottle by my bed. I used to sing to them as soon as the first star came out. We had a song we used to sing down south, "*star light, star bright, first star I see tonight, I wish I may, I wish I might, have this wish tonight.*"'

'And did your wish come true?'

'Look around you,' she replied with an expansive gesture. 'I guess I have. Not bad for a poor lil' girl from Georgia who used to dress up mops because her Mom couldn't afford to buy her a baby doll. Every time she wanted to clean up, she had to remove those clothes.' She sighed heavily as if the memory weighed on her like an anvil, and then smiled it away with a grin that was half hurt and half pride. 'But let's not dwell on the past, Jonathan. I'm a woman who lives for now and plans for the future. I think I happen to be in the most exciting job in the world. There are millions of people out there who rely on us to help cure their ills and ease their pain.'

'That's a pretty big responsibility.'

'Of course it is, and that's why Parados prides itself on the quality of its staff.'

Tring accepted her implied compliment diffidently. He felt that Sharon Proctor's expectations might outweigh his ability to fulfil them, especially as far as a new method of contraception was concerned. 'It's a tall order I've been set, Mrs Proctor.'

'Call me Sharon,' she smiled. 'Please.'

'Er, Sharon,' he said awkwardly. Somehow it didn't feel right. He had always found it difficult to call any boss's wife by her Christian name. It had been easier to resist with the wives of his previous employers. They had all been on the wrong side of fifty and had the sort of faces that would make a lemon weep. Anyway, he felt he had to know her a little better before he would feel comfortable with first name terms, at least in their professional capacity. He was also troubled by a general uneasiness and a marked stirring in the area of his groin.

'Jack and I have the fullest confidence in you, Jonathan,' she went on. 'We must innovate or perish, and neither Jack nor I is the suicidal type.'

Tring knew then that, despite the confidence she displayed, Sharon Proctor was a worried woman. Despite his fire-fighting job on Triamerol, it might only be a matter of time before the plug was pulled by the Department of Health. The contraceptive pill, the mainstay of the company, was also getting a bad Press. It gave the scientist scant solace that the Proctors looked upon him as their Great White Hope. 'I can only do my best,' he sighed.

'We realise that,' Sharon Proctor said supportively. 'And you can be sure that Jack and I will back you to the hilt. We have big plans for the future and an innovative male contraceptive will provide the blueprint.'

'Well, I suppose I'd better get back to work then,' Tring said unconvincingly. He was mesmerised by the woman.

'Just one thing, Jonathan....' Sharon Proctor stared at her visitor with eyes that were unusually expressionless. 'Many people find it hard to believe that I could truly love a man like Jack Proctor, or that I didn't marry him for his money. Let me just say that Jack and I are an item. He is everything I could wish for in a man.'

Tring felt himself blush. Her protestation was as much a disappointment to him as a surprise. The vision of a bloated bullfrog astride sleeping beauty had crossed his mind more than once, and Sharon Proctor's declaration of loyalty to her ugly sugar daddy stilled the pleasant warmth in his nether regions and replaced it with an unfamiliar pang of envy.

'Jack built this company from scratch,' she went on. 'He may have a few rough edges, but you don't succeed in this business by playing softball.'

Tring nodded in accord. Although others seemed to have an inordinate amount of faith in the breadth of his ability, he knew that he didn't possess the ruthlessness to run a company. He was not multi-talented like his friend, Abe Klein, who was as astute an industrialist as he was a scientist. Professor Jonathan Tring was simply a boffin who enjoyed the challenge of research and the buzz of creativity. He also knew what he liked, and began to appreciate Sharon Proctor's candour as well as her looks. He felt a need to know more about this beautiful woman and what made her tick. 'How did you meet Jack?' he ventured.

Sharon Proctor rose from behind her large mahogany desk and turned to peer through the window at the green swathe of Essex countryside beyond. 'What do you see out there, Jonathan?'

Tring approached the window, his sudden proximity to her sending his senses reeling. He couldn't put a name to the perfume she was wearing, but it reeked of class. The crisp cut of the Armani suit accentuated what he knew must be the perfect figure beneath. In heels she was almost as tall as him and her legs seemed to go on forever. 'I, er, don't know,' he flustered.

She turned to face him; the steel blue orbs barely a few inches from his face. Her breath caressed him with sweet incense. 'The environment,' she said simply. 'That's how I met Jack. I was a twenty-two-year-old journalist covering a conference on the environment in D.C. Jack was a key speaker on behalf of the pharmaceutical industry. I was as fascinated by his accent as by what he had to say. It was the first time I had heard an Englishman who didn't talk with a plum in his mouth.'

'Like me, you mean?' Tring smiled.

'Maybe,' she replied coyly. 'Anyway, I decided to get his personal viewpoint in an interview later that day. Then came supper, and the rest is history.'

'What about posterity?'

She smiled thinly. 'Oh, you mean children. No, neither Jack nor I have much time for kids. Other people's are okay, but we don't see many of them. My family is in Georgia and Jack was an only child. No, I've never had the maternal instinct.'

There were many more questions Tring wanted to ask, but her outstretched hand signalled that his audience was over. As he shook it gently, the professor noted how slender was her hand and how perfectly manicured the nails. Once again he felt a pang of jealousy that a man as repulsive as Jack Proctor could command the affections of this exquisite creature.

As Tring left her office, Sharon Proctor silently chided herself for being too open with him, for exposing her vulnerability to someone who was a relative stranger. Jonathan Tring would pay a price for her lapse. She would choose the time and the place, for she had pledged never to allow any man to exercise power over her again, not even the husband she secretly despised. For no one knew the real truth. Nobody would ever know the real truth: that all her subsequent actions had been guided by the memory of that sleeping man in the cotton field; the one who had jumped up and raped her.

Jonathan Tring walked a few paces down the corridor and paused to glance at the door bearing the name of his chairman. He could not help feel again a pang of jealousy towards the man who shared Sharon Proctor's bed. What the professor could not know was that the object of his envy had been listening intently to their conversation. Indeed, Jack Proctor was much more prone to this particular deadly sin than his employee. But on this occasion the chairman was smiling smugly, for his good wife had paid him due compliment, as he would have expected.

John Albert Proctor was essentially a man of simple desires, demanding loyalty from his staff and fealty from his spouse. In return, they might enjoy job security while she might share the keys to his kingdom. The operative word was 'might,' for virtue, as he was wont to say, is its own reward.

CHAPTER SIX

'We have no choice, Abe, simply no choice. Every time he cocks up it's costing us a fortune.'

The speaker, a tall, silver-haired man in his early fifties, threw up his hands in exasperation. The features of Kevin Kinloss· were bark-hard, slanted and angular. He was a Scotsman by birth and, the irreverent might say, a Scotsman by nature.

'I know, Kevin.' Klein swivelled uneasily in his chair. 'But I told you Tring is not interested at present. He's the only man I believe could fill the void. Great scientists like him are gold dust. Anyway, I don't think it's just a case of throwing more money at him. He's on a particular project at Parados and he wants to see it through. As you know, Jonathan is my best friend and if I can't persuade him, then nobody can.'

The Glaswegian stroked his angular jaw. 'So it's Bannister then,' he said. 'Temporarily.'

'Until I can persuade Jonathan, yes.'

The Scotsman's grey eyes narrowed. 'We won't tell Bannister he's on borrowed time. It'll affect his performance. You know how much he wants to be medical director. We'll let him assume he's got the job permanently and we can let him go as soon as we find a suitable replacement, whether it's Tring or no.'

Klein nodded. He knew his partner was right. That was why KleinKinloss was a success story. While he provided the scientific impetus, his associate looked after the business side of things. Hiring and firing was part of a game at which Kevin Kinloss excelled, although the duplicity of it all disturbed the American.

'Right then,' Kinloss said firmly, 'it's time to ring down the curtain on our Mr Sutton.'

Abe Klein sighed as he moved his hand to the intercom buzzer on his right.

'Maggie,' he called to his secretary.

'Yes, Mr Klein.'

'Ask Derek Sutton to come into my office, will you please.'

'I think he's taking an extended lunch, sir. I, er, was with him at the Bull an hour ago. Shall I call him there...hang on a minute, he just passed my office door.'

Klein and Kinloss could hear Maggie calling out. Then there were muffled voices and a scream. Within a few seconds there came a knock at the door of Klein's office.

'Lovely arse, that Maggie,' the purple-nosed face at the doorway enthused. The familiar gold pince-nez lay at a peculiar angle across his hooked nose, giving him a somewhat palsied visage. Derek Sutton was clearly inebriated.

'Come in, Derek, will you,' Kinloss ordered with a smile as thin as mist. Klein knew that smile well. It usually presaged the kiss-of-death for some poor soul. 'Take a seat,' the dour Scotsman added, offering the scientist his own chair and moving to take up a position alongside his partner at the top of the table. Bad tidings were always easier to impart when the responsibility was shared.

Sutton grinned like a Cheshire cat, wobbled unsteadily into the boardroom and half-fell into the vacant chair. Food stains on his tweed jacket and slate-grey trousers added to his general dishevelment. 'I'm shorry,' he slurred, 'over-indulged at lunch. Too mush wine in the Stroganoff.' The medical director then broke into a fit of giggling.

Kinloss cast a knowing glance towards his partner. Sutton was making it easier for them. It was faintly ridiculous to see such a renowned and respected scientist reduced to a barely coherent sop.

'How long is it that you've been with us, Derek?' Kinloss asked, already fully aware of the answer.

'Sinsh the beginning, old boy,' replied Sutton, beaming. 'What would the company be without me, eh?'

'Quite,' Kinloss replied, his smile thin-lipped and mean. 'And, of course, we are truly grateful for all your efforts, especially on Folitac.'

'Thank you, Kevin,' said Sutton, the veins of his florid complexion standing out like Danish Blue. 'I appreciate your appreciation. I know you appreciate me. Everyone loves old Derek, hee-hee.'

'Do you know who was the greatest heavyweight boxer of all time, Derek?' the Scotsman asked suddenly. The change of tack took both Sutton and Klein by surprise.

The scientist stroked his chin pensively. 'I, er, don't know mush about boxing, Kevin.'

'Rocky Marciano. And do you know why?'

Derek Sutton, already beginning to feel extremely queasy, shook his head. He was not in any state to indulge in trivial pursuit.

'He was the only one to retire undefeated, Derek.'

Abe Klein looked at his partner knowingly. So that was it. If there had to be a coup-de-grace, then why not make it self-inflicted.

'I don't know what you mean,' Sutton mumbled through his alcoholic haze.

'No false comebacks for Rocky, Derek,' explained the Scotsman. 'Got out at the top and stayed out. That's why he remains a legend.'

'I still don't know what you mean, Kevin,' said Sutton somewhat disingenuously.

The Scotsman's voice suddenly mellowed. 'Look, my friend, you've been going through a bit of a strain lately. Maybe it's time to hang up those test tubes and take things easy. You deserve a rest. Early retirement at fifty-five is no disgrace.'

'B-But I love my work, Kevin,' Sutton quailed. He was already feeling quite faint.

'Nevertheless, Abe and I feel that the company needs to move ahead and that the problems you're suffering are preventing this. I'm sure you can see it from our point of view.'

'But Kevin—'

Kinloss held up his left palm and, with his right hand, withdrew a folded letter from his inside pocket. 'I promise your golden handshake will not disappoint you, Derek. Just sign this.'

Derek Sutton, totally enfeebled by his inadequacy and the alcohol with which he sought to combat it, accepted the letter meekly. He fumbled for his pen, signed the letter of resignation without reading it and promptly slumped into oblivion over the desk. A dribble of saliva meandered down onto the letter, which was lodged under his right cheek.

Kevin Kinloss leant forward and delicately removed the piece of paper.

'You didn't have to make him resign, Kevin,' Abe Klein said sadly.

'Don't worry, Abe,' said the Scotsman firmly. 'He'll get his golden handshake. This just forestalls any complications that might arise in the future.'

The American sighed. It had not been pretty to watch a ruthless tactician at work. At that moment Abe Klein was thankful that *he* was the majority shareholder of KleinKinloss.

Barely forty miles south of the unassuming Cambridgeshire headquarters of KleinKinloss, the residence of John Albert Proctor stood out in the Essex village of Little Dunning like the Alamo. Its very size dwarfed even the lavish homes of the nouveau riche, the drug barons of East London who had moved there to acquire a semblance of respectability and, as an adjunct, to escape the prying eyes of the Metropolitan Police.

The huge wrought-iron gates began opening as soon as Tring pulled his silver-grey Mercedes SLK to within a few feet of them. Woven into the gates was the word 'Parados,' which Proctor had explained to him was an earthwork parapet thrown up behind a trench or other part of a fortified point to guard against attack or fire from the rear. The professor thought his boss's choice of title for both his company and his home quite apt. Considering the range of forces lined up against him, Parados presented just as big a target for his competitors as they did for him. Thus to protect his rear was indeed prudent.

The gravel road, flanked by ash and elm bedecked in fresh green shoots, seemed to wind interminably. Tring suddenly felt his stomach muscles tense. He was about to enter the wolf's lair for the first time, although it had been the wolverine that had dominated his thoughts since their meeting a couple of weeks earlier. He had passed her in the corridor a couple of times since, and on each occasion had felt a little weak-kneed, a giddiness which he recognised as the first signs of infatuation. Her fleeting smiles had been nothing other than formal, and yet he convinced himself that the fire in those incredible feline eyes contained a spark of desire for him. It had been six months since he had last bedded a member of the fairer sex and Sharon Proctor, wittingly or no, made the intensity of this abstinence almost unbearable.

Thus it was with a mixture of eagerness and trepidation that Tring drew up outside the extraordinary Palladian edifice, its tall white columns boasting proudly that this was the home of people of substance. The seventeenth-century architecture of Inigo Jones did not come cheap. Harold Spencer had spoken of the magnificence of the house atop what he called the Palatine Hill, having once attended a party in honour of the development of a new drug. 'I'd settle for just one of his minor works of art for a retirement gift,' the clinician had joked, adding, 'With my luck I won't even get a gold watch.'

Tring noted that alongside the conspicuous cream Rolls was ranged a number of cars of similar ilk as well as lesser vehicles, including those of Henry Cartwright, the head of sales, and Philip Brown, the finance director. The one absentee from the company's elite was Stanley Morris, the head of distribution, who had contrived to miss Jack Proctor's fancy-dress birthday bash by taking a winter break in the Bahamas.

Dressed as he was, Tring felt more than a little envious of his absent colleague. The professor felt faintly ridiculous in his eighteenth-century attire. From beneath his twentieth-century gabardine peeked the tightly fitting blue silk waistcoat. Frills and frothy lace sprouted at neck and wrists. When unencumbered by the overcoat, it would swing out over well-fitting knee breeches and the ghastly white tights that accentuated calf muscles set hard on the rugby field. In a box at Tring's side were the obligatory powdered white wig and tricorne hat and also a Venetian mask. It was made of the same sky-blue silk as his coat and was attached to a stick. The parcel of clothes had arrived by special courier at his home a week earlier, thus giving enough time to arrange replacements if they did not fit in accordance with the measurements he'd supplied to Jack Proctor's secretary. Spencer had warned him that Proctor was a stickler for authenticity and that his birthday parties were legendary. Previous bashes had seen the Wild West, The English Civil War and the Crusades visited upon this quiet corner of rural Essex.

Two suitably attired footmen ushered Tring through the portals of Parados and into a lobby that would have done justice to the nobility. Expensive-looking portraits of bejewelled princesses and their uniformed beaux stared down at him from the walls adjoining a spiral staircase to his right. The furniture was Regency and he had little doubt it was the real stuff. The prisms of the massive crystal chandeliers were ablaze and the whole arena reeked of style. He was sure that while the pocket of Proctor was the bottomless pit for this extravagance, it was his wife who had dictated the decor. Everything about the place shrieked of an American besotted with an idea of British aristocracy.

'This way, sir,' said one of the footmen, pointing him in the direction of the cloakroom. As Tring donned his wig and tricorne, he smiled sheepishly at a couple of other guests who were in various stages of attire.

'Do you feel as big a prick as I look,' joked one fop, who was struggling to fit his wig over a shock of red hair. 'I know it's all good fun, but these things are so damn uncomfortable.'

The professor smiled and preened himself again in the peach-tinted mirror. Not bad, he thought, straight out of the Age of Enlightenment. So was what greeted him a few moments later when, guided to it by the genteel sound of Purcell's The Fairy Queen, he entered the ballroom. It was like a scene from Amadeus. At least fifty dandies and their partners were standing around, drinks in hands. Most of the women wore pannier evening gowns with low décolletage, and Tring could not help thinking how this apparel could make even the most meagre of breasts inviting. On the other hand, a powdered face might flatter a crone. Should he be fortunate to attract the attention of one of these masked courtesans, he intended to check the lines on her neck most thoroughly.

The babble emanating from the pot pourri of guests almost drowned the music, which was being played somewhat forlornly by a small teahouse orchestra. To their right on the raised platform, the members of a more modern band were adjusting amplifiers and fiddling with guitars. This was more Tring's kind of music. It looked like the party was going to be far from dull.

The professor raised his mask frequently, using it like a pair of binoculars through which he could espy the multitude of bosoms. It was unabashed voyeurism. As his grey-green eyes swept the assembly for the second time, he spotted the unmistakable figure of his host. Like some Doge of ancient Venice, Proctor was seated on a dais around which his acolytes thronged. His fulsome robe was of golden cloth, as was his corno, the horned cap of office of those who had ruled the city of canals.

Tring noted that his beaming chairman had chosen not to wear a mask, thus making him instantly recognisable to the cognoscenti. Seated on Proctor's right was the object of Tring's lust. Sharon Proctor was simply stunning. Her gown of steel-blue satin matched the eyes that blinked coquettishly beneath a tall powdered wig. He stared at her for some minutes; entranced by the way she raised her silver-sequinned mask whenever she tired of an admirer's attention.

Still holding his mask to his eyes, Tring edged through the throng towards the regal couple. When directly in front of them, he lowered the mask gradually, as if reticent to give away his identity.

'Ah, Jonathan,' Jack Proctor enthused. 'Welcome, my boy, welcome to my humble abode.'

'Thanks JP,' the scientist said as warmly as he could. He felt a bit guilty about not buying a present, but then what could one buy an ostentatious multi-millionaire that he did not have already? 'Happy birthday and all that.'

'Thank you, my boy, now eat, drink and merry. That's an order.'

Tring smiled gracefully and then turned his attention to Sharon Proctor. He noted that she had not yet lowered her mask. The steel-blue eyes seemed to bore through him. 'Hello, Mrs Proctor,' he said blandly.

Her white-gloved hand hesitated a little before it glided downward. The high cheekbones and ample bosom, embellished as they were by fake beauty spots, made Tring catch his breath. She was achingly beautiful.

'Why, hello, Jonathan,' she smiled warmly. 'It was nice of you to come. I see you're unaccompanied.'

'Yes, I'm afraid I don't have a female companion at present,' the scientist shrugged.

'We'll have to do something about that, won't we Sharon,' Proctor beamed knowingly. He then winked, 'my wife's got a few friends who are footloose and fancy-free. By gum lad, some of them are real crackers.'

'Yes,' Sharon Proctor agreed, 'I'm sure one of my friends would love to meet you. Do you see that young lady in the corner...in the red dress?'

Tring followed the line of her gaze and looked over his shoulder. 'You mean the one with the gold mask?'

'Yes, her name's Fiona. She's very pretty, and unattached.'

ROGER RADFORD

It was more like an order than a suggestion, thought Tring. Still, considering the inaccessibility of his hostess, he was game for anything reasonably attractive. 'Thanks, I'll get myself a drink first and maybe chat her up later.'

'Splendid, Jonathan, splendid,' Proctor enthused. 'There's nowt so depressing as a wallflower at a party. You get stuck in, dear boy.'

Tring smiled bashfully. It was indeed a long time since he had got stuck in. He turned his head to say something to Sharon Proctor, but the mask had returned to base. 'Er, Fiona, you say...thanks.'

Two double whiskies and a half-hour later, Tring felt confident enough to make his first approach to the recommended Fiona. By this time the period music had given way to pseudo rock and the grand ballroom was a sea of gyrating bodies. Most of the revellers wore masks, some with huge hooked noses, and he could not help being reminded of the freaks in the Star Wars disco. Fiona, too, was still wearing her mask, a gold lamé full-faced affair with a cut-out mouth and deeply indented chin. He was by now close enough to check her neck. She was definitely no scrawny mother hen. The breasts, too, looked tight-skinned and youthful. She was dancing with an elderly man who was much shorter than her and clearly beginning to look the worse for wear. The professor chose his moment and, lowering his mask, entered the fray. The older man, his face ruddy and puffed, seemed glad to defer to the interloper.

'May I?' Tring said.

There was barely a nod from Fiona. Her eyes seemed to signal acquiescence but she did not break her dance routine. Tring, like most very tall men, felt more than a little awkward when it came to dancing. The two doubles, however, had contrived to loosen him up. The next dance, thankfully, was slow and she did not deter him from holding her close. She was quite tall, for which he was grateful. He tended to fight shy of petite women.

'Is there any chance of seeing what's beneath the mask?' he whispered into her ear.

She hesitated a little before replying, 'You might be disappointed.' The voice was sweet and the accent bore a hint of rural Cambridgeshire.

'I'll take my chances,' he said boldly.

83

She held him at arm's length and then slipped off her mask. Her demure smile begged his opinion.

'Very nice,' he said appreciatively. And she was. Her face had the freshness of a country girl with its high and slightly reddened cheeks and pert nose, and her medium length blonde hair provided a suitable frame for the large hazel eyes that sparkled mischievously.

'Thanks,' she said, pulling him close and burying her face in his cheek. 'You're Jonathan, aren't you,' she whispered. Her breath bore the scent of cachou.

'Yes, how did you know?'

'Sharon told me all about you.'

'Nice things, I hope.'

'She said you were like Little Bo-Peep.'

'I'm not that desperate.' Tring laughed, visions of his brother's Falkland follies rising to the fore. 'Anyway, maybe I'm like Georgie Porgie.'

'Do you kiss the girls and run away?'

'Not when they're as pretty as you.'

She smiled demurely. 'My name's Fiona.' she said, nestling closer.

'Nice to meet you,' Tring said, deciding it served no purpose to reveal that he already knew this. Allied with the effects of drink, the sheer proximity of her lithe body made Tring feel light-headed. They danced silently and sensually until she suddenly held him at arm's length. 'I'm afraid I have to put this back on.'

'But why?' Tring shook his head. She was too pretty to cover it all up with that ugly mask.

'There's someone I'm trying to avoid. I'm sorry, I can't explain.'

After donning the mask, she pressed herself even closer to him, as if making some kind of recompense. Tring's slightly befuddled mind fought to come to terms with it all as he felt her body grind into his. He knew she could feel the physical aspects of his arousal and it made him slightly embarrassed.

'It's okay, Fiona,' was all he could think to say.

At the end of the dance, Tring felt the mask scrape his face as she kissed him on the cheek. 'I must go and powder my nose,' she said urgently. 'I'll be back shortly. Wait for me by the bar.'

The professor stood dumbstruck for a few seconds as she swished away. He could not get the feel of her body against his out of his mind, and yet her insistence on wearing a mask for the rest of the evening concerned him. Who was she afraid of? Maybe there was an angry old boyfriend around at the party. Tring could look after himself, although he abhorred any kind of violence except that permitted on the rugby field.

Eventually, curiosity and a thirst that needed slaking led him to the bar. Propping it up and dressed like the Sun King was Philip Brown, the beady-eyed company finance director and a veteran of Proctor extravaganzas.

'How goes it, Jonathan?' he gushed. 'Bloody good party, what? See you dancing with that lovely girl in the red dress. Bit of all right. *Hic.*'

'You look terrible, Phil. Here, take this.' The scientist thrust the silly mask into his colleague's hand.

'What am I going to do with two masks?'

Tring ignored his inebriated colleague and ordered another double whisky. The drink burned its way down his throat and within a few seconds he, too, was feeling somewhat woozy. He also felt a little maudlin, for he did not believe his secretive masked companion would return.

Suddenly he felt a hand tug at his cuff.

'Ah, the Lady in Red, herself,' Brown blurted.

'Oh, hello, Fiona, I—' Tring was cut short by the slender finger raised to her lips. The hazel eyes stared at him beseechingly from within the golden visage. She pulled him away from the bar and led him firmly out into the lobby.

'Where are we going?' he asked groggily.

Within a few seconds they had descended some stairs, swirled along a narrow corridor and entered a musty room on their right. Once inside, he heard the door being locked. And hear was all he could do, for the room was pitch black. 'What's going on?' he bleated.

'Shh,' came the urgent reply, followed quickly by the pleasant odour of cachou as she pressed her lips against his. Pinning him against the door, she attacked his mouth voraciously with her tongue. She had removed her mask of course, although she might still have been wearing it for all the difference it made.

Tring felt himself harden, the tight breeches making his ardour almost exquisitely unbearable. Almost on cue, his companion's busy fingers deftly undid the constricting buttons and released their captive. He groaned as she slid down his body, the rustling of her dress almost deafening in the blackness. Her mouth and tongue quickly brought him to the verge of ejaculation. She stopped suddenly and then squeezed him hard. 'Fiona,' he groaned as she dragged him to the floor.

Still gripping his penis, she lowered herself onto it and began pumping rhythmically, her groans almost drowning out his. Tring, almost suffocated by the dress that had billowed over his face, gripped her buttocks hard. She had obviously prepared herself for she wore no underwear. The professor, his other senses honed by his virtual blindness, reeled under her onslaught. Soon they were making so much noise that he was sure they'd be discovered. He could not recall having ever experienced such a sexual high.

The beast with two backs continued its thrashings until it was totally spent. Fiona, her sweet breath caressing his ear, lay atop him for what seemed like an age.

Tring: was the first to speak. 'Jesus Christ,' he croaked, 'that was unbelievable.' He felt her finger against his lips, followed by further frantic rustling as she raised herself from him. He heard the door being unlocked, followed by a chink of light entering the room. This was succeeded by a flood that blinded him temporarily before the blackness returned. Tring lay where he was for some minutes reflecting on the most bizarre event of his life. His lover had come and gone like a thief in the night. Whoever she had wanted to avoid, it certainly hadn't been him. He figured that she had desperately sought sex and yet was obviously petrified of being caught in the act; hence the cover of darkness. Still, the subterfuge posed as many questions as it answered and he felt he needed to find out more about the mercurial Fiona.

The professor eventually hauled himself to his feet and readjusted his dishevelled clothing. He opened the door and peered into the corridor. It took a couple of seconds for his eyes to adjust to the light. To his relief no one was around. He closed the door gently and made his way groggily to the men's room, which, thankfully, was empty. Tring washed his face in an attempt to clear his addled brain and then straightened the preposterous wig. Bleary-eyed, he gaped at his pallid face in the mirror. Coincidentally, the band was playing A Whiter Shade of Pale.

The professor, satiated but confused, rejoined the throng in the ballroom, where the dancing Proctors appeared to be the centre of attraction.

Of the mercurial Fiona there was neither hide nor hair.

A world away from the frivolity but on the fringe of the same county, another man was about to engage in a little fancy dressing of his own. Kieran Kelly entered a toilet adjacent to the Plane Tree Centre day surgical ward at Whipps Cross hospital, whipped a freshly starched blue theatre gown from the plastic bag he was carrying and quickly donned it over his own clothes. He then tied on a mask and left it dangling around his neck. There was little reason to suppose that anything would go wrong, thought the Irishman. It had all been so easy to discover the best way to achieve his immediate aim. He had simply told his local pharmacist that he was writing a screenplay and needed some info on how the main protagonist would go about procuring certain drugs from a hospital. The chemist knew him well and was totally unsuspecting of any ulterior motive. He had even given him an old copy of MIMS, the monthly index of available drugs. Everyone loved a writer.

He had already carried out a dummy run the previous evening. It was amazing how accommodating people could be, especially hospital porters. They appeared to know everything, but were not suspicious by nature. Chatting to one, he had received an unwanted biography of the man's life and, by the way, information that there were only five security guards covering the hospital's forty-eight acres over a twenty-four hour period. By the time he had finished with the man, he knew all he needed to know and had made a friend for life. It was truly amazing what Irish blarney could achieve. Within a few minutes of them parting, he was in and out of the laundry with the surgeons' gear.

The hospital, a vast Victorian edifice, was one of the busiest generals in the country. There were hundreds of doctors who coursed through its corridors on a daily basis. It would have been asking too much of the staff of the dispensary to be able to identify every doctor.

Front, thought Kelly as he swept into the day unit, all one needed was front. 'Nurse, quickly,' he ordered, 'I need a blank drug chart right away. I've got an op in five minutes. And I need four syringes.'

'You surgeons are all the same,' said the nurse, a West Indian with a thick Jamaican accent, 'you're always forgetting something.' A paragon of efficiency, she scurried away to fulfil his request.

'Thanks,' he called out, 'you're a diamond.'

'Not even me husband call me that,' she called back to him, noting that she wouldn't mind assisting such a handsome man in theatre. Within a few seconds, the pseudo surgeon was on his way out of the unit replete with chart in hand and syringes in his pocket..

So far, so good, thought Kelly, as he made his way to the dispensary. The biggest test was about to come. He had been advised that his fictional protagonist should act with belligerence. If the dispensing pharmacist thought he was facing a surgeon in a fit of apoplexy because some nurse or other had not procured him the drugs needed in the operating theatre, then that pharmacist would be more likely to hand over the necessary without requesting written documentation. Basically, it wasn't only the public who were frightened of stern-faced physicians. 'Act with authority, Kelly,' he muttered to himself. He approached the dispensary window. Glancing down at his drug sheet, he called out in demand mode, 'Four vials *of brietal sodium* and four of Triamerol, and be quick about it.' The pharmacist, a weedy looking young man, visibly appeared to quake before scuttling away to bring him his request. Inside a minute the Irishman's request had been fulfilled and he was heading towards the toilet again to rid himself of his surgeon's paraphernalia. It had all gone like clockwork.

Kelly was about halfway along the corridor when his heart suddenly skipped a beat. Swiftly approaching him was a familiar figure. The Irishman instinctively ducked into an alcove. Thankfully, Dr Martin Townsend seemed engaged in animated conversation with a couple of housemen. As the trio passed him, the Irishman's eyes fleetingly engaged those of the man he held directly responsible for his wife's death. Townsend's were rheumy and tired and he looked like shit, thought Kelly. The doctor's nose was a bulbous kaleidoscope of brightly coloured veins. He knew a lush when he saw one. The Irishman did not look back, but carried on walking down the corridor, patting the vials in his pocket. 'A couple of these are for you, you bastard,' he mouthed silently.

CHAPTER SEVEN

The following day, thankfully, was a Sunday, and Jonathan Tring slept later than usual. He awoke sometime after three in the afternoon, still in his frippery but minus his wig. The mother of all hangovers was beating a drum roll in his head. He vaguely remembered being driven home by a colleague, although he was too far gone to remember anything other than that the Good Samaritan had had the face of the devil. Whoever it was who had helped him up the stairs to his flat and guided him to his bed at least had had the sense to disconnect his phone line. Tring looked forlornly at the disconnected cord in his hand. Old Chigwellians seconds had been robbed of their star forward that morning and they had been probably trying like mad to contact him. It was the first time he could recall letting them down and it made him feel even worse.

The professor slid the cord into its socket, scratched his unkempt thatch like a demon and staggered into the bathroom. 'Tring, you look like shit,' he told himself in the mirror. At least he was recognisable, which was more than could be said for most of the aliens at Proctor's extraordinary party. Had it all been some kind of existential dream? Had he really allowed himself to be debauched in pitch darkness by a country girl with whom he had exchanged only a few words? Who was she? Where was she? Somehow he felt the Proctors had all the answers. After all, they had set him up with her.

The urgent ringing of the telephone brought an abrupt end to his musing. It was Abe Klein.

'How goes it, my fine English friend?' The voice was bright and breezy.

'Could be better, Abe,' he groaned. Tring didn't believe Klein had ever been hung over in his life. He'd abstained at Oxford. Jews don't drink, his friend had once said, because getting stoned was bad for business.

'You sound like shit. What happened?'

'I was savaged by two Pit bulls, and one of them was in heat.'

'I don't understand.'

The professor cackled. 'Neither do I, actually.'

'Listen, Jonathan, you can tell me all about it on Friday night. Rachel's making her usual chicken soup and stuff. She won't take no for an answer.'

Tring smiled, despite himself. 'How can I ever say no Jewish penicillin and gefilte fish, Abe?'

'Friday, then,' said the American.

'You got it, Yank,' Tring replied in his best mock New York.

Jack Proctor was in mixed mood. His birthday party had been its usual glittering success. And so it damn well should have been. It had cost him enough. But then the dour Yorkshireman had always been prepared to entertain the troops, enjoying the homage engendered by wealth. Riches, however, could be ephemeral. If Parados did not grow, it would flounder or, worse still, be taken over. There could be vast profits in the pharmaceutical industry, which accounted for the many piranhas it attracted. Some of the big boys were already making overtures towards him. Sure, the money they were offering made the National Lottery look like a poor relation, but with a hundred million in the bank and no Parados, he knew he would be like a fish out of water. Jack Albert Proctor would rather go down with his ship than surrender the bridge. He was also enough of a realist to know that his good lady would desert that ship ahead of the rodents. Sharon had learned to love power more than money. She had demanded to be brought into the company soon after they married, and he had to admit she had proven a damn good businesswoman. He also knew that a woman as young and as beautiful as his wife was open to temptation. Potential seducers were legion and her chastity had had to be guarded, constantly and diligently. She never complained about his over-protectiveness, nor refused his advances, which admittedly had become less frequent with the years. Yet behind those steely eyes lurked a mystery that was as considerable as Southern hospitality.

The chairman suddenly leaned across his desk and pressed a button on the intercom. 'Jonathan?' he barked. Daydreaming was unproductive.

There was a few seconds delay before the scientist's tinny reply.

'Come into my office, will you,' Proctor boomed.

'Right away, JP,' Tring replied with a false brightness. The last thing he needed that morning was an interruption from his leader. He was due in the animal lab in five minutes and there were some rodents who needed his attention, particularly a couple of over-sexed rats.

'When His Master's Voice summons, one must but obey,' Harold Spencer said resignedly. 'Don't worry, I'll mind the store.'

'Thanks Harold, I'll meet you by the rat emporium in ten minutes. By the way, how do I look?'

The Mancunian twiddled his bow tie, leaned back in his chair and carefully surveyed the white-coated professor. 'From the neck down you look great.'

'And from the neck up?'

'You look like one of our rats just after he's serviced a dozen females.'

'That good, eh,' said Tring while doing some mock tidying of his hair. Spencer would never know how close he was to the truth. 'See you soon.'

'Don't forget to take your sleeping bag,' Spencer called out as the professor shut the lab door behind him. 'Nobody gets out of JP's office in under an hour.'

When Tring knocked on Proctor's door he felt more than a little uneasy. He still had no clue how he had arrived home from the party, and yet he felt sure his boss must have been involved.

'Sit down, dear boy,' said his host, beaming. 'Well, what did you think of your first Jack Proctor birthday party?'

'Truly amazing,' Tring replied honestly, 'although I don't quite remember all of it.'

'Don't I know it, my boy.' Proctor jowls danced a jig as he guffawed. 'You were so far gone I had to arrange for one of my friends to take you home.'

'I hope I didn't disgrace myself.'

Proctor laughed again. 'Oh, no, *you* put up very little resistance.' The chairman's tiny eyes narrowed and a sly grin cracked his ugly visage. 'Did *she?*' he asked with raised eyebrow.

'Who do you mean?' Tring replied disingenuously.

'You know, the country bumpkin, the farmer's daughter, my wife's friend, Fiona.'

The professor moved uneasily in his chair. Thankfully, Proctor appeared to be unaware of the sexual shenanigans that had taken place. 'I'm afraid I only had a few dances with her.'

'Perhaps it's just as well.'

'What do you mean?'

'Sharon got a phone call from Fiona this morning. Apparently her company's sending her to Hong Kong. Works in IT. Sales side. Wish she was working for us.'

Tring felt deflated. He had wanted to see Fiona again, if only because the sex had been so great. He was also intrigued by her secretiveness. There was something about the girl's vulnerability that appealed to him. 'Pity,' he said, 'I didn't even know her full name.'

'Harrington. Fiona Harrington. Anyway, enough of girls,' Proctor said with finality. 'What about sex in the laboratory, how go the rats?'

'I was about to try a new formula this morning,' Tring replied. As a scientist, he could not afford to be maudlin about the fate of his laboratory animals. They were specially bred in carefully controlled environments and the tests were important to discover which drugs were likely to be the most effective and safe when given to Man. Although the use of animals in laboratory experiments was controversial and generally undesirable, there was currently no other system that allowed the evaluation of new drugs with the same degree of reliability or acceptability to government Boards of Health. The professor was currently undertaking a study on a new compound to determine whether or not it caused cancer or other serious toxicity and, most importantly, its effect on reproduction, or teratology. They were all constantly aware of the thalidomide and benoxaprofen disasters.

'Good, good,' Proctor enthused. 'We all have the fullest confidence in you, Jonathan.' The chairman's mood suddenly turned more serious. 'I need you to work your boys harder, lad.'

Tring scratched his head defensively. 'But some of them are already putting in sixteen-hour days, JP. There's not much more they can do.'

'How far are we away from trials on humans?'

'Three, maybe four months,' Tring replied, trying hard to cover the gnawing doubt in his mind. Small amounts of the new synthetic hormone would be administered in controlled circumstances to a few carefully selected and screened healthy volunteers. Then blood levels of drug, the excretion characteristics and any beneficial or unwanted effects would be monitored in order to evaluate the behaviour of the new drug in Man. It all took time and could not be rushed.

'Then we have Phase Two trials followed by study of the Risk-Benefit Ratio,' the chairman went on. 'And then we have to decide whether the whole thing's worth further development, don't we?'

'Yes, sir.'

'And how much money has the project already cost us by then, Jonathan?'

Tring shifted uncomfortably. 'I don't really know, JP, but it must be considerable.'

'Hundreds of millions, Jonathan, and nobody can really understand the pressure that implies for me.'

The professor nodded. He could see that Proctor was hurting. There could be any number of reasons for discontinuation of a project: poor tolerability leading to a high number of side effects, formulation of the drug being unstable or unpalatable, little or no effectiveness, the cost of production outweighing the projected income or, maybe, the drug being inferior to other compounds.

'Then, as you know, we have large-scale clinical trials in hospitals and general practice,' Proctor continued, 'and only then can we apply for a product licence.'

Tring was fully aware of the procedure. He'd been involved many times in the compilation and evaluation of data on thousands of treated subjects. He hated the preparation of the phases two and three reports which, together with all the pre-clinical data from animal and laboratory studies, were sent to the Department of Health's Medicines Control Agency for evaluation by a team of experts. Usually, this evaluation took many months, even years, before a Product Licence was granted. Whoever thought up the phrase 'time is money' must have had the pharmaceutical industry in mind.

'What do you think of Parados, lad?'

Tring was nonplussed by the question.

'You know, you've been here a while now,' Proctor went on. 'I value your opinion. What are your impressions?'

Tring thought carefully before answering. He thought Parados had been an amazing success story, but he didn't want to sound sycophantic. 'I think you and Mrs Proctor run a tight ship,' he said simply.

Proctor's gimlet eyes narrowed. 'What if I told you the ship was floundering, the sharks were gathering and there was blood in the water.'

'I'd say that maybe they're underestimating you.'

Tring's comment forced a thin-lipped smile from the chairman. 'Maybe, Jonathan, maybe, but the fact remains that Glaxo is putting out feelers.' Proctor held up the palms of his hands. 'This is strictly confidential, of course.'

'Of course.'

Proctor swivelled out of his chair and waddled over to a model of the Parados headquarters that lay astride a large table. 'I just had this delivered, lad. Do you know why I had it made?'

Tring shook his head and joined his master at the table. The model was accurate, right down to the toy cars. A miniature cream Rolls dominated the parking bays.

'I had this made to remind me of who I am and what I am. I had it made to remind me that without Parados I am nothing. I had it made to remind me that money alone can never mean as much as the creation and sustenance of this company. Can you understand that, lad?'

'Yes, JP, I think I can,' Tring replied, visibly moved by the chairman's impassioned speech. Whatever antipathy Proctor's physical attributes and gruffness engendered in others, there could no doubt the sincerity of his love for his company.

The chairman leaned over the model and picked up the toy Rolls. 'This means nothing to me without this,' he said, gesturing towards the cardboard factory with his free hand. He then replaced the Rolls and returned to his chair. 'Sit down, lad. Sit down. I haven't finished yet.'

Tring returned to his own chair unsure of where all this was leading. Although he was flattered that his chairman chose to trust him with information that, in truth, had been unnecessary to impart, the professor felt that there was a purpose to it.

'You know, Jonathan,' the safely ensconced Proctor went on, 'at some point in their lives, most of the great leaders of our industry have had some tough times. What makes them great is that they don't wait their entire lives for Christmas to come. Leaders don't wait for someone else to change before they do. They act decisively. You know what I do when I feel under threat, lad?'

Tring shook his head, wondering what pearl of wisdom was coming next.

'I go out and buy, lad. While the bigger fish are looking to swallow me up, I look around for some minnows myself. That way I might get too large for the big boys and get stuck in their craw. You either eat or get eaten in this business.'

Get to the point, thought Tring. His chairman's pontificating was becoming irksome.

Proctor eyes narrowed again until the pupils were barely discernible. 'What do you know about KleinKinloss?'

So that was it. Proctor was out to swallow up Abe's company. 'They make Folitac,' Tring said unblinkingly.

'And Folitac is a patch with a great reputation,' Proctor stated with a smile that could freeze mustard.

'And one great reputation deserves another.'

'Quite.'

'So…'

'So how well do you know Abe Klein?'

Tring smiled thinly. 'You already know that, JP.'

The Pit bull gave a sort of half-laugh, somewhere between a snigger and a snort. 'Of course, lad, of course. I've done my homework. You two are pretty close.'

Tring leaned forward. 'He won't sell, JP. You might as well forget it.'

Proctor sat back in his chair and folded his arms over his ample girth. 'Every man, as they say, has his price,' he growled.

'You don't,' Tring said, perhaps a little too boldly.

'Maybe, maybe not, but we're not talking about me. I'd like you to have a little chat with Mr Klein. I'm not asking you to compromise your friendship. Just find out his thoughts about the matter. No numbers yet. Just a tentative inquiry.'

'He has a partner, JP.'

'A junior partner.'

'Yes.'

'Kinloss is the smaller fish. He doesn't interest me. When are you seeing Klein next?'

'Friday night; I'm invited for supper.'

Proctor smiled wistfully. 'Ah, Jewish cooking! Nearly as good as roast beef and Yorkshire pudding. Enjoy your meal, lad, and let me know what happens.'

Tring guessed by Proctor's demeanour that his audience was over. He stood up, and nodded to the chairman. So be it. Abe Klein wanted Jonathan Tring and Jack Proctor wanted Abe Klein. Business was business.

It was just that he hated to be in the middle.

CHAPTER EIGHT

'How is it, Jonathan?'

Tring's wide smile said it all. Rachel Klein made the best chicken soup north of Watford.

'Don't ask rhetorical questions, darling,' said the professor's host, tapping his good lady on her ample bottom as she ladled some more of the broth into his plate. Abe Klein was never happier than when entertaining his best friend for a traditional Sabbath eve meal.

'It's good you're staying overnight, Jon. I made cholent for tomorrow. Fancy some?' Rachel playfully ignored her husband's demand. She was a *balabusta*, a Yiddishe Momma from New York who doted on her spouse and their two children. Plain in looks and plain by nature, she gained complete fulfilment from her role of dutiful housewife and parent. Not for her the title of working mother, with latchkey children and a husband who thought homemade food came out of a packet.

Tring sipped the stock, and its warmth was the same as he felt for this wonderful family. True, Rachel was a bit of a fusspot, but she had the knack of making a guest feel like the most important person in the world. And what's more, it was genuine.

Tring beamed. 'Wild horses couldn't drag me away from a plate of your cholent, Rachel,'

'Enough talk,' Abe Klein chimed in. 'Eat, eat.'

The younger Kleins, Warren and Rebecca, needed little encouragement. They were already halfway through the course. Tring could see that while his mother's cooking would have little effect on ten-year-old Warren, who would probably grow up to be as dapper as his father, Rebecca was already showing signs at nine that she was destined for the fuller figure boutiques. The professor envied the children the warmth of their upbringing. Perhaps that was why he was so drawn to this family, because family was what they were, in every positive sense of the word.

'Do you recall the time old Dalgleish cooked that haggis his uncle sent him from Scotland?' Klein asked his guest with a twinkle in his eye.

'Here we go again,' Rachel said. 'Do you two never tire of talking of Oxford?'

'Charcoal on a bed of crispy rice,' said Tring wistfully, as the memory resurrected itself from the treasure trove of university life. Perhaps that's why Klein and himself were so close. Friendships forged in student salad days often provided a bond that surpassed time and distance. Many old friends had drifted apart, but the mere mention of their names was enough to rekindle the fires of shared experiences. Oxford University had been a gothic time capsule that had been polishing minds and confounding outsiders in equal measure for eight hundred years. Thanks to a uniquely British blend of tradition, first-rate scholarship, and, often, inspired eccentricity, it was in every sense a place apart. Klein, a Rhodes scholar, had fallen in love with the place, never fully comprehending its mystique, or the fact that students were not required to attend lectures, did not receive grades, seldom studied anything outside their chosen subject, and took just three sets of exams during the course of their college careers – 'one to get in and two to get out,' as his English friend had put it. Both men had graduated spectacularly, with Tring preferring to continue in academia while the American returned to Brooklyn. Within six months he was married and back in England. The Sceptred Isle, its habits and traditions, had proved too great a lure. Small-time posts with minor drugs firms had given way to a fervent desire to run his own company. A couple of years of steady success saw the need for an extra hand on the tiller. Abe had wanted to devote more of his time to research and development and needed an experienced businessman to guide the finances. Kevin Kinloss seemed to fit the bill. He knew little about pharmaceuticals, but was ruthless in business. That, plus a million pounds to buy in as a junior partner, and the marriage was made. So far it had been made in heaven, although Klein had never felt totally at ease with the Scotsman, who was fifteen years his senior. Theirs was strictly a formal relationship, a case of opposites that attracted, but only in the workplace.

The diners continued their reminiscing until Rachel disappeared into the kitchen to attend to the dishes and the kids into a bedroom to play with their computer. Despite the general bonhomie, Tring was keenly aware of the task that Proctor had set him. He felt a little like a Trojan horse.

'You look a bit like Dalgleish's haggis,' Klein said, noting his friend's sudden frown. 'I hope that black look isn't because of Rachel's cooking.' Tring smiled uncomfortably. Unlike his mother, he was never much good at hiding his feelings. 'No, no, the food was great as usual, Abe.'

'Have another Drambuie. You know Kinloss swears by it.'

Tring proffered his glass and then downed the whisky liqueur in one go.

'Steady on, old chap,' said Klein in mock Received English.

His guest felt the warming liquid further release the inhibitors that had been plaguing him all evening. 'Abe, there's something I've been asked to ask you,' he said at last.

'Shoot,' said the American, his hazel eyes bright with inquisitiveness.

'It's Jack Proctor.'

Klein beamed knowingly. 'Ah, the Pit bull. What's he up to now?'

'I don't know how to put this, Abe,' Tring prevaricated.

'Say it straight, Jon. That's always the best way.'

Tring shrugged. 'He wants you, Abe.'

Klein pursed his lips and tilted his head. He removed his horn-rims and sucked on one of the sides. Tring recognised the ritual his friend used when contemplating any serious issue. 'How much does he reckon I'm worth?' he said at length.

'No figures yet, Abe. It's just a tentative inquiry at present.'

'Tell him I'm willing to sell.'

Tring's square jaw dropped.

'Yeah, Jon, tell him to think of a number between one and ten, multiply by a billion and take away the number he first thought of.' With this, the American burst into a guffaw.

'I told him you wouldn't be interested, but he's used to getting his own way.'

'And will you help him, Jon?'

Klein's question cut the professor to the quick. 'I would resign before he could make me compromise our friendship,' he said firmly. 'You know that.'

The American blushed. It was true. If there was one man in the world he could trust, it was Jonathan Tring. 'I'm sorry, man,' he apologised. 'It's just that the Proctors of this world have a habit of corrupting those around them.'

Tring looked solidly at his friend. 'I don't believe Jack Proctor is evil, Abe. Ruthless, yes, but not evil.'

'You can tell him from me that he hasn't a cat in hell's chance.'

'He might approach Kinloss,' Tring suggested. 'Nearly everybody is rich in somebody else's eyes and poor in his own.'

'That sounds Talmudic,' said Klein. The American then frowned and shifted uneasily in his chair. 'Jack Proctor can promise Kevin Kinloss the crown jewels of the Queen of England, but as long as I'm majority shareholder, the jewel in my crown'll remain safely under lock and key.'

Tring nodded. He could see that this would be a case of an unstoppable force hitting an immovable object. He was just about to comment when the matronly figure of Rachel Klein appeared at the dining room doorway.

'Shop talk again, boys? Now who wants black coffee?'

When Jonathan Tring relayed Klein's unambiguous message to the chairman of Parados Pharmaceuticals the following day, Jack Proctor had simply smiled knowingly and then muttered something about other ways to skin a cat. The glint in Proctor's eye had made the professor uncomfortable, but Tring believed his boss was mistaken if he thought he could manipulate the American. Abe was nobody's fool.

The scientist returned to his laboratory troubled both by Proctor's comment and the vision of the globetrotting Fiona. He knew it was a waste of energy to concern himself with a woman who had simply used him for sex. And yet he couldn't get the pretty, fresh-faced farm girl out of his mind. Perhaps it was simply the memory of the sex, coming as it did after such prolonged abstinence. One thing was for sure: Hong Kong was too far away to conduct a meaningful relationship.

As he plunged into his work, professor Jonathan Tring began to feel more and more like one of his laboratory rats. Others had used him for experimental purposes, one in business and the other in sex.

In a Cambridgeshire boardroom, another man was seeing himself portrayed as a victim, albeit potential rather than actual.

101

'Who told you?' Abe Klein seethed.

'Proctor himself,' came the calm reply.

'First he sends an intermediary and then he goes behind my back. No deal, man. No deal.'

'Let's at least hear what his offer is, Abe,' the Scotsman said sternly. 'We canna lose anything by it.'

'There's no point, Kevin. I wouldn't sell out to anyone, let alone that ugly leech.'

If Kevin Kinloss was disappointed by Klein's reaction, he was not surprised. While the American saw the company through the pink spectacles of altruism, the Scotsman was more sanguine about approaches from predators. He was first and foremost a businessman. He looked for return on investment. 'Proctor intimated that it could be in the tens of millions,' he said with raised eyebrows that almost demanded acceptance of an offer.

'Money,' Klein said through gritted teeth. 'It's always money. Doesn't this company mean more to you than that?'

The Scotsman's steely eyes narrowed. 'You're not the only one who helped build this company, my friend.'

Abe Klein scratched his baldpate defensively. It was true. While he may have formulated a winning product, it took sales and marketing skills to fully realise its potential. Kinloss had every right to have his say. 'Look, Kevin,' the American said in more conciliatory tone, 'our potential is enormous. One day we could be a Parados. We might even build an empire.'

The Scotsman's angular features betrayed little emotion. 'We are basically a one-product company. I think we at least ought to hear what Proctor has to say. If word gets out, we'll have the other shareholders on our necks anyway.'

'If word gets out, our share price will rise and Proctor will be looking at a bigger bill. I'll issue an immediate denial and the price will probably drop lower than originally. Then some other sharks might move in to screw Proctor. Speculation is in no-one's interest.'

'You have ultimate control, Abe,' Kinloss said calmly. 'I'm just asking you to think about it.'

'There's really nothing to think about. Jack Proctor may think he can screw anyone he likes, but I'm one helluva tight end.'

It was just after noon on a sparklingly crisp Sunday. The Old Chigs clubhouse was resounding to the robust singing of ditties, their bawdiness designed to instil in friend and foe alike a comradeship that could only be found in those who had just spent eighty minutes battering one another in the pursuit of an oval ball.

For Jonathan Tring, a prop forward of no meagre skill, the game was a welcome release from the scheming of Jack Proctor. Rugby was the most physical of team sports, and yet there tended to be little gratuitous violence involved. Foul play was not cricket, so to speak, and part of the mystique of Union was that it was a game invented by gentlemen for gentlemen. Not that Tring was surrounded by a bevy of squires and aristos. Many of his team mates were brokers in the financial markets. Rough and ready Cockneys, they were just as well suited to flogging cutlery down Petticoat Lane. Buying and selling was their game and the venue didn't matter one jot. As he raised his glass along with theirs, Tring couldn't help thinking that Proctor would be well suited to this melange of machismo, although his boss would no doubt have felt more at home among practitioners of the Northern code.

Tring downed his glass of lager and bade farewell to the pink faces and glassy eyes. Expletives abounded among those who possessed limited vocabulary and he felt the need for more cerebral company. He'd pop home, rustle up an omelette, have a nap and then settle down to the current biography and a little Bach. The only thing missing was something warm and soft tucked close to him; someone like Fiona Harrington.

The big man sighed as he brushed past a collection of desirable Cabriolets and stepped into his silver-grey Mercedes. He had never felt more alone. Work had become the dominant theme of his life and he was becoming a little too long in the tooth to remain 'one of the lads.' He needed a woman. Period.

As the professor eased his car into Chigwell High Road, he was forced to brake sharply as a black Audi Cabriolet appeared from nowhere. The scientist cursed as the driver of the Audi screeched almost to a halt and then swung wildly to the other side of the road. In the split second that the other car was stationary, Tring could make out the features of its driver. 'Fiona!' he gasped.

The fresh-faced driver of the Audi had grimaced but otherwise had shown no hint of recognition. The next thing Tring saw was a flash of her blonde hair as the car raced away.

Tring never fully understood why he did it. Instinct took over. Fiona Harrington was supposed to be in Hong Kong and Fiona Harrington was driving along a country road in Essex. He also happened to have made love to the girl and he wanted to do so again, dammit! In a rush of testosterone, he slammed his foot to the floor. With a screech of tyres and a protesting roar, the Mercedes spun into the main road. The black Audi disappeared around a bend and then once more came into view as he steadily gained. It was heading towards Abridge at a fast but not entirely hectic pace. Within a few seconds Tring had made up the distance. He gave a couple of toots on his horn and flashed his lights, at the same time raising his left hand in a semi-wave.

Instead of slowing down, the driver of the Audi dropped a gear and the two-point-eight litre engine smoothly thrust the car forward. Tring's square jaw dropped open. He couldn't understand why she was trying to avoid him. 'Maybe I'm wearing the wrong after-shave,' he half-joked to himself, pressing his foot to the floor. He wasn't about to give up the chase.. The automatic smoothly slipped a gear and within seconds the Audi was once again in view. Thankfully, traffic was light, although both drivers were forced into manoeuvres that required no little skill. Her driving skill surprised him, as the black Audi meandered along the country road. This was one of those occasions when he would have preferred a manual car.

The pursuit continued for a further three miles, during which Tring twice came within scraping distance of the Audi's bumper. Further flashing of lights and tooting of horn seemed only to spur his quarry to greater effort. In the end, it was a mundane circumstance that brought an end to the pursuit. A motorised haywain had broken down and was blocking the narrow lane. The driver of the tractor, bent over the engine and busily engaged in repairs, launched himself backwards in a defensive manoeuvre as the Audi and the Mercedes screeched to a halt almost simultaneously. Cursing, he picked himself up and moved threateningly towards the two vehicles.

'Here, what d'yer think you two are doing,' he shouted. 'You'll kill someone.'

Both drivers remained sitting in their cars, seemingly oblivious of the farm worker's ranting. The sudden release from the tension of the chase had left them drained physically and mentally. Tring was the first to react, although his exit from the Mercedes was laboured. He felt as if he had just spent some minutes at the bottom of a collapsed scrum. Ignoring the tractor driver, a weedy middle-aged man, he walked a little unsteadily towards the Audi. Resting his left arm on the cloth roof, he stooped to peer at its driver.

The expression on Fiona Harrington's face was a mixture of surprise, relief and apprehension. 'Oh, it's you,' she mouthed.

Tring half-smiled and tapped on the window. As it lowered, the farm worker once again made his bellicose presence felt. 'Here, are you listening to me?'

The professor straightened to stand face to face, or rather face to chest with the man. 'Piss off,' Tring hissed uncharacteristically. He may have been a gentle giant, but his protagonist was not to know this. All the farm worker saw was a younger man of muscle and sinew who seemed almost twice his size. It was a no contest. Grumbling, the tractor driver returned to his stricken vehicle.

Tring stooped once again to face his quarry. 'What do you mean, "oh, it's you," Fiona. Surely you recognised me.'

'No, I didn't actually,' she replied coolly. 'Your car windows are tinted. All I thought was that some maniac was overcome by road rage and was chasing me. You're lucky my mobile phone is out of order or I'd have called the police.'

Tring glanced back his car. She was right, of course. The tinted glass had been an extra. 'I'm sorry, Fiona,' he said sheepishly. 'It's just that I thought you were avoiding me and I couldn't understand why. Anyway, I thought you were supposed to be in Hong Kong.'

'Who told you that?' she asked defensively.

'Jack Proctor.'

'What else did he tell you?'

Tring stared at her. God, she was pretty. The hazel eyes were bright with inquisitiveness. Her cheeks were high and slightly flushed, the pert nose flaring like a Newmarket thoroughbred's. This was one filly he desperately wanted to ride again. 'He said your company was sending you to Hong Kong on an assignment.'

Fiona Harrington remained silent, her fresh face showing no emotion.

'Listen,' said Tring, 'I'm getting a crick in my neck.' He moved swiftly around the front of her car and eased himself into the passenger seat. There was silence for a few seconds, then, 'Well?'

'Well what?'

'Are you going to Hong Kong?'

Fiona gave a shuffle of indignation. 'I don't see what business that is of yours,' she said testily.

Tring rubbed his square jaw in exasperation. 'Look, why are you being so damn touchy? I'll say it straight. I can't forget that night at the party. I want to see you again. Dammit I want to make love to you again.'

Fiona looked at him with eyes that betrayed a confusion of emotions. 'I like you Jonathan,' she said almost demurely, her voice suddenly soft and warm. She then sighed, deeply and with Job-like sadness. 'It's just that I can't see you again.'

'Can't or won't.'

'Can't.'

'Then it's not because you don't want to.'

'No...I mean, yes.'

'Fiona,' he said sternly, 'I don't know what you mean.'

'I can't explain,' she said with a pained expression.

'It's that other man, isn't it,' Tring said with a kind of finality. 'The one you've been trying to avoid.'

'No...I mean, yes. Please, Jonathan, don't press me any further.'

Tring was nothing if not a stubborn character when it came to something he truly desired. 'Look,' he cajoled, 'I promise I won't ask questions. I just want to see you again.'

Fiona Harrington's pretty face contorted into a mixture of longing and apprehension. She tore off a strip from a notepad attached to the

dashboard and scribbled a telephone number. 'Here,' she said handing it to him, 'you can contact me on this number. Just promise me one thing.'
'What's that?'
'Call me only from a phone box.'

As Tring took the slip of paper, the throaty noise of a tractor engine broke the quiet of the country lane and the haywain began to creep forward. The driver almost immediately turned left onto a muddy track that led across open fields.

'I have to go now, Jonathan. Give me a ring.' With that, she depressed the clutch, thrust the gearshift into first and revved the engine.

Tring yearned to kiss her, but thought better of it. He was not the type to force himself physically on a woman. She had been the one who had made love to him with such unbridled passion. Yet now her manner was full of contradictions. There were so many unanswered questions, but he knew this was neither the time nor the place to seek answers. The scientist , feeling slightly giddy from her perfume, nodded his head and hauled himself from the car. She slipped the clutch and roared away.

Tring stood rooted for a good half minute; long after the object of his desire had disappeared from view. He then looked at the note she had given him. He recognised the number. She lived in Chigwell, a stone's throw from his own home. The whole thing had been bizarre, but now at least he had something to look forward to.

CHAPTER NINE

'How much will it take?' Sharon Proctor's Southern drawl was tinged with trepidation. Money for others meant less for her. Less only became more if there was a payoff later along the line. And for Sharon Proctor there always had to be a payoff.

'He's no fool, my dear,' her husband cautioned. 'It'll probably take ten million to buy him out.'

She whistled through her pursed ruby red lips. 'Ten million, why I could buy whole towns in Georgia for that kinda money.'

Jack Proctor prodded the juicy Scotch fillet she had cooked him. 'You see this piece of steak, Sharon. If you tried to eat it all at once you would choke. But slice by slice, it's a different proposition.'

Sharon Proctor needed convincing. She was street smart, having survived a white trash childhood that had led her peers into crime, prostitution and drugs. She eschewed their twisted values through dint of hard labour, spending unearthly hours as a waitress or cleaner to pay her way through college. She saw education as the key to a brighter future, a future that would be as far removed from the milieu of 'Poortown,' Savannah. Not for her the solace of the bottle or a few bucks for selling her body, either up against a wall or on a greasy bed while the kids slept in the next room. Early deaths had been her parents' reward for dissolute lives that took no account of their effect on her and her twin sister. Undernourished and abused, Tracy-Lee Baker had succumbed to meningitis at the age of ten, leaving her sister to bear the brunt of the family's excesses. By the age of seventeen, Sharon Baker was alone, a family of one. Through force of circumstance, she became the great survivor. The vicissitudes of life had hardened her; her only true feeling of affection was reserved for the memory of her little sister. Since her marriage to Jack Proctor, she had revelled in the trappings of affluence and corporate power. The choice between staying with an ugly older man and giving up her lifestyle was no choice. 'Look at me now, Tracy-Lee,' she thought. 'I did it for you.'

'Well, Sharon,' Proctor chewed vigorously on his steak, 'what do you think?'

Sharon Proctor remained glassy-eyed for a few more seconds as she bathed in bittersweet memories.

'Well...?'

'I'm still thinking that's a helluva lotta dough,' she said at last, lapsing into white trash-speak and giving a flick of her newly coiffured blonde hair. The steel-blue eyes, too, seemed to flicker whenever the subject turned to money. 'How are we going to bankroll this guy?'

'Look, Sharon, KleinKinloss has a hundred million turnover and a price-earnings ratio of thirty. Put into perspective, ten million is about right.'

'So?'

'So I'll sell a few shares, offer him five million in cash, the rest in Parados stock and a place on our board.'

'And what if he wants more? Sharon Proctor had met the object of her husband's proposed largesse a couple of times at national conferences. She had taken an instant dislike to the man.

The pug-face broke into a sly smile. His beautiful wife was a born sceptic, a not altogether negative trait in the world of big business. 'Look, my plan is to let our friend continue on the inside as if nothing had happened, until the time is right for a complete takeover. We don't want their share price to go through the roof, do we? Once KleinKinloss is a subsidiary of Parados, I'll let him run his former company. Now tell me how he can refuse that.'

'Kevin Kinloss is a shit and you know it, Jack,' she said scooping some more roast potatoes onto his plate.

Jack Proctor chuckled. 'They say it's lucky to step on shit, my love.'

Jonathan Tring had had a hard time controlling an urge to telephone the mercurial Fiona straight after the fortuitous if rather bizarre roadside encounter that had served only to increase his lust for her. He had left it a couple of days, only to then suffer mounting frustration when his calls were met with an answer phone jingle that was both inane and irritating. Sorties in all weathers to the public phone box near his home were not conducive to maintaining an even temper. Thus it was with considerable relief when he had at last managed to make a contact of sorts. The elderly female voice at the other end of the line had said she had been expecting his call and that she was Fiona's great aunt. She had also named a wine bar in Chigwell village where he could meet the young lady in question at nine the following evening.

As Tring entered Blades Wine Bar, he couldn't help wondering when all this cloak and dagger stuff might end. At first his eyes caught only a few disparate figures propping up the bar. Three middle-aged men and a considerably younger brunette were engaged in animated conversation about the effects of the male menopause. He was about to order a drink and suffer more of their psychobabble when he noticed a lone female figure deep in one of the bar's dimly lit alcoves. She had her back to him.

He edged tentatively towards her. 'Fiona?' he half-whispered. He felt his face flush as she turned towards him. The mellow light glazed her high cheekbones like egg yolk on alabaster.

'Hello, Jonathan,' she said demurely. Her smile then broadened to show off the two perfect rows of teeth that complemented her generous mouth.

Tring, feeling more besotted than ever, edged his large frame between table and bench to sit opposite her. Two full glasses of red wine sat regally awaiting consumption. 'I see you were expecting company,' he joked.

'Claret,' she said sipping the nectar. 'The same colour as your rugby shirt.'

Tring's eyes widened in surprise, 'I didn't think you'd know much about that.'

'I've seen you play.'

Now he really *was* surprised.

'When I found out you played for a local team, I came to watch you. It was a few Sundays ago. The other team was wearing green and brown hoops.'

'Why didn't you say anything?' Tring queried.

'I didn't feel the time was right.'

'And now?'

'I felt I'd like to get to know you a little better.'

'You already know me pretty well,' he winked mischievously.

She looked at him wistfully. 'That...' she began to reply, then stopped abruptly. 'I didn't mean in that way,' she said quietly.

'I'm sorry,' Tring said quickly. 'It's just that I couldn't get you out of my mind after that night.'

Fiona raised the wine glass and sipped slowly and sensuously, staring at him all the while with eyes brimming with promise. He was indeed her type of man, tall and masculine with thick blond wavy hair. Thankfully, the rigours of rugby had not marked his features with the usual cauliflower ear or off-centre nose. He was, however, square-jawed and this gave his face a somewhat rugged look. She liked his eyes, which were a delicate grey-green. If only life was not so complicated, she thought.

'Tell me about yourself, Fiona,' he continued. 'First of all, is your company sending you to Hong Kong?'

She grimaced in mock sadness and then broke into a broad smile. 'Yes, but only for three weeks.'

Tring beamed with relief. He'd had visions of a brief but intense encounter followed by forced abstinence. 'You're in IT sales aren't you?'

'Yes.'

The professor frowned. 'I might me a scientist, but some of that new-fangled stuff baffles me. I'm more at home with molecules.'

'Selling is selling,' she said. 'Once you get your mind around the product, the rest is pretty straightforward. People buy from people they like.'

'Do you eventually want a posting abroad?' Tring asked with just a hint of trepidation.

'Depends.'

'On what?'

'On whether there was anything to keep me here,' she smiled.

'There are so many questions I want to ask you, Fiona,' he said, covering her slender delicate fingers with his large hand.

She let his hand linger a little before pulling hers away. 'As long as they don't include any about the Proctors, or why I've gone to all this trouble to keep our meetings secret.'

'I promised,' Tring held up his hands, 'and I'll keep my promise.'

There was no denying this beautiful young woman and her secrets intrigued him, but he decided to change tack by introducing the theme of their respective upbringings.

Fiona Harrington was indeed more forthcoming on what appeared to have been an idyllic childhood spent on a fifty-acre Fenland farm. 'You know,' she said wistfully, 'people say that the Fens are featureless. But to me, all that flat land has a magical quality. It was always brooding and melancholy in winter. As a child I always imagined witches were abroad at night.'

'And in summer?'

'In summer, there was this sense of freedom. You could cycle on the level for miles. Of course the wind was ever-present, but it was warm and caressing.'

Jonathan Tring was captivated both by her beauty and her eloquence. He could not describe his feelings for her at that moment, but he was sure that he had not experienced them about any girl before. 'I think I know what you mean about the country,' he said at length. 'I spent a few years at boarding school in Broadstairs. Kent's very hilly, as you know. I used to love walking down to the sea. There's this magical place called Stone Gap. It's a broad flight of stairs cut into the cliff and leading down to the sea.'

'Maybe that's where Broadstairs got its name from,' she smiled.

Tring ran a hand through his wavy blond hair. 'You know, I never thought about that before. Maybe you're right.'

'Did you like boarding school?'

Tring hesitated before answering. His childhood had been fraught with apprehension and uncertainty, and yet nostalgia had helped to gloss over the time he had spent away from home. Now it was his turn to look wistful. He told her how the melancholic lament of the foghorn aboard the Goodwin Sands lightship had comforted the lonely and homesick schoolboys tucked up in their beds; how the light, flashing every twenty seconds, had cast a spell every time it penetrated the darkness of the dormitory; how, on wet and windy nights, he, too, had dreamt of witches and warlocks.

An hour flew by; sixty minutes which brought them ever closer and culminated in Tring virtually proposing that they sleep together that night. Fiona had gripped his fingers, assuring him that she wanted that more than anything, but that she needed a little more time. The scientist tried hard to hide his disappointment as they kissed goodbye. They agreed to meet that Saturday at the same time and place.

Fiona Harrington gave the professor a farewell wave and climbed into her car. She felt a strange emptiness. She had loved the scientist's company, hanging on his every word. Rather than a boring boffin, he seemed to her a kindred spirit and a man she could trust implicitly. Yet there were so many things she could not tell him, things that might alter his perception of her.

Duplicity pressed on her shoulders like a ton weight.

CHAPTER TEN

Kevin Kinloss felt as if he had just won the National Lottery in a rollover week. The events of the day had left him euphoric and not a little bemused. Lunch with the Proctors had set his silvery hair on end. What they were offering was truly beyond his wildest dreams. Overnight he would become a multi-millionaire, not just on paper, but in readies. Sure, he had told the blonde bombshell and her sugar daddy that he needed time to think things over. After all, they were asking him to betray a man with whom he had cast his lot over several years. He did not dislike Abe Klein. In fact, he admired the New Yorker's tenacity. But Klein was too honest to survive forever in a world infested with sharks such as the Proctors.

Kevin Kinloss, however, was Scottish, and Scots were a prudent people. He was ever careful of being penny-wise and pound-foolish. While it would be tempting to go on a spending spree, he knew that he would have to pursue a policy of husbandry. To flaunt his newfound wealth too soon would send out dangerous signals, both to his naïve business partner and to the Inland Revenue.

'Well,' said his other half, 'go on.'

Kinloss leaned back in his favourite armchair, took another sip of Scotch and surveyed his wife with the satisfaction of a cat licking cream. Looks could be so deceptive. Her features were plain and pale, her eyes a cold blue, and her mousy hair was pulled back into an austere bun. To the outside world, Jean Kinloss was prim and proper, as befitted the daughter of a Presbyterian minister. However, what she may have lacked in looks she made up for in passion. She was twelve years younger than her husband and a veritable firebrand between the sheets, two facts that suited both his ego and his libido.

'We won't be able to touch the money for a while, of course,' he said with just a hint of disappointment.

'Of course,' she said knowingly. 'Offshore, I presume.'

'Aye. The Caymans.'

114

'Nice place for a winter break,' she smiled.

'No expense spared, my darling.'

'But not yet.'

'No.'

'We should set aside something for the boys.'

'Of course, my dear,' said Kevin Kinloss, smiling thinly. The twins were away at Harrow and were already well catered for. She clucked like a mother hen wherever Gregor and Grant were concerned, but he wouldn't have had it any other way. 'There's more than enough for everyone,' he added reassuringly.

Jean Kinloss re-filled he husband's glass with the golden liquid. She knew he was devious in business, but that only added to the attraction. He gave her everything she wanted, and more. He may have been an old Scottish skinflint to outsiders, but he never kept her or their sons short. The warm glow of her own dram coursed through her veins as she gazed admiringly at her spouse. She was suddenly reminded of the first drink he had ever bought her. It had been thirteen years earlier. He had simply walked into the Edinburgh Chamber of Commerce where she worked as a secretary and had, very directly, asked her out to lunch. Although he was much older than her, his clothes and style were immaculate. But then Jean was as much taken with the style of others that she lacked in herself. One Chateaubriand and several aperitifs later, the then Jean Muir had been swept off her feet. That evening she had willingly succumbed to the advances of this aggressive businessman and the rest was history.

'You're so clever, Mr Kinloss,' she said, raising her pencil-thin eyebrows. 'Daddy deserves an extra special reward tonight.'

'Daddy does?' he asked mockingly.

'Come, my cleverkins,' she said, pouting like a freshly caught sea bass. She put aside his glass and pulled him to his feet. 'It's time to celebrate.'

Some fifty miles from the ebullient Kinloss household, another couple not wholly unconnected to the saga of cunning takeover bids and deceit were about to consummate a reunion of sorts. Fiona Harrington had contacted Jonathan Tring immediately upon her premature return from

Hong Kong, and with almost breathless speed was now on his bed and in his arms.

Tring had been bemused by the turn of events. She had returned after only one week instead of three, had telephoned him the following day and, despite the jet lag, was about to make his dreams come true. The girl was truly remarkable.

Fiona Harrington herself had never been so sure of anything in her life as the moment she had agreed to return to his flat. Once more they had met at the wine bar, only this time their conversation had been peremptory, subsumed by the mutual sexual attraction flooding their senses. Tring had stammered a few times during his exhortations of ardour and this had endeared him to her even more.

That was why, upon entering Tring's flat, she had urged him to shower, promising to join him after seeing to her own toilet. Within a minute, she had checked every phone and socket in the apartment with an electronic detector that emitted a tinny shriek if a bug were present. She was half-expecting to find something, but thankfully the place was clean. Jonathan Tring may have been a six-foot rugby-playing hulk and a superb scientist, but he was as naïve as hell. She had never felt more protective of him as she did at that moment and yet, in reality, she hardly knew him. Yet she knew instinctively that sleeping with him was the right thing to do.

Fiona removed her clothes and folded them in a neat pile on a chair by his bed. Thankfully, the flat was as warm as toast, although she still shivered in expectation of what lay ahead. As she entered the bathroom, the sight of his naked body behind the glass partition sent a further quiver down her spine.

'May I?' she poked her head round the screen.

'Please do,' said Tring, grinning knowingly through the steam.

She stepped over the lip of the cubicle and joined him under the stream.

Tring placed his arms around her and brought his lips to hers. The kiss was so incredibly sensual that she was almost unaware of the growing hardness against her abdomen. They luxuriated in the caress of the spray as it penetrated the seal between their mouths and besieged their bodies with its sensual warmth. Taking it in turns, they licked each other's bodies, relishing the saltiness. Oblivious of the cascade, this mutually exquisite scrutiny continued for some minutes until it seemed that no part had been left unexplored.

Jonathan,' she moaned finally, her country accent sending him even wilder with desire, 'I want you so much.' She felt the ripple of his biceps as he gripped her tightly. His manhood was hard against her, urgent and demanding.

Tring, almost delirious with lust, lifted her perfect body and in almost one movement stepped out of the cubicle. He lowered her gently onto the bathroom carpet. Pinning himself to her, he exalted in her very essence, a mixture of sea salt and country air that took him back to his childhood. Once again he licked the moisture from her body and sucked her breasts until the nipples were long and pliant. Then his fingers slid to the very quick of her.

'I want you,' she groaned. 'I want you now.'

'Do it to me again,' he pleaded suddenly.

'Do what?'

'What you did at the ball.' Without waiting for her to act, he rolled over and gently made her sit astride him.

'Oh, that,' she said with a look that was both quizzical and cognitive. So that's what he wanted. Well, she wanted it to. She would show him that she was the best, that no one could match her in lovemaking. She rocked and rocked, slowly at first, and then with ever increasing fervour until they were both at the point of no return.

As the final paroxysm overwhelmed him, Tring gripped Fiona's buttocks with a ferocity that was almost brutal. Despite her nakedness, all he could think of was the rustle of a pannier evening gown.

Abe Klein knew that he had to get independent advice as soon as word was out that Proctor the piranha was trying to sink his teeth into his company. That was why the two pinstripes from Peterson Consulting were in his boardroom. They had been given a brief and the run of the place for a couple of weeks, poking into the nooks and crannies of corporate identity in an attempt to get to the core of KleinKinloss. They had to know everything in order to prepare a defensive strategy for the company. And expertise did not come cheap. The American knew that by the time the dust would settle in this battle, the bill for accountants, solicitors, merchant banks, stockbrokers et al might run into seven figures. The amount these guys charged for their time made him think he was in the wrong business.

'Basically, Mr Klein and Mr Kinloss,' the first pinstripe began, 'you hold between you sixty-five percent of the company. This gives you control of management and dividend policy, but it would not allow you to alter the articles of the company, or for that matter place it into voluntary liquidation.'

'What this means in effect,' the second man cut in, 'is that you are in quite a strong position vis-à-vis a takeover bid as long as you maintain a united front. You have enough shark repellent in your company by-laws to almost guarantee safety. With change of ownership having to be approved by at least seventy percent of the shareholders, it would just be a case of whether you could stand the pressures from all sides that would result from a concerted bid.'

Klein looked at his partner. 'Kevin and I are determined to ride this out,' he said. 'There's no way we would willingly allow anyone else to take control.'

'That's right, gentlemen,' Kinloss chipped in, 'this company has a great future and we canna allow ourselves to be browbeaten into submission. Certainly not by the likes of Jack Proctor.'

'Quite, quite,' said the first pinstripe, a weedy, balding man with horn-rims. 'Nevertheless, it would be prudent to discuss ways in which a defence could be mounted, especially as the potential acquirer is well-versed in the techniques of takeovers, whether hostile or otherwise.'

'Now look,' said the second man, holding up his palms, 'we are just looking at this hypothetically, you understand.' He was larger and more imposing than his colleague, and his voice boomed. 'Let's just suppose that when the heat is turned up, you two fall out over strategy...'

Klein glanced at his partner. They had spent hours discussing the ramifications of Proctor domination and Kinloss had pledged to stand foursquare with him. He had no reason to doubt the Scotsman's word. 'I don't think that—'

'No, no, of course not,' the weedy man cut the American short, 'but we are just advising you on all possible scenarios. In effect, to defeat any takeover bid, the management has to convince the shareholders that their best interests lie with the existing management rather than the company making the bid. This process cannot start too early and should certainly start well before any takeover begins.'

The second adviser then cut in. 'The management-shareholder relationship should be a continuous process so that when support is needed, early shareholder education will not take too much time and can quickly focus directly on the takeover issues. Communication isn't always easy and it largely depends on who your shareholders are. In your case, the majority apart from yourselves are institutional. This can be both a blessing and a curse, depending on whom they have the most confidence in.'

'At the end of the day,' the first man counselled, 'money normally sorts these situations out. But if the pros and cons of a bid are marginal, then the situation cannot be too clearly put to the shareholders and an effective media campaign could win the day.'

Gobbledegook, thought Klein. Basically, as long as the main players stood firm, Proctor could take a hike.

'There is, of course, always the poison pill defence,' the first pinstripe went on. 'But that's pretty rare in the U.K.'

The American's quizzical look spoke volumes. He was a scientist, and the only poison pill he knew about came in tablet form.

The consultant smiled. 'In certain circumstances, you might want to take action before or during negotiations to make the business less attractive for the bidder.'

'Like what for instance?' Kinloss asked, as if he didn't already know. It had been Klein's idea to bring these jokers in, and if it gave his partner false security, then so much the better.

'Well, there's a number of things you might do,' said the visitor, clearly warming to his subject. 'You could sign large-scale long-term contracts, extend personal service contracts for all the main board directors, make a bid for, or actually buy other companies.'

The second man, not to be outdone, cut in eagerly. 'You should always ensure that assets are reflected accurately in the balance sheet and that there's constant communication with stockbrokers and financial journalists who'll help maximise your share price.'

Abe Klein sat through a further hour of the anatomy of fighting and defending takeovers with the patience of a scientist who had just discovered how to regenerate brain cells. His own brain was almost dead with the effort of listening to his two fee-charging guests. He distrusted all pinstripes and knew they were really only interested in the bottom line for themselves. Eventually, the American glanced right at his partner with a look that said he had heard enough.

'Thank you, gentleman,' the Scotsman said firmly, 'I think we get the gist.' As Kevin Kinloss began to rise, he accidentally nudged his half-full cup of tea. 'Drat,' he blurted as a few drops splattered onto his trousers. They were his best pinstripes.

Further south, two predators were formulating policy for the struggle that lay ahead. While Klein was more or less an amateur at takeover tactics, Jack Proctor and his wife were past masters at corralling all the internal and external forces that came into play in a game where the stakes were so high. The Yorkshireman was an arch manipulator. Trade unions, the Stock Exchange, media, competitors and pressure groups would all have to be addressed, and it was inevitable that a few palms would need to be greased, some old and some new. The Government was already in his pocket. Every man had his price and the Secretary of State for Health was no exception. However, there was one flaw in Jack Proctor's character that could prove fatal. And no one was more aware of this than his good lady. While Sharon Proctor was as driven by greed and ego, she possessed a 'reality' filter, a cynicism born from being raised on the wrong side of the tracks. Hostile takeover battles were costly and the failure rate high. She believed in always having an insurance policy and had already begun to set one in place.

'Be careful, Jack,' she counselled. 'Rumours are bound to push up their share price.'

'Sure. Sure. We'll let Klein enjoy his moment of glory. Let him think he's safe. Our Scottish woodworm will play along for as long as he can. When Klein and the media find out the truth, there'll be a massive lack of confidence. That's when we step in and take over. Simple.'

But Sharon Proctor knew that nothing in business was ever that easy. There was any number of things that might go wrong. She did not underestimate her fellow American. He was a Yankee kike, and they were clever and dangerous. In the normal run of things he might eat a dumb blonde Southerner for breakfast. But this Southerner was no dummy and she was not about to become anyone's hash browns.

CHAPTER ELEVEN

Food was furthest from Kieran Kelly's mind as he sat pensively in his car outside a bungalow in northwest London. He knew he shouldn't be there. Years of practising subterfuge, of calculating the risk-benefit ratio of every action, screamed a warning that what he was about to do might somehow put his scheme in danger; that unnecessary friendships might influence his decisions, might eat into his resolve. But he was human. He needed the comfort of a woman. Teresa would have wanted it for him. It was not so much sex that he craved, but the sound of a woman's voice, the sound of compassion, of caring, of warmth. Ever since he had met the Countess he couldn't get her out of his mind. He'd kept asking himself why he should be attracted to someone who was suffering the same agonies as his beloved wife. What possible benefit could be achieved by starting a relationship with anyone when there was a distinct possibility that that relationship would have only one outcome: a sad one?

The Irishman sighed deeply and opened his car door. The decision was made and there was no going back. He trod slowly up the front garden path and rang the doorbell. The chimes played Big Ben twice and it seemed an age before he heard the noise of the lock being opened. He chided himself for bothering her, thinking that she had had to struggle in pain to reach the front door.

'Who's there?' came a strange voice from behind the portal.

'Kieran O'Donaghue,' he replied quickly, adding, 'a friend of Magda's.'

Then the visitor heard another voice, its Germanic tone instantly recognisable.

'It's okay, Christine, please let him in.'

The door opened wide and Kelly found before him a pretty fresh-faced black girl with eyes as wide as saucers. Dressed in an overcoat that appeared two sizes too large for her, she looked as though she had just arrived or was about to leave. Standing a few feet behind her and leaning on a stick was the stunningly beautiful Countess Magda von Esterhazy.

'Hello, Kieran,' she said warmly. 'This is Christine, my carer, please do come in. It's okay, Christine, you can go. I'll see you tomorrow.'

The carer's saucer eyes narrowed as she gave Kelly a suspicious look on her way past him. ''Bye, Magda,' she called out and walked down the path without looking back.

'Come in, Kieran,' Magda said warmly. 'It's lovely to see you again. I was just making a cup of tea. Would you like one.'

'Thanks, milk and no sugar. I was just driving through the area and thought I might pop in. I hope it's not inconvenient.'

'*Nein, nein,* of course not. *Wilkommen.* Please go straight through into the lounge. The kettle's nearly boiling.'

Kelly walked into the lounge and was immediately stunned by its decor. Completely at odds with the plainness of the hall, the room in which he now found himself was a microcosm of the great salon of some eighteenth century French chateau. The wallpaper was red velvet flecked with gold and the furniture appeared to be reproduction Louis XV. Two magnificent crystal chandeliers hung down from the ceiling to add to the total incongruity of the setting. He sat on a grand chaise longue. A Bach violin concerto playing in the background was almost de rigueur.

'Strange, isn't it,' she called out. 'Not every one's cup of tea, as the English say.'

'It's amazing,' he called back. 'Not exactly what one would expect to find in this neck of the woods.'

'The furniture's real,' she said, appearing suddenly in the doorway and carrying a tray bearing two cups of tea.

Kelly sprang to his feet. 'Here, let me take that.' He took the tray from her and placed it gingerly on the eighteenth century equivalent of a coffee table, thinking that any mark he might make would be a desecration.

The Countess hobbled over and half-slumped next to him. 'This furniture was the only thing my family managed to get out of Hungary before the Communists took over. It's worth a fortune and would solve all my money problems, but I could never part with it. It's the only link I have now with my past.'

'It's all magnificent,' Kelly said patting the settee, 'and comfortable.'
The Irishman spent the next few minutes listening to a fascinating history of eighteenth century French furniture. The woman was as erudite as she was beautiful, and he could feel himself becoming more and more captivated by her. He hung on her every word as if it was a polished gem, wondering whether the feelings he was harbouring towards her were being reciprocated.

What Kelly could not know at that moment was that the mind of the Countess was in turmoil. Magda felt herself slipping into automatic mode. She had given scores of lectures on period furniture and so the words that came from her lips were as well rehearsed as they could be. Meanwhile she could feel a tingling in the pit of her stomach that she hadn't felt for years. Her visitor was so extraordinarily handsome and he exuded a kind of magnetism she had never experienced before. Yet she knew her personal ethics would never allow herself to entertain a relationship with a married man, especially one whose wife was a fellow sufferer.

Kelly paused to sip tea as an opportunity to change tack. He told her how he had gone on-line to the America-based help group and how the stories of the sufferers had angered him intensely.

'Yes,' she said quietly, 'so many of them are on morphine. There's a grandmother's tale that sufferers become addicted, but those who are in chronic pain don't become addicted. Only someone with an addictive personality does.'

'You mean it's the mind that causes the addiction and not the drug.'

'Yes - ' The Countess stopped short, suddenly realising that she hadn't asked about his wife. 'Oh, how remiss of me,' she said, 'I haven't asked you yet how Frau O'Donaghue is. I hope she's having a low pain day.'

Every cell in the Irishman's brain shrieked a warning that he should beware of revealing the truth to her. There was a possibility that she might regard any confession as an attempt by him to ingratiate himself with her, to play on her sympathy. There was also the fact that he had lied to her, and honest people did not take kindly to liars. Kelly lowered his eyes.

'I would love to meet her,' she went on. 'Perhaps I could offer her some comfort. What procedure did she undergo and what symptoms does she have?'

Kelly, who sheltered the hardest of hearts when it came to those he perceived as enemies, suddenly found himself overcome by the emotions that he had kept pent up for so long. Despite himself, he felt a tear begin to trickle down his cheek.

Magda silently chided herself for being so inquisitive. 'I'm so sorry, Kieran, if you'd rather not talk about it, I'll understand. I know how devastating this can all be to those closest to us.'

The Irishman sighed heavily. He so wanted to open his heart to this brave woman, to unload his pain onto her however unfair. 'Magda—'

'You know,' she went on, cutting short his confession, 'many people ask me for advice about sustaining relationships when this terrible disease hits. I can only pass on what I have gleaned from others. Never assume what your loved one feels or thinks. That is the road to nowhere, except heartache. Always keep the channels of communication open. Chronic pain twists the soul, and if you don't communicate, a chasm will appear and grow ever wider until it cannot be bridged.'

Kelly remained silent. She might have been with them during Teresa's final days; the long silences; his wife's hopelessness feeding his helplessness; the chasm that could now never be bridged.

'Please tell your good wife that being disabled doesn't mean she is unable. She should avoid using the word invalid for it has a more sinister meaning, *in*-valid, and *that* she's certainly not and never will be. Tell her to concentrate on what she can do and not what she can't. Tell her that we all get depressed and have our moments or days when the future looks bleak. But she should remember that the future only happens one day at a time. Grab hold of the good days and cherish them. If you agree, I'd like to meet her. I'd like to help, but only if you agree.'

Kelly felt like someone who had missed the last bus. He felt an overwhelming sense of guilt. He'd not done enough for Teresa, not searched for support groups like Magda's. He had always protected his wife, always been the macho Irish husband who had all the answers. Nothing could happen to Teresa Kelly while he was around. He looked into Magda's eyes and saw the earnest goodness shining through the patina of pain. It was time to end the charade. 'Magda, my wife is dead,' he said dully.

There were a few moments silence as Magda von Esterhazy was engulfed by a succession of emotions: first compassion, then a fleeting thankfulness followed by flash of guilt that a stranger's demise might be her gain. 'I don't understand,' she said at length.

The Irishman took a deep breath. 'Teresa committed suicide a few months ago after an epidural they gave her before the birth of our fourth child. She couldn't stand the pain any more.'

'*Oh mein Gott,*' sighed the Countess, cradling his hand in hers. '*Es tut mir so leid.* I'm so sorry.'

She continued holding his hand as he poured out his heart to her. It was more a gushing. Everything he told her surrounded Teresa: how they met, how they fell in love, how they decided to come to London to look for work, how their lives were devastated, how he had sent the children to live with her sister even though it made him feel as guilty as hell, and, finally, how he now felt like jetsam in a sea of loneliness. It must have been all of twenty minutes before he fell silent.

The Irishman felt as if a great burden had been lifted from his shoulders. In reality, Magda was the only person to whom he could relate the tragedy of Teresa's death. Only a sufferer could truly understand what his wife had gone through. Try as he might, he would never be able to put himself in their place. Pain that was beyond normal comprehension, the pain of a body at war with itself, was unfathomable to those whose life had always been healthy. He gripped her hand tightly and looked into kindly eyes that seemed to flicker from green to blue in the light refracted from the chandeliers. He stammered her name, his mind once more in turmoil.

The Countess, almost overcome by the poignancy of his grief, brought his hand to her lips and kissed it gently. She felt the hormones flood her entire being, driving the pain of her illness to a remote corner of her mind. Nothing was consuming her more than desire for this man she hardly knew.

The Irishman moved closer to her. He slowly released his hand from hers and, putting his arm around her shoulder, cradled her head in the pit of his neck, the smell of her long newly-shampooed blonde hair further adding to the senses raging within him. For what seemed an age they sat in that position, both desperate to take the initiative but neither sure of the other's true intentions. Kelly then lifted her head gently so that their eyes could meet. They became diffused in recognition of their mutual need. The crimson bow of her own delicate lips parted almost agonisingly slowly, as if in final affirmation that she was prepared to accept the caress of his. The kiss was long, its tenderness almost unbearable, the salt of her tears sharpening itself on her tongue. He was still kissing her as he placed his strong arms under her thighs. In one movement he lifted her and stood erect.

Magda gasped as a lancinating pain ran through her spine to the tips of her toes. But she was determined that this would offer no excuse to resist his advances. She would not allow it to happen. She would not permit the pain to invade the heady feelings of womanhood that had lain dormant for too long.

There might not have been a word between them as they entered the bedroom, but there was a dictionary of understanding. He laid her gently on the bed. Despite their mutual abstinence almost demanding an animal-like response, Kelly unbuttoned her plain turquoise dress slowly and deliberately. He then leant over and again kissed her lips, followed by the hollow of her neck and then the gentle curves of her full and heaving breasts. He undressed her slowly and with the utmost care, knowing that any sharp movement might cause her agonies. He was still fully clothed when she lay before him naked and vulnerable. She was truly stunning, a milky oasis on a duvet of flamingo pink. Only the legs, slightly thin and lacking muscular tone gave any hint of her illness.

Unashamed of her own nakedness, Magda watched him undress. She knew her body was perfect apart from her legs. She also knew that this gentle man would explore it with the utmost care. He seemed to her to be incapable of hurting anyone. Within a few seconds, he was standing before her. His body was taut and sinewy and he was already fully erect. For a fleeting few moments their eyes were locked onto their respective forms, revelling in the splendour of the human anatomy.

The Irishman then slid alongside her. He felt himself hard against her, but then pulled away. Rising on all fours and, making sure not to be rough in any way, he began kissing her all over her body, starting with the neck, then into the cleavage of her breasts whose pink pinnacles were already as hard as steel. He then descended to the mound of venus and luxuriated in its downiness for a few seconds before proceeding onto the legs which were the recipients of so much referred agony. These he kissed from thigh to toe.

Magda felt her senses entering overload as he once more came level with her. She kissed him with unbridled passion before allowing his lips to descend to her nipples. Meanwhile she felt his finger gently begin rubbing her. She was already wet and her legs parted languidly, invitingly. She needed him inside her. She needed to feel the power of a man so that she could finally reinforce her womanhood.

'Now,' she gasped, suddenly aware of Bach's Concerto in D Minor as it headed out of *Largo ma non tanto* and into *Allegro*. 'Please, now.'

Kelly took his cue and gently spread her legs apart. He positioned himself between them and entered her with the expertise of one who had had experience of making love to a disabled person. It was an expertise he thought he would never have to use again. 'No, don't you move,' he whispered. 'Let *me* do it, dear Magda.'

The Countess could feel the burning pain in her legs beginning to break through, but she was determined not to reveal this to him. The battle between pain and ecstasy could not afford to be lost. 'More,' she gasped. 'More.'

His thrusting became more and more urgent until it seemed he was trying to keep pace with the *Allegro* and within a few seconds the able and the disabled had reached a simultaneous orgasm which left them both not only exhausted, but with a satisfaction that was utterly profound.

Magda sighed deeply. Ecstasy had indeed triumphed over Agony. Here in her arms was a man who had fulfilled an urgent need, both emotional and physical. Their mutual pain had been subsumed in sublime moments of passion; moments that she desperately wanted to believe would be repeated.

Furthest from Magda von Esterhazy's mind was there any notion that her kind and gentle lover had once been a cruel and calculating killer.

CHAPTER TWELVE

The trattoria was almost empty when Fiona Harrington took her place at a corner table and faced the man who had so recently become her lover. She leaned forward and kissed Tring lightly on the lips. After a fortnight of almost incessant, wonderful sex, she had had to admit to herself that she'd become infatuated with the man. She believed that he, too, held similar feelings towards her and that was why she had decided to reveal to him the truth about her duplicity and the reasons for it. Quite simply, she trusted the scientist. Nothing in his manner or his words led her to believe that he was anything other than the antithesis of what she had so far discovered among the denizens of Parados Pharmaceuticals. Yet she knew that some of her revelations might place him in danger and that one in particular might make him want to end their relationship there and then. The time was now right and it was a chance she had decided to take.

'If we're going to have a working lunch,' her lover said jokingly, 'then we should be at my place. As you know, I can rustle up a wicked tagliatelli con funghi and then we can get down to afters.'

'I thought you said you could spare only a few minutes for lunch. I'm not interested in a wham-bang-thanky-mam, my dear sir.'

Tring laughed. 'If you're not careful, my girl, I'll talk shop and bore you to death.'

Fiona smiled knowingly. He was about to find out that this was exactly what she intended they do.

The waiter, a weasel-like man with a pencil-thin moustache, sidled over to them for their order. They both decided to go for Scaloppini Milanese accompanied by a bottle of Montepulicano.

Fiona was grateful when the wine arrived. She needed to loosen up. It was clear that so far she had successfully concealed the tension that was gnawing at her. The poor man didn't have an inkling of what was about to hit him. She downed the first glass in almost one gulp.

129

'Hey, go easy there, my little fresh-faced country girl,' said Tring. 'Save some for the meal.'

Almost immediately, Fiona felt the effects of the alcohol invade her brain. Her eyes fixed on the empty glass in her hand. She felt her cheeks flush like a robin's breast on a cold winter's day. She suddenly felt almost overwhelmed by guilt.

'Hey, what's wrong Fiona?' Tring asked, noticing the uncharacteristic change in her mood.

'I think I'm falling for you big time, Jonathan,' she said quietly, at the same time cursing the lifting of inhibition brought about by the wine. What a stupid thing to say. They hardly knew anything about one another. It was not the way she had planned to go about the matter.

If Tring was taken aback by her confession, he didn't show it. He gently took both of her hands in his and looked into her glistening eyes. 'The feeling's mutual,' he said kindly. 'I think you know that.'

In one way, Fiona felt relieved, but in another it made the whole thing worse. Once she revealed to him the truth, he might feel that she'd used his affection for her to further her own ends; that her words of endearment were as empty as the lies she had told.

'There's a lot about me that you don't know, Jonathan.'

'Ah, those secrets you once mentioned. Well, I promised I'd never ask, right?'

She looked into the grey-green eyes that reflected both learning and naiveté. He was simply a scientist who was about to get caught up in something, the consequences of which neither of them could foretell.

'I'm not an IT sales consultant, Jonathan,' she confessed. 'I'm an investigative journalist.'

If Tring was surprised, he didn't show it, for if that was her secret, then it was no big deal. He paused for a moment before, 'so who are you investigating? Me?'

'In a way, yes, but only because you happen to be at Parados.'

'Now you really have to explain,' said the scientist apprehensively.

'The Proctors are who I'm really after.'

'But I thought you were Sharon Proctor's best buddy.'

'She thinks so, yes.'

'You'd better begin at the beginning.'

'Martin Locke.'

'My predecessor?'

'Yes.' Fiona hesitated and breathed deeply. She was about to play consequences. 'Locke contacted me the day before he died. He said he'd found out about me through a mutual friend. He said he had some information for me, information that would put his boss in jail and could possibly bring down the government.'

Tring whistled. He knew Proctor was ruthless, but if what she were saying were true, then Locke's untimely death might take on more sinister proportions. *He killed him you know.* The words of his colleague, Harold Spencer, flooded his mind. Spoken months ago and soon after he had arrived at Parados, he had dismissed the Lancastrian's misgivings as pure conjecture. Tring looked squarely at Fiona. 'Do you think Locke was murdered?'

'I don't know, but whatever Locke had on the Proctors is dynamite.'

'Do we have any clue where this information might be?'

'That's the problem. I've been drawing blanks and I thought you could help.'

'Become a whistleblower, you mean?'

'Look, Jonathan, my job is to expose wrongdoing wherever I find it. You know as well as I do that there is so much evil and corruption in this world that if we weren't there to reveal it, then it would be a far sorrier world than it is already.'

'A rather romantic view of the media, if you don't mind me saying so.'

She flushed in anger. 'Well, if you're not going to help me—'

'I didn't say I wouldn't,' he said quickly. 'But this is not without its risks. I could lose my job.'

'If you found out the truth, I would think you'd want to.'

There was certainly logic in that, thought Tring. 'Okay, my little investigative reporter, tell me all you know.'

In between bites of the scaloppini, Fiona Harrington told her lover how she had ingratiated herself into the Proctor circle; how she had met Sharon Proctor at a cocktail party and how they had quickly become firm friends.

'She's only thirty-one, six years older than me, and married to an ugly old brute nearly twice her age.'

'Money,' Tring said bluntly. 'She told me she was born on the wrong side of the tracks.'

'Yes, you're right, although, in her way, I think she loves ... maybe that's the wrong word ... maybe she's very fond of him.'

'I think it's the power and money she's very fond of,' he said, polishing off the last of the wine. 'They're the most powerful of aphrodisiacs.'

'And power is what drives the pharmaceutical industry.'

'What do you mean?'

'I've learnt a lot about the industry over the last few months and what I've learnt stinks.'

Tring was taken aback by her vehemence. 'Hey, hold on a minute. I work in it, you know.'

Fiona, her small nostrils flaring, was champing at the bit. 'I'm not talking about the scientists, I'm talking about the suits and the marketing men; the guys who promote the scandalous practice of bribing GPs to prescribe particular medicines while most patients are never told why they might suddenly and mysteriously receive a new medicine for a long-standing illness, or that these medicines could conceivably put them at risk. It's a way of discovering very rare adverse reactions that may not have shown up in clinical trials. They set up promotional studies, pretend they're science and damn the consequences.'

Tring was not a monk. He knew that in the past some companies had targeted doctors with potentially dangerous drugs, and also that tragedies like Thalidomide were embedded in the public psyche. There were also other disasters: the first Pill scare, pressurised aerosol inhalers that killed thousands of asthma sufferers and the link between the anti-arthritic drug Opren and jaundice. 'I didn't think post-marketing surveillance went on any more,' he said meekly.

'Post-marketing surveillance,' she said sarcastically. 'The usual gobbledegook they come up with to provide a smoke screen for wrongdoing.'

'Don't tell me this is happening at Parados,' Tring said with a tinge of apprehension.

'No, I don't think it is, but it's rife elsewhere.'

'Well that's a relief then ... that it's not us, I mean.'

'Not so quick, Jonathan Tring, your company is still too close to the Medicines Control Agency and the drug committees. There are even a couple of minor shareholders who serve on those committees.'

'Well, I don't know who they are. Who told you all this, anyway?'

'Sharon Proctor.'

'My, you have been a busybody, young lady.'

'Maybe, but I'm more interested in what she hasn't told me.'

'I think you might have to do that woman a big favour to get any more out of her.'

Fiona's heart pounded. Her lover had hit the mark, albeit unwittingly. This was the moment she had dreaded. Was it really necessary for her to tell him when she knew it could destroy their relationship? Would he understand that she had sold herself to the devil for the sake of a higher ideal: truth? Sharon Proctor had expected her every whim to be satisfied. Not to accede to her request might have placed the journalist's whole endeavour in jeopardy. Sure, the American had told her that her interest in the professor had been only transient; that what she had done was for a sexual high, a feeling of consummate power. But would Jonathan understand that?

'Hey, you're shivering, darling,' he said and rubbed her right hand. 'I'll tell them to turn the heating up.'

'No, it's not that,' she said quickly. 'There's something else I have to tell you.'

Tring smiled. It was certainly a day for surprises.

'You remember Proctor's fancy dress birthday bash where we met?'

'How could I ever forget?' Visions of rampant sex in the dark and the rustling of the pannier evening gown flooded his mind.

She took a deep breath. It was now or never. 'Jonathan,' she said almost inaudibly, 'it wasn't me.'

From the comfort of his car, Kieran Kelly watched with feigned insouciance as his prey left the Italian restaurant. The man may have been a boffin but he was certainly tall and strong enough to represent a potential problem when it came to the snatch. The Irishman had already watched the scientist parade his expertise on the rugby field. For the junior level at which he played, Tring was as hard as they came. But few men were as those portrayed by the movies. He found that when confronted by a shooter, most targets preferred to practise pragmatism rather than heroics. And there was nothing like a pistol in the face to bring a recalcitrant to order.

From a distance of only a few yards, Kelly noted that the scientist wore a worried frown. Maybe he'd just had a tiff with his girlfriend, he thought. She was certainly a looker; with a figure that most women would die for, and some men might kill for. But he was not interested in the perfect, the unblemished and the pristine. As he drew away to follow his quarry's silver Mercedes, the Irishman leaned forward to increase the sound on his car's CD player. Bach's violin concertos had possessed him ever since he had made love to Magda von Esterhazy. The music was at once both comforting and a torture. It had now been two weeks since he had seen her; two weeks in which he had forsaken her to track Jonathan Tring's every move, monitor his every habit; two weeks in which the single-mindedness of his purpose was being gradually eroded by his desire for the woman. But the Irishman knew deep in his heart that he would have to bear this complication; that he would have to take this unnecessary risk. He yearned for Magda's voice and the silky softness of her milk-white skin. What must she be thinking of him? A man who was interested only in a one-night stand; a man who got his kicks from making love to a cripple and then dumped her. The music pounded his brain, each cadence pummelling a message of love, of guilt, of subterfuge. 'Damn you,' he screamed aloud and veered away from his quarry. Tring could wait. So could Dr Martin Townsend and the Secretary of State for Health.

Kelly pressed the 'on' button on his mobile phone. As the bleeps made their connection, his mind raced to concoct a suitable excuse. He had told the Countess that he had had to fly to Belfast for a few days to see his children. A few days, however, was not two weeks. He recalled that her telephone number was ex-directory. It might offer him a way out, but would she still want to see him? His heart leapt as she answered the call and he immediately found himself tongue-tied.

'Hello, who is this please?' she enquired, her voice tinged with apprehension. 'Is there anyone there?'

'Magda?' he said at last.

'Yes,' she answered, her heart missing a beat as she recognised his voice.

Kelly decided to launch into his excuse immediately in order to allay her fears. 'Hello, Magda, how are you? I'm so sorry not to have called you. My boy was sick so I had to stay on. As you know, I programmed your number into my mobile phone and then mislaid the damn thing - the phone, that is. I couldn't remember your number and as you're ex-directory, I was like an Irishman who'd mislaid his pint of Guinness.'

Her laughter was a mixture of relief and concern. 'Is the baby okay?'

'Yes, he's fine now. It was touch of bronchitis. It's all that damn wet weather we have.'

'Are you calling from Belfast?'

'No, I've just got back.' He steeled himself for the vital question, suppressing the dichotomy raging in his mind because deep down he knew he *had* to see her again. It was every much a need as was his compulsion for revenge. 'Can I see you this evening?' It was almost a whisper.

For Countess Magda von Esterhazy, the Irishman's plea was affirmation that she had not misread his intentions after all, that her days of self-doubt could be consigned to the recycle bin and then emptied. She could tell by his tone that he bore her genuine affection, and at that moment she pledged to herself that she would never ask more of him than that which he was prepared to give.

Try as he might, Jonathan Tring could not get Fiona's revelation out of his mind. Gunning his SLK out of the slip lane and onto the M11 motorway, he was glad that he had allowed his initial shock to be replaced by pragmatism. He'd reassured Fiona that it wouldn't make any difference to their relationship. At the time Fiona and Sharon Proctor had carried out their switch, his new girl friend had been a complete stranger. In a way, it had laid to rest a nagging doubt about a girl who would ravish a strange man without a word between them. He liked to think of himself as a liberated individual, but the actions that night had been disturbing as well as exhilarating, and he was glad that the demon at the ball had not been her. However much he could understand Fiona's ulterior motive in doing Sharon Proctor's bidding, he found less fathomable the dark sexual forces that would impel the American to carry out such an act of subterfuge. He was honest enough with himself to admit that prior to his affair with Fiona, he had found Sharon Proctor alluring. This feeling had been compounded when she had told him of her devotion to her ugly husband. Her words, chosen to forestall approach, had, in effect, issued a challenge. But Fiona had changed all that and Tring now looked upon his employer with a mixture of contempt and pity.

Within fifteen minutes, the professor was pulling into his parking space at Parados. He had just switched off his engine when Harold Spencer approached. The beetle-browed head of clinical research was obviously enjoying a pipe-smoking break.

'Nobody smokes those things any more you know, Harold,' said Tring, laughing through his open window.

'One of the delights of life, my friend,' replied the bluff Mancunian. 'Oh, and another of the delights of life is looking for you, Jonathan.'

Tring's raised eyebrows begged an explanation.

'When the blonde goddess summons a devotee, he shall obey,' Spencer said with mock pomposity.

'Shit,' muttered the scientist. Sharon Proctor was the last person he wanted to see. He climbed out of his car, pressed the remote to lock it and turned to face Spencer. 'Harold?'

'Yes, you lucky man.'

'Let's go for a drink tonight after work.'

'Uncle Harold would be delighted, dear friend.' Then winking, 'you can tell me all about the delights of your meeting with our Sharon. Some people say she fancies you, y'know.'

Tring smiled. 'Don't get your bow-tie in a twist over that one, Harold,' he said, slapping his colleague on the arm. 'She'd eat me alive. See you later in the lab.' The professor then made towards the entrance, temporarily replacing thoughts of Sharon Proctor with his plans to quiz Harold Spencer more deeply over the demise of his predecessor. The Mancunian might just be the key to unlocking the Locke affair, thought Tring, chuckling to himself at the pun. He had to admit that Fiona's request that he play amateur detective had created within him a bubble of excitement as well as of apprehension. He calmed himself by deciding to approach the matter as he would when researching a new drug. Explore the theories and then test them. It was with this in mind that he knocked on Sharon Proctor's door. A CCTV camera stared down at him from above the lintel.

'Please enter, Jonathan,' came the Southern drawl.

He could feel a few butterflies as he went in. Sharon Proctor, dressed in one of the myriad dark designer suits whose cut only served to enhance her stunning beauty, smiled at him benignly. 'Good afternoon, Sharon,' he said with false bonhomie.

'Enjoy your lunch?' she queried.

'Yes, it was splendid, thanks.'

'Jack's very pleased that you and Fiona are hitting it off. We both like her immensely.'

God, thought Tring, was there nothing the Proctors did not know? And then he grinned, more to himself than to Sharon Proctor, for indeed there was. 'Yes, she's a lovely girl. I'm very fond of her.'

'Good,' said the American.

Prior to his lunch with Fiona, Tring would have regarded Sharon Proctor's glacial smile as purely enigmatic. But now he knew what lay behind it, and this gave him a certain sense of power over her.

'Jonathan, I'd like to come down to the laboratory and look over a few things,' she said. 'You can explain to me all the technicalities.'

'Of course,' said Tring, who then watched bemused as she lifted a polished fingernail to her lips and bade him to be silent. She rose from her desk and walked over to the door, which she first opened and then closed with an exaggerated bang. The American then removed her shoes and tiptoed over towards a wall socket sporting a plug whose wire led to a table lamp. Resting sideways on her haunches, she gently removed the plug containing the listening device. 'That's better,' she said, replacing her shoes. 'Just one of Jack's silly games.'

Tring stood dumbfounded as she retook her seat and beckoned him to sit down. It was clear that there was no real trust among the Parados elite.

'Jonathan, I meant what I said about coming down to see your work. I know that I'm more concerned with the business end of the company, but I'd sure like to learn the workings of molecules, however mundane.'

Tring wanted to say that molecule moulding was far from mundane for him, but decided to keep his own counsel. 'You're very welcome, Sharon,' he said simply.

'We all need a little excitement in our lives, Jonathan, a change from the routine.'

Alarm bells began resounding in the scientist's brain. He was desperately hoping that this beautiful but dangerous woman was not about to make a play for him. If she did, and he rejected her, it might jeopardise everything.

'How do you get your kicks, Jonathan?'

'Rugby,' he blurted. It was the first thing that came into his mind. Anything but weird sex.

Sharon Proctor sighed wistfully. 'Ah, men and their sport. You know, I once dated a football player back home in Georgia. As tall as you, but built like a Redwood. Wanted to marry me. But his brain was the size of a pea. I can't abide stupid men.'

Tring said nothing, but he felt sorry for any man who had had to try to fulfil Sharon Proctor's exacting standards.

'You're not stupid, Jonathan, are you?'

'I would like to think not,' he said wondering where the hell this was all leading.

She breathed deeply. 'Look, I know you and Klein are friends, and I also know that you're an honourable man, but the future of this company is at stake.' She noted the concerned look in his eyes and quickly added, 'Don't worry, I'm not going to ask you to do anything against your conscience.'

Sharon Proctor then launched into an explanation of how her husband's headstrong actions might lead to ruination, that intrigue in the pharmaceutical industry made politics look like a teddy bear's picnic. By her very tone, Tring could see that there was something else; something very damning that was worrying the boss's wife.

'I believe I understand you much better that you think, Jonathan,' she said knowingly. 'I know that you wouldn't let our company go under if you could help it.'

'What do you want me to do?' he said bluntly.

'I want you to try to find out if your friend Klein has anything on us,' she said steely-eyed.

So that was it, thought Tring. The Proctors were running scared over something and Abe Klein or someone connected to him was involved. It was a golden opportunity for him to legitimately engage in a little non-scientific research, ostensibly on behalf of his bosses but effectively against them. But he also knew that he mustn't show over-eagerness to accede to her request or Sharon Proctor might smell a rat. The blonde bombshell from Georgia was as wily as they came.

'You're asking me to spy on my friend?' Tring said gravely.

'Not exactly, Jonathan,' she drawled. 'We're not after information which might undermine him. We want information that might undermine us. Anyway, we all enjoy a little excitement from time to time, don't we.'

You sure do, thought Tring. He leaned forward and placed his left hand on the table for support. 'As you mentioned before, I won't do anything that conflicts with my conscience.'

Sharon Proctor smiled through the teeth that were achingly faultless, and then leaned towards him, placing a hand of sculptured white marble over his. 'I wouldn't expect you to.'

The professor stared at the hand for a moment, recalling that it had once held his sex in a darkened room. Ordinarily, her touch would have brought an immediate response in the vicinity of his groin. Instead, it left him as frozen as a Waynesboro cotton picker stranded in Alaska.

Only slightly less chilly was the cold and musty garage in which Kieran Kelly now found himself. It was a derelict lock-up in Islington, tucked away in a cul-de-sac used by no one. It was one of those odd sites that had not yet been snapped up by property developers, and it had changed little since he had last visited it a year earlier. There were still dormant cells of the IRA, decommissioning or no decommissioning, that maintained arms and ammunition sites in and around the English capital. He doubted whether their whereabouts would ever be revealed. Only he and his friends in Belfast knew the existence of this one, and they were not about to compromise themselves for the sake of a peace that might turn out to be as ephemeral as a leprechaun in a Donegal mist.

The Irishman's first task was to avail himself of emergency funds. He opened the top drawer of a dust-covered chest in the far corner. The money, ten thousand pounds' worth of superbly crafted and suitably grubby twenty-pound notes, was still as he had left it, wrapped in a Tesco shopping bag. He placed the bag in his briefcase. The money, albeit counterfeit, would come in handy when he left his job. He then moved around the garage to inspect the crates, the contents of which he thought he'd never have to use again. The first one he opened contained a selection of handguns, mostly stolen from the British Army. He picked out his weapon of choice, a 9mm Browning High Power, and played with it, tossing it from his right hand to his left and back again. Made in Belgium by Fabrique Nationale, the Browning had become synonymous with the SAS. The weapon had a semi-automatic action, considerable stopping power and fourteen-round box magazine. Kelly liked this, the latest version, because it had a double action. The hammer could be cocked manually before the trigger was pulled, or alternatively cocked and fired by continuous pressure on the trigger. Still with weapon in hand, he found an empty crate and placed it inside. The Beretta he kept at home would be used as back up.

Next on the Irishman's agenda came his preferred weapon for sniping. He couldn't help smiling to himself as he packed away the 7.62mm LA96A1. The rifle had a plastic stock, a light bipod under the barrel and a monopod under the stock so that it could be laid on the target for long periods without tiring the firer. The Schmidt and Bender telescopic sights provided accuracy to a distance of one thousand metres. He stroked the rifle sensually and smiled, for he knew it was the SAS's own choice for counter-revolutionary and hostage-rescue operations, where a first-round kill at a range as short as one hundred metres was critical. 'Tuché, my friends,' he said through pursed lips. 'Tuché.'

Kelly then collected a pair of night-vision goggles before moving on to the last two items for his armoury. The first was a 66mm M72 one-shot, throwaway anti-tank weapon. It was the only one he had, but at less than two-and-a-half kilos it was extraordinarily light. Its one-kilo rocket could penetrate armour to more than three hundred millimetres at any range. Although he doubted that he would be forced to use it, the British authorities might be tempted to bring in armoured vehicles of some description if things got hairy. It might be prudent for him to disabuse them from the start.

The final item was something the Irishman definitely hoped he would never have to use. Resembling some innocuous putty, the two kilos of Semtex would be the last resort of a desperate man, but he was prepared to blow himself and everyone else to kingdom come if the British Government and the pharmaceutical companies did not accede to his demands. He placed the explosive and a few detonators into the crate, along with the appropriate rounds of ammunition for his weapons.

All was now ready for him to collect when the time was right.

'Well,' said Harold Spencer raising his glass towards his lips and his voice above the hubbub, 'what did she who shall be obeyed have to say for herself?'

Tring downed a few gulps of his Worthington Best while he pondered again whether he should tell the truth to his head of clinical research. He decided it might be prudent to be economical with the precise facts. 'Mrs Proctor wants to come down and visit us in the lab.'

'Does she, by heck,' said the gruff Mancunian with a hint of cynicism. 'What the hell does she know about science and chemicals. She just rings the bloody till.'

Tring smiled. 'Sure, but you know what it is with the new, liberated women. They like to have a finger in every pie.'

'As long as she keeps her finger out my Petri dish, I don't mind.'

'I'll handle her, Harold, don't you worry. It's just that's she's concerned for the new pill to be a success.'

'Aren't we all?'

Tring decided it was time to jump in. 'Look, Harold,' he said conspiratorially, 'between you and me, she's a bit concerned that the opposition might have stolen a march on us. It has something to do with Locke.'

The portly Mancunian leaned against the bar and fingered his trademark bow tie nervously. 'No, your predecessor wouldn't have sold out the company however much he was scared of Jack Proctor. Martin Locke was as loyal as they came.'

'Then perhaps he knew something that had nothing to do with the product, something that could harm the company in another way. Perhaps he told someone else before he died.'

'Well it certainly wasn't me.'

'But you knew him as well as anyone at Parados.'

Spencer shrugged. 'Sure, but I didn't socialise much with him. I'm married and I always thought he was queer, so—'

'So was there anyone else he was close to?'

Spencer frowned and shook his head. 'Not that I knew about, although hold on a minute.'

Tring waited with bated breath while his colleague searched the inner recesses of his memory. Give me a name, the professor pleaded silently, any name.

'I don't know *who* he was,' Spencer said at length, 'but I do recall someone telling me where he worked.'

Tring found he wanting to scream at the Mancunian as the older man decided at that precise moment to take another long swig of lager.

Harold Spencer burped loudly before adding, 'Yes, that's right. The bloke worked at KleinKinloss.'

While Jonathan Tring and his colleague were enjoying a last beverage before the pub closed, Kieran Kelly was cradling the head of his lover in his powerful arms. The Countess moaned as he moved his lips towards her forehead and planted a kiss gently beneath the hairline. Once again, their lovemaking had been of extraordinary tenderness followed by ferocity of need that surprised them both.

Magda von Esterhazy felt she was as near to Nirvana as she would ever be. She was once again a real woman, and the sense of fulfilment was totally overwhelming. Her main satisfaction had come from being able to fulfil the needs of her partner despite her disability. She'd been afraid that the first time might just have been a one-off, a brief encounter between two people trying to dissolve their respective hurts in the sunburst of lust. It had seemed to her that they had been like two fireflies desperately seeking to mate before the lights went out. But now it was different. Kieran had come back to her. She was not just a one-night stand. She recognised his terrible need to fill the void left by the death of his wife. Strangely, she found the Irishman's protestations of his eternal love for Teresa only made her more attracted to him. However, she felt she still needed to know more about this man named Kieran O'Donaghue: his likes, his dislikes, his plans for the future and whether they included her or not. But she also knew that she would never be the first to raise these issues.

. 'Secrets and lies,' he said suddenly.

'What do you mean, Kieran?'

'The world is full of secrets and lies.'

She snuggled closer to him. 'You mean the general attitude towards arachnoiditis?'

'Not only that,' he said with a tinge of bitterness. 'There is so much evil out there. So little honour.'

'But, *liebling*, didn't someone say that honour was the last refuge of a scoundrel.'

'I think it was patriotism that Samuel Johnson was talking about.'

'That too.'

Kelly felt a desperate need to gain her support for his rationale. 'You know, some unknown Vietnamese said it was better to die with honour than live in disgrace. Honour is the highest plane to which man can aspire. No wrongs would ever be righted unless there were men who acted in its interest.'

She leaned on one elbow and gazed lovingly at his strong profile. 'But surely honour is only satisfied when it is just.'

'Precisely.'

'So when an Arab villager slaughters his own daughter because she has been raped, that is just?'

'Yes, in his eyes it is.'

'So honour is only in the eye of the beholder.'

'Who are we to judge other cultures and their codes of honour?'
'Can we agree to disagree on that one,' she smiled and leaned her head
back on the pillow.
'So you don't believe in the concept of revenge,' he said.
'I believe in the concept, but I don't practise it.'
He stroked her long blonde hair. 'But don't you hate the people who did
this to you. Don't you ever wish you could get back at them?'
She shook her head. 'A grudge only destroys the bearer. It eats away at
him like a cancer.' She snuggled deeper into his shoulder, then, 'you see,
we too are culpable. We have an emergency and then expect that the
medical community will somehow have all the answers. We need to stop
treating our physicians as gods and recognise them as human beings. We
all need to ask the questions that need to be asked.'
Kelly kissed her again. 'I don't quite understand your drift,' he said.
Magda von Esterhazy smiled. She loved intellectual conversation. It
was something she had desperately missed until the Irishman had come
along. 'There are so, so many questions we all need to ask, Kieran. Why,
for instance, are cigarettes still legal when each of us knows that they are
harmful to our health and that it drives the cost of medical care through
the roof? Why haven't the citizens of the world demanded that the
manufacture and sale of this killer be banned? Why are mobile phones
still legal to use while driving when we know that the results are worse
than drunk driving? I don't think many people are investing time and
effort in this country to make things right. Most people sit around hoping
that someone else will do it. In the end, we seem to get what we deserve,
whether it be inept governments, poor medical standards or, how you
say, dodgy pharmaceutical companies.'
'Magda, are you telling me you deserve the pain you suffer?'
'No, *liebchen*, no one deserves to suffer, but it is a fact of life
nevertheless. The trouble is, no one can truly understand another
person's suffering. My ex-husband used to say, "Magda, surely it can't
hurt all *that* much." I asked him if he'd invented a machine that he
attached to the pain centre of my brain that somehow broadcast the pain I
was feeling to him. I told him that if suddenly, out of the blue, he had
just five seconds where he went from normal to my pain level, he would
think he was dying. He'd fall to the floor screaming and do pee-pee in

his pants. Then, at the end of those five seconds, when he went back to normal, he would never again doubt me.' She hesitated, then, vehemently, 'that's the trouble with pain. *Aus den Augen, aus dem Sinn.* Out of sight, out of mind. You can't prove it, so people are prone to doubt it. When I fell on that ice, it was the worst agony I'd ever experienced, but that day would now seem like a day off. Am I boring you, Kieran?'

'No, please go on. I want and *need* to understand everything, every single thing about this disease.'

'You know, the bizarre symptoms we suffer have been compared to a burglar alarm that goes off for nothing. The injured nerve bombards the brain with repetitive painful impulses. Because our brain just can't ignore the impulses any better than our ears can stop listening to the shrill of the alarm, nerve pain will remind itself as long as it hasn't been switched off. In our case, of course, the pain becomes chronic. The wiring starts to go haywire. In response to the damaged nerve fibres, new ones sprout out all over the place but keep making the wrong connections. It's like a spaghetti junction with all the roads making wrong connections. What this means for us is that practically anything we do develops into an attack of pain.'

The Irishman was silent for a few seconds, then, 'Magda?'

'Yes.'

'What about suffering for a cause?'

'What do you mean?'

'What do you think about the IRA?'

'I think,' she answered unhesitatingly, 'that after years of war, peace is the better option.'

'Did you think their cause was just?'

'Maybe, but not the manner in which they expressed it. I can understand loyalty to a cause, but not when it makes innocent people suffer.'

'Loyalty is the principle that guides my life, Magda. I think those who are disloyal to a cause are the scum of the earth.'

Magda was surprised by his sudden vehemence, but did not respond.

'You know, I was a Catholic living in a sea of Protestant bigotry,' he went on. 'You don't know what it's like to live as a minority.'

'What do you mean?' she said with feigned indignation. She was eager to lighten the conversation, 'I'm a down-at-heel aristocrat. If that isn't a minority, then I don't know what is.'

Kelly laughed. He realised that he was being too open and was thankful that she had steered the discussion into humour. He leaned over and pressed his lips against hers. He felt the familiar stirring of an ardour that he knew must be finite. Magda von Esterhazy would never divert him from his course, and there was no doubt that he would hurt her in the process. And it was tearing him apart.

CHAPTER THIRTEEN

'Fuck Derek Sutton,' screamed Kevin Kinloss like an off-key bagpipe. His wrath caused the Scotsman's angular features to pull tight until he resembled a Highlands Goshawk who had just dropped a field mouse lunch in mid-flight. Kinloss then turned on his unfortunate minion with a steely-eyed glare that would have unsettled William Wallace. 'What d'ya mean, you found nothing, man. I know for sure he was working on a new formula.'

Although no Braveheart, Michael Bannister was enjoying a newfound self-assurance, the confidence of a man who knew he held an ace up his sleeve. 'Then you shouldn't have fired him,' he said with unusual bravado.

Kinloss glared at Bannister with undisguised contempt. The untalented interim director of science was of little use to him now, but the Scotsman knew Klein would take a more lenient view. His soon-to-be erstwhile partner was just too damn soft when it came to hiring and firing. When Jack Proctor took over the company, Bannister would rapidly find himself the star of a downsizing operation.

'So, Michael, d'ya think you're capable of carrying the day with our new patch?'

Bannister smiled wanly at the sarcasm in Kinloss's voice. 'I'm sure of it, Kevin. I've been working on a few ideas of my own, and I believe I can crack the present problems.'

'I've got the greatest faith in you, Michael,' Kinloss said unconvincingly. He knew the dick brain couldn't crack an egg with a sledgehammer.

'I won't disappoint you,' said Bannister, who then wheeled around and left the Scotsman's office with as confident a stride as he could muster.

Damn them all, thought Kinloss. There was no proof that Sutton had taken his work in progress home with him. If he had done so, then theoretically that belonged to the company, although there was no way he could force the old drunk to divulge anything. It would, however, have been nice to take a little bonus for Jack Proctor when he crossed sides. The chairman of Parados had told him to be ready to act at a moment's notice. Timing was everything, and the Scotsman knew that all hell was about to break loose sooner rather than later.

'Something's afoot,' said Fiona Harrington. 'I had lunch with Sharon Proctor today and she's more uptight than I've ever seen her.'

Tring smiled. 'The plot thickens,' he said mockingly. 'She must have a lot to hide.'

'What do you mean?'

'I thought I'd save it all for a bedside story.'

'No give, no bed, Mister Tring.'

The professor laughed heartily and then looked around the restaurant self-consciously. 'Shh,' he whispered, 'you don't want anyone to hear what a brazen little vixen you are.'

'Jonathan,' she said with a glare, 'if you don't tell me this minute, I'll stand on this table and strip naked.'

He laughed again. 'Promises, promises.'

Only when Fiona started to undo the top buttons of her blouse did Tring realise his lover meant every word. 'Heh, hold on, girl, that's for my eyes only.' Without further ado, the scientist recounted his meeting with Sharon Proctor, interrupting it only for mouthfuls of a particularly succulent fillet mignon.

Fiona Harrington, her reporter's instincts rising to the fore, slammed her hand on the table. 'I *knew* something wasn't kosher. So Sharon's worried that when the dirty tricks start, Abe Klein might have something up his sleeve.'

'Klein might not have, but someone who works, or worked, at KleinKinross might.'

'What do you mean?'

Tring ran his fingers through his thick wavy hair and scratched the back of his head. Conspiracy did not weigh easily with him, and yet he felt committed to both Fiona and to her cause. After a short pause, he told her about his conversation with Harold Spencer.

'I've also got a gut feeling that this unknown guy could be the key,' said Fiona, unable to disguise the excitement in her voice, 'but how on earth do we find out who he is? There must be more than three hundred employees at KleinKinloss and who knows which one of them might have been a homosexual partner of Locke's. They both seem to have been eager to keep their relationship in the closet.'

'So how do we start?'

'You'll have to ask Klein,' she replied baldly.

'Just like that?'

'He's your best friend.'

Tring shifted uncomfortably. 'I find it awkward bringing up anything to do with our respective companies, considering mine is trying to take over his. It would be unethical. Abe would expect me to be loyal to my employer.'

'All's fair in love and war, Jonathan. You owe the Proctors nothing.'

'Then I should resign first.'

Fiona Harrington squirmed. It was her job to be pushy, but not with the man with whom she knew she had fallen in love. He was just too damned altruistic. 'You can't resign,' she squealed. 'Then they really would smell a rat.'

'Fiona?'

'Yes.'

'You're not using me, are you?' Tring regretted the words as soon as he had uttered them.

Tears welled in Fiona Harrington's large hazel eyes and her fresh cheeks flushed with indignation. She stayed silent though, if only because her emotions were trapped. She was angry, but at the same time she could understand why he might think of her in such a way. Everything she had done up to now bore the taint of subterfuge, everything except her feelings for the scientist.

'I-I'm sorry, Fiona,' he stuttered.

'No, it's okay,' she said with a smile. 'In a way, I'm glad you'd make a lousy spy.'

'Then you'll give me time to think it over?'

'How long will you need?'

'A couple of days.'

'What's a couple of days between friends,' she said coyly.

'I think it might seem like a lifetime to an eager beaver reporter like yourself.' Tring then laughed, thankful that a possible crisis in their relationship had been averted.

What neither of them knew was that events at the London Stock Exchange were about to test relationships to the limit.

The shop, apart from its name, was as nondescript as the parade in which it stood. Double-fronted and with mirrored glass that shielded it from prying eyes, *I-Spy* was a haven for all items connected to the art of surveillance. For art it most certainly was, and in the eyes of one particular practitioner, it was as good a toy store as he was likely to find anywhere.

Kieran Kelly, dressed in navy-blue pin stripes and looking every much the executive with industrial espionage high on his agenda, inspected himself in the mirrored door. He re-arranged his tie slightly, knowing full well that he was being watched from within, and then rang the doorbell. It seemed an age before the door opened and a dapper man in his early forties beckoned him to enter. The man sported unfashionable horn-rimmed glasses, greasy black hair and a pencil-thin moustache. These combined to give him the anachronistic appearance of a throwback to the sixties and the world of Harry Palmer.

'Good morning, sir,' said the salesman, 'and how may we help you.'

The Irishman looked around the salon. On a shelf to his left stood three CCTV monitors. Below them was a counter that was in effect a glass cabinet containing items with which any self-respecting spy would arm himself. Kelly's shopping list was in his head. He knew the items he wanted. 'Good morning,' he replied confidently, 'I'm in charge of security at my company and we're moving premises. We need to get our new security up and running.'

'Of course, sir, I'm sure we can find something to suit your needs. Are you looking for transmitting or hard-wired devices?'

'Hard-wired,' the Irishman replied. Transmitters could be detected and then disabled. He wanted to have eyes and ears at all times.

'We have some excellent CCTV cameras to go with the monitors you can see on the top shelf.

'I'm more interested in your pinholes. Can you show me your self-focusing ones?'

'Of course, sir,' said the throwback, adding obsequiously, 'I see you have an excellent knowledge of our trade.' He then turned to open a drawer and withdrew a black camera the size of a postage stamp and with wires attached.

Kelly played the device through his fingers. 'I'll take twelve,' he said coldly. The cameras were Japanese and had infrared motion sensors adjustable to twenty-five metres. 'Give me two toggles as well as those three monitors.

The salesman beamed. 'Three screens into quadrants. Good idea.'

'I'd also like four radio mikes with audio threshold trips, a joystick and an A/V mixer.' Kelly knew that the microphones would work only if background noise was ambient. Rustling leaves in a high wind would make them useless. Still, as he wasn't paying for anything, the more toys the better.

The salesman arranged everything on the counter and then eagerly began totting up while the Irishman looked on with apparent indifference. 'That'll be seven thousand two hundred and thirty pounds, please, sir, including VAT. How would sir like to pay?'

'Amex Gold card,' said Kelly flatly.

'That'll do nicely, sir.' The salesman giggled, then, 'always did like that advert.'

'Perhaps you'd like to help me load up the monitors.'

The salesman looked down at the card. 'Of course, er, Mr Flynn.'

Within a few moments the transaction had been completed and the goods were being neatly stowed in the rear of a Range Rover. Kelly was under no illusion that both he and the car were being captured on the shop's CCTV, but this did not bother him in the slightest. He had stolen the vehicle ten minutes earlier, and within a few more minutes he would transfer the goods to his own car that was parked in a quiet corner of a nearby run-down industrial estate. As for the Gold card, they were two-a-penny if one knew the right people.

'The motherfuckin' Scotch bastard,' seethed Abe Klein and slammed down the phone. His broker had been the first to alert him of events that were rocking the pharmaceutical sector of the Stock Exchange. Soon the world and its neighbour would be contacting him for a quote. The press would have a field day. He was just about to dial his partner's extension when there came a knock at the door.

'Who is it?' he screamed, his churning anger almost uncontrollable.

The door opened and the American's nemesis stood before him with a grin that would have curled the whiskers of a Cheshire cat. 'Don't tell me you didn't expect something like this, Abe,' Kinloss said smugly. 'I've been telling you for weeks to accept Proctor's approaches.'

'You asshole.' Klein was boiling, his saucer-like brown eyes bulging from beneath his shining pate. 'Proctor must have offered you a pretty penny for you to dump all your shares.'

The Scotsman was unfazed by the outburst of his Bilkoesque former partner. 'That's for me to tell and you to find out.'

Klein stood up behind his desk and tried to make himself appear taller to the lanky Scotsman. 'I oughta wipe that fucking supercilious grin off your face.'

'You don't frighten me, Klein.' It was now a case of surnames only.

'Don't you ever heard of loyalty, you Scotch sonofabitch.'

'Scottish ,' Kinloss corrected. This time it was his turn to seethe with indignation. 'Don't speak to me about loyalty. While you immersed yourself in your laboratory, I was the one who kept this company afloat. If it wasn't for me massaging the investors, you would have gone under ages ago.'

The American leaned forward onto his desk and stared squarely at Kinloss. 'I'll still not sell out to that ugly fucking bulldog.'

'You're pissing in the wind, Klein. The institutions won't let you hold out for long. They've seen their investment drop forty per cent in minutes. The only way they can recover their money and make a premium is if Proctor steps in.'

'You're a fool, Kinloss. What makes you think Glaxo and the rest of them won't outbid Parados.'

The Scotsman smirked but remained silent. Nice try, he thought, but the KleinKinloss profile did not support any bid other than that of Parados.

'You'd better clear your desk and get out,' said the younger man through gritted teeth.

Kinloss, still standing by the door, turned to go and then halted. 'To paraphrase you Yanks, science is softball and finance is hardball. The bottom line always wins in the ninth inning.'

'Get out,' Klein said quietly, suddenly deflated by what he knew to be an economic truth. The American watched his erstwhile partner leave and then held his head in his hands. Everything he had worked for was about to be swallowed up. Kinloss just could not see that sometimes the realisation of a dream was more important than money. Yet the boy from Brooklyn knew that finance directors who were not motivated solely by the bottom line were few and far between. It was just that the betrayal had been so crass. He wearily switched on his intercom. 'Maggie, if any members of the media call, just tell them I'll be issuing a statement at one p.m.'

'Right,' Mr Klein,' said the secretary. 'By the way, your wife said to ring home as soon as you can, and I've got Jonathan Tring on hold. He insists on speaking to you.'

Abe Klein hesitated. Who knew if his best friend was also an enemy from within. He then quickly dismissed the thought, although he feared that the events of the last few minutes could drive a wedge between them. He would prefer to believe that Tring would have had nothing to do with Proctor's plots. A further betrayal would be too much to bear. 'Put him on,' the American sighed.

'Hello, Abe.'

'Yes, Jonathan,' he answered, sensing the coolness in his own voice.

'I'm calling from home,' Tring said gravely. 'My girl friend's a reporter and she just rang me with the news. Abe, I want you to know that I didn't know anything about this.'

Klein hesitated, then, 'I believe you, Jonathan, but I may soon find myself sojourning with the ladies of the borscht belt in a Miami Beach advanced age recreational facility.'

Tring laughed, thankful that his friend still retained his indomitable Jewish humour. 'They won't be putting you out to grass just yet, Abe.'

'What do you mean?'

'I need to see you. I know all the shit's starting to hit the fan and I want to help.'

'But you're pitching for the enemy.'

'Well, to paraphrase the Arabs, Abe, your friend is now your enemy's enemy.'

'I don't understand.'

'Is Rachel's chicken soup still on for Friday night?'

'You know it is.'

'I'll explain everything then - oh, Abe?'

'Yes.'

'I'd like to bring my girl friend - you'll like her, especially what she has to say.'

'But you said she was a reporter.'

'She's on your side, Abe, believe me.'

Normally Abe Klein would have burrowed away until his intrigue had been satisfied. But this time his mind was too full of the consequences of his partner's actions. 'The more the merrier,' he said. 'Roll up for the Last Supper.'

'Just one thing you can be sure of,' Tring said.

'What's that?'

'There'll be no Judas present.'

'Pity,' said Klein sneeringly, unaware that Tring was alluding to himself. 'Maybe I should invite that bastard. Chicken soup laced with arsenic. Speciality of the house for that Scotch sonofabitch.'

'Friday night, then,' said the professor and replaced his handset, little knowing that it contained yet another of a phalanx of bugs installed on the orders of a pug-faced Yorkshireman who had to satisfy a pathological need to spy on everyone and everything.

When Jack Proctor discovered that his own director of science was intent on betrayal, it neither surprised nor fazed him. Every man had his price, whether that price was in gold or in women. In fact, he reckoned that what appeared at first to be a disadvantage might be turned to his own favour. Fiona Harrington, however, was a different kettle of fish. She

154

was the surprise packet, and he knew he had no control over the little bitch. All that nonsense about being an IT sales executive. She was a journalist, and reporters were the scum of the earth, always poking their noses into other people's business and writing lies. He had debated with himself whether to let his wife in on his discovery, knowing that it would hurt Sharon more than anything to know the truth about her so-called friend. On the other hand, if there was one person who could wheedle information out of anyone, it was his very own Southern belle.

'Sharon, my dear,' he called out loudly from his study. It was within megaphone distance of the enormous kitchen in which Mrs Proctor was enjoying rustling up her husband's favourite dinner dish, the ubiquitous roast beef and Yorkshire pudding.

'It's ready, Jack,' she called back, placing the last of the hash browns on his plate instead of roast potatoes. They were her husband's only condescension to Southern cooking. But then she always believed that the man who paid the piper called the tune. Thus she would make anything he damn well wanted.

'Coming, my dear, coming.' Jack Proctor took a final satisfying glance at the headlines in the Financial Times, and placed the newspaper on a small mahogany side table. He then pressed the button on the arm of his deep leather orthopaedic recliner. The electronic armchair allowed him to extricate his not inconsiderable bulk with the minimum of effort. Undue physical exertion of any kind was anathema to John Albert Proctor.

He waddled into the kitchen and over to the Aga, where his towering wife was carefully wiping one of the hot plates with a damp cloth. He wrapped his short arms around her slim waist and sank his gleaming pate into the crook of her back. 'Mmm, smells good, my dear, and I'm not talking about your cooking. That's a new perfume, isn't it?'

'Now, now, Jack,' she said with an air of resignation, 'your dinner's on the table. You know how you hate it if it gets cold.'

'Well, stop your fussing, my love, and come and join me.' He released his iron grip and took his place at one end of a long oak table. Sharon Proctor dutifully ceased her tidying and sat facing her husband. They ate their meal in silence.

Sharon Proctor knew better than to engage her husband in conversation before he had finished eating. Jack was a quick eater and hated being interrupted. He had once divulged that his habit of wolfing down his food stemmed from a childhood spent in a bleak orphanage on the Yorkshire Moors. The food was crap, he had said, but the portions were meagre. The fastest eaters got any seconds on offer. Thus hunger, in its many guises, had become the driving force of his life. That's why her husband had to have the most of everything. Not unlike herself.

'That was delicious as usual, my dear,' he said, using the obligatory toothpick to dislodge a stubborn shred of beef stuck. 'A pleasant end to an interesting day.'

'You mean the headlines about Kinloss?'

'Yes, in the main. The way's now open for us to make our bid. Klein won't be able to resist us, unless...'

'Yes.'

'...Unless he's got something on us that we don't know about.'

Sharon Proctor's steel-blue eyes narrowed. She recalled her conversation with Jonathan Tring, a conversation she had not revealed to her husband. Unless, of course, he'd had bugs in her office other than the one she'd found. 'What are you getting at, Jack?'

'I had Tring's home phone bugged,' Jack Proctor replied with a smirk of self-satisfaction. 'You know me. It's better not to trust anyone.' He then proceeded to relay most of the details to his wife, but omitted mention of Fiona Harrington.

Sharon Proctor shrugged. 'So Tring has something to tell Klein. What could he possibly know that could harm us?'

'Whatever it is, we mustn't let him know that we know that he knows.' The chairman of Parados could see his wife's mind switching into overdrive.

'Jack, you're paying off that many people, any one of whom could blow the whistle.'

'Cash in brown envelopes is no problem,' Jack Proctor cackled. 'If al-Fayed can get away with it, then so can we.'

Sharon Proctor was less sure than her husband. It was true that the case of Harrison against the boss of Harrods had gone against the errant MP, but that was a civil case brought for libel. But if Jack was bribing someone like a Government Minister, then that was a different matter altogether.

'Oh, don't worry, my dear, there's nowt that can link me to any wrongdoing - not unless someone rifled through my golfing partner's bag on the eighteenth tee.'

'Your golfing partner isn't exactly the most judicious person in the world. Stephen Sellars has got a big mouth on him, like most of those damned politicians.'

'Don't you worry about our fat Secretary of State for Health, my dear. He's as pure as the driven snow and, anyway, except when he's in the Commons, his lips are sealed tighter than a duck's arse.' With this, the Yorkshireman let out a guffaw that rebounded off the kitchen walls. The small mouth on his pug-face then turned downward and his jowls ceased wobbling. The time had come to reveal all to his wife. 'How well do you think you know Fiona Harrington?' he asked, his gimlet eyes narrowing to mere slits.

It was an unwritten rule in the Klein household that food and piety, however diluted, must always come before shoptalk during any given Friday night Sabbath bash. While Tring was used to the formalities, Fiona Harrington had to fight hard to conceal her eagerness to expound on the reason she was there. She found the Hebrew liturgy of the kiddush quaint and the warmth of the family gathering uplifting, but it was only when the Klein kids had been packed off to bed that the coiled spring could be released. Given the signal by her lover, she launched into a potted history of who she was and how she had inveigled herself into the Proctor milieu. It lasted a breathless ten minutes.

'Bit like a dog with a bone,' Tring said proudly, but also with a tinge of apprehension. The farmer's daughter was wont to exhaust any current hobbyhorse on anyone who would listen.

'So you think old man Proctor has got something to hide?' said Klein

'Look, I can't prove anything yet,' she replied. 'It could be any number of things. You know as well anyone that there's been a dramatic rise recently in the number of prescription drugs taken off the market. Catastrophic side effects have shaken the public's confidence in the pharmaceutical industry.'

157

'I think the good ol' profit motive is going to rear its ugly head pretty soon,' the American suggested without a trace of rancour.

'Always does,' Fiona said affably.

Tring shifted uneasily. Why did she always want to get involved in polemics?

'Do you know how much it costs to bring a new drug to market, young lady?' Klein asked, safe in the knowledge that she probably did.

'Yup, hundreds of millions of dollars.'

'For research and development alone,' Tring chipped in.

'You need a pretty big profit motive to cover *those* costs,' said the dapper American.

'Yes,' said Fiona defiantly, 'but if you can get a great new drug to market fast and keep it there you're talking in terms of billions.'

'And speed sometimes kills,' Klein said quickly.

'You said it, Mr Klein.'

'Call me Abe, please.'

'You see, Abe,' she said entering overdrive, 'this mentality has really hit people. Loads of drugs have been marketed without sufficient testing and adequate warnings. Even where a drug is potentially dangerous and may result in litigation, drug companies will market it anyway if they believe the profit from the sale of the drug will exceed the cost of the litigation and any damage awards in settlements to injured users.'

'Fiona!' Tring said gruffly, his mind addled somewhat by too much sweet kosher wine. 'Surely you're not accusing Abe of such practises.'

'Calm down, Jonathan,' said Klein. 'I think it's a fat ugly Yorkshireman she's alluding to. But you need proof, young lady, and plenty of it.'

'Don't worry,' the professor said with some pride, 'if it's there, Fiona Harrington will find it.'

'Times have changed, gentleman,' said Fiona in what was almost becoming a diatribe. 'At no time in history has so much information been available to so many people from so many sources and at such speed.'

'You sound like Churchill,' said Klein.

Fiona was unfazed. 'And how much the old man would have welcomed the Internet. We now have immediate dissemination of information to every corner of the globe in a matter of seconds.'

'Not very good news for totalitarians of any ilk,' said Tring.

'And not very good news also for drug companies like Parados either,' said Fiona. 'The bigger they get and the more minnows they swallow, the more arrogant they become.'

Klein nodded in agreement. 'These gargantuans are becoming like multi-national soft drink companies where the bottom-line is the only consideration.'

'Yes,' she nodded, 'but whereas a can of Coke might ruin your teeth, a dangerous drug with harmful side effects might kill or injure an extremely large number of people in a relatively short time and without much warning.'

The American could feel the warm glow of the wine wearing off. It was time to talk turkey. 'So, ace reporter, what can I do to help bring the bulldog to heel?'

Fiona Harrington flicked a stray blonde lock from her eyes and launched into information on Jonathan Tring's predecessor and the possible link between his demise and the Proctors. 'We know that Locke was a homosexual and that he had fairly intimate relations with one of your staff. The problem is which one.'

'We've got upwards of three hundred workers here, Fiona,' Klein said almost apologetically, 'half of them men. It could be anyone. We've also had a bit of a turnover since Locke died.'

'Perhaps you could send out a letter to each one,' Tring suggested. 'Something to the effect that lawyers for the estate of Martin Locke are looking for a friend of his at this company.'

Klein grunted dismissively. 'Every Joe Shmo would think he was being left a fortune in the will.'

'No, we have to keep this investigation as quiet as possible,' Fiona cautioned. 'There's no way the Proctors must discover what we're doing. I can't afford to blow my cover.'

The three of them sat mute for a few seconds as they pondered a way to solve the problem. Then the American scratched his bald pate and nodded to himself. 'Tell me, Jonathan,' he said, 'do you have a direct line into your office.'

'Yes,' Tring said. 'It was there when I moved in.'

'Fine. I'll check our phone records. Whoever made calls to that number during the months prior to your arrival at Parados is our man. Each department here has its own line, so at least we'll be able to narrow it down a bit.'

'How long will it take you?' Tring asked.

'Give me a couple of days,' replied Klein, 'and with any luck the young lady will have her story and I might still have my company.

CHAPTER FOURTEEN

The cottage was pleasant enough, better even than on his first two visits. *Rosedale* was two-up, two-down and set in a couple of acres of lush Surrey greenery. It would be easy for them to surround him and just as easy for him to see them coming. Standoff. Exactly the way he wanted it.

'Well, here are the keys, Mr O'Donaghue,' said the letting agent, a young Pakistani kid with slick ebony hair and an attitude to match. 'Remember, if you want to extend, just give us a month's notice. As you know, the landlord's an ex-pat out in the Gulf. Says he's got no intention of returning, but you never know.'

'Once a Brit gets out in that Middle Eastern sun, it's hard to drag him away,' said the Irishman.

The young man smiled. 'Only mad dogs and Englishmen, as they say.'

Probably born and bred in Southall, Kelly thought as he pocketed the keys.

'Do you need any help with your luggage, sir. You look as though you must have a bit of a load there.'

'No, I'll be managing okay, thank you. Wouldn't want to charge you for breakage.'

The Asian laughed, displaying a wide set of Steinway ivories.

Kelly exchanged a few more pleasantries with the lad before watching him roar away in a salubrious silver fox BMW coupe. He couldn't help thinking that the boy would go far. Good luck to him. He was a little pushy, but that was okay as long as it was accompanied by good manners. Not like those lazy English yobs that thought everyone owed them a living.

The Irishman unlocked the back doors of the white Mercedes van. Under the green tarpaulin was everything he needed. He reckoned it would take him the best part of the day to set it all up. First thing was to get all the arms and ammunition and communications equipment safely inside. His personal effects could wait until later.

A full four hours had elapsed before he was satisfied that the cottage was as good as he could get it. He'd decided to set up the main console on the walnut dining table in the open plan lounge. Fully extended, it had proved large enough for him to position two camera monitors to the left of his computer monitor and web cam and one more to the right. In front of all the monitors were mouse, keyboard and A/V mixer.

Next had come the installation of the pinhole cameras. He had placed one under the gable at each corner of the cottage and five more at various strategic spots under ivy-embraced soffits. He installed a further camera in the top corner of each of the three bedrooms.. Despite the luxuriant ivy, the cameras had an unrestricted field of vision but were themselves virtually impossible to detect from the outside. Nothing less than three-hundred-and-sixty degrees would do. Lastly, he had installed the four directional microphones. These might prove of limited value, but he reckoned that if he had them, he might as well use them. As far as the non-technical equipment was concerned, he'd used his second visit to the cottage, sans agent, to take measurements of its eleven windows. Two large windows were either side of the front door, with two smaller ones on the second storey. The same was repeated at the rear with an extra small toilet window. One end of the cottage was a blank wall, while the other had a medium sized window in line with the landing. The last window was in effect a skylight in the roof. Ever the Irish handyman, he had drilled and filled in order to erect the blinds that he knew would drive his adversaries to distraction. There was nothing worse than seeing your reflection in a mirrored glass or blind knowing that the person the other side could see you as clear as day.

Hardest work of all had been drilling the holes for the external stays in the main load-bearing walls of the three bedrooms. Four stays per bedroom, two for the hand and two for the leg irons. The chains had to be just long enough for a prisoner to use his slop bucket or lie on a mattress, but short enough to prevent him from reaching the window.

Already sweating and exhausted, Kelly pulled up a chair and sat in front of the console in the lounge. He leaned forward and switched on the monitors and the A/V console. He flicked another switch and the three screens divided into quadrants, giving him the panoramic view he desired. The tree line around *Rosedale* was set well back, maybe by an average of thirty metres all round. Facing the front of the cottage was a large oak that might support a police hide for their snipers. Little matter, he thought, for he didn't intend to present them with much to fire at.

The Irishman then flicked the toggle switch that brought the microphones crackling into life. It was a hot and windless summer's day, and they were sensitive enough to pick up distant birdsong. He was experienced enough to know that even a slight breeze would distort any sounds made by those laying siege, and that the microphones were more a psychological prop than a useful one. Still, he loved the toys of surveillance and they gave him a certain sense of security.

Kelly switched off the technological paraphernalia and headed back towards his vehicle. His work was about to get even more physical and it was time for a well-earned lunch break. He picked up the box of sandwiches he'd prepared earlier walked towards a trestle table and bench in the garden at the rear of the cottage. It was already after two when he sat down to eat his farmhouse cheese meal. The satisfying of his hunger and the heady essences of the countryside combined to give him a sense of well being he hadn't enjoyed since Teresa's death. He gazed at the idyllic view around him, silently thanking the Internet for finding him such a place within hours of logging on. The website had been magnificent, providing him with the photographs, details and measurements that had enabled him to plan almost everything in advance.

Downing a can of draught Guinness, Kelly turned his attention to the five kilos of Semtex and associated detonators nestling in a polythene bag in the rear of the van. More than enough to blow the whole shebang to kingdom come, it was his pièce de résistance. He returned to the table and began separating the malleable plastic explosive into half-kilo mounds. Playing with it through his fingers, Kelly never ceased to wonder how safe the material was to handle and yet how devastating it could be on detonation. The regular IRA loved it because it was so relatively stable, not to mention the fact that airport X-ray machines had a hard time detecting it. Chemical 'sniffers' were also easily fooled, and it was only trained dogs that had any luck in detecting its weak odour. But then, if you knew what to do, there was never any need to buy the stuff from the Czech Republic, Libya or wherever. If the general public knew how relatively easy it was to make, they'd shit themselves. Mix a little cyclonite with pentaerythrite tetranitrate in a simple laboratory and bingo. Not that he was ever in favour of its gratuitous use. The atrocities of Lockerbie, Riyadh, Nairobi, Dar es Salaam and, especially, Omagh, appalled him. The so-called Real IRA were unprincipled bastards who simply enjoyed killing.

Into each parcel of explosive, the Irishman set blasting caps which could be capacity detonated by remote control. Ten of the caps operated on different frequencies, giving him the ability to make controlled blasts at any of the sites he would choose in the grounds surrounding the cottage. He would also install infrared alarms that would alert him if anyone came within thirty yards of the cottage. No, the British government would capitulate to his demands in double quick time. After all, some of these demands were the same as theirs had been of the Tories nearly a decade earlier. What goes around comes around, as somebody once said.

He moved back to the van to retrieve a shovel and sat on the tailgate, where he'd left his mobile phone. He took a deep breath and dialled the number. Within a couple of rings, a familiar voice answered.

'Sean, is that you?' Kelly queried.

'Is that his master's voice,' joked the older man.

'How are you and Gerry?'

'Champing at the bit, Kieran-boy,' Callaghan lied. If the truth were known, he and O'Connor were shitting themselves about what they were volunteering to do. And yet, in some strange way, there was also a mixture of elation, a sort of adrenaline rush that he hadn't had since accompanying their leader on his very last action, the despatching of two informers who had been a thorn in their sides for a long time. The only thing that had left a sour taste was the fact that the victims were twin brothers. Kelly had insisted that they be executed within minutes of one another, but at different locations. It was a logistics nightmare, but Kieran had insisted that neither brother should know about the other's demise. 'I don't delight in Schadenfreude,' he had said. Callaghan remembered spending a few minutes that evening leafing through a dictionary to find out what the word meant.

'Next Friday, Sean, my place.'

'Do you want me to tell Gerry?'

'Yes.'

'How many days will it be, Kieran?'

'A week.'

'Not a couple of days then?'

Kelly thought he could sense reticence in his comrade's voice. He prayed that they wouldn't let him down at this late stage. 'Five days' preparation, two days' action. Are you still game, Sean?'

'Of course I am, man.'

'My place, Friday, then.'

'Friday it is, Kieran.' *Click.*

Kelly felt a tingle of excitement mixed with a twinge of apprehension. He knew that he could rely on his comrades, but if anything went wrong before they were in the clear, he didn't think he could forgive himself. Apart from his children and his sister-in-law, he regarded Sean and Gerry as his only true family. It was funny how shared experience of violence tended to unite people whether they were perpetrator or victim. Old soldiers were always saying that friendships forged in war were everlasting, even though they might never see their former comrades for decades, if ever. The Irishman wiped the sweat from his brow and dialled another number.

'*Ja?*' came the Germanic reply.

'Hi, Magda.'

'Kieran, *liebling*, how are you?

'I'm okay. Look, I'm sorry I haven't contacted you for a few days. Something came up at work.'

'There's no need to explain,' she said perhaps a little too quickly. She didn't like the hint of desperation in her own voice.

'Look,' he said, 'the weather forecast says tomorrow's also going to be hot and sunny. I've got a day off, so why don't we head off to the coast for the day.'

'That'll be nice, Kieran, thank you. My pain levels are always much lower in the good weather.'

'I'll pick you up at about ten. Is that okay?'

'I'll look forward to it.'

'See you then.' With this, Kelly turned off the mobile and stared at it balefully for a while. He could simply have written Magda a 'dear John' letter, telling her how much he'd enjoyed their short relationship. But he owed her more than that. He would tell her face to face that he'd decided to return to Belfast to take care of his kids. He missed them greatly, and that was the truth. It was all a bluff, of course, but should he die, then they would all know that he remained true to his principles to the end. He lived his life in black and white. Shades were for the vacillators, the wimps who would never be found standing up for themselves, let alone for anyone else. And, anyway, he was doing this for the two women he cared most about in the world. If he succeeded, the damned disease that killed one and haunted the other would at least gain the sort of world recognition that might lead to further research and a possible cure. As things now stood, the only man who gave a fuck was Kieran Patrick Kelly.

'So what do *you* think?' Sharon Proctor queried, as she waved aside the obsequious saleslady and stood resplendent in the black, backless Versace creation with its howling price tag. Jewel-encrusted, with a bias cut and asymmetric floor-length hemline, the dress shrieked 'buy me.'

'Stunning,' Fiona Harrington replied. 'Simply stunning, but then you'd look good in anything, Sharon.'

The American smiled. 'Flattery will get you everywhere, and let's face it, I trust your opinion more than any of these people.'

The store's saleslady, a bat-like matron with Bram Stoker make-up, visibly wilted at the barb. Sharon Proctor wasn't the easiest of customers, but then new money never was.

'You don't know how important your friendship has been to me, Fiona,' the statuesque blonde drawled. 'There seem to be so few people one can trust nowadays.'

Fiona Harrington felt herself blushing, a dead give away for someone who could spot the difference between embarrassment and duplicity.

Sharon Proctor continued parading herself in front of the full-length mirror. 'You know, Fiona, Jack and I have been under a lot of strain

lately, what with the takeover and all. You know all about that, don't
you.'

Fiona had to think fast. She could deny it, but then that might appear
incongruous taking into account that she was sleeping with the
company's chief scientist. 'Yes,' she said matter-of-factly, 'Jonathan did
mention it. He said you were trying to take over a company,
KleinKinloss, I think he said.'

Sharon Proctor disrobed and handed the Versace to the bat. 'Wrap it
up,' she said curtly, 'and here's my card.' The saleslady took the plastic
and dress and scurried out of the fitting room, hoping against hope that
her testy customer wouldn't change her mind.

'Fiona, my dear,' the American continued, 'how much do they pay you
at that IT company of yours?'

'Thirty thousand plus my Audi Cabriolet.'

'Not much, really.'

'I can't complain. I'm still young and the prospects are good.'

The American laughed. 'I bet they ain't gonna offer you no share
options, though.'

'Maybe not, but I'm happy enough.'

'You'd be a lot happier running public relations at Parados along with
half a percent in share options.'

If Fiona Harrington was taken aback, she did not show it. 'But I don't
know anything about public relations,' she said quickly.

'There's nothing to know. You spout the party line and you look good.
That's about it. Salary seventy grand and a guaranteed bonus of another
thirty at the end of the year and, of course, your shares will probably be
worth a million if this deal comes off.'

'I-I don't know what to say,' Fiona stuttered. 'It's mind-blowing.'

'It's the least I can do.'

'I just don't understand.'

'Look, you've been like a younger sister to me over the past couple of
years. Whenever I've had problems, I've been able to discuss them with
you. Strange, really, when you consider I'm six years older than you. But
the thing I like about you is that you're completely non-judgemental.
Anyone the same age or older than me would have probably given me a
hard time. Perhaps that's why I've always liked to be surrounded by

young blood. Maybe I hope some of that youth will rub off on me, or maybe its because I'm looking for a substitute for my twin sister. I don't believe I ever told you this before, but Tracy-Lee died from meningitis when we were ten. I don't think I've ever gotten over it.'

At that moment Fiona Harrington felt truly sorry for the American. She realised how desperately unhappy Sharon Proctor really was; that despite all the trappings of great wealth, her proposed benefactor was trapped in a loveless marriage, longing for a youth that had passed her by. 'I don't know what to say, Sharon,' she said quietly.

The American put her arm around her young companion. 'It's simple, really. I believe loyalty should be rewarded.'

Again Fiona felt distinctly uncomfortable. Whatever dirt she could dig up on Jack Proctor was by its very nature going to smear Mrs Proctor. She would have liked to believe that Sharon was an innocent party in any conspiracy at Parados.

'I need a couple of days,' the younger woman lied.

'There's just one thing I'd like you to do for me, though,' the Southerner drawled. 'Your boyfriend's best friend is Abe Klein. Tring seems incorruptible, but that damned little Yankee has got something on us that might ruin our company. Maybe you can work on Tring. If you can find out what it is, it'll be worth millions to you, I promise.'

'Wow,' Fiona Harrington gasped. If she gave up her mission, she'd be made for life. If she swapped sides, she would never have to take an editor's bullshit again. Regaining her composure, she looked Mrs Proctor squarely in the eye. 'As I said, Sharon, give me a few days to think about it.'

It was perhaps because she hailed from a land-locked country that the sea held more of a fascination for Magda von Esterhazy than it did for her companion. Westcliff-on-Sea wouldn't have won many prizes for resort of the year, she thought, but the blustery air was bracing enough. The tide was in and the small boats were gaily bobbing about on their moorings as if glad to be free of the mud that had ensnared them for half the day.

'That's the Isle of Grain over there,' Kelly said, leaning over the wheelchair to speak into her ear. 'It's a huge oil refinery. You see the flame atop that chimney?'

'Yes,' she shouted above the wind.

'They say that if that goes out, the island would blow up and take the whole of Southend and Westcliff with it.'

Magda stared at the flame with rekindled intensity, almost wishing it to go out because she knew it wouldn't.

'You must be feeling cold,' he said with concern, knowing that poor blood circulation was always a problem for those who could not walk well. Not waiting for affirmation, he pushed the wheelchair briskly towards a Victorian pavilion that acted as a windbreak. Both the pavilion and the promenade on which it stood were deserted.

She shivered. 'Lift me out, Kieran, and let me snuggle close to you.'

Kelly gently lifted her from the wheelchair and placed her on the bench which faced the sea but was recessed just enough to shield them from the elements. He then spread a thick tartan blanket to cover them both from the waist down. A few spots of rain began to fall, heightening their sense of cosiness, and at that moment, the Irishman experienced an extraordinary and overwhelming feeling of peace. 'I used to bring the wife and kids down here on summer Sundays,' he said wistfully. 'This place has always been a sort of refuge for east Londoners. In the old days before package holidays, it was about the only bit of seawater the working class would ever get to see. Back home the sea was an integral part of our lives. Up until the age of ten we lived n a little seaside village called Donaghadee. I used to look out over the North Channel and watch the ferries making for the Isle of Man or Liverpool or returning to Belfast. Then, one day, out of the blue, my father has a massive stroke and our whole lives turned upside down. It took just a week for him to die. He was thirty.'

'I'm so sorry, Kieran,' she said. 'It must have been terribly hard for you.'

'Yes, it was. I was the youngest of three brothers and a sister. We had an elderly great aunt who lived off the Falls Road, a little back-to-back that you couldn't swing a cat round. She invited me ma and us to live with her. I guess she was lonely and she would always say we kids gave her a new lease on life. She died when I was fifteen and me ma got the house. By that time all of us were working.'

'So life became easier.'

'Financially, yes, but—'

'Politically, no.'

'How did you guess?'

'You were a Catholic living in the Falls Road area. It was the time of the Troubles. I read up on it when you mentioned it soon after we met.'

What did it matter now, thought the Irishman? If he told Magda the truth about himself, it might make her despise him and make it easier for her to accept his going away. She would probably be appalled to learn the truth.

Magda snuggled close to him and sought to change the subject. . 'I never saw the sea as a child, you know. Boating on the Danube was about as close as we got and it's making me feel *Heimweh*.'

'What's that?'

'Homesick.'

The very mention of the word was like a dagger in Kelly's heart. He missed his children so much and the fact that he might never see them again filled him with a deep melancholy. 'Magda,' he said quietly, 'there's something I have to tell you.'

She turned her head to look at him and even this slight movement caused a wave of pain to suffuse her lower limbs. The tone of his voice created a sense of foreboding that frightened her.

'There's no easy way to say this,' he said, already hating himself for the pain it would bring her. 'It's just that the kids miss me as much as I miss them. I *have* to return home.'

Magda took a deep breath. Knowing how close he was to his children, she had secretly dreaded this moment. She knew he loved her, but she also knew it was too soon for him to introduce her as a replacement for his children's mother. 'I understand, Kieran,' she said quietly. 'You need your space, time to think. Anyway, if it meant that you could only get away to visit me a few times a year, I would have to accept that. I love you, Kieran, with all my heart and soul. You know that, don't you?'

Ordinarily, her words would have found a positive response, but for Kieran Kelly the expression of her love instilled in him only unbearable guilt. Yet he knew only that he would have to be cruel to be kind. 'Magda,' he said, his voice almost breaking, 'I don't know whether we should see each other again.'

The Countess gasped, the hurt suddenly exacerbating the pins and needles cascading down her legs. She remained silent, unable to muster the words that would do justice to the desolation she felt. As if in response to his declaration, the lowering sky began to darken further and the rain to intensify.

'Is it because of my illness?'

'Yes,' he lied. 'I don't think I could cope a second time.'

'I understand,' she said simply.

'*Why* do you understand, Countess Magda von Esterhazy?' It was the first time he had raised his voice towards her. 'For God's sake, woman, be angry with me. Hate me, make it easy.'

She was frightened by his controlled vehemence. 'What can hate achieve,' she said quietly. 'I have no strength to hate.'

'I have more than enough hate for both of us. There's so little you know about me, Magda.'

'I only know what I see, a kind and loving man who has been torn apart by tragedy. My pain is physical and yours is mental, but it is still pain.'

'My pain is caused by injustice, Magda. It eats away at me like a cancer. I must have revenge.'

She smiled wanly. 'We have a saying in German: *Rache bringt keine Frucht*, revenge brings no fruit.'

'No, Magda, when justice fails, revenge is the only option, and its fruit tastes very sweet indeed. To my enemies I am nemesis.'

'What do you mean?' she asked, a twinge of apprehension knotting her stomach.

Dammit, thought Kelly, he had to tell her. Then maybe she would hate him enough to free him from the responsibility of hurting her. 'I am a killer, Magda,' he said almost in a whisper. 'A callous murderer to some and a hero to others.'

For a moment, Magda's mind went blank. Then it began to reel with the enormity of his confession. The heaviness in her heart plummeted still further. She was in love with a man about whom she had known so little, a man who had brought her to an ecstasy she believed she would never feel again. Yet now he was confessing to the worst of all sins. What demons he must be suffering, she thought, what torture.

Kelly held his head in his hands for a few moments, before looking into eyes whose hurt mirrored his own. 'Magda, I have executed seven men in cold blood,' he said baldly. 'Can you understand what it's like to look a man in the eyes and know that you are going to be responsible for snuffing out his life within the next few seconds?' There, it was out. Hate me, Magda. Hate me.

Despite the dreadful nature of his revelation, the Countess found herself strangely composed. It was as if a steel curtain had been lowered to prevent further hurt. She was intelligent enough to realise that the Irishman's actions had been politically motivated; that he had been an executioner for the IRA; that she would never be able to fight the twisted logic that people like him used to rationalise their appalling deeds. Cradling his face in her hands she gazed directly into his uneasy eyes. 'The Troubles are over, Kieran. Whatever the merits of your cause, there is peace now, a new beginning. Life goes on.'

'Life goes on,' he repeated bitterly, 'and one injustice gets replaced by another.'

'There will always be injustice, *liebling*, and no one can fight every war. Maybe it will be best for you to return home to your family. Perhaps you will find peace there.' The hollowness of her own words suddenly frightened her. She desperately wanted him not to leave her.

'Forget me, Magda. There's a contract out on my life. There are still plenty of people like me in Belfast even if the Troubles are over. But I must go back.'

'I don't want to hear any more. Take me home, Kieran,' she said with calm finality.

The rain had ceased and there was a break in the clouds, but not even the warmth of the sun could dispel their mutual despair.

172

CHAPTER FIFTEEN

The rain began to beat against his car even more vehemently as Jonathan Tring skidded to a halt outside the cottage, a lone sentinel in the middle of Cambridgeshire's brooding fens. The lowering skies were already beginning to darken as dusk approached, adding an air of the surreal to a location that was already famous for its witches, warlocks and other whimsies.

The wait for this moment had been almost unbearable for Tring. More than a week had passed since he had first tried to contact Derek Sutton, the erstwhile director of science at KleinKinloss. Abe Klein's comb through company records had discovered quite quickly that it was Sutton who had made an inordinate number of direct phone calls, three hundred and sixty-seven to be precise, to either the home or office of his opposite number at Parados Pharmaceuticals. The calls between Sutton and Martin Locke had begun seventeen months earlier, and it was reasonable to assume that this coincided with the beginning of the liaison that was cruelly cut short by Locke's untimely death.

Eager to quiz Sutton, the professor had immediately telephoned his fellow scientist, only to be told by his housekeeper that he was on holiday in Thailand. Sutton had probably been in the arms of some lady-boy in the back streets of Bangkok while the fate of his former employers hung in the balance. Nevertheless, all that had changed yesterday, when the inebriate had welcomed Tring's request for them to meet.

When Tring had informed Fiona Harrington of his intended visit, she had barely contained her excitement. She'd wanted to accompany him and it had taken all his powers of persuasion to convince her that he should act alone. If certain scientific papers were involved, then only he would be able to understand their relevance. As luck would have it, her parents' farm was less than twenty miles away and he had arranged to meet her there after his meeting with Sutton. She had already retreated there anyway in order to free herself of the pressure from an increasingly agitated Sharon Proctor.

As Tring rang the doorbell, he just hoped the old man was sober enough to be coherent.

'Hold on, I'm coming,' slurred a voice beyond the door. 'Just putting me slippers on.'

Rain dripping from the lintel bathed Tring's face as he waited patiently for Sutton to let him in. When the door finally opened, the professor gasped at the sight before him. The old man was in his pyjamas. They were grubby and soiled; although pristine by comparison to a face that was a mass of red blotches. The hooked purple-veined nose was almost incandescent and the beady eyes rheumy and baleful. The Thai lady-boys probably hadn't cared as long as the old man's money was good. Sutton's shock of white hair looked as if he had plugged himself into the nearest socket. In his right hand he held the requisite brandy glass. It was empty.

'Come in my friend,' Sutton gushed, 'come in. *Hic.*'

'My God, you're a state, Mr Sutton,' said Tring, entering premises that were clearly in need of renewed attention from the old boy's housekeeper. Tables and chairs lay on their sides, pillows and cushions lay scattered like confetti and the haberdashery was grubby and torn.

'Excuse the mess, excuse the mess,' Sutton repeated contritely. 'My housekeeper only comes Tuesdays. I haven't been feeling too well lately. How about a little drink? I'm sure you'll join me in a brandy, mister, er …'

'Baker – no thanks.'

'Baker,' Sutton mumbled and shuffled unsteadily towards a drinks cabinet that was already open. Bottles, most of them empty, stood gloomily on the opened shelf. Others lay on the floor where they had keeled over. Tring thought his host was about to do the same. 'Are you sure you're okay, Mr Sutton?' he asked with genuine concern.

'Call me Derek,' Sutton hiccupped as he poured himself a further large draught of Cognac. 'Ah, this is the staff of life,' the older man enthused, and downed the potion in one gulp. 'That's better, now what can I do you for?'

174

'As I told you on the phone, I'm a private investigator searching for the truth about your partner's death.'

Sutton slumped into an armchair. 'He was murdered, you know,' he said balefully, 'although you'll never prove it.'

'The Coroner recorded a verdict of suicide.'

'That's what I mean. That fuck Proctor was too clever for the police. Listen, my friend, if you want to get rid of someone cleanly, call in a calculating chemist from Castleford.' Sutton began to giggle. 'Hey, that's what they call an allit- an allit-'

'Alliteration.'

'Yeah, couldn't think of it for a mo'.'

'So what makes you believe Proctor had him killed?'

'Martin had something on that ugly bastard. He told me as much just before he died.'

'But he didn't give you any details.'

'No.'

'Try to think, Derek,' Tring said forlornly. It was the clear the man was in no state to exercise a brain addled by years of alcohol abuse.

Sutton stared morosely at his brandy glass. 'He was the best thing that ever happened to me,' he said with a melancholy that threatened to engulf him. 'I even went on the wagon.'

'Surely if you lived together, he must have given you a few clues.' Tring could sense the desperation in his own voice.

'We never lived together.'

'I don't understand.'

'We had a relationship, but we didn't live together. We both wanted it that way. We kept our relationship secret.'

'Why didn't you go to the police?'

'I couldn't come out of the closet. That Scotch shit Kinloss would have crucified me. Now it doesn't matter any more.'

Tring felt the icy fingers of disappointment knot his stomach. The shell that was before him was proving useless. 'Think, man,' he ordered with more than a hint of desperation. 'Did Locke leave you anything? Did he send you anything before he died?'

'I don't remember, old boy. *Hic.* Are you sure you don't want a brandy?'

'Surely he must have left you something in his will.'

'A cousin of his got the lot,' Sutton said without rancour. 'It doesn't matter any more, anyway.'

'Shit,' Tring muttered under his breath. Sutton looked like being a waste of time.

'Nice chap, his cousin. Knew Martin and I were into jazz, so he gave me all the CDs and cassettes. Said he couldn't stand jazz himself. I had my housekeeper stack them all in that display cabinet over there. Haven't even gone near them, though. Music doesn't matter anymore.' With this, Sutton picked up the bottle of brandy and seemed to down half of it in one long gulp.

'God, man,' thought Tring, 'what are you raving on about.' The professor didn't know why he moved over to the display. Perhaps it was just a natural inquisitiveness; the sort of thing one does when one enters the home of stranger, such as looking at photographs on the mantelpiece or perusing a bookshelf. He ran his eye almost peremptorily over the spines of the cassette boxes. There were three or four Charlie Parkers, a few Dizzy Gillespies and some Duke Ellingtons that immediately caught his eye. Some of the spines had writing on them; they obviously contained cassette copies of originals. Most of them were of musicians he'd never heard of. Tring was just about to turn away when the spine of a box near the bottom of the rack caught his attention. Written on it were the names 'Proctor & Sellars' His first instinct was to think what a coincidence it was that there was a jazz musician who had the same name as his tone-deaf boss. Then Tring's heart skipped a beat as the enormity of his discovery suddenly hit home. Stephen Sellars must be none other than the Secretary of State for Health.

The sound of alcohol-induced snoring suddenly punctured the professor's thrill of expectation. He looked round to see Sutton spark out in his armchair. He withdrew the cassette case and opened it. Inside was a min-cassette, the type used in a portable Dictaphone he always carried in his car, just in case he might come up with some inspirational new formula. Tring walked over to the old man, gently released the empty bottle from his grasp and straightened his head a little to make him more comfortable. 'God bless you, you old sop,' he muttered kindly, and quietly let himself out.

As Jonathan Tring reversed out of Sutton's driveway, furthest from his mind was the notion that his sleek company Mercedes SLK might host a tracking device and be wired for sound, or that his every move was being surveyed by a variety of people who did not have his best interests at heart.

'Bob, you and Trevor go into the house and grill them. Maximum coercion, minimum force. I don't want it messy unless it's absolutely necessary.' The voice of Jack Proctor boomed out its order to the occupants of one of two vehicles containing his henchmen. Meanwhile the chairman himself continued to keep his Roller a discreet distance from Tring's car, reassured by the ping-ping of the tracker and its on-board display module. Directly behind the Yorkshireman's Rolls Royce was an altogether different car, one more suited to pursuit along twisting country roads. The latest Porsche 911 was as mean as the men inside it. They were Jack Proctor's personal bodyguards, paid to cater to the chairman's whim when it came to matters of persuasion. The aptly named Bill and Ben were two Cockney ex-pugilists whose loyalty was in direct proportion to their salaries, and they were paid very well indeed.

'You've got the fix on him okay, Bill?' said Proctor.

'Yes, boss, mile ahead, straight.'

Proctor then turned his attention elsewhere. 'Ian, let me know as soon as you find out anything,' he told the man who was just about to press the doorbell of Derek Sutton's home. Mobile phone conferencing was a truly wonderful thing.

'They're not answering,' said the man named Ian after a few seconds. 'We'll have to force entry. Shouldn't be too hard.'

Proctor heard a crash and what seemed like the splintering of wood, then, after a few more seconds, a staccato of slapping sounds. 'The man's drunk, boss, paralytic. I can't even get him to wake up.'

'Shit,' Proctor cursed, 'stay with him until he sobers up. Look around and see if you can find out anything about him from his papers.'

At that moment, Proctor came within range of picking up the microphone in Tring's car. He was surprised at suddenly hearing his own voice. 'I'm going off air for a few minutes,' he screamed at his minions and switched off his mobile in order to concentrate.

PROCTOR: ..put the word in with the agency, Stephen?
SELLARS: Are you sure it's safe to talk, Jack?
PROCTOR: Safe as aspirin (loud laugh).
SELLARS: They'll pass it, don't you worry. Just don't let there be another fuck-up like Triamerol.
PROCTOR: You worry too much, Stephen. They'll never get us to court on that one. Anyway, as far as the agency's concerned, the new drug'll be okay. No comebacks, don't you worry, my lad.
SELLARS: Did you, er, make the payment?
PROCTOR: You'll be a much richer man by Thursday.
SELLARS: I don't like talking about it.
PROCTOR: But you like getting it.
SELLARS: I wish you wouldn't talk like that, Jack.
PROCTOR: We both know you can't live on a ministerial salary today, Stephen. Every man has his price. You're just more expensive than most, that's all.
SELLARS (nervous): Must go, Jack. Another call.
PROCTOR: Give my regards to the gnomes in Zurich, Stephen (loud laugh).

For the first time in his life, Jack Proctor felt naked, exposed. His jowls quivered as the rage within him began to mount. He had been betrayed, by who did not matter – for now. He had to have that recording, at any price. He was just about to send in his dogs when he heard the sound of Tring's voice.

TRING: Hello, Fiona.
FIONA: Jonathan, how goes it?
TRING: Jackpot!
FIONA: What do you mean?
TRING: Locke sent Sutton a tape. It's damning.'
FIONA: For God's sake tell me, will you.
TRING: Jack Proctor and Stephen Sellars.

FIONA: I knew it!
TRING: Proctor bribed Sellars to influence the Medical Controls Agency. Stay on the line and I'll play you the tape.

'Fuck those bastards!' Proctor screamed to the roof of his Rolls. He quickly dialled his heavies. 'Bill,' he growled, 'move in now. He's got a cassette tape I want. Make it look like an accident.' The chairman slowed slightly as the Porsche sped by him. 'Make it good lads, make it good.'

Jonathan Tring had just concluded his conversation with Fiona and switched off his hands-free mobile when he noticed the lights of a car behind him. It was almost eerie that he had driven thus far without seeing another vehicle. Not that it surprised him much for the night was so bleak that anyone in his or her right mind would be tucked in front of the television up with a hot totty. The monotonous tone of the wipers accentuated the brooding loneliness of driving across the Fens. If anything, the rain was lashing down even harder. The replay of the conversation ended quickly and Fiona's excited voice came through loud and clear.

'Fantastic, darling! We've finally got them. How long will it take you to get here?'

'Half an hour, probably. The weather's crap, and I don't want to drive too fast along these winding lanes.'

'I'll have a whisky mac waiting for you.'

'Okay. I'll tell you the full story when I get there. Bye, love.'

'Bye – oh, Jonathan.'

'Yes.'

'Be careful.'

'Everything's okay, I promise.'

'I'll play the recording over to my answer phone at work as soon as you arrive.'

'Yeah, we'll make a few copies, just in case. I'd love to see Proctor's face when he reads about this in your paper and hears his voice on the ten o'clock news.

'Jonathan?'

179

'Yes?'
'I love you.'
'I love you, too. You know that.'
'Bye, darling.'
'Bye.'
Tring switched off his mobile, and with the vision of his lover in his mind, stepped a little more firmly on the accelerator. The Mercedes glided around a bend and for a brief moment the following headlights disappeared. When they next came in sight he was startled to see the car right up his backside. The headlights were then flashed continuously, not something somebody would do if he wanted to overtake. Tring's first instinct was to believe it might be a police car, so he slowed. But then fear gripped the pit of his stomach. What if Proctor were on to him? He didn't know what made him do it, but he ejected the cassette, leaned forward and placed it in his sock just above the left ankle. He then switched to full headlights and gunned the SLK forward.

Jack Proctor could only watch in dismay as the tracker signal indicated his prey was speeding up. The urgent voice of his Cockney henchman cut through on the mobile.
    'He's taken off like a fuckin' bat out o' hell, boss.'
    'Catch him, you fools. Don't let him get away or you're both fucking history.' With this, Proctor too began to accelerate, although the Rolls was soon complaining about the sharpness of some of the bends. Normally cool under pressure and self-reliant, the Yorkshireman began feeling the twinge of fear that came whenever he delegated responsibility to others. Failure could mean the collapse of his empire, everything that he had worked for all his life. Various rationalisations flooded his mind. Firstly, Tring had to be stopped at all costs. Fiona Harrington had heard the incriminating evidence, but she had no case without that tape. That shit Locke had sold him down the river. The irony was that he had had nothing to do with the man's death. Who knew what demons had possessed him to top himself, but it was unlikely to have involved money, for Locke would have known the value of that tape to his ex-boss. Then again, some people were incapable of blackmail; they just

didn't have the bottle. He also knew that he would be pissing in the wind if he tried to negotiate a deal with the likes of Tring and Fiona Harrington. Investigative reporters were single-minded buggers who would sell their souls for a scoop and, anyway, his chief scientist was besotted with the girl.

The chairman of Parados Pharmaceuticals also knew that if the tape saw the light of day, it would be the end of his marriage. He was under no illusion that Sharon would abandon him as soon as there was a sniff of ruination in the air. His Southern Belle could be as manipulative and as ruthless as anyone in business, but she would never countenance corruption of a Government Minister, or for that fact murder.

'Bastards,' Jack Proctor growled, 'they're all bastards.'

Jonathan Tring felt his heart pounding as he negotiated the next bend at high speed. He couldn't afford to take his eyes off the road ahead for a fraction of a second, and if he took a hand off the wheel in order to dial Fiona, or 999, he might lose control.

'Jesus!' he screamed as he swerved to narrowly avoid a pair of glowing animal eyes that came up on him like a hazard in an arcade game. Dammit, he was a rugby player, not a Grand Prix driver. And it wasn't a Sony Playstation he was driving either. The lane was so narrow that Tring felt that unless his pursuers intended to blow him off the road with shotguns, they couldn't hope to force him to a stop. The question was how long he could keep up this speed and also how far it would be before the road might widen and present them with an overtaking opportunity. He didn't know this countryside that well, and for the first time it dawned on him that he had lost all sense of direction. He'd probably missed the turn that would take him to Fiona's. Then again, she would be the last person he would endanger, and to expect a police car to suddenly appear and come to his rescue was the stuff of fiction. For the first time he felt a fear that was almost sickening in its intensity.

With thoughts of doom racing through his mind, the professor fought to regain his concentration. Raindrops were now pounding on his windscreen like demented hobgoblins with pickaxes. There was no way he could keep this up for much longer. Mesmerised by the brooding black shapes of the hedgerows flashing past him, it was a good half-minute before he realised that the lights behind him had disappeared. The scientist could scarcely believe that he was alone again. He drove on for a few more seconds at about sixty miles an hour, before slowing down to about forty. His whole body gradually began to relax. The nerve endings that had hitherto tingled with adrenaline began to suffuse him with warmth that was as debilitating as it was comforting. He felt totally spent and suddenly became aware of the damp caused by his sweat on the leather seat. His pursuer must have been some crazy country yokel who'd decided to play games with him. They said the Fens had a weird effect on people.

Tring slowed almost to a halt and was just about to hit the buttons on his mobile to call Fiona when blinding lights suddenly appeared from his right and forced his car, almost in slow motion, into a nearside ditch. The minor impact did little more than propel him sideways onto the front passenger seat. The element of surprise was so great and angle of his posture so acute that he found himself totally disorientated. By the time he fought free of the seatbelt, the front door had been opened and professor Jonathan Tring found himself facing a man in a balaclava. In the man's right hand was a gun.

'He's stopped dead, boss. We've got him now, the fuckin' arse'ole.'

Jack Proctor felt the blood drain back into his body. Cockney villains had their virtues, after all. He then heard the sound of a strange voice from the microphone in Tring's Mercedes.

'Get out of the car quietly, Professor Tring, and we won't hurt you. Do anything stupid and you're a dead man.'

The chairman of Parados suddenly felt the blood drain to his feet.

The voice was Irish.

There was little that Jonathan Tring could do other than comply with the gunman. His car was in a ditch, so a getaway was out of the question. The pistol in the man's hand was also extremely persuasive. As the professor struggled to get out of his car, he felt the strong arms of another man grab him and haul him upright. Within seconds his hands had been cuffed behind his back and plaster stuck over his mouth. For a moment the eyes of the man holding the gun sparkled blue in the headlights. Those eyes, cold and impersonal, were the last things Tring saw before a blindfold plunged him into darkness.

'Can you breathe, okay?' asked the man with the gun.

Tring nodded.

'Okay, get him in the car.'

Tring felt the splatter of rain on his head as he was led into his attacker's vehicle. The smell of the upholstery told him that it must have been a fairly new model. He was aware of a man sitting beside him, but it was the voice of the man who held the gun that he heard next. It was in front and to his left. That meant there was a third man, the driver.

'Now, Professor,' said the gunman in an accent that was clearly northern Irish, 'from now on you don't speak without permission. Is that clear?'

Tring nodded.

'It's a big vehicle, Professor, so feel free to have a lie down.'

With this, Tring felt a tug on his sleeve and then his hair. He tried to shout 'ouch' but it just came out as a muffled moan.

'My, you're a big lad,' came the voice again. 'I'm afraid it's not going to be too comfortable, so we're going to give you a little something to help you relax.'

Tring suddenly felt a sharp stab in his thigh. He gave another muffled moan and almost immediately felt himself being suffused by a welcoming warmth. Blackness swiftly followed.

Fiona Harrington was beside herself with worry. She'd tried repeatedly to raise Tring on his mobile. He had said half an hour max, and yet ninety minutes had gone by and he still hadn't arrived.

'Might have broken down, love,' her father said comfortingly. 'If you like, I'll go out and look for him.'

'No, dad, if his car had broken down, he would have called me right away.'

'Unless…'

'Unless he's had an accident.' The sound of her own words shook her to the core. It was the first time she had enunciated her fears. Perhaps

Jonathan was lying broken and bleeding in some godforsaken country lane. Visions of mutilation and even death flashed through her mind. Then the bulldog spectre of Jack Proctor appeared. She couldn't help thinking that the ruthless Yorkshireman was behind whatever had happened, especially now that she knew Martin Locke's secret.

'Shall we call the police, love?'

'I think it's time,' she said quietly. She moved towards the phone in the lounge when it suddenly rang. She picked up the receiver.

'Is that six-seven-three-five-one and is your name Fiona?' asked an officious voice.

'Yes,' she answered apprehensively. 'Who's that?'

'Police Constable Brian Little, Miss.'

'Oh, my God, what's happened?'

'Presumably you know the driver of a Mercedes SLK, reg. number PAR 3 and owned by Parados Pharmaceuticals.

'Jonathan,' she half-screamed, 'what's happened to him?'

'We've found his car abandoned in a ditch, Miss. We found a cell phone still inside. Yours was the last number he dialled. What relation is he to you?'

'He's my boyfriend.'

'What are his full name, address and date of birth?'

Fiona gave Tring's details and thanked the officer for his help.

'Strange that he left his mobile phone in the car, Miss. He doesn't appear to have called the emergency services or the AA. The car is hardly damaged and there are no signs of blood inside. He might have got a knock on the head and wandered off somewhere. We'd like you to come to the car's location if at all possible, or we can send someone to collect you.'

'Of course, officer, of course. I'll come in my own car. It'll be quicker.'

The policeman then proceeded to give her the details. 'Are you sure you know where it is, Miss?'

'No problem, I'm a local girl. It'll take me about twenty minutes.'

'We'll see you in twenty minutes, then.'

Fiona replaced the receiver, her mind racing with ideas. If Jonathan had indeed been abducted, then the tape might still be in the car. The police would hardly think that CDs and cassette tapes could have any relevance.

If that bastard Proctor was behind it, then the tape might prove a useful bargaining chip. 'What am I thinking about,' she chided herself under her breath, 'this whole thing is preposterous.'

'Who was that, Fiona?' Bill Harrington asked with growing concern.

'Police, Dad,' she said donning her hat and coat. 'You hold the fort. Jonathan may have been in some kind of accident. Nothing serious. Don't worry, I'll be back soon.' She kissed him and swept out of the front door. Thankfully, the rain had stopped and the cloud had cleared enough to allow a full moon to cast its silvery aura over the countryside.

Fiona Harrington knew the Fenland roads like the back of her hand and in less than twenty minutes she had drawn up alongside the abandoned Mercedes. There was neither hide nor hair of the police. She opened the car's offside door and peered inside. Almost choking with emotion, she first checked the cassette player and then other possible receptacles for the damning tape. She withdrew Tring's driving gloves from their box, stared at them for a few seconds and then sniffed the lining. The faint lingering odour of him made her feel even more desperate.

'I wouldn't bother if I were you?'

The gruff Cockney voice behind her came as such a surprise that she bumped her head on the door frame as she hauled herself out of the car. Standing before her was a brute of a man.

'My boss would like a word with you, Miss Harrington.'

With this the man grabbed her arm and roughly pulled her towards some headlights that had suddenly been switched on. It was only when she was a yard or two from it that she saw that the car was a Rolls Royce bearing the registration number PAR 1. Jack Proctor's wagon.

'You're hurting me,' she cried as the man opened the nearside front door of the Rolls.

'Fiona, my dear,' came the familiar Yorkshire growl from the driver's side. 'How nice to see you.' With this, Proctor's heavy pushed her into the front seat.

'Bill, you follow in her car and let Ben drive the Porsche.'

'Right, boss,' said the man named Bill and firmly closed the door of the Rolls.

'Where's Jonathan, you bastard?' hissed Fiona, surprised at the sudden fearlessness in her own voice.'

'I wish I knew.'

'Don't fuck with me, Jack. You're not here just by coincidence.'

Jack Proctor smiled as he accelerated the Rolls away.

'You won't get away with this, Jack, the police – '

'You're referring of course to Constable Brian Little. My man did a pretty good impersonation, don't you think, lass?'

'What have you done with Jonathan?'

Proctor took a deep breath. 'Look lass, why don't *you* tell *me.*'

'What do you mean?'

'Maybe you faked his disappearance because of that tape.'

'So you know about the tape?'

Proctor spent the next few minutes relating to her details of his various surveillance techniques and how he had heard the Irishman taking Tring hostage, then, 'so you see, I wouldn't be wasting my time with you now if I had the tape, would I?'

Fiona could see the logic of Proctor's argument. As far as they both knew, there was only one copy of that tape and there was no knowing where it was now or with whom.

'Look, lass, I admit I was tailing your boy friend.'

'You would have killed him, wouldn't you?'

'Not necessarily, not if I had that tape. Without it you haven't got a case. You wouldn't be able to prove a thing.'

'Why don't I believe you, Jack?'

'All that's redundant now, my girl. All we both want to know is where the hell is Jonathan Tring.'

'I assure you, Jack, I don't have the faintest idea and I intend to inform the police – the real police – right away.'

Proctor sniggered. 'You're assuming I intend to let you go.'

For the umpteenth time that evening, Fiona Harrington felt the icy grip of fear. She knew Jack Proctor was capable of anything in order to protect his interests.

'So, let's continue this conversation, shall we. Who, my dear, are our prime suspects? Maybe Abe Klein or that Scotch shit Kinloss who now works for me. Blackmail is the sort of game he *would* play.'

'And see the value of his share options disappear. I don't think so, Jack. And Klein would never stoop to anything this low.'

'Then who?'

'I said I don't know. One thing is for sure though – '

'Yes?'

'Unless that tape reappears, I can't write a thing about you or your nefarious deeds.'

Proctor smiled. 'That's why I'm going to let you go, lass.'

Fiona Harrington felt a surge of relief as Proctor brought the Rolls to a halt. The pug-face turned towards her. His voice was sad, almost poignant.

'For the first time, Fiona, I'm not in control of my own destiny. Both you and I will have to hope and pray, but for opposite things. There's never owt for nowt in this world. There's always a payback.'

'You shouldn't have done the things you did, Jack. You could have made it without all that corruption.'

'Don't be so naïve, lass. There isn't a major pharmaceutical company in the world that hasn't corrupted itself in the search for profits. It's the name of the game.'

'And you've lost.'

'Not yet, lass, not yet.' With this, Proctor motioned for her to step out of the Rolls. 'By the way,' he added, 'Sharon doesn't know the ins and outs of all this. She's feeling betrayed by you, as it is. Just leave her alone, will you.'

Fiona nodded and closed the door of the Rolls Royce behind her.

'Your keys, Miss,' hissed the brute that was now standing before her.

She took them from him and, feeling more alone and desperate than ever, walked towards her car at the rear of the convoy. As she pulled out, she heard the thug call out sarcastically, 'drive carefully.'

CHAPTER SIXTEEN

Jonathan Tring felt as if his body weighed a ton and his head had been crushed by a stampede of rogue elephants. It was a good few minutes before he was savvy enough to be aware of his surroundings. The first thing he realised was that his mouth was stuck fast and that breathing through his nose was uncomfortable. His first instinct was to try to remove the offensive plaster, a move thwarted instantly by the fact that his hands were tied behind his back. Lying on his left side on a mattress, he twisted his body to peer at the rope that was binding his legs. Lying close to them on the parquet floor, like a nest of resting snakes, were two sets of chains and shackles. There was what he guessed was a bucket for slops. A window set in ochre-coloured walls was about two eight feet away. Rolling over onto his right, he was greeted by another set of shackles and chains. A white door was about twelve feet away. Apart from the mattress, the bucket and the arresting metalwork, the rest of the room was bare. It was only when he looked up into the far corner that he noticed a small CCTV camera. It suddenly dawned on him that with all this paraphernalia, his captors intended for his stay to be a lengthy one. But why? What on earth could Proctor's henchmen hope to gain by this? Why not just kill him and be done with it?

It was only then that the professor remembered the tiny cassette nestling between sock and skin just above his right ankle. They hadn't found it and they *must* not find it. It might prove his only trump card. If their intention was to kill him, then he could only hope that they would dump his body where it, and the incriminating tape, could be found. Overcome by morbid thoughts, he imagined Fiona standing stoically at his funeral in a windswept Fenland graveyard, her garments billowing like some black Bedouin tent; his brother looking on completely crestfallen; the church bell ringing balefully as he watched his coffin being lowered into the ground; earth hitting the coffin lid. The came a vision of the Pit bull hovering over Fiona with malevolent intent, willing to torture her for information about her meddlesome boyfriend. He rolled once more onto his left side and tried in vain to slip back into a kind of semi-consciousness that might release him from this nightmare. Immersed in his own black thoughts, he failed to notice that someone had entered the room.

'Penny for your thoughts, Professor,' came an Irish voice.

It took a few seconds for Tring to register that he was no longer alone. He slowly rolled over. A shortish figure wearing a balaclava stood before him, his right hand resting on the back of a wooden chair. The scientist stared at the hand, which appeared to be inside some sort of surgical glove.

'Oh, I forgot,' said the man with a giggle, 'you can't answer, can you?' He moved towards his captive and struggled to get him to his feet. 'My, you're a big one, ain't you?'

Tring swayed groggily, trying in vain to make some kind of intelligible response.

'Now,' said balaclava-man, 'just do as I say and you won't get hurt. I want you to drape your body over the back of that chair and rest your chest on the rim.'

Tring did as he was told, although the position was uncomfortable, especially if he tried to raise his head to stare out of the window.

'Okay,' the Irishman said. 'He's ready.'

Jonathan Tring heard the door open and another man enter the room.

'Hold it like that,' came the man's voice. It was both familiar and threatening.

Tring then heard footsteps as the man passed his chair and stood between him and the window. Craning his neck, the scientist was surprised to see that the man before him did not wear the ubiquitous balaclava. He was of above average height, probably in his early thirties and with jet-black hair and piercing blue eyes. The slight hook to the nose gave masculinity to features that were otherwise finely drawn. Around the man's neck hung two cameras and in his right hand was a pistol.

'Polaroid and digital video,' said the man as if reading his thoughts. The voice was the same as he remembered when he had first been abducted. Proctor seemed to like hiring Irishmen to do his dirty work.

'Now just stare up at me. Try not to blink at the light. I want those eyes of yours wide open. Look scared.'

That shouldn't be too hard, thought Tring, his attempt at a wry smile stifled by the tape. His handsome captor then clicked the Polaroid.

'Just a few seconds with the camcorder, my friend, and that'll do nicely.'

The scientist began to feel close to collapse with the strain and was relieved when a rough pair of arms hauled him off the chair rim and guided him over to the mattress. While balaclava-man began untying the rope around his wrists, Tring peered up at the other protagonist facing him. A pistol was in the man's hand.

'Don't even think about it,' said the man laconically.

Once his hands were free, the scientist felt a welcome rush of blood back into his sore wrists.

'Now strip,' ordered balaclava-man.

Tring muffled a protest.

'Down to your underwear,' said camera-man. 'We'll at least grant you that dignity.'

'And your socks. You can keep them on as well,' said balaclava-man. 'We don't want you catching a cold now, do we?'

Tring's first thought was that they were bound to find the tiny cassette. Undressing slowly, he managed to manoeuvre it round to rest against his lower calf. Balaclava-man then grabbed hold of his captive's right wrist and, after unclasping the expensive Dunhill watch, clamped a shackle around it. He locked the shackle and removed the key. The man then proceeded to clamp Tring's left wrist, followed quickly by his legs. The scientist's stomach knotted as his jailer grabbed his right heel in order to clamp the ankle, but balaclava-man was so intent on his task that he failed to notice the slight bulge caused by the mini-cassette. With a silent sigh of relief, the professor squirmed to rest his naked back against the wall. The man with the cameras lowered his gun and leant towards him. Tring flinched, as the sticky tape was torn from his mouth in one swift movement.

'Now, my friend,' said camera-man in a voice that commanded respect, 'just remember that you are never to speak unless given permission, otherwise the tape goes back on.'

Camera-man turned to leave and then suddenly halted. 'Oh, I almost forgot,' he said swivelling to face his captive. He pressed a button on the Polaroid and the picture whirred out. He waited a few seconds and then tore off the backing paper. 'Hmm, nice one. You look good, Professor. I'm sure you'll appreciate it. In fact, it's so good I'll leave it with you.'

Tring stared at the photograph. In it, his eyes truly reflected the fear that he felt; only now it became apparent just why, for behind him stood balaclava-man with a raised syringe in one hand and a drug phial in the other.

'Triamerol, just in case you were wondering,' said camera-man. 'You know all about that, Professor, don't you, especially if it hits the arachnoid membrane?'

'But—'

'Shh, Professor, not a word, remember.'

Fiona Harrington looked squarely into the eyes of the stocky country bumpkin standing before and said firmly, 'I know he's been abducted, Inspector.'

'You say, Miss, that you received a call from Professor Tring saying he was being chased by another car.'

'Yes,' she lied, 'he told me this on his mobile. I could hear the screeching of tyres and then the connection went down. That was the last I heard from him. Anyway, you found his car abandoned in that ditch. You know all this. I told it all to the first copper who questioned me. For God's sake, it's been almost twenty-four hours since Jonathan went missing.'

Detective Inspector Keith Barnard bit hard on the stem of his pipe. The thing was an anachronism he used solely as an aid to thinking. Anyway, smoking was an evil habit he'd given up years ago. 'We've got every available man on this, Miss,' he said importantly.

'You mean the one man and his dog at the local nick.'

'Look, Miss,' the policeman drawled, trying hard to disregard her facetiousness, 'don't you think it might be a bit early to assume the worst?'

'No, I don't, Inspector. My boyfriend has been abducted and if you don't believe me, then read the newspapers in the morning.'

'Okay, so let's assume – er, say – he's been abducted. Who by and for what reason?'

'How should I know, probably something to do with his work.'

'Did he ever say to you that he might be in some danger?'

'No.'

'What was he working on?'

'You'd better ask his boss?'

'We already have.'

Fiona's raised eyebrows begged an answer. She was intrigued by how the Proctors would handle an incident in which they were so closely involved.

'Mr Proctor said he'd had a few crank calls recently from some anti-vivisectionists. Said the voices were Irish.'

'Irish?'

'Yes, although that doesn't mean much nowadays. There's more Irish living here than in Ireland.'

'So what do you intend to do, Inspector?'

'We'll have to go through the phone records. The company's, Tring's … and yours, of course.'

'Be my guest,' Fiona said, her mind still racing with the revelation about Animal Rights activists. Somehow, the whole idea just didn't gel.

The Inspector put the empty pipe in his pocket. The time had come for him to get personal. 'Miss Harrington, I'm afraid I'm going to have to ask you some questions about your relationship with Professor Tring. It's necessary, I'm afraid.'

'To eliminate me from your list of possible suspects?'

'Well, if you put it so bluntly. You know the score, after all, you're an investigative journalist, aren't you?'

For the first time Fiona Harrington felt uneasy. If the police found out she was working on a story to expose Parados Pharmaceuticals, they might see an ulterior motive lurking somewhere in her relationship with Jonathan and direct their investigation down the wrong channels. It was important not to reveal even a trace of culpability. 'Fire away, Inspector,' she said firmly.

For the next hour, Fiona Harrington fielded Barnard's questions as best she could. Thankfully, there was no mention of any investigation into Parados, but she reckoned it might be just a matter of time before they found out.

Apart from mealtimes and the emptying of his slops bucket, Tring was left alone to reflect on his predicament. The meals were nutritious, if a little bland, and were brought to him by balaclava-man. There had not even been a hint of the torture suggested by the photograph, and he reckoned around twenty-four hours had elapsed since his abduction. The shackles were annoying, but were infinitely preferable to the ropes that had cut into his wrists and ankles. He had been dying to ask questions of balaclava-man but was dissuaded by fear of the return of the mouth plaster. He almost thought it would be a relief to see Jack Proctor walk through the door. At least then he might be allowed to find out what the Pit bull wanted of him.

For most of his waking hours, Tring had thought about how Fiona would be coping. She must have been beside herself with worry when he didn't show after his phone call. He reckoned she would have called the police immediately and given them the full story of Proctor and his machinations. His boss would have denied everything of course, but there was no smoke without fire and the police would be forced to look into every nook and cranny of Proctor's alibi. The scientist thought it strange, that his captors had not mentioned one word about why he was there. As for location, he didn't know whether he was in a residential building or a factory or, indeed, where he was in the United Kingdom. The threat of using Triamerol was intriguing. He knew the effects of injecting it in the wrong place would be catastrophic, but why Triamerol particularly? Perhaps it was just Proctor's sick sense of humour.

Suddenly, Tring was shaken from his morbid thoughts by a commotion coming from below. He heard the words 'stop yer fuckin' struggling, you bastard' being shouted by balaclava-man followed by the sound of clumping boots on a staircase. There were a few muffled grunts from what appeared to be an adjacent room, followed by the familiar sound of chains and shackles. It didn't take a brain surgeon to figure out that he was no longer the only captive in the building.

Stephen Sellars was in a hurry to get home. It had been a gruelling day at the Department, made none the better by news of the abduction of Proctor's man. The Yorkshireman had had the temerity to ring him at the office and rant on about his fears that something untoward was about to happen to them both. The nerve of the man! There were eavesdroppers everywhere at Richmond House and two plus two usually made four where he came from. He had cut Proctor short and told him he would stop off at a public telephone box on the way home to discuss the events with him. It was already quite late and he would probably have to face a barrage from Linda when he got home. She didn't take kindly to resurrecting yet another burnt offering in the kitchen. There was, however, one advantage to leaving Whitehall late in that he missed the God-awful rush-hour traffic. If he left the office at a 'normal' time it might take him two hours to reach home, but travel time could be cut in half if he left the after seven. He preferred motorways, picking up the westbound M4 at Chiswick, then onto the M25 at West Drayton and off again at junction 16 for the M40. It would then take him a few minutes to reach the turnoff that eventually led to his palatial bungalow off the Amersham road. Some days he took an overcrowded train, but he preferred the car. Travel at a reasonable speed on an empty motorway meant that he could mull over the events of the day in cocooned seclusion. Apart from Proctor's hyperactive intervention, it had been an extremely good day. The Prime Minister had hinted that he was preparing to groom his obedient servant to be his successor. 'You've done an excellent job at Health, Stephen,' the PM had said. 'I don't want a third term and I'm looking towards someone who is popular with the public. Anyone who can take on the poisoned chalice of your Ministry and still remain popular has more than an even chance.' He had thanked the PM for his support and said he would do everything in his power to justify his leader's faith. He could have telephoned Linda with the exciting news, but he wanted to save it for a bedtime story. The promise of ultimate power would prove a powerful aphrodisiac.

The drizzle had ceased and a full moon could be seen breaking through the clouds by the time the Secretary of State for Health drew his Volvo up alongside a telephone box in a village that was just a short detour from his main route home. He just hoped Proctor would not delay him too long. The gruff Yorkshireman on the other end of the line sounded agitated.

'Stephen, is that you?'

'Yes, Jack. *Now* what's up?'

'I wish I knew, Stephen, but I don't like it.'

'Look, Jack, I'm sorry this has happened to one of your men, but there must be a rational explanation as to why anyone would want to abduct him. Was there a new drug he was working on? Maybe it was over a lover's tiff or something. You know how those things can get out of hand.'

'No lover's tiff, Stephen.'

'What do you mean?'

'You mean you don't know?'

'Know what, man, stop talking in riddles.'

'He knows about us.'

Stephen Sellars turned cold, the icy grip of fear beginning to tie his stomach in knots. 'How?' he croaked.

'He has a tape.'

'Oh my God, Jack, you and your big mouth.'

'And I thought – '

'You thought maybe I had something to do with it, you bastard.'

'Well it damn well wasn't me, Stephen, and there's no need to get abusive, my lad.'

'You'd better explain, Jack.'

'Not over the phone. I'll see you at the golf club tomorrow, midday.

The Health Secretary suddenly became aware of a tapping on the pane of the booth. Ten o'clock at night in a deserted village and there was a queue to use the phone. Ridiculous. 'Okay, Jack, got to go. I'll see you tomorrow.'

Sellars' mind was such a hotchpotch as he hung up the telephone that he failed to hear Proctor's parting admonition: 'be careful, Stephen, be very careful.'

Sharon Proctor was apoplectic. 'Jack, you're a fucking idiot,' she fumed. 'You're so busy bugging everyone else that you can't even imagine them doing the same to you.'

'But I –'

'But nothing. You fouled up big time, buddy. If that tape is ever made public, we're all washed up.'

Jack Proctor had sworn he would never tell his wife what had happened, but now he had poured out his heart to her. What could he do? He'd felt the loneliest man in the world and he desperately needed the support of the only woman he had ever loved.

'Maybe they'll just want money, my dear.'

'These guys ain't Chechen terrorists, Jack. Anyway, if they knew about that damned tape, they would have had it by now. Presumably it was still in the car when they stopped Tring. Maybe they listened to it and it didn't mean a damn thing to them.'

'Tring would have told them. He had nothing to lose.'

'He had plenty to lose,' she said.

'What do you mean?'

'His life. Maybe they killed Tring, dumped his body and then played the tape. There are a thousand and one scenarios.'

'Maybe the police found the tape, my dear.'

'Bullshit. That hillbilly cop who came to see us didn't have a clue.'

'I just don't understand it.'

'There's a lot you don't understand, Jack.'

'What do you mean, Sharon?' Proctor queried, his voice quavering.

Sharon Proctor's eyes narrowed in contempt. She didn't need to go down with a sinking ship. She hadn't clawed her way from the back of the freight yards in Savannah to the high society of a European capital for nothing. If Jack Proctor was heading for the jailhouse, she sure as hell wasn't planning to join him. 'If you're stupid enough to bribe a government Minister, then you can go to the devil – alone.'

'You wouldn't leave me,' Proctor said, scared by the doubt in his own voice.

'God knows what the Parados empire will be worth if the truth comes out, but at least I'd be entitled to half of it. I sweated just as much as you did, Jack. The company means everything to me, and you go and jeopardise everything with your damn stupid mouth.'

'We're in this together, my love,' Proctor said meekly.

So that was it, she thought. Her good husband was planning to take her down with him. He would try to implicate her, try to make out that she was a corrupting influence, the reason why he did what he did. 'You bastard,' she seethed.

'I won't let you leave me without a fight, lass,' Jack Proctor threatened unconvincingly. 'You're all I've got.' The chairman of Parados Pharmaceuticals already felt a beaten man, his whole world crumbling around him. He could take anything from any man, but he could not take his wife's scorn.

Sharon Proctor finally lost the self-control that had guided her through the barren years of her sham marriage. 'You're a pitiful motherfucker, Jack,' she hissed, slipping into the vernacular of the trackside urchins of Savannah. 'You're an old man with a limp dick. You talk a good game, Jack, but you can't cut the mustard.'

'Stop it,' he cried. 'Stop it.'

But Sharon Proctor had no intention of stopping. Years of pent-up frustration were about to be vented in a way that she knew would destroy him, for nothing could hurt a jealous man more than the knowledge of his wife's infidelity.

'I fucked them all, Jack,' she hissed contemptuously.

'What do you mean?'

'All your friends, I fucked each and every one of them. They laughed at you behind your back because they knew they'd had the one thing you prized above all else – me.'

Jack Proctor slumped deeper into the dralon armchair, hoping that somehow it would swallow him up. He covered his ears, 'Stop, Sharon, stop.'

'Look at me, Jack!' she thundered. 'Look at me!'

He looked up at his exquisitely beautiful wife with the anxious eyes of a submissive lap dog. 'I'll do anything you want,' he quivered, 'anything.'

'There's nothing more you can do for me, Jack Proctor. I put up with your petty jealousies and your intrigues for years. Sure I married you for your money, but I was just a trophy wife. I looked good on your arm, Jack, that's all.'

'But I love you, Sharon. Don't do this to me.'

'Love!' she spat, 'you don't know the meaning of the word.'

'Tell me you're lying about those other men,' he pleaded.

'Your fucking ego, that's all you care about. Don't worry, I was selective in who I chose to service me. They had to be tall and lean and with dicks the size of baseball bats. Oh, and I almost forgot. You remember your birthday, the fancy dress party? I fucked Jonathan Tring. I fucked him so hard, his powdered wig nearly blew off.'

With this, the statuesque Sharon Proctor turned on her heels and stormed out of the room. Whether the incriminating tape surfaced or not, her marriage was over.

CHAPTER SEVENTEEN

'I can't thank you enough,' Kelly told the two men slumped exhausted in armchairs before him. 'You're to take the first available flight back to Belfast. It's my show from here on in.'

'How are you going to cope, Kieran?' the shorter man asked. 'There's three of them to take care of. You can't manage on your own.'

'Sean, I promised you and Gerry that once I had these bastards in chains, you were free to go.'

'But if the police know there's just you here, they'll be more likely to storm the place.'

'There's no reason they should believe that I'm on my own. Anyway, I can't go wrong, can I.'

'What do you mean?' Callaghan queried.

'Well, I've got everything I need in-house,' said Kelly, smiling. 'If I feel ill I can visit the doctor, if I need a pill I can go to the chemist and if I need advice on how to lie to the police, I've got the politician.'

The three of them laughed, a welcome break in the tension that had enveloped them in the last few days.

'When do you intend to go public?' Gerry O'Connor asked.

'As soon as you and Sean are safely back home. Now are you two sure your alibis are watertight?'

O'Connor nodded, 'I'll get the first Ryanair flight out of Stansted in the morning, Kieran. God bless you.' If the truth was known, he couldn't wait to get out of there. Friendship and loyalty was one thing, suicide was another. Kelly was in a no-win situation. Even if the whole affair ended peaceably, his comrade would probably get life imprisonment. He suspected that Kelly planned to go out in a blaze of glory, taking some members of the establishment with him. The British government would not take lightly the kidnap and incarceration of one of its own. The might of the authorities would be brought to bear on this little cottage, but then so would the eyes of the world.

'I suggest, Sean, that you get the flight after Gerry's,' Kelly said, turning to Callaghan for confirmation. He would miss them both, especially the wiry older man. There was an endearing quality about Callaghan. He was the kindest of men to his friends and that was all that mattered.

'I'm not going anywhere, Kieran,' Callaghan said quietly.

'What do you mean?'

'I mean that I'm staying with you. There's no way you can handle this situation on your own.'

'Do you know what you're saying, man?'

'Yes, Kieran. Look, my friend, there's nothing for me back in Belfast. Times are hard. I'm out of work and living off the state. I'm on my own and it's been a dull and lonely life one way or another since the peace. I need the adrenaline, man.'

'I can't accept it,' Kelly declared. 'It'd be unfair of me to endanger your life. This is now my battle and my battle alone.'

'Look, Kieran,' said the older man, 'the only way you're going to get me to leave you is to shoot me and I don't think that's an option.'

Kelly, normally cool and calculating, was almost overcome by emotion. 'I don't know what to say, Sean,' he said almost in a whisper.

Callaghan looked at his leader squarely, 'I loved Teresa, too, you know, Kieran. She treated me better than a favourite uncle. That girl was a saint. When you moved to London I was devastated. I felt I'd lost the only two people in the world who cared about me. I was a lonely middle-aged bachelor who's never known the sort of love you two shared. She had this gift, you know, the gift of listening. Here was a woman twenty years younger than me who let me pour out my heart to her. I was so uneducated. You know how much I found filling in forms a nightmare. I used to turn to her for help. She was never judgmental, never condescending. She had the sort of wisdom that all the money in the world can't buy. She never deserved what happened and she deserves justice now.'

Visibly moved by his friend's words, Kelly's mind flooded with images and memories of his dead wife. Like most men, he had often been selfish, especially through his involvement with the Republican cause. Teresa had never criticised him for the days he went missing. She never questioned his actions or his motives. She, too, had been a committed Republican, but she also knew that the best way she could serve her husband and the cause was to be a dutiful wife and mother. She had accepted that the real battle for a united Ireland was man's work. 'I don't know what to say, Sean,' he said again.

'Say nothing and let's get some sleep,' said Callaghan. 'I'll look after our guests in the morning and you can concentrate on letting the world know what a bunch of arseholes they are.'

Jonathan Tring had not been altogether sure whether he'd been dreaming but he could have sworn he had heard a commotion in the night, as if a further guest or guests had arrived. He thought he had heard the sound of shackles, although they might have been his own as he moved in his sleep. He had also been vaguely aware of a gentle sobbing followed by a shout and a slap. Now the morning sunlight was once again streaming through his window and for a few moments there was an unearthly silence. He guessed it was somewhere around eight a.m., but there really was no way of knowing. Suddenly he heard the sound of shackles again and this time they were definitely not his own. The strange thing was that there were two sets of sounds, coming from either side of his room. The whole affair was becoming increasingly bizarre. Suddenly his door swung open and a small wiry man stood before him carrying a breakfast tray. By the nature of his stature and clothing it was balaclava-man sans the hood.

'Room service,' said the man with bonhomie. 'Bacon, eggs and two slices, wholemeal of course.' With this, he stooped to place the tray at the foot of the mattress.

The voice confirmed that it was indeed the man who had worn the balaclava, though his decision to remove it seemed to defeat the object of wearing it in the first place. Tring's immediate thought was that if his captors no longer cared about revealing their identities, then things did not augur well. He reckoned the man was probably in his early fifties. He had small pointed features and eyes that were grey studs but not unkind. A receding hairline and widow's peak gave him somewhat of an elfin appearance.

'Thank you,' the scientist responded automatically, forgetting momentarily that he was meant to be seen and not heard.

His visitor laughed. 'And the condemned man ate a hearty breakfast,'

'Why am I here?'

'Now you know better than that, Professor,' the Irishman said, putting his finger to his lips. 'You'll have plenty of chance to have your say.' He then added cryptically, 'after all, a man cannot be expected to atone for his sins if he is not allowed to confess, now can he. My name's Callaghan, by the way, but my friends call me Sean.' He giggled, then, 'so you can call me Callaghan. I drew the short straw, so it's been me who's been seein' to your every need and even removing your slops bucket for you. Now isn't that nice of me. Of course, that's why we Irish are famous for our hospitality. Now enjoy the food. It may be the last hot meal you get.'

With an enigmatic smile, Sean Callaghan left his guest and made his way down the stairs. There were two other breakfasts to serve, although the cut lip on one of his guests might make eating for him somewhat difficult. He descended the stairs and entered the kitchen. It was more of a galley really and not altogether conducive to preparing meals for five people. He reckoned it was going to have to be sandwiches all round for his guests from now on.

'How is he?' Kelly asked.

'Sweet as a bird,' Callaghan replied. 'I think we'll have more trouble from the other two. The good doctor's already having the DTs and the Minister's got a big mouth on him, but I soon put him straight. Anything on the news yet?'

'No, I reckon it'll be another few hours before any announcement is made. They'll try to sit on it for as long as possible just in case our politician is found in some bordello somewhere with his trousers round his ankles.'

'So you're going to let them stew?'

'Yup. As soon as the news breaks, I'll post a video of their confessions to the BBC. That'll set the cat amongst the pigeons. I want to make them sweat before I reveal our whereabouts; prime the world so that international pressure is brought to bear on the wonderful Prime Minister. There's nothing better than having world opinion on your side.'

'Who are you seeing first?'

'The professor. Each one of them will be able to present his defence, but there's only one judge and one jury – me.'

'Do you want me with you, Kieran?'

'No. You keep a watching brief on the news.'

'Besides the cooking.'

'That too.' Kelly smiled and glanced at his watch, then, 'I reckon he's finished his breakfast, don't you. He must be going crazy trying to figure out why he's here. With this, the Irishman pushed aside his breakfast plate and rose to his feet. 'Well, he's about to find out.'

Tring had had to admit that the man who called himself Sean could make a mean English breakfast. It was the first decent meal he'd had since his incarceration and he'd wolfed it down with gusto. Although he desperately wanted someone to tell him why he was being held, he was more preoccupied with trying to guess the identities of his fellow prisoners. His greatest fear was that one of them might be Fiona. This was the only logical conclusion he could draw from the rattling chains. He imagined killing them if they harmed a hair on her head, a vision curtailed by the irons around his wrists and ankles. His imagination worked overtime as he thought of fanciful ways of escape. A file would mysteriously appear by his side; the stays holding the chains to the walls would fortuitously come loose; even a heavily bearded Count of Monte Cristo character appeared in front of him, pledging to help him escape. The scientist was so wrapped up by visions of the impossible that he failed to notice the door being opened.

'Sean makes a great breakfast, don't you think?'

Startled from his daydream, Tring looked round to see camera-man standing in front of him. The man then took the chair that was in the corner of the room, swivelled its back towards him and sat astride it.

'I think it's about time I introduced myself formally,' said the man. 'My name is Kieran Kelly and I don't expect you ever to forget it.'

'Why am I here, Mr Kelly, and who are the others?'

'I will reveal everything to you, Professor Tring, but I ask you not to interrupt until I tell you about my wife and what happened to her.'

Tring, a captive audience in the fullest sense, listened intently to the Irishman's story of the medical negligence that had caused his wife's suffering and her ultimate suicide. He could see the hurt in his captor's piercing blue eyes and the man's sense of loss was tangible.

'I'm sorry,' Tring said genuinely when his captor had finished. 'It's an awful tragedy.'

'But you don't see how you come into the equation?'

'Frankly, no, I've never had anything to do with any drug used in spinal anaesthesia.'

'Do you have any opinions at all on the use of spinal injections?'

The chains rattled as Tring scratched his head, unsure of where all this was leading. 'I can't say that I've given it much thought.'   .

'What about Triamerol?'

Tring had an immediate vision of the syringe and phial his inquisitor had shown him earlier. 'It's not an anaesthetic and, anyway, we inform doctors that it should not be used intrathecally.'

'It took you twenty-five years to issue that warning, and doctors are still using it epidurally.'

'I had nothing to do with that. The new warning came in two years before I joined the company.'

'Oh, so that's all right then,' Kelly said sarcastically.

'It's not my field of expertise. I'm researching male contraceptives. I really haven't had time to concern myself with Triamerol.'

'There's a lot you haven't concerned yourself with, Professor,' said the Irishman, his eyes narrowing in contempt. 'Medicine is just a dog wagged by your industry's tail. That Triamerol stuff is crap just like those diagnostic dyes that corrode ceramic tiles. They put it in people's spines for years because it gave pretty x-ray pictures. The drug companies knew they were super toxic, but they disregarded the results of tests on animals. They fucked up monkeys and then claimed that as monkeys weren't humans...get my drift? Hundreds of thousands have been maimed for life because companies like yours put profit before people.'

Tring's mind began to race. This angry Irishman was not working *for* Jack Proctor; he was railing *against* him. 'Look, Kelly, I don't know who the hell you are, but if you are against Parados and what it stands for, then so am I.'

Kelly, his eyes like blue lasers, glared at his prisoner. 'You've got a fucking nerve trying to ingratiate yourself with me, you bastard,' he spat.

Tring didn't know where he got the courage from, but he decided to call the Irishman's bluff. 'Maybe you're trying to ingratiate yourself with *me*. Maybe you're working for my boss; maybe you're Jack Proctor's protector.'

'What the fuck are you talking about, man?' Kelly said, taken aback.

'You know who Jack Proctor is, don't you?'

'I know he's your boss.'

'So why didn't you take *him* hostage.'

'We thought about that, but he always seem to surround himself with heavies. Frankly, you were an easier target.'

The Irishman's reaction appeared to Tring to be genuine. If it wasn't, and all of this had been an elaborate bluff, then what he was about to do could be the biggest mistake of his life. The scientist took a deep breath and for the next few minutes told his captor about the machinations of Jack Proctor, how he had thought his boss was out to get him and how he had believed that the Yorkshireman had been behind his current incarceration.

Kelly listened intently to the story with increasing scepticism. After all, he was used to captives concocting cock and bull tales in order to save their own skins. His victims had always begged him for mercy during the Troubles. They all had had an excuse and it was always someone else's fault. The person who would admit to his own culpability was a rare bird indeed, unless it was at the point of a gun, of course. 'Why should I believe a word you're saying?' the Irishman sneered.

'Because I have proof.'

'I don't need any more proof that your company is owned by a greedy bastard or that the Health Secretary is probably the most corrupt man in the British government.'

Tring noted the slight inflection of his captor's head towards the right. My God, he suddenly realised, one of the other captives was none other than Stephen Sellars. The professor's chains rattled as he reached inside his sock and pulled out the cassette. 'I mean I have proof *on* me,' he said bluntly.

There was not much in life that surprised Kieran Kelly, but the sight of the tiny cassette being proffered by his captive took him aback. Here before him was a man he was prepared to maim or kill if necessary and yet this same man appeared to be on his side in fighting the forces of evil; unless, of course, it was all an elaborate ploy. Maybe Tring was exploiting the Stockholm Syndrome. The Irishman was a master of hostage taking and was fully aware of the phenomenon. Back in the early seventies, four hostages had been taken in a botched bank robbery in Sweden. At the end of their captivity, six days later, the hostages had actively resisted rescue. They had refused to testify against their captors and raised money for their legal defence. Psychologists had given the phenomenon its name and defined it as a hostage's strategy of trying to please the captor in order to stay alive. It had never worked for the Irishman's victims in the past. Although this time the circumstances might be different, the principles were the same. Kelly took the cassette, 'I'll pay you the courtesy of listening to this, but don't expect too many brownie points. You've seen too much.'

'I've only seen the inside of this room.'

'That's enough.'

'He's here, isn't he,' Tring said, hoping he wasn't taking his inquisitiveness too far.

'If you mean the Right Honourable Secretary of State for Health, yes. Soon the whole world is going to know everything so there's no reason to keep any of you in the dark. The lush who injected my wife is also here. I want you all to know why and what will happen to you if the government, the pharmaceutical companies and the medical profession don't meet my demands.'

Tring didn't need to be a brain surgeon to figure that one out. The man had already made it clear that he meant to take his revenge with a syringe. 'They'll trace you to this place and they'll use every means to defeat you, if not for me then for Sellars.'

'They won't have to trace me.'

'What do you mean?'

'I intend to let them know the exact location. I want the maximum exposure I can get over this. You can only defeat a government by embarrassing it.'

'So what are your demands?'

'Enough questions for now, my friend,' Kelly replied, 'you'll find out soon enough. We're not unreasonable. Each one of you will be given a television and radio so you can keep in touch with the news. You'll have a ball-by-ball commentary on how much your government and your employers care about your lives. My guess is, very little.'

With this Kelly rose from the chair and silently left the room. There were further fish to fry and he doubted whether his other two guests would provide the sort of surprise Tring had sprung. He couldn't wait to play the professor's tape to Stephen Sellars and then to the world.

Less than twenty miles away and in a more or less northerly direction lay the hub of the British Government's answer to one of its own coming under threat. The Diplomatic Protection Group was based at Charing Cross, the true centre of London and, indeed, the fulcrum for measurement of distances to all points north, south, east and west. Its remit, among other things, was to guard the liberty of ministers of the Crown. Needless to say, secretaries of state for health did not come high up in the pecking order for guarding. The Prime Minister, of course, received twenty-four hour protection, but lesser lights were mostly left to fend for themselves if any threat against them was deemed unlikely.

The DPG was set up in nineteen seventy-four, essentially to protect London's diplomatic community under the Vienna Convention. It also provided for an armed contingency reserve for the Metropolitan Police Service. But the DPG was just one facet of five interactive groupings under the banner of Specialist Operations. Directly responsible to the Assistant Commissioner, these included the anti-terrorist squad and the Serious Crime Group (SO7). Within the ranks of SO7 was the Hostage and Extortion Unit. These included highly trained negotiators whose main purpose was to extricate hostages with minimal collateral damage. On most occasions this would revolve around family disputes involving desperate and vulnerable people whose very vulnerability gave the negotiator more than an even chance of coming out on top. The biggest challenge always came from the politically motivated terrorist, the man who thought of his own death as secondary to the cause that he represented. The Unit was about to face its greatest challenge.

'I need a drink.'

Kelly looked with disdain at the speaker, a pathetically thin figure with rheumy tortured eyes. The good doctor was still reeking from the alcohol he had imbibed before they had picked him up. This was the man directly responsible for Teresa's suffering, the man who was a disgrace to himself and to his profession. 'Whisky and water's your favourite tipple isn't it, Townsend,' the Irishman said with a sneer. 'Well, the good news is we've got the water.'

The Gobi desert that was Martin Townsend's mouth emitted little more than a croak.

'You know,' Kelly went on, 'I don't know whether I blame you as much as the governing body that allows people like you anywhere near a scalpel or a needle. The General Medical Council gives a little rap on the knuckles and in no time the drunks, the butchers and the molesters are back in their surgeries creating more mayhem for the sick and vulnerable.'

Townsend remained silent. The mention of the word whisky had created an overwhelming craving that subsumed any inclination he might have had to argue the toss with his captor. He had recognised the Irishman as soon as the man had taken off his balaclava. There hadn't been a night when the obstetrician had not thought of Teresa Kelly and her husband. The drink that had guided the epidural syringe into the wrong location had also tried to obliterate memory of the deed. Guilt, however, had proved a thirsty demon.

'What should always be your first concern as a doctor, Townsend?' his inquisitor sneered. 'I'll tell you, never to do harm. We come to you at our most vulnerable and we put you on a pedestal. We put our trust in you. If you abuse that trust, then you're not fit to touch another person with a feather duster, let alone a syringe.'

'It was a mistake,' Townsend whimpered. 'For God's sake, give me a drink.'

'*It* was my wife, you bastard,' Kelly seethed. 'You were drunk, weren't you?'

'I-I don't know what you mean.'

'You were drunk that day, you low-life. You were drunk when you had that syringe in your hand. You put her through so much pain that she ended up taking her life. You killed her, Townsend, not the damn paracetamol. You left four children without their ma. You left me a widower at thirty-seven, you scum.'

'Please, I never meant to do any harm.'

Kelly laughed sardonically. '*Harm?* You became a lethal weapon the moment you put a whisky bottle to your lips, man. God knows how many others you've maimed. How many babies have you lost, Townsend? How many mothers will ever know that their infants died from your negligence? It's so easy to cover it up, isn't it? After all, God's infallible and you arrogant bastards play God all the time. The worse thing is that when you make mistakes, you try to cover them up. You know what a doctor says when he tears through the dura? He says 'sorry'. But just a little while later he says, 'what me?' You all do it. You go into denial mode and treat your victims like shit. Look what happened at Bristol Royal Infirmary.'

'That had nothing to do with me.'

Kelly, ignoring the doctor's plea, felt the familiar anger within him reaching boiling point. 'Thirty-five babies butchered by heart surgeons who then clubbed together to cover up their ineptitude. Funny, that, don't you think? Heart surgeons without a heart.' The Irishman laughed again, this time with a bitterness that sliced through his captive. 'On the other hand, they had plenty of hearts. They took them out of those poor babies and gave the bits and pieces back to the parents for burial. Without telling them, of course.'

'Please, I feel so bad,' the doctor beseeched.

'You're going to feel a lot worse by the time I'm through with you, scumbag. You're going to feel what a misplaced needle full of toxins is going to do to your central nervous system. In your case, we might even use alcohol. Now that would be fitting, wouldn't it. I don't have to tell you what a few fluid ounces of whisky would do to your spinal cord, you lush,'

With this, Kieran Kelly swept out of the room, leaving in the wake of his condemnation one painfully thin, middle-aged physician drained of energy and hope. Lying crumpled on the mattress, Townsend resembled little more than the husk of a dead arachnid.

The vitriol was still coursing through the Irishman's veins as he entered the room containing his biggest prize. He had little doubt that of his three captives, the politician was the most devious. However, the little matter of Tring's cassette in his pocket was likely to prove a great leveller.

Stephen Sellars was physically the opposite of Dr Martin Townsend. While the physician could be regarded as emaciated, the cabinet minister sported an expansive girth that owed much to the rich fare provided by some of London's more salubrious eating establishments. Words of contrition were also not likely to be found readily in the Minister's lexicon. He regarded any admission of mistakes as a sign of weakness. Indeed his peers regarded him as a master of spin. At the first hint of trouble, the slick Sellars machine would slip effortlessly into gear with arrant journalists being wined, dined and fed the party line. It had worked most of the time. True, the situation in which he now found himself was different, but the same principles applied. It was all a question of psychology. Mind games.

'Ah, the good Secretary of State for Health,' the Irishman sneered. 'My God, you're really quite gross, aren't you. Why are most greedy bastards fat? You know what your epitaph will be when you die? Here Lies Stephen Sellars. He Denied Himself Nothing.'

Sellars was unmoved. He regarded himself as a master at dealing with such jibes. They were part and parcel of the political arena. 'I don't know why I am here or what you want from me,' he said trying to present a brave front, 'but I'm sure you won't deny me the satisfaction of knowing.'

'Oh, I'll tell you all right, Minister,' said Kelly, smiling wryly. 'I promise I won't keep any secrets from you. You're a corrupt bastard, Sellars, although that's really not why you're here. You see, you represent a malaise that's been endemic in British governments for years. It doesn't matter whether you're Tory or Labour, you all kow-tow to big business. It's money that calls the shots, not the needs of the sick and disabled. You all just pay lip service to them. You so-called Socialists even brought in the rule that makes the disabled undergo a grilling every three years. You said it was to curb benefit cheats, but what about the other side of the coin?'

Sellars shifted his massive bulk uneasily. 'I'm afraid I don't quite understand,' he said genuinely.

'What about those people who're in terrible agony but look normal. What about those who are turned down for benefit because some bureaucrat thinks they're swinging the lead. All you people ever think of is saving a buck.'

'I still don't see your point.'

'Teresa Kelly is my point,' the Irishman said, and fell silent for a few seconds as the bitter memories flooded back. He then gave his captive a potted history of the suffering and subsequent demise of his wife and those like her. It didn't get any easier with each telling.

Sellars listened intently to his captor. The man was obviously hurting. He couldn't bring his wife back, but he could make promises. A politician could always make promises. 'I'm sorry about your wife, and I promise to raise all your grievances with the Prime Minister personally.'

'Your promises ain't worth jack-shit, Minister, and you know it.'

'Then what do you intend to do with me?'

'You saw the syringe.'

'You wouldn't dare.'

'Maybe, but that's for you to guess and me to know.'

'The police will find us. You'll go to jail for the rest of your life unless—'

'Unless what?'

'Unless I give evidence on your behalf. You know, mitigating circumstances.'

'You assume too much, Minister. You assume that I care about saving my skin as much as you care about saving yours. I only care that my demands are met.'

'And what are they?'

'You'll find out soon enough and, by the way, I'll be informing the police of our exact whereabouts. They'll be very interested in trying to make sure that both of us spend time at Her Majesty's pleasure.'

'I don't know what you mean,' Sellars said, his stomach churning.

'One of my other guests is Professor Jonathan Tring. You know who he is, don't you? You know, Sellars, for such a shit you're underwear's pretty clean. But not for long. This is a tape of you being bought off by Jack Proctor. You'll hear it when the media'll broadcast it. Until then I'll leave it to your imagination.'

The Secretary of State for Health broke into a cold sweat. He knew that no amount of spin could wipe clean the tiny cassette now raised high in his captor's right hand.

Kelly, enjoying Sellars' obvious discomfort, turned on his heels and left the room. He almost skipped down the stairs. The time had come to inform the police and he felt more purposeful and more determined than ever to remain true to his wife's memory. The world was about to be educated about the dangers of invasive spinal procedures. Only God knew how it was all going to end.

CHAPTER EIGHTEEN
THE SIEGE – DAY ONE

The explosion, when it happened, took everyone by surprise. It was not that they didn't take the hostage takers seriously; it was that the threat of violence usually remained just that. .

'Jesus Christ, these guys really mean business,' Commander Bob Simmons growled, as he ducked behind one of the ubiquitous red DPG vehicles. Sods of rudely disturbed soil crashed all around him. The man in charge at the sharp end of Operation Whitehall, the codename hurriedly given to the task of bringing this particular incident to a peaceful end, looked nervously around him. Other members of the various units within Specialist Ops could be seen either lying flat on the ground or crouching behind their own cars. My God, he thought, they'd only just got there and the shit was already hitting the fan. This one was definitely not going by the book.

'You okay, Bob?' came a familiar voice alongside him.

Simmons was glad to see the rotund figure of a veritable legend within the ranks of SO7, the Hostage and Extortion Unit. A proud Welshman from the Rhonda, Dai Hopkin was the hostage negotiator's negotiator, a man who could talk himself into a desperate man's psyche, unravel it and put it together again to construct the perfect pussycat.

'They must have known I was coming,' the fat man said jokingly as he straightened up and tucked an errant shirttail into his voluminous trousers. 'What do we know so far?'

Simmons stared pensively at the cottage. 'He told us not to approach the building closer than fifty yards or we'd get a nasty surprise.'

'He wasn't joking.'

'He was using an electronic voice disguiser, but I think he's Irish.'

'IRA?'

'I don't think so. What would he be doing holding a scientist and a doctor as well as Sellars?'

'He told you?'

'Yeah, he mentioned them by name. Said he'd use the Internet to broadcast his demands. He said everything would become abundantly clear. Gave us the domain. The web cam just shows a chair and the back wall of the room. Impossible to tell which room, although I'd guess it's at the front of the cottage. I hate those fucking mirror blinds.'

'Have you got his phone number?'

'Yeah, it's a mobile.'

'Did you give him yours?'

'Yeah. I told him to call anytime he wanted.'

'Has he got a landline?'

'Yeah, but he says that it's dedicated for the web. He's adamant that he won't use the line for calls.'

Hopkin rubbed his chin pensively. While cellular phones could be monitored using a short-wave radio receiver and scanner, it was a two-edged sword. The media might also find the frequency and listen to the whole caboodle. They would be better off if they could get a throw phone in there.

'He's not alone, Dai,' Simmons said, cutting into the Welshman's train of thought. 'If there was only one hostage, maybe, but more will take some controlling.'

'Yeah, I agree, but how many?'

'The bare minimum's got to be two, probably more. They'd need to keep an eye on every angle. He told us the perimeter was mined and that he'd got surveillance cameras and mikes everywhere. A real gadget man.'

'Well, we've got some new toys of our own, boyo,' Hopkin growled. 'What about the MDR?' Thanks to Hughes Missile Systems, entry rescue units now had access to a compact Motion Detection Radar, which could penetrate non-metallic walls and tell them how many people were in *Rosedale* cottage and also their locations.

'We've got to get it within thirty yards,' Simmons grunted. 'He'll probably blow it to smithereens if we used it during daylight.'

'Hmm,' Hopkin pondered, running his finger and thumb along his neatly trimmed moustache. 'Run it up at night and get it back before it gets light.'

'What if he's got night vision?'

'It's a chance we've got to take, Bob. This one's a pro all right, and it's political.'

'But you said—'

'No, not the IRA or the Middle East. Politics of a different kind, maybe Animal Rights. Anyway, he's soon going to enlighten us. How well armed do you think he is?'

'To the hilt,' Simmons grunted, 'judging by that welcome. Whatever he's got he knows how to use it. I believe he must have a military background.'

Hopkin glanced around. The police presence was massive. There must have been at least twenty cars and vans surrounding the cottage, albeit at a radius of fifty yards. Soon they'd be more. Support vehicles, ambulances, and a couple of fire engines. Then would come the media circus, clamouring to get as close as it could. He could see the snipers searching for good vantage points to construct their hides. Soon they would be straining every sinew to get a pot shot at God knows who. He had never liked the use of force. In most cases it proved unnecessary. He also didn't like handling huge negotiating teams. The Assistant Commissioner in charge of Specialist Operations had ordered everything but the kitchen sink: sixteen people and a dog, presumably in case the hostage takers spoke bow-wow. There were also two negotiating mobile command posts, an equipment trailer and enough incidental stuff to open a shopping mall. He himself was of the old school, believing that negotiators who lacked the bells and whistles often came up trumps because they had to work extra hard and be super-creative in resolving incidents. Negotiators could become complacent when surrounded by a large assisting team and expensive equipment. 'Keep this lot under control, Bill,' he said quietly. 'Our only friend at the moment is time.'

Kieran Kelly surveyed the scene with a quiet satisfaction. The first stage had gone according to plan. The remote controlled explosion had worked and his adversaries now knew that he meant business. He stared at the console in front of him, gratified that he could see their every move, while they could see nothing.

'They must be dying to know how many there are of us and what we're about,' said Sean Callaghan over his friend's shoulder.

Kelly smiled and tapped the computer screen in front of him. 'God bless broadband technology,' he said. 'Power to the people.' Ever since he had bought the machine, he had become hooked on its ability to garner information. Someone had once said that knowledge was power and the Internet could provide as much knowledge as anyone could ever need. The beauty was that with a web cam you could put yourself online to the world. Streaming had reached such a level of sophistication that it was as if every computer owner could run his own TV station. In the last year, photon technology had made all this possible. He'd read somewhere that the whole of the world's population could watch one man's web cast without it overloading the service provider. They were in only the fifth year of the new century and all this recent innovation meant that he, Kieran Patrick Kelly, could reach the world with his message. The only thing that could prevent this would be if the service provider pulled the plug, so it was time to make sure that that was unlikely to happen. He inclined his head slightly towards the thin sliver of plastic attached to the top pocket of his shirt. 'Baldrick,' he said firmly. There was a beep as the codeword activated the brand new paper-thin mobile phone. He then spoke the numbers clearly and precisely and waited.

Bob Simmons was startled by the sudden ringing tone of the mobile he'd dedicated solely for dealing with the hostage takers. He spoke his own particular codeword and acknowledged his caller.

The Irishman brought the voice distorter level with his throat. 'Good morning once again, Commander,' he said, almost with bonhomie. 'It's time for me to give you information about tonight's broadcast. At nine o'clock this evening you and the rest of the world will find out what this is all about. Just make sure the ISP keeps me live. I'll be watching myself anyway.'

Hopkin brought a closed fist to his right ear and mouthed the words 'throw phone'. He knew that this piece of equipment could be more useful than a firearm. They were purpose-built with around one thousand feet of military-grade field cable and they could work off an internal battery. These units included headsets for the negotiator with an on/off switch, outlets for additional headsets, jacks for external speakers and

.

tape recording facilities. But some of them had another, more vital weapon in the chief negotiator's armoury: an internal, highly sensitive microphone that would allow them to monitor conversations in the cottage, even when the phone was not in use. The only problem was that any information gleaned from the bug would have to be denied a chief negotiator in order to prevent him from inadvertently using it with the hostage takers. They would immediately smell a rat and put the whole operation in jeopardy. Another useful facet of the system was that it also contained a signalling light so that team members could readily tell when the phone was active. The field cable could also be marked in measured increments so that when the hostage taker was on the telephone, his exact position could be accurately determined. The big question was whether or not the men in Rosedale Cottage would buy the proposal.

'Er, listen,' Simmons said hesitantly into his mobile, 'we don't want the press picking up on our conversations. How about letting us get a throw phone into you. It's just a line between you and us. Everything could then be private.'

'So that you can bug it and listen to everything we say?' Kelly laughed. What kind of fool did they take him for?

Simmons looked at Hopkin and shook his head. 'Okay, listen, the next call you get will be from our chief negotiator. His name's Dai Hopkin and he's a good man.'

'You mean I can trust him,' said Kelly with heavy sarcasm.

'Look, we're going to need a name for you, any name.'

'Okay. You can call me Spinal Tap.'

'But that's a rock group.'

'I have my reasons. It's either Spinal Tap or Mr X, and I prefer the former.'

Simmons snarled with undisguised contempt. 'Okay, Mr Tap, or would you prefer Spinal?'

Hopkin shook his head. His boss was using the wrong tone with the man. Everything had to be kept very smooth, very unthreatening. With a circular motion of his index finger, the Welshman intimated to his colleague to wind up the conversation.

Kelly was enjoying himself. There was nothing he liked better than taunting authority. 'You can try calling me after the broadcast. Whenever my phone is off it means I don't want to talk to you. Don't try any games. We can see and hear everything you do. Keep your monkeys at least fifty yards away or the hostages get it.'

'But—'

'Bye for now,' croaked the strange voice.

Simmons shrugged. 'He's rung off. He'll only talk to us when *he* wants to. I guess it's down to you guys now. We're sure going to need a lot of patience.'

The Welshman grimaced. 'I've got all the patience in the world, boyo.' The question is, does Her Majesty's Government?'

'I'll do my best to keep them off your back, Dai, but you know governments exist to make every simple situation difficult.'

'The fucking Government,' said Hopkin. He sighed deeply, and began moving towards the nearest mobile negotiating post. As always, there was much to organise before the real work could begin. He was a stickler for organisation and that meant everything had to be correct down to the last detail. Woe betides any member of his team who didn't equip himself with a briefcase, notebook, pencils and pens, and a clipboard and folders. He was also pedantic when it came to such minutiae as paper clips, a stapler and markers. He also insisted that each person should have a pocket tape recorder to keep track of conversations, decisions and suggestions. It was surprising when the shit began to hit the fan how many officers forgot suggestions or failed to write down important decisions and details. As for weaponry, each of his team was equipped with a concealable pistol and full body armour. Their clothing had to be comfortable and rugged, such as jeans, trainers or boots with heavy socks, gloves and woollen hats. The vagaries of the English weather meant that windcheaters were normally worn. These bore the logo 'Negotiator' so that everyone else would know that they had a right to be there. Each man brought with him an overnight bag with a washcloth, toothbrush, small towel, toilet paper, basic foodstuffs and, of course, aspirin and antacids if things started to get out of hand. Experience told him that this was going to be a prolonged standoff, so he'd arranged for runners to bring the team plenty of hot beverages and light meals.

Hopkin hauled his bulk into the rear of nearest van. 'Are the tape recorders and the laptops linked up to the mainframe?' he asked one of

ROGER RADFORD

the two men who was sitting at a desk littered with surveillance paraphernalia.

'Yes, sir,' the man replied with some trepidation. The Welshman was renowned for being a slow burner with hostage takers but quick-tempered with his own staff. A native of Camarthen, he was often called the Dyfed Dragon, although never to his face.

'Clear that fucking mess up,' Hopkin exploded. 'An untidy desk means an untidy mind, and we can't afford untidy minds in our business, can we, *boys bach.*'

'Yes, sir – I mean no, sir,' the constable rejoined, as others in the van began an exaggerated cleaning up operation.

The Welshman began to fiddle with the knobs on one of the video cams. Two of his staff would be responsible for keeping a historical record of the negotiations. Team discussions and command decisions could also be videotaped. Sometimes a vital detail might go unnoticed in real time, so keeping a thorough record of events gave the negotiator a second chance, and when it came to desperate men, a second chance might mean a life saved. 'Where's the VSA?' he grumbled irritably.

'In the other van, boss,' a hesitant voice piped.

'I want it in here with me.' The Voice Stress Analyser was an Israeli-made machine that was virtually a polygraph. It could even register deception from a cassette tape, thus enabling him to analyse a hostage taker's frame of mind if it became impossible to monitor communications in real time.

'What about the robots, boss?' another of his men asked.

'Sod the robots, *boyo*, they're a fucking waste of time.' Hopkin preferred using his mind to outwit his opponents rather than a lump of dumb metal. The use of robots had never been very successful, anyway. Hostage takers often refused to allow robots within range, believing the machine contained various exotic devices that could be used against them. Some of these ranged from guns and cameras to lasers and chemical agents. The first and last time he'd used a robot, the hostage taker had believed it contained radioactive X-rays that would not only see through walls, but would make him sterile in the process. No, there were some things far more useful than robots. 'Where's the most important piece of equipment in our arsenal?' he growled.

A set of blank faces turned towards the Welshman, who met them with a look of feigned hurt.

'My sandwich box, boyos, my sandwich box.'

It was already dark by the time Kieran Kelly had put the finishing touches to his announcement to the world. Besides the police, he had also contacted the Press Association. Within minutes the news had flashed around the globe. He thrilled as he watched television pictures of the siege outside *Rosedale*. His captives, too, were privileged to see their plight in real time, a fact that he'd imparted to the media. The authorities would soon be wheeling in the wives and kids to make impassioned pleas on their behalf, something that would have little effect on Kieran Patrick Kelly, but would create turmoil in the minds of those shackled upstairs. Their emotions would be running the full gamut, from visions of joyful liberation to those of a horrible death. Let them suffer, as his Teresa had suffered.

The Irishman was under no illusion that his true identity would remain secret for very long. Nevertheless, there was no way he was going to make it easy for them. He'd used a hundred and one aliases in his time. Whilst Kelly might have been the name on his birth certificate, he'd rarely used it in his 'business' dealings. True, he had reverted to it in London, but then that was simply because the Troubles were over, and there was no need for subterfuge any more, or so he had thought. Anyway, there was a lot to be said for having one of the most popular Irish names if you wanted to veil your identity. There were a million and one Kellys out there. Why, in India, he would probably have been a Patel. He smiled and donned his balaclava. It was exactly nine o'clock and the game was about to begin in earnest. He adjusted his web cam slightly until he could see himself taking up the centre of the screen. A sudden rush of adrenaline made him light-headed as he dialled the number that would give him access to the world. He placed the voice distorter at his throat. Maybe it would soon make him as popular as Stephen Hawking.

'Good evening, world,' he began, 'the waiting is over, and I'm now going to explain to you why we are holding three men hostage. These three men, as you know, are the Secretary of State for Health, a research director of a leading pharmaceutical company and an obstetrician. Each in his own way is guilty of flagrant disregard for the lives of those whose safety he purports to hold dear. Our protest is also threefold. We protest at the British Government's blatant refusal to instigate an inquiry into the carnage caused by invasive spinal procedures; we protest at the policies of the pharmaceutical companies that put profits before people; we protest at the doctors who seek to cover up their crass ineptitude with lies and subterfuge. Britain is a secret society. The general public is constantly kept in the dark, whether it's about mad cows, foot and mouth, injections into the spine or a million and one other things that affect our daily lives. We demand freedom of information as a prerequisite for bringing about the reforms that are so sorely needed.'

Kelly paused to shuffle his papers importantly before continuing, 'I will now go into more detail in order to convince the British people, and indeed the world, that our cause is just and that pressure must be brought to bear on the authorities to right these terrible wrongs. Firstly, how many of you women out there are soon to give birth and are contemplating having an epidural to ease the pain?' The Irishman paused, as if waiting for thousands of 'mes' to erupt from the screen before him. 'Did you know that common painkilling injections used in childbirth have left thousands of women disabled or even paralysed? Did you know that damage caused by injections into the spine is one of the NHS's most closely guarded secrets? Remember Thalidomide and HIV-infected blood given to haemophiliacs? They're nothing compared to this scandal. Nearly two hundred thousand epidurals are given every year. They've almost become a bloody fashion statement. Well let me tell you something future mothers of the world, you don't need them. What's a few hours of the pain of childbirth compared to a possible lifetime of agony? Let me tell you what an injection into the spine can give you. It doesn't matter whether it's an epidural for childbirth, a dye to see if you've got a slipped disc or a steroid that's supposed to relieve your back pain, the result is the same. It's called adhesive arachnoiditis and it's one of the worst medical-caused diseases in the world. There's no difference in the symptoms whether you're injected by a doctor or attacked with a chemical warfare agent by some tin-pot Arab dictator. If you're one of the unlucky ones, your central nervous system will be shot to pieces. The chemicals in the injection will poison delicate nerve endings inside your spinal column and cause them to stick together. Your immune system will then go haywire trying to deal with it. That chemical reaction can leave you unable to walk, incontinent, blind and in the most God-awful pain that not even morphine can help. How would you like to feel that you're hobbling on broken glass or that your legs feel as though they're being incinerated? How would you like to know that there is no cure – that they're not even looking for a cure – and that you'll have to put up with this terrible condition for the rest of your life? How would you like it if doctors refused to diagnose you, telling you that it's all in your head, in order to avoid admitting *their* culpability in *your* suffering? Most of our so-called doctors aren't even trained to recognise the symptoms. This means that patients get the wrong treatments or get little or no help. Our wonderful government cites statistics as the reason they're unable to institute action. They say that not enough cases are reported. Not surprising is it when you consider that if the true statistics were known, it would lead to calls for legal action, which of course they don't want. Please understand that most victims don't want money, they just want an admission of fault and an apology.'

The Irishman paused again to clear his throat and also to let his message sink in. He knew he had to pace himself and it helped that he could see himself both on the computer screen and CNN. Auntie BBC was, as usual, kowtowing to the Government and refusing to air his statement live. More fool them.

'Now,' he continued, 'let me tell you what some of the stuff they used to pump into your spine did to a couple of inanimate objects. Pharmaceutical companies made a dye used in x-rays of the spine. They put some of it in a Styrofoam cup and it melted. Then some of the crap fell by accident onto a ceramic tiled floor and began eating the tiles away. Still, they said, plastic cups and ceramic tiles ain't no human spine, so they carried on their merry way. Next they tried it out on dogs and monkeys and it devastated their spinal cords. Still, dogs and monkeys ain't human, they said, so let's market it anyway. In the last fifty years, twenty million people around the world have been injected with that dye and they reckon five per cent got adhesive arachnoiditis from it. Figure it out for yourselves.' Again, the Irishman paused to allow millions of minds to do the mental calculation.

Kelly could feel the familiar anger mounting within him, but he knew he would achieve much more by remaining cool, by presenting a reasoned case. He spent the next few minutes explaining how successive governments had shirked their responsibility when it came to invasive spinal procedures. By the time he had finished, the general public knew as much about the issue as he did. Now it was time to list his demands and, of course, the consequences if these were not met.

'So what do we want in order for our three guests to be returned to their families unharmed?' he continued. 'Firstly, we want the Government to set up a full inquiry into invasive spinal procedures, especially those concerning epidurals in childbirth and steroids given for relieving back pain. There is no doubt that if this inquiry does its job properly, it will come to the conclusion that most spinal injections are dangerous and unnecessary. The reason that we do not demand the immediate cessation of all invasive spinal procedures is that this would be unrealistic. Any restrictions must be sanctioned by a government that purports to be of the people, by the people and for the people. We are not anarchists. Secondly, we demand that compensatory funds be set up for victims past, present and future. These funds shall be financed solely by those pharmaceutical companies that have been actively engaged, and continue to be engaged, in the production of intra-spinal products. The initial fund should be for those who've already fallen victim to the injection of dangerous chemicals into their spines. This will include all those who have yet to be diagnosed because of medical incompetence and/or vacillation. The Department of Health will give strict orders to radiographers and doctors to treat each case with the respect it deserves. This initial fund shall be set at ten billion pounds. The pharmaceutical companies shall also be obliged to set aside annually one billion pounds no-fault compensation, this sum to be index-linked. If due caution is exercised, this sum should more than cover the number of inevitable mistakes. Thirdly, a further five hundred million pounds annually should be earmarked for research into the causes of adhesive arachnoiditis, effective treatments and a possible cure. Fourthly, every necessary spinal procedure should be preceded by the patient having informed consent. It should be remembered that not one of the scores of millions of people injected with iophendylate dyes or steroids containing preservatives was ever informed that they could cripple him or her for life. This was scandalous, an absolute disgrace to the medical profession.

'We demand that legislation be introduced that would ensure, as a statutory right, that patients are fully informed about proposed treatments, the possible alternatives and any substantial risks so that they can make a balanced judgment.

'Remember that informed consent is a legal doctrine that has been developed by the courts over a number of years. It is your right and your government has to make sure you enjoy that right.'

The Irishman had concluded his soliloquy. Now it was time to warn the authorities of the price that would have to be paid if his demands were not met. He did not want to risk the empathy of the general public by using the photographs he'd taken of his hostages. Those had been used simply to strike terror into them, to make them more compliant. He once again stared into the eye of the web cam. 'I do not have to tell you what will happen to these three men if our demands are not met. Their lives are in the hands of the Government and the pharmaceutical companies who, in effect, almost represent a state within a state. In order to prove the collusion between our elected leaders and the drug companies, I shall invite you all to log on or watch your televisions tomorrow at nine p.m. I can promise you an astounding revelation. Thank you for your attention.'

Kelly instructed his computer to log off. So far, so good. The world now knew what he was about, but it was also important to maintain the interest of the media by offering them the prospect of fresh headlines. He also knew that to be effective, the siege must achieve its aims within a limited period. Too long, and people would become bored. The ongoing saga would be relegated to a paragraph at the foot of an inside page under a headline that might read, 'siege enters thirtieth day.' Ho-hum. No, he had plans to keep it fresh; to keep it alive until he was sure he'd won over the hearts of the people and the minds of the powers that be. In the end, it might come down to whomever possessed the strongest will. However, of one thing Kieran Patrick Kelly was still certain: right was indisputably on his side.

No sooner had the broadcast finished than Dai Hopkin was being quizzed by his boss.

'Well, Dai,' Simmons said over the link, 'what did you make of that?'

'I'd say that we're in for a long haul, Bob,' the negotiator replied. 'This man is no fool. It's not a case of some crazy or a guy who's only interested in money for himself. This man has a cause and it's clear he's willing to kill or be killed for it. They're the toughest kind to crack, boyo.'

'What do you propose to do?'

'Sleep on it. Nothing will be gained by acting like a bull in a china shop. It's getting late. The best negotiating time is in the morning. If our hostage takers suffer sleep deprivation, they're likely to do something irrational. They'll probably have a couple awake during the night. I guess our main man will keep to his normal sleep pattern.'

'They're a few clues in the speech.'

'Yeah, the guy in the balaclava is hurting. I think he's had a relative, probably a close one, who's suffered from some kind of spinal procedure.'

'The doctor?'

'Yeah, we wondered why he in particular was involved. I guess you'd better get someone to go through his records.'

'I can feel my stress levels rising,' Simmons grunted.

'It's the name of the game, boyo,' replied Hopkin, 'for everyone.' The Welshman was well aware that stress was one of the few constants in the hostage situation. At the onset, the hostages whose safety, after all, was his main concern, had been confronted with loss of life or serious injury, loss of freedom and loss of self-respect. They were bound to be panicky, anxious, uncertain and fearful. They would see themselves as victims of circumstance. At one moment they were going about their normal, everyday activities in an orderly world; then that order had been roughly displaced by an uncertain, and possibly short, future. More importantly, they were in a situation in which somebody else was controlling their actions and emotions. Hopkin also knew that the very presence of the police produced stress in the hostages, who would not know how or if the police could differentiate them from their captors. They might do things that would get themselves killed.

Then there was the stress from both the public and the Government. When hostages were taken, the incident evoked a combination of horror and empathy among a country's population. At the same time, unless a response was carefully planned and successfully carried out, a government could appear impotent or non-responsive to the dangers facing its citizens.

But before he could deal with the stress in others, a negotiator had to deal with his own, and it was often higher than that of the hostage taker. Hopkin knew that he would be talking to a person who might kill people, and that this, in itself, represented a kind of role ambiguity. On the one hand, as a police officer, he was expected to uphold the law, arrest criminals and protect the public. As a negotiator, on the other hand, he was expected to be able to talk to and become friendly with a criminal. He had to set aside his values and beliefs and operate from a different structure. In effect, he'd be negotiating for the freedom of the hostage taker as well as his captives. The Welshman knew that every word he spoke, every action he took and every decision he made might cost the lives of not only the hostages and their captors, but also those of his own colleagues. To make matters worse, the negotiator was expected to internalise his fears. He couldn't let these fears show either to fellow officers or to the hostage takers. At the same time, he was constantly aware that his superiors were monitoring and evaluating his every move.

'Stress,' the Welshman grumbled, 'you buggers don't know the fucking meaning of the word.'

While Dai Hopkin wrestled with his demons, three other people closely connected to events at the cottage in the heart of the Surrey countryside were caught up in their own maelstroms of emotion. Glued to the television screen in her father's Fenland home, Fiona Harrington quickly realised that the hostage takers had taken possession of the incriminating tape that Jonathan had played her. She asked herself whether there was any point in giving the police forewarning of the revelations that were planned for the following evening. Her journalistic instincts screamed for her to write a pre-emptive sidebar exclusive detailing her involvement in the quest to expose corruption at the heart of government. Yet she reckoned that if she spoiled the hostage taker's party, it might jeopardise Jonathan Tring's safety. Therefore, she convinced herself, she had to let the man in the balaclava enjoy his moment of glory. Despite her fears, she was forced to admit to harbouring a sneaking admiration for him. The plain fact was that he'd outlined many of the issues she had raised in her unpublished article. They were both in the business of exposing graft and corruption. It was just his methods she abhorred. She decided she would re-write her article in time to catch the front page of the morning edition, knowing full well that this would spark a frenzy among the electronic media. Although the police were bound to be pissed off that she hadn't revealed all to them sooner, she would beg them to allow her to make a personal televised appeal to the hostage takers. They had to be told that at least one of the men they were holding was innocent of any wrongdoing. She could forgive the hostage takers everything as long as Jonathan came out of that cottage alive.

Meanwhile, in a northern suburb of London another beautiful woman was confronted by a quandary that was even more profound. The hostage taker's distorted voice did not fool Countess Magda von Esterhazy, for it was the man's piercing blue eyes that leapt from the television screen and screamed his identity. 'Oh, Kieran,' she had cried out, 'why have you done this terrible thing?'

Her first instinct had been to telephone the police. She had even lifted the receiver and begun dialling, but was then overcome by apprehension and a deep melancholy. However misguided were his actions, Kieran was fighting her cause. He had seen that all her conventional efforts had failed to stir the conscience of the authorities. He believed his way was better. He believed his way would right wrongs that had gone uncorrected and unpunished for too long. It was only now that she could understand his strange behaviour, his decision to end their relationship. It had not been because he had not loved her, but because he was consumed by a greater passion. Kieran was probably going to such extraordinary lengths to conceal his identity in order to protect his children, although he must surely have known that it was just a matter of time before the police discovered it.

Magda slumped back in her bed as the burning in her legs reached a new intensity. She ripped open a morphine patch and placed it on her thigh, praying silently to God that no one would be harmed and that people would understand her lover's desperate action. Within a few moments she began to drift off to sleep, her last conscious image being the steely intensity of her lover's eyes framed by the black wool of the balaclava.

Unlike the Countess, millions of people continued to stay glued to their computer screens, albeit that they now portrayed only an empty chair and a poster on a wall. The poster showed a human spine and a syringe with a large red cross through it. Many were afraid that they might miss a scintilla of action if they switched off, for it was now possible to see major events as they unfolded. It was just a case of logging on to the live drama of your choice, whether it was on a fixed screen or on the slivers of plastic that were mobile phones. No longer could the traditional media apply editorial control. True power now resided with the service providers who could throw the switch at any time, although with human lives at stake this was unlikely to happen. The phenomenon was so new that the Government was still locked in battle with the ISPs as to who should have the last word. The fight was about to become even more intense, for although there were a myriad of newsworthy dramas on any given day, this was the first time the perpetrators of a crime had sought to enlist the sympathy of the public by running their own live web cast.

One of the countless numbers who continued to watch their monitors was a man who had more interest than most in the events being played out in a cottage just south of London. Jack Proctor was almost catatonic. Sitting in his office at Parados headquarters, he had not moved a millimetre since the start of the broadcast. In less than forty-eight hours the Yorkshireman had seen his world turn upside down. His wife had declared that she was leaving him, and now true nemesis was staring him in the face. The bastard in the balaclava had Tring's tape and tomorrow his dreams of becoming a true giant of the pharmaceutical industry would be over. While Sharon's disloyalty had devastated him, in the end she was a woman, and a woman could be replaced. What could never be replaced was a lifetime of effort which was about to be shattered into thousands of little pieces, each shard a dagger through his heart. What did the world know of what it took to claw one's way out of a grimy orphanage in a godforsaken mining town where the main topics of conversation surrounded the pit and its brass band? Working down the mines was not for Jack Albert Proctor. There was no difference between a miner and a soldier at the Battle of the Somme. One may have gone down to the bottom and the other over the top, but a horrible death awaited them both. No, he mused, nobody knew how hard it had been for him to scrimp and save from part-time jobs in order to finance his studies. Nobody knew how difficult it had been to reach the top of his profession. And now, dammit, it was all about to come to an end. He would have to suffer a jail sentence and stand the opprobrium of his peers. Even more humiliating was the knowledge that sharks like Kevin Kinloss would go on a feeding frenzy, tearing lumps out of his company and leading it to eventual ruination. Didn't they understand that *he*, Jack Albert Proctor, was Parados and vice versa? Didn't they know that it had taken him more than thirty years to propel the company from a run-down lab on a derelict industrial estate to a beautiful state-of-the-art complex covering hundreds of acres. Sure, he had made mistakes, but he'd supplied jobs for thousands of people, produced drugs that had helped millions more. Well, fuck them all. He wouldn't give them the satisfaction of revelling in his downfall. He wouldn't bear the humiliation of having to witness the dismemberment of his baby while he rotted helplessly in some godforsaken jail.

Jack Proctor took a deep breath, opened the drawer on his right and withdrew the Beretta from its nest of green lint. Without hesitation, he placed the barrel in his mouth.

CHAPTER NINETEEN
THE SIEGE – DAY TWO

Jack Proctor's body was discovered early enough to make the first editions of the morning papers. What had begun as a sensational event had now entered the stratosphere of speculation. The media had immediately made the connection between the suicide and the hostage taker's promised revelation that would shake the Government to its foundations. They had also speculated that it was no coincidence that the Health Secretary was one of the hostages, and that the doctor was also in some way involved with his captors. Some suggested that the whole military-style operation indicated that the hostage takers were ex-SAS commandos. Two and two made four in anybody's language, but they all realised that the true answers could only be found in the detail.

While the media scrum was concentrated around the cottage, there was no shortage of reporters outside the residences of Fiona Harrington and Sharon Proctor. Not wishing to allow pressure to be brought to bear on her parents, Fiona had decided to drive back to her London flat in the early hours of the morning. She had steadfastly ignored the throng of badgering colleagues, and once safely in her own bed had quickly succumbed to a deep and dreamless sleep. It was already about eleven when she awoke and groggily replaced the telephone cord in its socket. Within seconds, the phone was ringing urgently.

'Harrington,' she mumbled wearily.

'I hope you're satisfied,' came the cold and familiar drawl.

'Is that you, Sharon?' she quizzed with more than a tinge of apprehension.

'Yes, it's me. I said I hope you're satisfied.'

'Look, I, er, was only doing my job. What Jack did was wrong. He has to pay the price, even if it means going to jail.'

There was a long pause before, 'My God, you don't know, do you?'

'Know what?'

'Jack killed himself last night.'

Fiona Harrington felt the stuffing knocked out of her. She would never have believed that a man like Proctor would be capable of such a thing. 'I, er, don't know what to say,' she said at length. 'I'm truly sorry. How, why?'

'He shot himself in his office. Where else? The company was his life. It was more important to him than anything else in this goddamnn world, even me.'

'But he loved you in his own way.'

'Maybe, but I was just a trophy wife,' the American said without rancour. 'Look, Fiona, I never loved him, but I respected what he'd achieved. He was a self-made man who came from nothing, just like myself. When he told me what he'd done with Sellars, I just flipped. I told him I was going to leave him.'

'You think—'

'No, Jack didn't love me that much. He knew his empire was about to crumble. He just couldn't see any other way out.'

Fiona tried to imagine the last desperate minutes of Jack Proctor's life. It was clear that the man who always gave the impression that only a ten-ton truck could stop him was as vulnerable as anyone else. 'I'm sorry, Sharon, that I betrayed your confidence, but I had no other choice.'

'I know that you did what you had to do, but that doesn't make it any easier. I'll always feel a sense of betrayal when I remember you.'

The words cut deeply into Fiona Harrington, for she liked Sharon Proctor. She knew the American could be ruthless, but her strong will coupled with her stunning beauty made for a magnetic personality. 'What will you do, Sharon, when this is all over?'

'I've decided to go back to good ol' Savannah, Georgia. Only this time the girl from the wrong side of the tracks'll be able to buy up half the city. At least Jack made sure of that.'

'But Parados was just as much your baby as his. He would never have succeeded without your support. Anyway, it's your company now.'

'I don't want it anymore. Let Kinloss and the other piranhas have it. I hope it chokes them. There just one more thing, Fiona—.'

'Yes.'

'You were like a younger sister to me, but I don't ever want to see you again. Can you understand that?'

'Yes, I think I can. I'm sorry. Under different circumstances—'
'We would never have met under different circumstances.'
'Yes, I suppose that's true.'
Sharon Proctor sighed. 'Anyway, I hope your boyfriend gets out of this mess in one piece. He's a good man, if a little naive. So long, Fiona.'
Fiona Harrington wished the American well and replaced the receiver. She could not help but feel an inordinate sense of loss.

Inside the cottage, Jonathan Tring had been privy to his captor's extraordinary performance the previous evening. True to his word, the Irishman had supplied him with a television and a radio. The reports of Proctor's suicide had shaken the scientist to the core. Kelly's threat to broadcast the tape had obviously been enough to tip the Yorkshireman over the edge and, in the end, like most bullies, Proctor had taken the cowardly option. In a way he was thankful that it was his captor's action and not his own that had precipitated the suicide. Kelly was either half-mad or extraordinarily clever and the professor found himself playing out all sorts of scenarios in his mind, most of them concerned with how the police would conduct themselves. He just prayed that they wouldn't botch any rescue operation. He couldn't help but think of the Munich Olympics and the demise of the Israeli athletes through the rank amateurishness of the German police. Those poor bastards had all died because of an ill advised and poorly timed attack and he could see from the TV pictures that the authorities had surrounded them with all manner of sophisticated firepower. Chained as he was, he felt like a helpless pawn in a game played between two chess masters, with the police probably not realising they were confronted by a man who was as calculating as a computer. He had little doubt that Kelly would be ready to sacrifice one or two of his pawns if things got rough. Just as he began to envision the worst of all scenarios, his captor opened the door and ambled into the room.'
'Well, Professor, what did you think?'
'Look, Kelly, if that's your real name, if you want to know the truth, I don't think you've got a hope in hell of them agreeing to that package.'

232

The Irishman sneered in mock derision. 'Oh, dear me, if the great Professor Tring thinks that then who am I to argue? Opening gambit, man, opening gambit. It's all a game after all, isn't it? They'll soon be starting the old psychological approach, getting some negotiator to try to sweet-talk me into surrendering. Do you think I'll ever surrender before my demands are met?'

Tring looked directly at the steely blue eyes and a hesitated a few seconds before shaking his head.

'So it's death or glory then, isn't it Professor. Now what do you prefer? You don't really want to join your boss in that great laboratory in the sky, do you?'

Tring again shook his head.

'No, I didn't think so. You'd better pray that the authorities eventually come around to my way of thinking, otherwise you might not get to taste lunch which, by the way, is corned beef.' Kelly then winked slyly at his captive, 'white bread or rye?'

The House of Commons

'Mr Speaker, is it the Prime Minister's intention to stand firm against this unbridled example of modern terrorism or will he allow anyone with a grievance to bring this great democracy to its knees?'

The Prime Minister, a dour Scotsman not given to outbursts of hyperbole, rose to the despatch box and gazed at the Leader of the Opposition with undisguised disdain. 'I have already assured the right honourable Gentleman that Her Majesty's Government will do everything in its power to bring about a peaceful resolution of this incident. The hostage takers are clearly determined to hold this Government to ransom and I can assure the House that we intend to act firmly in this matter. However, I should like to remind my right honourable friend that while we should not be cowed by threats, we must bear in mind that the lives of three innocent people are at stake here and, therefore, it would be imprudent to use inflammatory language.'

The Leader of the Opposition, a slack-jawed balding man in his early fifties, jumped to his feet eager to embarrass his counterpart. 'I am sure the Prime Minister is aware of rumours in the media that the death of Mr Jack Proctor is linked in some way to the Secretary of State for Health. Can the Prime Minister shed any further light on this matter, or do we have to wait for the man in the balaclava to enlighten us?'

'I am unaware of any such link, and I should advise the right honourable Gentleman not to engage in unwarranted speculation that might endanger the lives of the hostages.'

'Hear, hear,' the Government benches bayed, followed by cries of, 'shame, shame.'

'Order, order,' cried the Speaker. 'Order, order.'

'They're all over the fucking place, Kieran,' Sean Callaghan groaned. 'I've never seen so much hardware.'

Kelly peered through slits in the silver-coated blinds. It looked like most of Police Special Forces and half the British Army had turned out on his parade. 'Fuck them all, Sean. They can posture all they like. Using a fucking sledgehammer to kill a fly is fucking nonsense. They won't make a move unless I give them the impression that I'm a madman whose going to kill their goddamn people anyway.'

Callaghan looked at the younger man questioningly.

'Carrot and stick, my friend.' Kelly then cackled somewhat maniacally. 'I'll feed the public the carrot and I'll leave them to turn it into a stick with which to beat the authorities.'

'What do you mean?'

'Listen, my friend, at the moment the British public is against me. That's good, and I'll tell you for why. When people have a certain view of things and then you enlighten them, they tend to switch sides, and you know there's no more passionate a believer than a convert.'

'I'm sorry, Kieran, you've lost me.'

Kelly moved away from the window and returned to the panel of screens from which he could survey the whole shebang. He sat down in the chair and swivelled to face his companion. 'Look, Sean, they might not be able to find out your identity that easily, but I'm not foolish enough to believe that they won't have mine within a few hours.'

'So what are you going to do?'

.

'I'm going to announce it myself and I'm going to tell Teresa's story.'

'But Kieran, you can't tell them you're ex-IRA. The British public'll hate you for it,'

'We were internal affairs, Sean, you know that. We never laid a finger on a Brit. The British Army has no record of us.'

'What about our own, Kieran? We have enemies.'

'It was an unwritten law. We did what we had to do. There was no room for traitors. Anyone who grasses, even now, is a dead man walking. Anyway, there were only two people who knew our true identities and they've both passed on.'

Callaghan again looked questioningly at his leader.

Kelly laughed. 'Don't worry, man, they died with their boots off. One of them was a guy from Derry. Had a heart attack. Died the next day in hospital without regaining consciousness,'

'And the other?'

'The other was Father Seamus O'Hare. I heard that he died in his own bed from old age a year ago.'

Callaghan was shocked. He knew that O'Hare had administered the last rites at all of their executions,, but they had always remained fully disguised in their balaclavas. There was never a hint that the priest knew the identities of the executioners. Kieran had always said someone from the outside had hired the cleric.

'God, that priest must have been one tormented individual,' Kelly went on.

'What do you mean?'

'He'd be forced to administer the last rites to our victims and then he'd have to hear my confession.'

'You mean—'

'Yeah, I knew that he couldn't tell anyone else. You might say that absolution was my insurance policy. It was our little secret.'

Callaghan found himself shaking his head in disbelief. He knew that the man before him was a highly complex individual, but there was a dark side that seemed to extend beyond the bounds of duty. Nevertheless, he was not about to question the motives of a mind that was far more intelligent and more ruthless than his own. 'It was a dirty business we did, to be sure,' he said simply.

'It was necessary, Sean, just as this is necessary. There are some things in life where the end justifies the means. When you know that injustice will never be corrected without coercion, you use coercion. Anyway, one man can make all the difference. Take Herzl for instance.'

'Who?' the older man queried.

'Herzl was a bearded Jew who said more than a hundred years ago that if you will it, it is no dream. There would have been no State of Israel if that man hadn't inspired his people with the dream of their own country.'

'We dreamed of a united Ireland, Kieran, but it didn't come.'

'Not yet, my friend, but it will.' Kelly leaned back in his chair, clasped his hands around the back of his neck and gazed at the ceiling. In a saintly murmur, he repeated the mantra of Theodore Herzl.

'Three up, two down,' Commander Bob Simmons smiled, and handed his colleague a five-page dossier containing an assortment of graphs. 'And I'm not referring to the rooms.'

Dai Hopkin studied the report. The radar had done its job well. 'The three upstairs are obviously the hostages because this shows extremely limited movement. The other two appear to be moving around freely. Only two, that's a relief.' The negotiator was suddenly distracted by the familiar throb of a helicopter that appeared to be heading their way. 'For fuck's sake, Bob, get that damned chopper away from here.'

'But—'

'Listen, Bob, you're either with me or against me. You know how I operate. I don't want some kudos-seeking fly-boy giving my hostage-takers the eeby-jeebies. They hear that thing and they might panic. I want calm, dead calm. Jesus, they'll fuck everything up before I even get a chance to talk to the bastards.'

Simmons was reticent about confronting a man who had become a living legend in the Met, but he felt he had to stand his ground. 'Look, Dai, they're pros in there. They expect choppers to be flying around. If we let them get used to the idea, it'll make it easier if we ever have to use one.'

To give Hopkin his due, he recognised the sense in what Simmons was saying, but it still made him uneasy. He hated edgy hostage takers.

'Okay, but if Kelly objects and lets off any more fireworks, we pull them out.'

'Okay, Dai,' Simmons compromised. He knew that the Welshman had a hundred per cent record for saving lives in these sorts of situations. That's why he'd put the man in charge in the field. There had been more than a few raised eyebrows among his men, but reputation counted for everything in the Met. They had to understand that you couldn't afford to fuck about with the mediocre, not with the whole world looking on. He'd never worked with the fat man before and he was eager to find out what made him tick. 'Dai,' he asked hesitantly, 'what made you go into this line of work?'

'Why did *you* become a copper, Bob?' the Welshman countered.

Simmons breathed deeply and stroked his lantern jaw. He pondered for a few seconds, then, 'for the public good. Anyway, I was born to it. My father was a copper.'

'Yep, for the public good, boyo,' Hopkin repeated, 'although sometimes I think they don't appreciate us.' He swivelled in his chair and peered out at the cottage. 'No, I was once an ordinary bobby on the beat just like your good self. I was wet behind the ears. I was slimmer and fitter then. I thought I could handle any situation. You know, brute force and all that. It all changed one day when I was the first copper on the scene at an abduction. It was a cottage not much different from this. It involved a kid. The man was the kid's father. He had a shotgun and was threatening to kill the boy and himself. The kid was only five. The father was a schizoid. The shit could have hit the fan at any time and we were all vulnerable. I was all for taking the guy out.' The Welshman hesitated, as if overwhelmed by the memory.

'So what happened?'

Hopkin swivelled back to face his gangling colleague. 'A man called Tommy Smith is what happened. He was the first negotiator I'd ever seen in action. You know the hardest job is to sweet-talk a crazy; they're totally unpredictable. Anyway, it took two days of painstaking negotiating to secure the boy's release. Smith didn't get flustered, not once. He just played the anchor for the man to latch onto in one of his saner moments. It was an education, a real education. You ask me why I'm a negotiator. It's because it saves lives more effectively than any other course of action open to us. That boy, his father and God knows how many coppers could have died if it wasn't for Tommy Smith. It proved to me that one man could make a difference, and I wanted to be that man.'

Simmons shook his head in awe, then, 'rather you than me, Dai.'

'It's common sense really, boyo. You put yourself in the hostage takers shoes and try to think like he does. People like people like themselves. It's the old salesman's adage.'

'What about the poor buggers being held in there?'

'They'll either be survivors or succumbers.'

'What do you mean?'

'Well, it works like this: survivors engage in activity, physically *and* mentally, that lead to a greater chance of surviving a hostage situation, while succumbers engage in activities that increase the probability of their being harmed or killed.'

'That covers a multitude of sins or virtues, Dai.'

The Welshman stroked his heavy jowls. 'Look, Bob, survivors try to hide any hatred or anger they might feel towards their captors. They don't act with any hostility. They don't get fucking uppity. They stay confident, but they don't flaunt it. They concentrate on survival and on doing what's necessary to survive.'

'And succumbers?'

'Ah,' Hopkin sighed, 'those poor bastards do everything to stand out to their captors. They might be too subservient or they might be the opposite. They might plead or beg or they might show open hostility. For them the future holds only negatives and all they succeed in doing is fucking with the heads of the people I'm trying to talk into letting them go.'

'I wonder which of those poor bastards over there fall into which category.'

'If I do my job right, they'll all be survivors despite themselves.'

Just as the Welshman finished speaking, an excited constable entered the van waving a piece of paper. 'I think we've got a name, sir. A man called Parsons rang in to say he used to work with a guy whose wife committed suicide after being given an epidural by Dr Townsend during childbirth.'

'What's his name, dammit?' Simmons spat through pursed lips.

'Kieran Kelly, sir.'

'An Irishman,' said Hopkin. 'A fucking Irishman.'

'Ex-IRA, Dai?'

'Maybe. I want to know everything about him. I want to know what he eats for breakfast and I want to know how many times a day he craps. Meanwhile, keep everything under wraps.'

'What do you mean?'

'I mean do not under any circumstances reveal his identity at this stage,' said the Welshman forcefully. 'Do you understand me, Bob? I must be allowed to judge the timing of any revelation. Get the media and tell them that if any of them steps out of line, they might end up facing charges of being accessories to murder.'

It was fast approaching nine in the evening and Kieran Kelly was eager to make his second broadcast to the world. The helicopters flying overhead had been a minor distraction. They could buzz around all they wanted, as long as nobody interfered with the transmission of his message. This time he'd rock the establishment to its very foundations. He'd already dangled the carrot in front of the media, and with Proctor's death adding a little spice, they were falling over themselves in a frenzy of speculation. He had prepared the tape to feed directly into his website. With a single click, people would be able to listen to the damning evidence as many times as they cared. The voice of Jack Proctor was about to rise from the grave and haunt a swathe of politicians, not least the pompous bastard upstairs.

Kelly donned his headset and cleared his throat. He picked up the voice distorter. This would be the last time he would use it. The next time the world would have a real voice, a real face, a real person; not some maniac in a balaclava.

'Good evening world,' he began stridently, 'here I am again as promised. As you all know, the chairman of Parados Pharmaceuticals is no longer with us. What I am about to play to you is the reason why Mr Proctor took his own life. It is a recording of a conversation between himself and one of my guests, the Right honourable, or rather dishonourable, Secretary of State for Health, You may wish to hear this recording a few times to make sure your ears aren't deceiving you. To do so, press the play icon at the bottom left of your screens. Here goes...' With this, the Irishman activated the recording and sat back to listen to Stephen Sellars talking his way out of politics. The conversation between the Minister and Proctor may have lasted less than a minute, but the Irishman believed it would be enough to switch the public from anti-balaclava to pro-balaclava.

'So there you have it, ladies and gentleman,' Kelly said when the recording had finished, 'corruption in all its glory. Kickbacks to help get a new drug on its merry way down our throats, regardless of whether we might choke on it. Time is money, folks, when you've got to get a new drug on the shelves. You all know the nursery rhyme, don't you: this little piggy went to market, this little piggy went home, and that fat little piggy upstairs went squealing all the way to the bank. Tomorrow evening at the same time I will make another revelation. Meanwhile, over to you Prime Minister.'

Kelly rose from his chair. It was time to visit a couple of his guests. He had told Sean to deal with Townsend. He couldn't even bare to be in the same room as the man who had crippled his Teresa. He removed his balaclava and swung firstly into the room containing the errant politician. Sellars looked up at him with the eyes of a Basset hound who had just crapped on his owner's new carpet. 'What price the Premiership now, fat man?' said the Irishman contemptuously.

Sellars turned away from the accusing glare. He had already known his career was over, but listening to the evidence of his own corruption was about as chastening as it could get.

'Maybe a spell in jail will make you a reformed man, Sellars,' Kelly went on, 'or perhaps hara-kiri would put you out of your misery. No, you're not the suicidal type, are you? I think you might need an injection into the spine. It's a painkiller you know. However, injected into the wrong place it doesn't kill pain; it kills you. Makes you wonder why it ever got passed by the Government, doesn't it?'

It was not that the Irishman's heavy sarcasm was lost on his hostage. It was just that Stephen Henry Sellars no longer had the energy to defend what was in essence indefensible. The Health Secretary simply no longer cared what happened to him.

'Cat got your tongue, shit-face?' Kelly spat and left the room. This was another one that he'd leave to Sean. He entered the room opposite and stood facing Jonathan Tring, who was still engrossed in the television punditry that had followed the broadcast. 'Look's like the shit's hit the fan, Professor, doesn't it?'

Tring used his remote to turn down the sound before replying, 'I hope it gets the Government to meet your demands.'

'But you still don't think they will.'

'It doesn't really matter what I think, does it?'

The Irishman scratched the back of his neck. 'You know, Tring, I don't really know what to think of you. You're pretty cool under pressure, aren't you?'

'Don't let appearances fool you.'

'You know when I was a boy in Belfast, we used to play a game. We'd see who could hold their hand over a candle the longest. The pressure was never on the weakest guys. It was always on the strongest, those who needed to win in order to gain their place in the hierarchy. Do you need to win, Professor?'

'I just want to get out of this alive and in one piece.'

'So do I, Professor, so do I. But there are some things more important than life or death.'

'Like what?'

'Like principles. One should be prepared to die for one's principles.'

'That's fine by me. As long as you don't take anyone else with you.'

'Innocents, you mean.'

'Yes, innocents.'

'Show me one person in this world who says he's innocent, Mr Tring, and I'll show you a liar.'

'Surely, it's a question of degree. If everyone were punished for their mistakes it would be the end of civilisation. It's civilised to show mercy.'

'It's Christian to show mercy, Mr Tring.'

'You're a Christian, aren't you?'

'I'm a Catholic, Mr Tring. I kill people and then I go to confession. God is in the mercy business, not me. And He's not much good at it either.'

'What do you mean?'

'Watch tomorrow night's broadcast and you'll see what I mean.' With this, Kelly turned and left the room. He felt a grudging respect for the scientist, but that was all. When push came to shove, Tring was as expendable as any man that got in his way.

CHAPTER TWENTY
THE SIEGE – DAY THREE

'Have you read this?' stormed Dai Hopkin flinging the newspaper onto the ops control table.

Bill Simmons looked down at the London Evening Standard headline: 'BALACLAVA' EXPOSES CORRUPT MINISTER. 'So they've given him a nickname, so what?'

'I don't care about *that* headline, I'm talking about the sidebar by Tring's girlfriend.'

The commander's eyes quickly scanned the article in which Fiona Harrington described how she and Jonathan Tring had sought to expose the corruption at the heart of the British Government, and how the hostage takers were now using it to their advantage. Fiona Harrington made clear that her lover was the true hero in the whole sordid affair. 'She's got a fucking nerve not informing us,' Simmons seethed. I'm going to read the bloody riot act to her editor.'

'Waste of time, boyo. Cat's out of the bag, look you. Anyway, it might work to our advantage. Our *Mister* Kelly has reason to be grateful to at least one of his captives. Maybe the Stockholm syndrome will come into play.' The Welshman was just about to continue with his theorising when his attention was drawn towards the awning of the ops van. Standing alongside a burly young constable was a fresh-faced blonde girl. He looked down at the front-page picture of Fiona Harrington and then looked up again. 'Well, talk of the devil.'

'May I come in, Commander?'

'No you may not, young lady. This is a restricted area.' The police chief's beady eyes narrowed as they turned towards his minion. 'You know that Constable.'

'Sorry, sir, but she said it was very important.'

Simmons scowled. He wasn't having any reporters in his own domain. 'Wait there,' he said gruffly, 'we'll come outside.'

Relieved at the opportunity to leave the fetid atmosphere of the van, Hopkin followed his colleague down the steps and out into air that had been freshened by an early morning shower.

'You must be very proud of yourself, young lady,' Simmons said scornfully.

If Fiona Harrington was intimidated by the man towering over her, she didn't show it. 'We had no idea about this planned abduction,' she said firmly. 'It was all just an incredible coincidence.'

'So your boyfriend's not in on it then?'

'Certainly not.'

'He soon might be,' Hopkin interjected.

Fiona Harrington stared at the rotund figure before her with a mixture of puzzlement and hurt.

'This is Inspector Dai Hopkin, Miss Harrington,' Simmons explained, 'he's our chief negotiator.'

Hopkin nodded, then, 'I mean it's not hard to see Professor Tring being sympathetic towards his captors.'

'He's not going to arse-lick a bunch of criminals if that's what you mean,' Fiona replied, surprised at her own indelicate use of language. 'Anyway, if there's one person who deserves his freedom it's Jonathan.'

'So you don't care about the other two?' the Welshman said cynically.

'I didn't say that.'

'Cut to the chase, Miss Harrington,' Simmons said irritably. 'What do you want?'

'I want to make a direct television appeal to the hostage takers.'

'And say what?' Hopkin asked with a hint of exasperation. Women always thought they could manipulate any situation involving men.

'I want to tell them that if they release all the hostages, Professor Tring and I will do everything in our power to see that their demands for justice are met.'

Hopkin smiled wryly. 'Missy, you're very earnest and you're very pretty, but I don't believe our balaclava-man will be persuaded by any argument you might put to him.'

'I can try.'

'Not without my permission you can't.'

'You can't muzzle the media.'

Hopkin was determined to remain calm. She was a feisty young lady and he could understand her concern for her boyfriend, but there was no way he would allow her to interfere in his game plan. 'You won't find anyone to run your appeal. The Government has issued strict orders.'

Fiona could sense that her request was falling on deaf ears, yet there appeared to be so little progress being made. 'May I ask you a question, Mr Hopkin?'

'Go ahead.'

'Have you even spoken to the hostage takers yet?'

'Not yet,' the Welshman answered coolly.

'Isn't it about time?'

'Listen, Missy, I can only speak to someone if he decides to speak to me and, believe me, sooner or later he will.'

Fiona looked at the fat man and raised her eyebrows. 'Let's hope it's sooner, Inspector,' she said turning away, 'just don't screw up.'

'Oh, Miss Harrington,' Hopkin called out, 'we didn't have this conversation, right?'

'I understand,' she said without looking back, and continued walking towards the throng of newsmen standing fifty yards away. She might not be permitted to appeal to the hostage takers through the electronic media, but that would not prevent her from making her appeal in print. The TV and radio stations might not quote her in full, but at least the men holding Jonathan would get the gist of her message.

Hopkin watched Fiona Harrington with a mixture of admiration and consternation. She was right. Unless he could make some contact with Kelly, this was becoming a one-way street. That might be all right in the early days, but the longer the siege went on without him being able to exercise his skills, the greater the pressure would become for force to be used. The Government wasn't helping either. There had been a lot of waffle from the Prime Minister, but nothing that could be construed as a sweetener to the hostage takers. Predictably, the drug companies had spouted the formula that no one should surrender to terrorist demands; the thin edge of the wedge and all that. They were the ones who were being asked to give up some of their profits and they didn't like it. The Welshman realised, however, that in the final analysis it was the Government that would decide how this thing would be played out. It could impose a windfall tax on the pharmaceutical giants and leave them bleating all the way to the bank. The question was whether there would be the political will to do so. In the meantime everyone was silent except Kelly, and silence was never golden for a negotiator.

Kieran Kelly had spent most of the day preparing his evening address, formulating its content and rehearsing its delivery. He'd given scarcely a thought to the menagerie outside, leaving Sean to look after the shop while he prepared the updates for his website, which had now become more popular than CNN, the BBC and the whole media caboodle. He used the software to install biographies about himself, sans his unofficial work, and Teresa. She would have pride of place: a photo gallery of her and the kids. He thought of the kids, and how they would be proud of their Da'; how they would understand that the success of his cause was for *their* future; how they would see that their Ma' had not suffered in vain. The madness of sticking needles into people's spines had to be stopped.

Once again he positioned himself in front of the web cam.

'Good evening, world,' he began as per usual, 'most of you must be wondering who I am and what I look like. You are about to find out.' With this, the Irishman removed his balaclava, straightened his hair and fixed his piercing blue eyes on the web cam. He placed the voice distorter on the table in front of him. Everything he was about to say would not only come from the heart, but would be uttered with the inflection and power of the one thing that could move men and mountains: the human voice.

'My name is Kieran Kelly,' he said, 'and I am from Belfast. However, in the great scheme of things, who I am and where I am from are of no consequence. The action my comrades and I have taken is not only about the deeds of the three men we are holding here; it is about this woman.' With this, Kelly held up a framed photograph of Teresa. It was his favourite of her, taken in the full bloom of early motherhood, just six months after the birth of their first child. Teresa's smile was as carefree and as pure as her bairn's. The camera angle had caught the innate kindness that radiated from within; the fullness of the flowing red hair;

the petite nose that turned up ever so slightly; the emerald green eyes that could captivate the hardest of men.

'This was my wife,' he said, speaking from behind the photograph. 'Her name was Teresa and she was only twenty-five years old when she died. She was the mother of four children who miss her terribly. She was the wife of a man who misses her more and more as each day passes.' He paused because of the lump that was forming in his throat. It was the truth, dammit.

'Teresa and I met at a dance,' he continued after regaining his composure. 'She was only seventeen, but I knew almost immediately that this girl would become my wife, that she would bear me the most beautiful children in the whole world. We came over two years ago. We were just an ordinary family living an ordinary life in east London. That was before late last year when Teresa decided to have an epidural for the birth of our fourth child. I didn't want her to have it, but she wanted to experience childbirth without pain. They told us Dr Martin Townsend was good, but they didn't tell us he was a drunk. They also didn't tell us what would happen if he injected the anaesthetic in the wrong place. They didn't tell us that there were thousands of women affected by these injections that no one ever got to find out about; they were told it was all in their heads; they were told they should stop their bleating and go away. That's what happened to my Teresa. No one believed her agony. She couldn't stand, she couldn't sit, and her waterworks wouldn't function properly. The burning pain in her legs tortured her remorselessly and if you ask me about the pain in her feet, I'd ask you whether you mean the kind where if you could bend easily enough you would gnaw them off; or the kind that makes you look to see if you're bleeding because it feels like they're being sliced with razor blades; or the kind where it feels like your toenails are being pulled out or wooden slivers are being shoved under them; or the kind that makes you think the balls of your feet are so swollen that your toes don't reach the floor, but then you look and they're digging into the hardwood; or do you mean the kind of pain that feels numb until you bang your foot into something and break a toe because you can't feel where it is? Teresa begged me to get a chainsaw and cut off her feet. She begged me to sever her spinal cord, thinking that would put an end to her agony. I had to tell her that if

I did that, her pains would continue. They'd simply call them by another name: phantom limb pains. She said she didn't mind; at least people would take her agony more seriously if she didn't have any legs. I did what I could, but it wasn't enough. She took an overdose. I shouldn't feel guilty, but I do. I feel as guilty as hell.'

The Irishman's voice had dropped almost to a whisper and a single tear worked its way down his cheek from his left eye and into the corner of his mouth. 'I pray to God that my Teresa will not have died in vain,' he rasped. He stood the framed photograph of his wife directly in front of the web cam. It would be all people would see for the duration of the siege.

'He's playing us like a fiddle, Dai,' Simmons growled with barely disguised frustration. 'With that performance he'll have the whole bloody nation baying for the PM to accede to his demands.'

Hopkin nodded. 'Amen to that. Nothing would please me more than if my efforts were redundant, boyo.'

The commander was just about to make a comment when his telephone rang. 'Simmons,' he said gruffly, then quickly covered the mouthpiece. 'It's him, Dai, and he wants to speak to you.'

'Well, that's a first,' said the Welshman, his heart pounding as he picked up the link and motioned to his staff to begin recording. 'Dai Hopkin here.'

'The negotiator?' came the now familiar voice.

'Yes.'

'Listen, Hopkin, I've seen the movie.'

'I'm sorry, I don't understand,' said the Welshman.

'The Negotiator, with Samuel L. Jackson. Great film.'

'Yes it was, but *it* was a movie and *this* for real.'

'Sammy was a pussy,' Kelly went on, 'he just pretended he was prepared to kill. I'm not pretending, Hopkin.'

'I believe you.'

'Of course you believe me. Never say no to a hostage taker, never use don't, won't or can't.'

'I see you've read the script.'

'You might as well throw away the manual when it comes to me, Hopkin. Unless my aims are met, I'm prepared to die and to take as many of you as I can with me.'

'That's not for public consumption, I guess,' the Welshman replied, a cold sweat breaking out on his forehead.

'You're right, Taffy. Bad PR.'

Hopkin felt a flicker of relief that Kelly had agreed with him early on. It was paramount that he did everything to win the man's trust. 'I think you've presented a convincing case.'

'What you think doesn't mean jack shit. It's what that bastard Scotsman does that matters.'

Hopkin glanced up at Simmons with a look that spoke volumes. As far as they knew at the moment, the Prime Minister was not for turning. He was a po-faced politician who thought compromise was a dirty word. Meanwhile, Kelly and his cohorts were like animals backed into a corner, fangs bared, seeing no way out. It was going to be an uphill task.

'*All* my demands must be met,' the Irishman said firmly. 'Make sure he understands that, Taff.'

'I understand how you feel, Mr Kelly. It's not easy to see a loved one suffer. I felt terrible watching my old man die of cancer.'

'God killed your father, Mr Hopkin. Man killed my wife.'

'Yes, medical malpractice is a tough call. Dr Townsend should never be allowed to practise medicine again.' Hopkin knew that he had to focus on the man's feelings. He had to demonstrate understanding of the Irishman's fear, anxiety and anger. He had to empathise without being judgmental or condescending. Just by having someone listen might reduce the man's stress.

'I wish I could believe that were true, Taffy,' Kelly said with a sigh. 'If I let hit him go, the GMC will give him a slap on the wrists and the drunken bastard will be out there ruining more people's lives.'

'Unfortunately, you're probably right,' Hopkin agreed. So far so good, he thought. He could feel that he was building what might be the beginnings of a rapport. It was all a case of active listening, the ability to see a circumstance from another's perspective and to let the other person know that the negotiator understood that perspective. Empathy, not sympathy, was the keyword. Sympathy implied pity and over-involvement. If the negotiator got too involved and showed pity, then the hostage taker might feel justified in how he was feeling about the actions he was taking. One thing was certain: the man was highly intelligent. Unfortunately, that could turn out to be more of a bane than a boon.

'Anyway,' Kelly said, 'how would any of you bastards know how it feels to lose someone you love so fucking unnecessarily.

Kelly's sudden vehemence did not fluster the Welshman. The 'how do you know how I feel?' response was common in people who were in crisis. It was possible to understand another's feelings without going through the same experience because, while experiences were not universal, feelings were. Degrees of feelings were also common. There wasn't a man alive who hadn't experienced shades of anger, sadness or depression.

'It's a good thing I can rely on my friends,' Kelly went on.

'Friends?' Hopkin repeated. The technique was called mirroring. By repeating the last word and adding a question mark, he was using the subject's own word to provide an exact response.

'Yeah, the –' Kelly halted dead in his tracks. He had just been about to say 'two.' There was a pregnant silence before, 'cute, Taffy. You almost had me there.'

'But not quite.'

Kelly laughed. He found himself admiring the man's honesty. This was going to be an intellectual challenge. 'That's enough for one day, Hopkin. I'll answer my phone again tomorrow at noon. By that time I hope the authorities have gained some wisdom.'

'Are you telling me that if they get wise, then there might be some room for compromise?'

'What I'm saying is that the prick you call a prime minister has to stop his waffling and come up with something concrete.'

It was a glimmer of hope, thought the Welshman, relieved that the rapport appeared to be still alive. 'Is there anything you need in the meantime, like food for instance?' he asked with genuine concern.

'Fully stocked for the duration and enough to feed Africa's starving for a year. And there's just one more thing. If you find out where my kids are, don't involve them or I'll shoot at least one of the hostages. Make sure they're not hassled by the media. Is that crystal clear?'

'Yes.'

'Good. And there's one other thing.'

'Yes.'

'I've just put an article on my website. It's from a book by some Yank doctor called Marsden Wagner. I want it published in full by every goddamn national newspaper. Tomorrow, get it, tomorrow, not the day after. Then I want the Prime Minister to agree to an inquiry.'

With this, Kieran Kelly switched off his mobile.

Hopkin frowned and turned to his staff in the control van. 'Okay, boyos, listen up. What do you think we've learned from this initial contact?'

'He might be prepared to lower his demands if the politicians make some concessions,' piped a chubby-faced copper manning the tape recorders.

'Which is a tad better than his earlier statement that *all* his demands must be met,' Hopkin agreed. 'But never forget, boyos, this guy is not only desperate, he's clever. He's got a manipulative personality. He's used to getting his own way.'

'How many men do you think he's got in there, boss?' asked a beak-nosed constable standing by the awning.

'Play back the tape, Jim,' Hopkin ordered.

They all listened intently when it reached the place where the Welshman almost caught his man out.

'Play it again,' Hopkin said, 'and watch the oscilloscope. There it is, look you.'

The Welshman was slightly amused by the sea of blank faces before him. 'I think our voice analyst will say that Kelly was just about to say "two". It's that nasal snort just before he cut himself short. You wouldn't get that with any other number. My guess is that Kelly and no more than two other hostage takers are in that cottage. Confirms more or less what the radar is telling us.'

'That'll make SO17 even more itchy to take him out,' Simmons grunted.

'Over my dead body,' retorted Hopkin. If the anti-terrorist unit went into action, it could only mean that he'd failed.

'I'm already getting flak from that quarter,' said the commander. 'How long can I stall them?'

'It's too early.'

'Unless he starts shooting,' Simmons warned. 'We know he must have a fucking arsenal in there.'

Hopkin looked at his boss anxiously. The Welshman's job was to stall as long as practicable, but there was a downside to the passage of time. A major problem would be exhaustion on the part of everyone involved, from the subject through to the negotiators, tactical personnel and commanders. He himself was already feeling the effects of sleep deprivation. Although twelve hours was probably too long to be actively negotiating, most teams established twelve-hour shifts, and his was no exception. Exhaustion could lead to fuzzy thinking at best and irrational thinking at worst. What sounded like a good idea at three in the morning after eighteen hours of high stress might not sound so good when it came to the day in court. Typically, however, the first few shifts in sieges were extraordinarily long. Most of his best men liked to believe that the standoff would end soon and itched to be on the scene when that happened. They just didn't want to miss out on any of the action. From past experience, he knew how difficult it was to get personnel to leave for rest or even to run errands. No one wanted to go home and have his son ask, 'Hey, Dad, when that bad man was shot today, what did you do?' and have to answer, 'Well son, I was down at McDonald's buying burgers for the team and missed the whole shebang.'

Lost in his own dark thoughts, Dai Hopkin had to be prodded back to awareness by one of his staff.

'Excuse me, sir, I've got his website article on screen.'

Hopkin and Simmons spent the next few minutes sitting in front of the screen engrossed in the article. 'Pretty impressive stuff,' said the Welshman. 'Do you think you can get the press to cooperate, Bob?'

'Believe me,' the commander replied, 'they'll fucking cooperate. It's the PM I'm worried about.'

CHAPTER TWENTY-ONE
THE SIEGE – DAY FOUR

True to his word, Commander Bob Simmons won the cooperation of the nation's newspaper owners. The leader writers were baying for the government to react positively. Every tabloid and broadsheet, from The Sun to The Times, carried the Wagner article in its entirety.

FISH CAN'T SEE WATER
By Dr Marsden Wagner
Former Regional Officer for Women's and Children's Health, World Health Organisation (WHO)
Humanising birth means understanding that the woman giving birth is a human being, not a machine and not just a container for making babies. Showing women, half of all people, that they are inferior and inadequate by taking away their power to give birth is a tragedy for all society. On the other hand, respecting the woman as an important and valuable human being and making certain that the woman's experience while giving birth is fulfilling and empowering is not just a nice extra, it is absolutely essential as it makes the woman strong and therefore makes society strong. But we do not have humanised birth in many places today. Why? Because fish can't see the water they swim in. Birth attendants, be they doctors, midwives or nurses, who have experienced only hospital-based, high interventionist, medicalised birth cannot see the profound effect their interventions are having on the birth. These hospital birth attendants have no idea what a birth looks like without all the interventions, a birth which is not dehumanised. This widespread inability to know what normal, humanised birth is has been summarized by the World Health Organization:

'By medicalising birth, i.e. separating a woman from her own environment and surrounding her with strange people using strange machines to do strange things to her in an effort to assist her, the woman's state of mind and body is so altered that her way of carrying

through this intimate act must also be altered and the state of the baby born must equally be altered. The result it that it is no longer possible to know what births would have been like before these manipulations. Most health care providers no longer know what 'non-medicalised' birth is. The entire modern obstetric and neonatological literature is essentially based on observations of 'medicalised' birth.'

Why is medicated birth necessarily dehumanising? In medicalised birth, the doctor is always in control, while the key elements in humanised birth is the woman in control of her own birthing and whatever happens to her. No patient has even been in complete control in the hospital. If a patient disagrees with the hospital management and has failed in attempts to negotiate the care, her only option is to sign herself out of the hospital. Giving women choice about certain maternity care procedures in not giving up control since doctors decide what choices women will be given and it is doctors who still have the power to decide whether or not they will acquiesce to a woman's choice.

To understand why there is now an epidemic of epidural block for normal labour pain, it is necessary to understand what happens to the woman before she is offered the epidural. The care she received when she comes to the hospital to give birth markedly increases the pain she will have. Scientific evidence shows labour pain is significantly increased by labouring in an unfamiliar place; by being surrounded by unfamiliar people; by having unfamiliar procedures done; by being unattended during labour; by being placed in a horizontal position and not allowed to walk about freely; by having the membrane artificially ruptured; by having induction or augmentation with drugs. Thus the woman comes into the hospital in labour, has number of things done which all increase her pain, is then offered an epidural and is so grateful to the staff for the relief of the pain, much of which the staff created.

The epidemic use of epidural block for normal labour pain has closely followed the rapid increase in the use of powerful and dangerous drugs for induction and augmentation. The predominant obstetric cascade of the 1990s has been pharmacological induction, leading to increased pain, leading to operative birth with forceps, vacuum extraction or caesarean section. Since each of these interventions carries significant risks, this cascade multiplies the risks for both the woman and the baby. For example, the contractions induced by the drugs have a different intensity and different interval, which not only increases the pain, but also increases chances of foetal hypoxia.

Why does epidural block lead to operative birth? Two reasons. Firstly, with the woman already having lost all feeling from the waist down because of the epidural, the temptation is great for the doctor to go right ahead and carry out surgical procedures. The second reason is fundamental to the basic understanding of the birth process. The pain of labour is an essential component of normal labour, as it stimulates the brain to release hormones that, in turn, stimulate the uterus to contract at normal levels of intensity so that placental blood flow will be maintained and there will be no foetal hypoxia. This is a delicate feedback process. With an epidural block there is an interruption of this process, leading to a slowing or cessation of normal labour. Attempts can be made to overcome this with more and more stimulation of the uterus with more and more drugs such as Oxycotin – a rather typical scenario found in high tech birth where one intervention required another intervention to try to overcome the problems of the first intervention.

Nevertheless, the scientific evidence is clear: even with such efforts to overcome the slowing of labour caused by epidural block, there is still a four times greater chance forceps or vacuum extraction will be necessary after epidural block and at least two times greater chance caesarean section will be required. This is no surprise since this is the inevitable result of using an intervention, namely epidural, which essentially stops the birth process in its tracks.

The only way an epidemic of epidural block for normal birth has been able to happen is because the procedure has been given a very 'hard sell' to women by doctors. The only way that so many women agree to an epidural for normal labour is they are told it is 'safe'.

Is epidural block safe? The single most important new trend in modern obstetrics is a universally agreed principle that all obstetric practice must be based on the best scientific evidence. What is the evidence on the safety of epidural block? Firstly, a procedure can hardly be called 'safe' when close to a quarter (23%) of women receiving epidural block have complications. The risks to the women are many and serious, starting with the possibility the woman will die because of the epidural. The maternal death rate for women having epidural block for normal labour pain is three times higher than for women with normal labour not having the block. For every 500 epidurals performed there will be one case of temporary paralysis and the paralysis will be permanent in one of every half million epidurals.

The woman has a fifteen to twenty percent chance of fever after receiving an epidural, necessitating a diagnostic evaluation for possible infection in the woman and baby that can sometimes be invasive, such as requiring a spinal tap. Between fifteen and thirty-five percent of women given an epidural will suffer from urinary retention after birth.

How effective is epidural block in relieving pain? In around 10% of epidural blocks it doesn't work and there is no pain relief. Even when it works, around a third of the women given an epidural during labour will have severe back pain after birth and 20% will still have back pain a year later.

A great deal of scientific research has shown that women receiving epidural block for normal labour pain will have a significantly longer second stage of labour. This, in turn, results in a four times greater risk if using forceps or vacuum extraction and at least a two times greater risk of caesarean section, and these interventions during birth carry their own serious risks as well.

While many women might be willing to take risks with their own bodies to gain pain relief, it is highly unlikely they are willing to put their babies at risk. One common complication in the woman after an epidural is started is sudden loss of blood pressure leading to a sharp drop in blood flow through the placenta to the foetus, resulting in mild to severe lack of oxygen to the foetus as shown on a foetal heart rate monitor. In another typical high-tech strategy of using a second intervention to try to stop the bad effects of the first intervention, doctors give the woman a great big dose of fluid through an IV to try to prevent the drop in blood pressure from the epidural, but this does not always work. So lack of oxygen to the baby during the epidural remains a possibility and the American College of Obstetricians and Gynaecologists reports that the electronic foetal heart monitor shows severe foetal hypoxia in eight to twelve percent of infants whose mothers are given an epidural block for normal labour pain.

There are other risks to the infant, including some data suggesting poor neurological function at one month of age in babies whose mothers had epidural blocks. More recent epidural block innovations, such as changing the type of drugs used or what the drug does or the 'walking epidural', do *not* eliminate these risks to the woman and her baby.

One reason for the evidence of epidural in many countries is that women are not told the scientific facts about all the risks to them and their babies when epidural block is used for normal labour pain. Indeed, at one meeting of obstetric anaesthesiologists in the US, discussions were held on how to prevent any information on risks of epidural from reaching the public. The excuse used was the typical patronising approach of some doctors: 'we don't want to scare the ladies.' It is absolutely essential that any women offered epidural must be told all the scientific facts about the risks before she gives informed consent to the procedure.

With all these risks of epidural block to woman and baby, why are doctors urging women to use it? Research shows that doctors prefer the woman to have an epidural because then she is quiet and compliant. Furthermore, it is the frequent use of epidural for normal labour that has created a new speciality, obstetric anaesthesiology, which is highly lucrative and flourishing – witness that obstetric anaesthesiology journals contain advertisement urging doctors to purchase private jet airplanes.

Adding epidural block to an already high-tech, highly invasive style of birth care is seen by many doctors as a logical next step. Efforts to contain this new invasive and risky procedure and prevent it from spreading as an epidemic in any country must begin with the education of doctors, midwives, nurses and the public to the reality that such a style of birth care has been shown scientifically to be truly dangerous and full of risks to women and babies. In other words, everyone must begin to see the water that many obstetricians and hospitals are swimming in and see that it is full of sharks that may not 'eat' the doctors, but will 'eat' some of the women and babies.

Countries must work hard not to allow visiting doctors from places like the US to try to sell them on their system of maternity care, a system where nearly every obstetrician and maternity hospital offers only one style of birth care – a style not based on scientific evidence, but on the absolute control of the system by the doctors.

Maternity care in the US is a form of care with extreme 'medicalisation' of birth. Doctors give primary care to over 90% of normal, healthy women giving birth. As a result, birth becomes a surgical procedure with high rates of unnecessary interventions. Women giving birth are disempowered and there are huge wastes of resources, financial and professional. Midwives are marginalized and more and more obstetricians are trained. This is not a system to emulate – the US maternal, perinatal and infant mortality rates are much higher than those of nearly every other industrialised country. Epidural block is part of such a system and this is not a direction that either health professionals or the public in any country wishes to take.

It is far more appropriate to develop strategies to avoid pain medication during labour – strategies that will empower the woman to believe in herself through experiencing what her own body can accomplish. One strategy to consider is not having the birth in a hospital, but in a birth centre or at home. Good scientific research shows such out-of-hospital birth at birth centres or at home staffed by midwives is a perfectly safe option to consider. Epidurals and other dangerous drugs are not used in such settings for controlling the pain of normal birth.

Another strategy is to have a midwife as the principle birth attendant, regardless of where the birth takes place. Scientific data prove that women giving birth who are continuously attended by a midwife have less pain and need less pain control. The midwife approach is to help the woman through the pain rather than the medical approach, which sees the pain as an evil to be eradicated.

Allowing relatives or friends to be continuously with the woman in labour is another strategy that scientific evidence has shown significantly reduces pain and the need for pain control.

In those places where epidural block is promoted, one never hears about the scientifically proven effective ways to control normal labour pain without turning to powerful and risky drugs. Warm water is another highly effective way to relieve labour pains, and having tubs available in maternity hospitals is now popular all over the industrialised world.

Massage is proven to relieve labour pain, as is acupressure, nerve stimulation (TENS) and, yes, walking.

Some doctors put birthing women on their backs in a horizontal position because this is what is done with surgical patients. This was never done to birthing women before surgeons started attending births. We have known scientifically for over twenty-five years that putting women on their backs and not allowing them freedom to move about increases pain, slows labour and increases foetal distress. So freedom to walk and assume various vertical positions is another effective labour pain strategy.

None of the non-drug methods of labour pain relief just described have any risks or dangers. They are examples of interventions that can be truly called 'safe, something which cannot be said about the drugs used to relieve labour pain.

Finally, how pain is perceived, endured or managed is highly cultural. In many places, women have a long history of coping with the pain of normal labour and will not rush to adopt epidural block, a highly invasive and dangerous American method that fits into the highly medicalised, dehumanising American birth care offered by obstetricians.

Birth, which has been taken from the community and slowly but surely changed into hospital-based care during the last hundred years, must be given back to the community, back to the woman and her family. Doctors are human; birthing women are human. To err is human. Women have the right to have any errors committed during their birthing be their own and not someone else's.

There was an addendum from Kelly that said that the issues discussed in the article applied to Britain as much as they did to America.

'Well, we've done our part,' Hopkin said, spreading out the morning's national newspapers before him. What time is the PM's statement due?'

'Noon,' Simmons replied. 'I don't know about you. But I feel like shit. I didn't get much shuteye last night, not after reading that article.'

The Welshman winked. 'Having a baby are we, then, Bob?'

'My daughter.'

'Sorry, boyo,' Hopkin apologised.

'Well, I for one am going to convince my Karen not to have an epidural. It's not worth the aggro. Her mother didn't have one and she never complained.'

'Trouble is, boyo, the youngsters of today are not as tough as they used to be. They've been conditioned to regard pain as always being unnecessary. They've been conditioned to popping pills at the slightest ache. Kelly was right when he said that epidurals have become a fashion statement.'

Simmons was just about to respond when one of his operatives reported that an email had been received from 10 Downing Street. 'It's embargoed for noon, sir,' said the constable. The two senior officers turned towards the screen, their eyes scurrying over the main points of the statement.

'Shit,' Hopkin seethed. 'Shit, shit, shit.'

Magda von Esterhazy wearily moved from the settee to the wheelchair. The pain was so intense that the whimpering sounds that escaped from her lips frightened her carer.

'Are you sure you want to do this, Magda?' asked the pretty West Indian girl. Christine Smith had become the Countess's constant companion since the Irishman had left. She had always had her doubts from the first time she had seen the man who now called himself Kieran Kelly.

'I must, Christine,' the Countess replied. 'Someone must save him from himself.'

'I don't think he wants to be saved.'

'What do you mean?' Magda queried, a knot of apprehension in the pit of her stomach.

'I think Kelly wants to become a martyr. However much his cause is just, he knows that the odds are against him.'

'No!' the Countess blurted in a response that bordered on panic. 'He wants to live. He's got four beautiful children.'

'How can he care about them?' Christine Smith said darkly. Despite her tender years, she was nobody's fool. 'They must be going through hell now that he's revealed his true identity. He's very handsome, but I still don't know what you see in him. He just used you, like he's using everyone.'

'It's not true, Christine. Our lives have been shattered. I lost my health and he lost his dear wife.'

'You must have known you could never replace her, Magda.'

'Of course I knew. But we both yearned for affection. I know that he loved me, even if it wasn't the same love that he had for Teresa. I also know that he would never do anything to hurt me.'

'He hurt you when he left you.'

'He had no choice.'

'Of course he had a choice.' Christine Smith was nothing if not frank. 'He could have given up his ridiculous plan of revenge and dedicated himself to helping you.' Then, feeling that she had overstepped the mark, she added softly, 'you know I really care about you, Magda. I couldn't bear it if anything happened to you.'

The Countess took her young companion's slender hand in her own. 'I promise I'll be okay. We don't even know whether the police will agree, anyway. Now, get a few things together and let's go.'

Kieran Kelly watched the noon TV news broadcast with a mixture of disbelief and consuming anger. The female newsreader's voice was flat and emotionless, as if the issues affected only women in the reaches of Outer Mongolia.

... the statement said Her Majesty's Government had complete confidence in the use of epidurals in childbirth and saw no reason to institute a general inquiry ...

The Irishman switched off the television and reached for his phone. He dialled the negotiator's number. Trying to remain cool, he took a deep breath. Threats delivered with emotion carried no weight. Only those delivered with deliberation and purpose would convince the recipients of his earnestness. 'Did you hear that Taffy?' he asked through gritted teeth.

'I heard.'

'Well you tell the Prime Minister that he bears direct responsibility for what's going to happen next.'

Hopkin's mind raced. He was desperate to know what his adversary was planning. In training, a negotiator learns not only to listen to the facts, but also to tune in to the emotion behind the words and facts. Emotion labelling was used to respond, not strictly to content, but to the emotions heard in the subject's voice. 'I hear your frustration and anger, Mr Kelly,' he said softly. He also knew that by paraphrasing what he had just been told demonstrated that he was listening intently, which in turn created empathy and didn't put the subject on the defensive. 'Are you telling me that you're going to take some kind of action?'

'You don't need to be a brain surgeon to figure that out, Taff.' replied Kelly wryly.

'May I make an observation?'

'You may.'

'According to the media, the British public is rapidly being converted to your cause.'

Kelly chuckled sinisterly. 'Not rapidly enough to convince the Government, it seems.'

'I agree, but then these things tend to have their own dynamics. They have a habit of progressing slowly until some sort of compromise is arrived at.'

'After that statement, there can be no compromise with that Scots shit.'

Hopkin needed to keep the man talking. 'Try seeing it from his point of view,' he cajoled. 'He needs to be seen to be tough before he inevitably bows to public pressure. I'm sure you wouldn't want to do anything that might lose you the advantage.'

'I wish I could believe you, Taffy, but I'm a suspicious person by nature. All politicians are liars. He might end up promising a lot, but he'll deliver little.'

'So you're going to do something to encourage him.'

'Yes.'

Hopkin decided to use silence this time. He would wait for Kelly to continue, hoping that he would give details of his proposed action.

The Irishman played the pause, then, 'you'll know what I've done as soon as I do it. Let's just say it'll involve one of the hostages.'

'Are you telling me that you 're going to harm one of them?' Hopkin queried, his heart racing. Usually he would ask open-ended questions, but this was rapidly becoming an emergency situation.

'You'll know when it happens,' Kelly replied noncommittally.

'Unless—'

'Yes?'

'Unless Downing Street issues a retraction by noon.'

'I'll see what I can do,' Hopkin said unconvincingly. For the first time he could feel his usual optimism fading. He could sense that the situation was slipping away from him.

'Noon,' Kelly repeated and switched off his mobile.

The Welshman's heavy jowls appeared to sag a few more centimetres in the direction of his ample girth. He turned to his colleagues and spoke quietly, 'we're pissing in the wind, boyos.'

'I've got some more bad news, Dai,' said Simmons. 'The powers that be are saying that if just one hostage is harmed, then we're going in.'

'That's madness, Bob, you know that.'

'Madness or not, that's the decision.'

Both men spent the next three hours waiting for a retraction from number 10 that they knew would not come. Military vehicles were scurrying to and fro and they were aware that the extra activity would not have been lost on the hostage takers.

At precisely noon a single shot rang out from the cottage.

'Faster, Christine,' urged Magda von Esterhazy, 'please, faster.' Despite the fact that every bump and bend from her north London home sent paroxysms of pain through her back and lower limbs, news on the radio about the shooting acted like an anaesthetic.

'We're nearly there,' said her young carer. 'I just hope the police will let us through.'

A minute later and the Toyota, which was specially adapted to carry a wheelchair, drew to a halt before a line of police cars.

'Where do you think you're going, Miss?' a burly sergeant asked gruffly.

'Please, sergeant,' Christine Smith begged, 'let us through. This is Countess Magda von Esterhazy. She is Kieran Kelly's girlfriend.'

'And I'm Count Dracula,' replied the policeman cynically.

'Let me speak to him, Christine,' Magda gasped. She looked squarely into the copper's cynical grey eyes and spoke as calmly as she could. 'Sergeant, I am disabled and in crippling pain. I have made the effort to come here in order to try to prevent a tragedy. Kelly is my lover. I believe I can make him see reason.'

'That bastard will never see reason,' the policeman growled. 'He's just shot one of the bloody hostages.'

Magda's heart sank, but she knew she could not give up now. 'Look, Sergeant, if this thing ends in more tragedy, I'll tell the whole world that you prevented the one person who might have made a difference from reaching the scene. It wouldn't look good on your CV.'

The Sergeant thought for a few seconds, then nodded. He relayed the information to central command and within a minute, the Toyota was being guided through the phalange of armoured vehicles towards a black van that was parked closest to the cottage but behind a clump of trees.

While Magda's wheelchair was being lowered, Dai Hopkin and Bob Simmons were already locked in a heated exchange.

The commander gasped with incredulity. 'What do you mean, he hasn't shot anyone?'

'Samuel L. Jackson,' Hopkin replied.

'What the fuck are you talking about?'

'Don't you remember, he said he saw the film The Negotiator.'

'So what.'

'Well, in the film Jackson is the hostage taker and he makes the police believe he's shot one of the hostages. It was all a bluff to make them think that he was serious.'

'That's crap, Dai, you can't be sure.' For the first time Simmons believed his own negotiator was losing the plot. 'We're going in unless this Countess von Hazy, or whatever her name is, is the real McCoy.'

'I don't like putting another member of the public at risk,' the Welshman said. 'It goes against everything I've ever learnt, or ever taught for that matter. As a general rule, direct civilian participation in negotiations is entirely unsupportable, Bob, you know that.'

'It's the last throw of the dice, Dai. If she is who she says she is, then maybe she can get that mad Irishman to see some sense.'

'We could ask her to speak to him by phone.'

The commander shook his head, 'No, Dai, she insists that she can convince him only if she sees him face-to-face.'

'She'll have to convince *me*, Bob.'

Just as Hopkin finished speaking, the two men were advised that their visitor was waiting outside. When the Welshman first laid eyes on the woman in the wheelchair, he thought Countess Magda von Esterhazy was the most beautiful woman he had ever seen.

'I don't fucking believe it,' Kieran Kelly cursed, as he zoomed his monitor in on the electric wheelchair trundling up the path. Shaking with rage, he snatched up his mobile and dialled the negotiator. 'What the fuck are you playing at, Hopkin,' he screamed. 'Get her out of here.' It was the first time he had failed to control his emotions.

'I understand how you must feel, Mr Kelly,' the Welshman said, his voice quivering with trepidation, 'but she insisted. She said you'd understand.'

'Understand!' Kelly yelled. 'You'll bear the consequences if she gets hurt, you Welsh bastard.' With this, the Irishman hurled the thin plastic mobile to the floor, where it shattered into a few jagged pieces.

Dai Hopkin felt as if he'd been hit by a truck. It was all over as far as rapport was concerned. For the first time in his life, the big man felt the icy grip of failure around his vitals. Unless a sick woman in a wheelchair could make a difference, the standoff could only end in chaos and death. He, for one, had no confidence in anti-terrorist squads however well trained. From Teheran to Waco, it had just been a succession of foul-ups. When the gun replaced the word, it was time to take to the hills.

Kelly opened the front door of *Rosedale*, aware that he was making himself a target for police snipers, although he reckoned they wouldn't shoot. They still didn't know how many men he had in the place and they wouldn't risk hitting Magda. He breathed in the fresh autumn air. In a way, it was a kind of freedom after being cooped up for so many days.

'Go away, Magda,' he said softly as she reached the front door. 'Please.' He could see the pain in her eyes and knew that the effort was causing her seven shades of hell.

'I can't, Kieran,' she replied. 'I'd rather die than live without you. Even if they sent you to prison, I would wait.'

'No one will ever put me in a prison,' he said with a determination that frightened her.

'You're already in a kind of prison, *liebling*,' she said softly.

'Yes, but here I'm the warden.'

'I didn't mean a physical prison.'

The Irishman stared at her in silence for a few seconds, once again captivated by her brittle beauty. A few spots of rain began to fall. 'You'd better come in,' he said, despite his inner misgivings. 'Turn your wheelchair around and I'll lift it over the step.'

Magda pressed a button on the right-hand arm of the wheelchair and it revolved on the spot. It was only then, while facing away from the cottage, that the magnitude of the forces arrayed against him really hit home. She was more afraid for his safety than she had ever been.

'Don't worry about them,' the Irishman said, reading her thoughts, 'they're just amateurs.' It was false bravado, and they both knew it.

Once inside the cottage, Magda found herself facing another arsenal of weapons. He was obviously prepared for a shootout. The whole thing was crazy.

'As luck would have it,' he said, changing the subject, 'we've got a recliner here. He knew the armchair was about the only item of furniture that would offer her some relief. 'Here, let me help you.' He took her hands in his and leaned back, slowly levering her out of the wheelchair. He then clasped her closely to him.

Magda winced as he held her tight. She had no trouble standing upright, or hobbling a few metres for that matter, but the closeness of his masculinity suffused her with a kind of sensual giddiness. They stood embraced in silence, his strong arms looped around her and his hands clasping her shoulder blades. Then his lips touched hers. It was merely a brush at first, but then it developed into a kiss that rekindled the deep yearning within her. She could feel his hand moving over her breasts in exaggerated circles. 'Don't!' she cried suddenly.

The Irishman stopped and was immediately overcome by a sense of deep shame. 'I'm sorry, Magda,' he said quietly.

'For God's sake, Kieran,' she hissed, 'you know I'm not wired. I'd never allow them to do that.'

He apologised again, and helped her into the recliner.

She peered deeply into the cold azure of his eyes and tried to fathom what lay behind them. Who really was this man who could combine tenderness with such suspicion? Her attention was suddenly distracted by a short wiry figure descending the stairs into the open plan kitchen-diner.

'Sean Callaghan,' Kelly explained. 'A true friend.'

Callaghan nodded. 'Pleased to meet you, Countess. Kieran told me you were beautiful, and it's no exaggeration, to be sure.'

Magda felt herself blush. She could never handle compliments well. It was always as if people had to say something positive when confronted by a cripple in a wheelchair.

'Magda's here to try to change our minds, Sean,' Kelly said. 'Knowing me as you do, do you think there's a chance?'

'I'd say there's more chance of the Secretary of State for Health becoming leader of the Free World.' The older man laughed. 'Which reminds me, I'm late with his lunch.' Ever tactful, Callaghan picked up a plate of ham sandwiches in the kitchen and began making his way up the stairs.

'Toss me your mobile, Sean,' Kelly said, 'mine's had a bit of an accident. Not as robust as the old ones.'

Magda turned her head back towards her lover just as he caught the phone. 'I'm not leaving here unless you give yourself up,' she said firmly.

'Why should I give myself up, Magda, when the government hasn't agreed to even one of my conditions?'

'Public opinion is on your side.'

'Public opinion is fickle. If I give up now, everyone will have forgotten this inside a week.'

'No, Kieran, the whole world is discussing invasive spinal procedures. You've set in motion a train that can't be stopped.'

Kelly began pacing up and down in front of her. 'Those bastards'll derail it at the first opportunity, you know that. I've never trusted the authorities my whole life and I don't see any reason to start now.' He suddenly stopped, pulled up a chair and sat facing her. His voice softened as he once more took her elegant pale hands in his. 'Anyway, what about all the people like you who deserve compensation?'

'I'm not looking for money, Kieran. I just want justice and mercy, not malice.'

'But can't you see that justice is what this is all about?'

'Not this way, Kieran. Too many people are hurting already, not least the families of those three men you are holding.'

'I can see the pain in your eyes, Magda. I wish I could take your pain.'

The Countess looked squarely at the man she loved. What could he or anyone else understand of the terrors of her illness? 'Don't say that,' she said in almost a whisper. 'Don't ever say that again.'

'I don't understand,' he said genuinely.

'It's condescending. The easiest thing in the world is for a healthy person to say they want to take on the suffering of a loved one. You can't experience my nightmare unless your spine is injected with toxic material. That's something neither of us are likely to agree to, however much you might love me. No, I don't want anyone sharing my pain, thank you.'

The Irishman released his right hand from hers and caressed her long blonde hair. She was truly an extraordinary woman. 'Look, Magda,' he said softly, 'I can't give this thing up. I must win.'

'So if you don't get your way, you'll kill another man,' she said resignedly, 'then another, then maybe even me.'

'Never you.'

'*Auch das Schöne muss sterben*,' she said, smiling wanly. 'It's a phrase by Schiller. Even the most beautiful must die.'

'I haven't killed anyone, anyway.'

'But the shot?'

'I was pretending. That was just to see if I could wake them up a bit.'

'Kieran, ' she said, shaking her head slowly in disbelief, 'you have enough weapons to destroy an army, and I don't think they're here for nothing.'

'I'll use them only if they attack.'

'They will if you don't make some kind of gesture. Let one of the hostages go. Professor Tring is on our side, him at least.'

The Irishman shook his head gravely. 'I couldn't let any of them go. It would show weakness.'

The Countess sensed that it was hopeless arguing with him. 'You're a stubborn man, Kieran Kelly,' she said sternly, 'and the definition of stubbornness is stupidity.'

'There's something else, Magda,' the Irishman said, ignoring her barb.

She looked at him quizzically. What other surprises could there be?

'I can't let you go back to the police,' he said flatly.

'You're frightened I might tell them too much?'

'They have their ways.'

'Don't be a *kleiner Mensch*, Kieran Kelly,' she said with rare bitterness. 'I had no intention of leaving here without you.'

Kelly nodded in acknowledgement of her devotion. He knew at that moment that whatever the outcome, he did not deserve this woman. In normal times, he could have allowed her to replace his darling Teresa. But these were not normal times, and the fires of revenge still burned too deeply to allow him the luxury of another woman's love. He needed her opprobrium if only because it helped prevent him from falling totally under her spell. He had to maintain a distance between them lest it impair his ability to achieve his aims. He also knew that despite the danger to which he was submitting her, he must do all he could to ensure her safety in the event of an attack.

'You'll sleep in my bed here in the lounge,' he said pointing to a divan in the far corner.

'But what about you?'

'I'll use the recliner. It's just as comfortable.'

The Countess nodded resignedly. 'I've only got one favour to ask of you, Kieran. I want to meet Jonathan Tring.'

'Fraternising with the enemy?'

'Will you agree, or won't you?'

Kelly hesitated. He stroked his chin pensively, then, 'why not. You'll have a captive audience, if you'll pardon the pun. Can you make the stairs?'

She looked at the staircase leading to the landing. The ceilings in the cottage were low, so there weren't that many stairs to negotiate. She would use the banister for support. 'I can manage,' she said. 'Second room on the right. You'll find a chair in there. He's chained up, but he's being well looked after.'

Kelly helped her rise from the recliner, her heady scent once more threatening to undermine his false coldness towards her. He watched her climb the stairs, knowing that each step was filled with pain. For the first time since the conception of his plan, he felt almost paralysed by self-doubt. He lowered his gaze and rubbed his eyes vigorously. He then stared ahead at the whitewashed wall. He thought he could see a vision of Edvard Munch's *The Scream*, only this ghost-like figure had long red hair. Teresa was still with him, guiding his every move. With renewed determination, he picked up Callaghan's mobile and dialled. The Irishman took small comfort from having to inform the negotiator that his ploy had failed.

'A visitor for you,' said Sean Callaghan, helping Magda von Esterhazy into Tring's room.

The scientist gasped in surprise when he saw her, not because he didn't know she was in the building – the running commentary on the TV saw to that - but because Kelly had allowed her to speak to him. 'I apologise for the lack of salubrious surroundings, Countess,' he said staring up from the mattress. 'It's probably not what you're used to.' He pressed the silence button on his TV remote control.

'Don't be fooled by the title, Professor,' she said with a nervous smile. 'The Austro-Hungarian aristocracy doesn't have much kudos nowadays. Anyway, I see that Kelly's allowed you to keep abreast of the news as it happens.'

'The media's having a field day,' he said grimly. 'There seems to be nothing like adding a touch of glamour to a drama.'

'There's nothing glamorous about being a cripple, Professor,' she said without rancour.

Tring lowered his head. Even if he was not directly responsible, his company had produced a drug that had caused chronic suffering like hers.

Sensing his discomfort, Magda was quick to reassure him. 'I wanted to thank you personally,' she said. 'It took great courage to do what you did.'

'Anyone in my position would have done the same, Countess – and you can call me Jonathan by the way.'

'That's not true. For every man willing to do what you did, there are many others who compound injustice by their silence. There is a tendency to condemn, how you say, whistleblowers, rather than praise them. In German we call it *Zivilcourage*; to have the courage of one's convictions and to express them without fear.'

'Then you have *Zivilcourage*, too, Countess.'

'Call me Magda, please.'

'Our situation doesn't look good, does it Magda?' he said, looking at her squarely. She was more beautiful in person than in the TV footage.

She laughed nervously. '*Immer schlimmer.* From bad to worse.'

'He won't listen to you, will he?'

'No, I'm afraid not.'

'He's mad, you know.'

'He's not mad, Jonathan,' Magda said, shaking her head. 'It's just that he sees everything in black and white. Anybody who is not for him is against him, that sort of thing. In some societies revenge is the most powerful of motives.' She looked at him sadly. It was horrible to see a man in chains.

'Don't worry about these,' he smiled knowingly, 'I've got used to them. I've been treated very well. I must be the only hostage who has his own butler.'

'Yes, Callaghan seems a nice man, but I think he would do anything Kieran would ask of him. The police believe there are more than just a couple of them here.'

'Then he can't let you go, can he?' Tring said. It was more of a statement than a question.

'No,' she said quietly, 'I'm here, as you English say, for the duration. For what it's worth--' she hesitated, debating with herself whether to tell him, 'for what it's worth, I asked him to let you go. I told him you didn't deserve to be involved in this, that you were on our side.'

'You're really in love with him, aren't you, Magda?' Tring said baldly.

'Yes, I suppose I am.'

The scientist could sense her hurt. He thought there wouldn't be much mileage in their relationship, even if the whole affair ended without bloodshed, but he kept silent. There seemed little point in compounding her sadness. 'I have a favour to ask of you,' he said at length. 'If I don't make it out of here in one piece, I want you to tell Fiona I loved her more than anything in the world.'

'Please don't speak like that,' she said, her heartbeat quickening with fear. 'The Government will see sense. They won' t endanger our lives by doing anything stupid.'

'Kelly thinks all governments are stupid.' Tring stroked his five-day stubble. 'He's probably right. Just as he finished speaking, it occurred to him that however devoted the Countess might be to her lover, her rare altruism might be put to his advantage. It was a long shot, he thought, but there was no harm in asking. 'Magda,' he said holding up his shackles, 'is there any way you can find the keys to these?'

CHAPTER TWENTY-TWO
ENDGAME

The night was unusually tranquil for early November. A sliver of moonlight barely enhanced the outlines of the cottage and the wagon train surrounding it. For Commander Bob Simmons the night reminded him of an Arsenal home match in the seventies; it simply begged for action.

He moved over to his chief negotiator's bunk and shook him gently. The fat man moaned with exhaustion. It was a full minute before he regained a semblance of consciousness.

'I'm sorry, Dai,' Simmons said genuinely. 'It's a go.'

The Welshman rubbed eyes that were rheumy through lack of sleep, his hangdog expression one of resignation and failure. His superiors had decided on a coordinated attack and no amount of verbal opposition on his part would make a blind bit of difference. Dai Hopkin knew that once the machinery of war swept into action, the outcome was simply a lottery. However well trained the anti-terrorist squad, the chance of everyone surviving without a scratch was minimal. The authorities had decided to replace jaw-jaw with war-war and, taking into consideration the expertise of the opposition, he believed that casualties were inevitable.

'The MAR is showing no movement in the cottage,' Simmons went on. 'Whichever one is on guard, he hasn't moved for half an hour. Let's hope he's fallen asleep.'

'I hope you lot aren't planning a frontal, boyo,' the Welshman said apprehensively. 'You know he's probably mined the whole area.' Up until now, all details of any planned action had been kept from him. This was because a negotiator, if he knew too much, might let something slip to a hostage taker. Now it just didn't matter any more.

'Choppers, Dai,' Simmons said bluntly. The fat man deserved to know everything. 'There's a skylight.'

The Welshman whistled. 'Jesus, that's risky. Can I have a look at the sketch?'

Simmons handed his colleague the drawing that was reproduced for every member of the attack squad. The sketch showed possible concealment points such as fences, bushes and corners. Each of the four sides of the cottage was colour coded with numbers for each storey, door and window from left to right and from top to bottom. By using the top-down method, everyone would remain consistent about which level was under discussion at any particular time. Each window and door had been labelled as to type, and the owner of *Rosedale* had given the police a full description of the interior.

'What about our snipers?' Hopkin asked.

'Purely diversionary, mate.'

They both knew that the sniper usually had myriad responsibilities at a hostage site, providing intelligence, protecting innocent bystanders or preventing the escape of a dangerous hostage-taker. In this case, central command had decided to get the marksmen to open fire on the sides of the building in order to create a diversion while the special team fast-roped through the skylight. It was a high-risk strategy, but no commander could sanction the possibility of his men being blown sky-high by buried ordnance, unless there was no choice other than to mount a full frontal assault. The 'Go Team' on the ground would be activated only if it appeared that all or many of the hostages would be killed or injured if they didn't carry out the assault immediately. The onus on the helicopter boys was enormous. Dynamic entry using speed, aggressiveness and surprise was their task and theirs alone. They would fast-rope down onto the skylight using a hands-free safety descender, and then employ a new rake and break implement that was simplicity itself. It would not only smash the window and rake the glass, but also insert distraction devices. These gizmos produced ear-splitting sound, millions of candlepower of flash and a certain amount of over pressure in the area. The combination usually disorientated the targets by causing ringing in the ears and contracting pupils. To be most effective, the device had to deployed in a darkened environment and Simmons had taken the decision to cut electricity to the cottage just before the choppers reached their target. Main weaponry, which he prayed would not have to be used, was the Heckler and Koch MP-5 submachine gun. The H & K had recently become the weapon of choice, if only because it fired a pistol round, which would not risk over-penetration and endanger hostages as much as a rifle round. The ammunition had been treated to reduce ricochet in confined spaces. If things started to go wrong, then the dynamics would revert to the ground units. They would also move in if Kelly set off all his ordnance.

'Give it to me straight, Bob,' the Welshman grunted, 'they've never done this in a real situation, have they?'

Simmons shook his head wearily.

'Plenty of scope for a fuck up then, boyo.'

The commander nodded. He knew that even in the most professional of units, which trained constantly and maintained a ready force twenty-four seven, dedication and hard work might be tested in a single incident. Even many of the most successful operations resulted in the death of one or more hostages. It was essentially a no-win situation. 'This is what they train for, Dai,' he said quietly. 'There has to be a first time for everything.'

'And maybe a last,' Hopkin sighed, the pessimism in his voice spreading through the command post like a grey mist. He hated himself for his negativity, but he was a man who couldn't pretend to his colleagues. He was still convinced that Kelly had not shot anyone and that it was too soon for the Hooray Henrys to have their way.

It was just past three in the morning when Magda von Esterhazy awoke. Her sleep had been fitful, wracked as it was both by pain and by conscience. She had foregone her usual dose of painkillers in order to remain fully compos mentis for the impossible task she had set herself. Tring had described the set of keys used for his shackles and she had seen them hanging on the wall in the kitchen. It was obvious from the size of the bunch that they included keys for the others as well. She felt she must try to set all the hostages free, although Tring would be the first. She lay on her bed with eyes still closed, imagining all sorts of scenarios, most of them ending in disaster. The whole ridiculous idea made her shiver with fear. It could never work.

It was only when she opened her eyes fully that Magda became aware of a pink glow in the room and the stereo sound of heavy snoring. It appeared that both Kieran Kelly and Sean Callaghan had succumbed to the mental and physical exhaustion engendered by the siege. She turned her head towards the console. Kieran was lying back on the recliner, his hands clasped across his chest. On one side of the desk stood the table lamp, its pink shade spreading a kind of eerie cosiness throughout the room. On the other lay a threatening black sub-machine gun. It had what looked like a torch attached, or it might have been a telescope. She turned her gaze back towards the profile of her sleeping lover. How very handsome he looked in repose. All the moments of their intimacy seemed to flash through her mind in a kaleidoscope of colours, sounds and emotions: the first time they had made love, Bach's violin concerto in D minor, the windswept pavilion in Westcliff where he told her he was leaving her. That decision had tormented her day and night until news of the kidnapping revealed his true reason. She was sure that he truly believed he was doing this for her and all the other sufferers; that he was their knight in shining armour. Such was Kieran's single-mindedness, that there seemed little point in attempting to disavow him of his mission. He had simply retreated into the forest of his own truth. She also knew that he would regard what she was about to attempt as the ultimate betrayal. He would never understand that she sought only to save him from himself, to rescue him from his destructive passion for revenge.

Magda continued to stare at the sleeping Irishman. He seemed so at peace, so assured of eventual victory, figuring that he had worked out all the angles. He'd even boasted to her that the police would never get to within a stone's throw of the cottage; that if they did, they would set off enough alarms to wake the dead. Even the distant drone of circling helicopters high above had failed to faze him. 'You get used to it,' he had said. And he was right. In a strange way, they were kind of comforting.

Still fully clothed, she swung her atrophied legs around and sat upright on the edge of the bed. She winced as the strangulated nerves in her lower spine shrieked their disapproval of the sudden movement. Magda took a deep breath and pushed herself upward. Now came the hard part.

'It's a go,' barked Police Pilot Officer Darren Green at the three black-clad figures perched behind him in the Aerospatiale Eurocopter Twin Squirrel. He glanced around to see eyes that were bulging with the sudden adrenaline rush. 'Don't worry, lads,' he said only half-jokingly, 'Her Majesty's Government has complete faith in you.' With this, Green slammed all the fuses in the overhead panel, pressed the engine start button and opened the throttle. The twin Allison turboshafts burst into life. He then pulled hard on the collective pitch lever and waited for the torque meter to reach red, at the same time keeping his eye on the front edge of the disc described by the whirling blades in relation to the skyline. The gas turbines roared as he lifted gently off the ground. Despite some minor drawbacks, he liked this particular chopper. The Twin Squirrel was fairly sedate as helicopters go, with a slight tendency to tuck the nose towards the ground and a distinct yet easily controlled yaw to the right. It tended to wobble a bit in the hover, but not enough to upset the guys in the rear when they rapelled into action. He thanked God for a windless night.

'Squirrel One airborne,' Green yelled into the mike, knowing that his back up, Squirrel Two, would be taking off a few seconds later. The French-made helicopter's maximum speed of a hundred and forty miles an hour was fairly redundant, given that mission target was only a few miles from Fairoaks airfield, Chobham, the base for the South East Region Police Air Support Unit. Once airborne, he moved the cyclic-pitch stick forward and the helicopter lurched ahead. It was a procedure he had carried out hundreds of times before. The only difference now was that this was no mundane sky patrol.

Operation Whitehall had gone dynamic.

Without the benefit of her sticks, Magda von Esterhazy was forced to hug the walls as she shuffled her way towards the open-plan kitchen. Every step sent a paroxysm of pain through her legs, and every step seemed to her to make enough noise to wake the dead. She continually kept her eyes on Kelly's slumbering form. At any moment he might awaken. She had a couple of ready-made excuses; such as she was going to get a glass of water to take another pain killer or on her way to the toilet. She knew that it wouldn't hold much credence if she was caught with the keys in her hands. There were a thousand reasons why it all might still go wrong.

Hardly daring to breath, the Countess finally reached the keys. She gingerly lifted the ring off its hook. The whole thing reminded her of an old fairground stall where one would have to pass an electrified loop over a wire without setting off the alarm. She clasped the six large keys hard so that they would not swing free and clang. She then inched her way back towards the staircase. Gripping the banister, she prayed that the stairs would not creak. Now which one was the bad one? One of them had groaned terribly when she had visited Tring, but which one? She looked intently at each stair, counting it mentally, as if that would aid her memory. The fifth one up, she told herself finally, more in hope than in certainty.

By the time Magda reached the fifth stair, she was already sweating profusely. She rested against the banister and glanced round at the Irishman. Thank God, he was still snoring gently. Now came the biggest test. She gripped the underneath of her left thigh and hauled her leg up a double flight in order to miss the fifth. Stifling a gasp at the unimaginable intensity of the pain, she was forced to maintain the awkward position for a few seconds in order to prepare herself for the next move. Gripping the banister with both hands, she hauled herself to stand more or less upright on the sixth stair. She swayed slightly as a cry sought desperately to burst from her throat. It was pure torture.

Once on the landing, she could see that Callaghan, too, was deep in exhausted sleep. The energy-saving light on the landing was bright enough for her to notice the holster bulging beneath his slumbering form. She knew she could never free the pistol without waking him. Operating on adrenaline alone, she inched her way past his fold-up bed to reach Tring's door. Gingerly she turned the handle.

The professor's room, too, was dimly lit. She left the door very slightly ajar and hobbled over to the mattress. She knelt down beside the slumbering scientist and whispered in his ear, 'Jonathan, Jonathan.'

Tring woke with a start though, thankfully, made very little noise. He nodded as she placed a finger over her lips and showed him the keys. There were two for each set of shackles; but which two?

'Callaghan's asleep on the landing,' she whispered. 'He's got a pistol, but I couldn't steal it from him.'

'Jesus, Magda,' Tring whispered back, 'I must have been mad to ask you to do this.'

'Shh,' she cautioned, and continued trying the first key. As luck would have it, it opened the foot shackles. Two keys later and she had released those around his wrists.

Jonathan Tring was just rubbing them when the room was suddenly plunged into pitch darkness. Then a deafening thrum seemed to be right above them.

Pilot officer Darren Green manoeuvred the Twin Squirrel into position about twenty feet above the roof of the cottage. There was simply no room for error. He had to be high enough not to blow debris everywhere and low enough to make entry as fast as possible for the men behind him who had to fast-rope down in rapid succession. They all knew that once entry was achieved and the distraction devices deployed, the team had, at most, seven seconds in which to neutralise the hostage-takers. After that, the odds that hostages would die increased dramatically. Green re-checked his position finder. 'Go!' he screamed.

The first black-clad figure slipped down the descender and landed inches to the left of the skylight. Still hooked onto the line, he used the rake and break to smash the window, and clear the jagged edges. The noise of the shattering glass was totally lost in the din of the chopper's rotors. Within a fraction of a second the rake and break had also inserted the distraction devices onto the upper landing. Facing away from the searing flashes that lit the cottage, the officer was also grateful for the earplugs that were protecting him from the cacophony above and below. He then unhooked from the descender and slipped through the skylight. As he landed, the flashlight attached to his H & K played on the startled figure of Sean Callaghan. Although totally disorientated, the Irishman managed to loose off a single wayward shot before a lethal burst scythed him down.

At the same time that the chopper was over the roof, Commander Bob Simmons ordered the snipers to open up with massive firepower into the bare exterior walls of the cottage. If that didn't confuse the hostage-takers, he thought, then nothing would.

It was funny how the simple switching off of a light could sometimes be enough to wake a sleeping person, for Kieran Kelly was already working on autopilot by the time the first volley hit the sides of the cottage. Even in the blackness, he had managed to grope for the sub-machine gun with one hand and a switch on the console with the other. Suddenly, loud booms shook the cottage as the buried ordnance exploded all around. 'The bastards!' he cursed, the words drowned in the mayhem. 'Sean, Sean!' His cries were cut short by the staccato of sub-machine gunfire from the landing. Switching on the torch fixed to his weapon, he bounded up the stairs two at a time, paying scant attention to the empty bed against the wall.

Knowing full well that the attackers would be wearing body armour, he fired a volley at head height in the direction of the torchlight facing his own. There was a loud scream and the black-clad figure slumped to the floor. The Irishman barely had time to make out the body of Sean Callaghan, which lay on the floor in front of him, before another black figure dropped down from above. Bullets flashed past him as he temporarily retreated to the stairs. He then aimed his sub machinegun around the corner and fired wildly. There came a further groan, mixed with a woman's scream – Magda's - that strangely appeared to becoming from the upper level. It was at that moment that Kelly decided that everyone must die.

Taking advantage of an apparent lull in the attack, he burst into the first bedroom. His flashlight made out the petrified figure of Martin Townsend. A short burst and the doctor slumped forward, the rattle of his chains just about audible above the thrum of the helicopter. Kelly then entered the second room and fired into the body of Stephen Sellars, who was already lying prostrate with his hands over his head. One more, thought the Irishman, and justice would be done. His kind of justice.

He almost fell over the bodies on the landing as he opened the door to Tring's room. The torch fixed to his weapon played on the figure on the mattress. 'Magda!' he gasped.

Professor Jonathan Tring, summoning all his strength as a prop forward, launched himself from the shadows at the dumbstruck figure in the doorway. As both men clattered to the floor, Kelly's weapon slithered across the parquet, shattering the torch and plunging the room back into darkness.

Magda von Esterhazy screamed as the two men grappled with each other, her mind completely frozen by fear for the safety of both of them. Suddenly, a strange voice burst from the landing. 'Turn the fucking lights on, boss, it's carnage in here.'

Kelly and Tring continued to wrestle for another few seconds until the sudden flood of light took both of them by surprise. The Irishman was the first to react. He pulled away and dived towards his sub machinegun.

'No, Kieran!' the Countess cried. The words were barely out of her lips before a burst of fire from the doorway cut through the Irishman just as his hand reached the stock. Kelly gasped and rolled over onto his back. Racking sobs punctured the cold mist of impending death. 'Please don't cry, Teresa,' he groaned. A vision of exquisite feminine beauty hovered above him. Strange, he thought, why had Magda dyed her hair red?

EPILOGUE

Professor Jonathan Tring and Fiona Harrington announced their engagement two weeks after the end of the siege and one day after the Prime Minister tended his government's resignation. Commander Bob Simmons and Inspector Dai Hopkin both declared that they were taking early retirement from the Metropolitan Police.

One month later, the Labour Party, under new leadership, was returned to power with an even greater mandate after pledging in its manifesto to institute an inquiry into invasive spinal procedures.

One year after the events at Rosedale Cottage, nothing had changed. Countess Magda von Esterhazy was continuing her lone battle for justice.

THE END

Printed in the United Kingdom
by Lightning Source UK Ltd.
9806000001B